the secrets we Keep

LOGAN MEREDITH

RIPTIDE
PUBLISHING

Riptide Publishing
PO Box 1537
Burnsville, NC 28714
www.riptidepublishing.com

The Secrets We Keep

Cover art: L.C. Chase, lcchase.com
Editor: Veronica Vega
Layout: L.C. Chase, lcchase.com

ISBN: 978-1-62649-953-9

First edition
October, 2021

Also available in ebook:
ISBN: 978-1-62649-954-6

the secrets we Keep

LOGAN MEREDITH

RIPTIDE PUBLISHING

For all the former secret-keepers helping to break the silence and stigma of mental illness.

Forgiving is not forgetting; it's actually remembering—remembering and not using your right to hit back. It's a second chance for a new beginning. And the remembering part is particularly important. Especially if you don't want to repeat what happened.
—Desmond Tutu

Table of Contents

Chapter One

Adam

The invitation came as I was brushing the taste of regret and day-old cigars out of my mouth. I forced open my eyes, which were more red than blue thanks to my neighbor, Bryan, and his friend Jose Cuervo. Blinking hard against the sunlight streaming in through the window, I read the message. *Guys trip to Hawaii?*

I spat and rinsed my mouth, then wiped my hands on my boxer briefs and popped off a response. *Hell yes, I want to go to Hawaii. When?*

My phone rang, and I answered it on the way back to my bedroom.

"Don't freak out," Brady said before I could say hello. "I'm going to propose to Josh, but I'm sort of worried it's too much."

"Hawaii for a proposal? No way. That is just the right amount of much. Josh will love it." I paced back and forth in my room, cradling the phone to my ear while looking for my bottle of ibuprofen. "But your text said a 'guys trip.' If you're dropping to your knees, shouldn't you two be alone?" Grinning despite my hangover, I listened to Brady stutter for a few breaths. I couldn't help myself. After all the years I'd had to be so careful about encouraging his crush on me, I loved that I didn't have to censor myself with him anymore. Not after he got his head out of his ass and realized his perfect match was actually the other six-foot, one-hundred-eighty-pound jock with sandy-blond hair we'd known since college. I might have been Brady's type, but Josh and Brady had some next-level-soul mate shit going on. Knowing I'd played a role in getting him to see that still filled me with pride.

"You propose on one knee, you perv. Get serious for a sec. This might be a horrible idea." I sat on my bed and rummaged through my bedside table while Brady walked me through his proposal dilemma. "I bought a ring, and I've been waiting for a big occasion to ask him for like months already. Since he's back in school full-time, we can't afford to go full balls-to-the-wall elaborate on things like vacations. But I don't want to do something generic."

Yes! I extracted the bottle and swallowed the capsules dry before returning my attention to my friend's faux crisis. Josh might have been the biggest romantic of the group, but he wasn't pretentious, and there was absolutely no way his response would be anything other than enthusiastic acceptance. "Josh doesn't care about how much you spend."

"Oh, yeah, I realize. But it's Josh, so he wants it to be perfect, and I want it to be perfect because he wants it to be perfect. I've been thinking about it for a while. I'd considered asking him on a hike or a run, but we're always rushed for work or school. Then yesterday, Matt mentioned he owned an investment property on Kauai that he wants to sell." The mention of Matt explained why Brady's brain had gone into overdrive. Since I was fairly sure this wasn't going to be a quick call, I fished some joggers out of my hamper and slid them on, then set the phone down to slip on a T-shirt. Brady unloaded every angsty detail on speakerphone.

"He's taking a private plane because he's Matt. He invited Sid to join him, then Sid wanted Cade to come, then Cade invited Josh and me, and there are four bedrooms, so tell it to me straight—is this perfect, or will I be sleeping on the couch all week?"

I rolled my eyes. Josh had turned Brady into the biggest overthinker. "Hmm. Let me think. Proposing to your man in one of the most romantic places on the earth or refusing a free trip because you'd be staying with your ex-turned-boss that your man is mad jealous of."

Brady huffed. "Yes, except one date does not an ex make, and Josh insists he's no longer jealous."

"Counterpoint—you still fucked on that one date, and Josh punched *me* in the jaw trying to punch Matt." I rubbed my stubbled jaw at the memory.

"Fuck. So I should pass, right? I knew it."

"No, I'm just busting your balls, man. It's risky but also kind of perfect. I mean, a practically free trip to Hawaii and the romantic proposal he's been dying for should soften any protest. Speaking of exes, does Cade know you invited me?"

Brady made an uncomfortable throat-clearing sound, which I took as a sign that our friends had already had multiple conversations about the potential awkwardness of the situation. "No progress on that front?"

"Nope."

Brady's sigh effectively handed me the angst baton, so I ran with it. Unlike Brady and Josh, who'd completed the friends-to-lovers journey, Cade and I were on a lovers-to-sort-of-friends-path by way of Heartbreak City. "I realized yesterday that it's been four years since we broke up. Since then, we've burned through every version of friends with benefits, fuck buddies, and casual dating trying to find something that works. Some days friendship seems like a mountain too big to climb."

Brady released a discontented huff. "Damn. You guys seemed like you'd finally made it to a good place when Josh and I first got together."

We had been, and that was the problem. We were always in a good place until I tried to get back what we had. "I asked him to move in again. He said he'd think about it, and a month later—kaboom. I love him so much, but . . . The last time was awful, man."

Cade knew how to land a verbal punch. All I had to do was complain about him flaking on me for dinner, and we were right back to the day after my drunken moment of immaturity ruined us. I'd lost count of how many times we'd tried.

"Don't lose hope. Look at Josh and me, how long did it take us to get here?" Brady asked.

A brief flicker of nostalgia made me smile. Some days it seemed like we'd all known each other forever, but in reality, it'd only been about eight years. We'd met freshman year of college. Josh and Brady were roommates, and I lived next door in a single on the second floor. We'd met Cade a week after the fall semester. Sid got inducted within a few weeks of classes beginning, and he and Cade became roommates not long after. The five of us were a unit throughout college. I would never not be happy for Josh and Brady, but there was one glaring difference for Cade and me that everyone seemed to gloss over.

I closed my eyes and recalled the way my heart had raced as I approached the short, sinewy twink from the fourth floor that Josh and Brady had nicknamed Tinkerbell. I'd never struggled with flirting before, but I was so sprung on him, my stomach did somersaults while I fumbled my way through an introduction. "You and Josh had that entire friendship foundation down solid. Cade and I burned hot from the first night. There's no safety net with Cade; it's like a free climb."

Brady grumbled. "Rock climbing? Dude, I swear you and Josh sit around dreaming up sports metaphors just to annoy me."

I rolled my eyes. Before Josh, Brady lacked the ability to distinguish a layup from a line drive. "You love it."

"No, but I love him. Please come. You're the only one who helps me think through these things. Nothing is stopping you and Cade from working on your relationship without your dicks getting in the way."

"Yeah, because we hadn't thought of that."

Brady huffed. "Yeah, but have you ever actually tried it?"

"Only ten billion times."

"Parading men in front of each other isn't exactly working on your friendship. What's the longest streak you and Cade have ever gone where you were both single, on speaking terms, and not fucking?"

I sighed. As dysfunctional as our romantic relationship was, our sexual relationship was crazy good. Cade and I had zero success in the platonic hanging out department. Even when pissed off, one drunken, *You up?* text, and it was game on. "Whatever, man. I don't care anymore."

"Uh-huh." Brady packed a lot of sarcasm into those few sounds. "Because you are *so* welcoming to the guys Cade's brought to Sunday Brunch."

I liked to think, like me, Cade had met no one he cared as deeply for, but it was more likely he couldn't find someone to dick him out as well, and I was just desperate enough for him that that distinction hadn't curbed my thirst. "I told him he's free to date whoever he wants."

"Well, if I had a dollar every time I heard one of you say that, I wouldn't be needing to bogart Matt's trip to propose to my man. Since you clearly care, he's definitely not seeing anyone right now, and you're single, so . . . I dunno, do whatever you want with that info, but I'm trying to not be single ever again, so will you please come to Hawaii?"

Brady's plea reminded me this wasn't about me and Cade. He and Josh were two of the best guys I knew. Of course I wanted to be there for that milestone. "If Cade's okay with it, then I'll come."

"He said the exact same thing about you. He knows I'm inviting you."

"Fine," I sighed. "I guess count me in."

I said my goodbye to Brady and pocketed my phone before throwing myself on my mattress. I grabbed a pillow, covered my mouth, and screamed.

A week in Hawaii with Cade?

We hadn't spoken since our latest falling out six weeks ago, but experience dictated stage one would last up to eight. We'd stay away as long as we could, until something would flip, and our magnetic field or our friends drew us back together. I'd gone out multiple times with my work buddies and some guys I'd met in my building, trying to stay busy. To not be the one who flipped. That had been hard enough, but face-to-face and on vacation? There was no way we'd be leaving Hawaii without serious regret.

Cade

The timing of this vacation could not have been worse. My seniors had a severe case of senioritis, and based on the first six research papers I'd graded, about half of my junior AP class would be surprised to learn that the Hulu version of *The Handmaid's Tale* did not strictly follow the book.

Still, I'd told Siddharth and Matt, who then told Brady and Josh that I'd go. Even if it would be the most awkward week for me personally, I'd been on a whole self-improvement kick—new healthier diet, regular exercise, better choices with men, and keeping my commitments.

I picked up another paper and sighed, forcing myself to write a parent-friendly critique instead of circling the entire paragraph about Offred's rebellious nature and writing one big *WTF* in red letters. I didn't care so much that they didn't read the book, but Atwood wrote it in 1984, so yeah . . . Offred didn't attend the Women's March.

Twelve papers later, I took a break to start packing. Siddharth lived closer to the airport, and since we had an early flight time, my plan was to pack, drop by my sister's, and get to Siddharth's late enough to go straight to bed. Hopefully, with no discussion of Adam—because I didn't fucking have a clue what to do about that situation.

History had proven it wouldn't matter. A plan for how to handle Adam was pretty well useless. I might well say what I wanted to do all the livelong day, but as soon as I saw him, that guy giving himself the insanity-must-end pep talks was full of shit.

I dug my suitcase out of its storage place, tossed it on my bed, and started gathering what I'd need: reading glasses, sunglasses, workout gear, a week's worth of shorts and T-shirts, and toiletries . . .

I headed to my bathroom and tossed my toothbrush and contact solution into my Dopp kit, then sorted through the bottles of products I'd amassed trying to find some magic combination that would give my baby-fine blond hair a chance at surviving a style that didn't involve an elastic band.

Returning to my bedroom, I dropped the Dopp kit into my bag and surveyed the room, considering what else . . . *Fuck.*

With a sigh, I pulled open the top drawer of my dresser and shoved the contents around, sifting through clothes I never wore in search of swimwear. A small splash of color gave me a weird, uneasy feeling. My eyes slammed closed as a memory rushed through me.

"Oh, you are so getting these." Adam smiled mischievously and dangled the hanger holding the tiny green briefs with a rainbow across the ass on his finger, letting it sway back and forth.

"I don't think Mexico is that gay-friendly." I caught a glimpse of the price tag. "Seventy bucks for a swimsuit? That's insane."

Adam pouted at me. "For St. Patrick's Day. C'mon. It's festive." He held it to my face. "It matches your eyes."

"No." I snatched the hanger from his hands and hooked it back on the rack.

"We leave in two weeks, and you've barely bought anything. You can't wear sweatpants and my hoodies to the beach." He gestured to my attire, which was getting harder and harder to explain as Winter yielded to Spring.

I hugged my arms around the bulky gray terry cloth sweatshirt that had practically become my uniform. My fingers found the edge of my last rib, and I followed it toward the swell of my gut, hiding my revulsion with a swallow. God, how was I going to tell him I couldn't go? Why I couldn't go. He was going to hate me. I gulped back the burn of acid racing up my throat. Closing my eyes, I tried to form the words. "Look, Adam—"

"Save it. I decided I need to see your fine ass in this. I'm buying it for you."

I shook the memory and the guilt out of my head and selected two pairs of board shorts and some rash guard shirts and tanks. While I packed, I worked on reminding myself that I had nothing to apologize for. Adam was . . . Fuck. Adam was not part of my program. I was moving on. Finding someone better. Being someone better.

By the time I finished justifying the sexy underwear and condoms I absolutely did not pack for Adam, I didn't feel prepared to see my family or my friends. Not until I worked off some of this energy vibrating through me.

Some ab and oblique work with the exercise ball I kept in my living room settled most of my anxiety. In the back of my mind, I knew I didn't really have time, but if I was going to be in a bathing suit, my stubborn winter blubber layer needed to go.

I was ninety-seven crunches in toward my hundred crunch goal when the phone rang. I sped up, pushing aside the burn as I hurled my upper body toward my lower half. *Ninety-eight, ninety-nine, one hundred.* I reached for the phone on the fourth ring and hit the Talk button. "Hello," I said breathlessly.

"Are you still coming over? Hayley is waiting up to see you, and I really need to get to bed." My sister sounded exhausted. I glanced at the clock. *Shit.* It was after nine o'clock. I'd exercised for far longer than I'd intended. Springing into action, I carried the phone with me to the bedroom to gather the rest of my things.

"I, um— Sorry, Maura. Not sure if I'm going to be able to stop by before I leave after all."

"Are you okay? You sound out of breath."

My lip slipped between my teeth. "I'm still packing," I lied.

"Cade, are you sure this is a good idea? I don't think—"

"Maura, I told you. It's under control. I'm being careful."

She sighed unhappily. "Fine. But please don't do anything stupid. I mean it, Cade. Promise me." I heard my niece's voice draw closer to the phone demanding to speak to me. "Stop it. Wait a minute, Hayley," Maura barked sharply.

"Maura, I told you already. You need to focus on you. I'm fine."

"Have you talked to Adam?"

"Not since the flip-flop debacle."

Maura exhaled a breath of exasperation. "You had every right to be angry. Telling you he wanted to fuck someone less complicated was some bullshit."

I cringed. Technically I'd been the one to tell Adam to find someone less complicated. He'd only agreed with me after I lost my shit at him. "Maura, I was throwing shoes at him, warning him not to leave in one breath and making him promise to stay away in the next. Nothing he said justifies me embracing the full trailer trash cliché. I sounded like Mom."

"You were spending time with your family! Hold on. Hayley, knock it off." Maura covered the phone as she scolded my niece; when she returned, I could hear she was reaching her limit. "Listen, Hayley is gonna lose her shit if I don't let her say goodbye. Have fun, Cade, but please . . ."

"I know, Sis. I'm good. Trust me."

I wasn't sure if Maura heard me, because Hayley grabbed the phone and talked a mile a minute about the book she'd finished reading. As much as I loved and shared my niece's passion for literature, I didn't have time for her detailed book report. By the time I managed to get off the phone, it was well after nine thirty.

Hurriedly, I loaded the car and drove thirty minutes across town to Siddharth's house. Unfortunately, it was too late to enjoy the canopy of trees that formed over the beautiful historic neighborhood not far from where we'd gone to school. I drove past row after row of charming houses in architectural styles from the late-nineteenth and early-twentieth centuries, any of which I'd kill to call my own. When Siddharth started house hunting, I'd pushed him toward the walkable neighborhood that primarily attracted young professionals with money just to have a reason to see inside some of them and dream.

I pulled into the driveway of Siddharth's Craftsman-styled home and parked in the rear, as usual. My chest tightened as I spied the group assembled around Siddharth's firepit.

"Cade's here. The Loman Hall reunion can begin," Josh cheered.

I exited my car, smiling as I unlatched the gate of the white picket fence leading to a yard that was so fucking quaint it'd actually been featured in a landscaping design magazine. My eyes searched out Siddharth, who was using his boyfriend, Matt, as a human jacket. My best friend did not fuck with cold, and even with the fire, the spring air still carried a chill.

"Just wait till we get to Hawaii." I said to Josh, as I hugged him and Brady, then dipped to kiss Siddharth.

"Hey, now," Matt protested, pouting at Siddharth. Siddharth twisted, his face full of affection, as he tilted his chin up toward Matt and chased my kiss with a much more passionate one.

I stiffened as a rush of cold hit my neck, instinctively reaching for whatever it was and finding only wetness. "What the—" I twisted around.

"Hey." Adam's playfulness dulled my irritation. He held an ice-cold bottle of beer in one hand and a stemless wine glass in the other, which he extended to me. "I still had a few bottles of the rosé you like."

That was my problem. Adam *could* be thoughtful when he wasn't a total dick. I swallowed as I accepted it with a gracious smile. Even through the worst of our fights, we'd always tried to keep our drama from making our friends uncomfortable. If he played nice, I would too.

"Thanks," I mumbled.

He nodded and took his seat on the other side of the pit next to Brady. The conversation was lively, and I tried to stay upbeat as I peppered Matt with questions about what to expect from a private plane and the area. I sensed Siddharth's curious brown eyes watching me or, more accurately, watching me not watch Adam. He was probably worried it annoyed me he didn't tell me the entire gang was attending our sleepover. And I was annoyed, but not at Siddharth. Only at myself for the steady flood of not-hateful thoughts I kept having as I listened to Adam dole out support, love, and charm to our friends.

I lost the battle with myself and allowed one glance. He was sitting next to Brady, wearing track pants and a fitted T-shirt, like he'd planned to go to the gym and hadn't made it. Relaxed, he leaned back in his chair with his long legs extended and ankles crossed, hands clasped behind his head, showing off drool-worthy biceps he didn't deserve. If I worked out until my arms fell off, they'd drop to the floor with the same level of definition, but Adam could lift an empty box and gain an inch. It was so unfair.

He somehow managed to appear even sexier through the smoky filter and crackles popping up from the fire. Brady said something in a near whisper that must have been off-color, because Adam tilted his back and laughed mischievously, and the sound traveled straight to my cock. When our eyes met, I knew he'd caught me lusting after him. The fucker gave me a little wink, which had never, ever failed to make me want him.

"Cade," Siddharth said, and my treacherous eyes whipped back to him. "Come inside with me. It's too cold."

I nodded, silently thanking him for the escape, before I followed him into the house. He led me to the little breakfast nook in his kitchen and started putting a plate together. I took a minute to admire the familiar elements of his home—the natural wood floors and exposed beams. It was perfect, modern, and welcoming. Not a hint of ostentatiousness.

He set the snacks down in front of me without a word. I sized it up, my stomach clenching. I did some quick math. With the wine, I had to be careful or I'd blow my diet. So I took an olive and popped it into my mouth.

Siddharth picked up some vegan cheese, put it on a cracker, then handed it to me. I made a face. "I'll never understand vegan cheese."

Siddharth laughed, prodding me to eat but saying nothing when I didn't. "How's Maura?" he asked, lowering his voice.

"Better," I said with a half smile. "She extended her medical leave a few more weeks. Her psychiatrist upped her antidepressant, and she's on the antipsychotic again, so she won't get manic."

"And Hayley?"

"She's good. Worried about her mom, you know? But Aislinn's coming on Tuesday to hang out."

"Aislinn's coming? Aw. I'm surprised she had time off already. How does she like Boston?"

"She doesn't have time off, but she works twelve-hour shifts, so she can group them to cobble four days together. She said the spring is much better. The winter almost killed her."

Sid laughed. "I still can't believe that tiny teenager who begged us to get her a fake ID is an emergency room nurse?"

"Right? I'm proud of her. Maura is too, although she's still upset that she moved to be near her dad."

Siddharth nodded. "It makes things harder for you."

I shrugged. Aislinn and Maura were technically my half sisters. Maura and I were three years apart and had grown up together with our mother. Aislinn's father had gotten custody of her when she was a baby, then remarried a lovely woman, whereas Maura's father was in prison and mine had fucked off before I was born. To say we had vastly different childhoods was an understatement. Aislinn pitched in when she had time, and she adored Hayley, but Maura didn't lean on her the way she did me.

The patio door slid open. Josh, Brady, Matt, and Adam filed in, carrying empty bottles and dishes and in hysterics.

"What did we miss?" I asked, focusing my attention on Josh, who seemed to be the one with the story.

"Oh, just Brady's face when I told him that the speedo I bought the other day was for him, not me. Adam asked him to model it for us."

"Not going to happen, beautiful." Brady's deadpan delivery didn't do much to cover for the blush on his cheeks or the small puff of his broad chest that he got when anyone commented on his weight loss.

"You're gorgeous, babe. If you really don't want to, then fine, but don't let old insecurities stop you from showing this body off." Josh's encouragement made my stomach clench. Brady's distinctly buffer physique was partially owed to Josh, who'd always kept all six feet of his enviable body in perfect condition and had gotten Brady into running and working out. It would be so much easier if I had someone like that supporting me during my program, but after Maura's overreaction, I decided it was just something I'd keep to myself.

"I show it off . . ." Brady said to Josh with an indulgent smile. "For you."

Josh shimmied up to Brady, wrapped his arms around him, and kissed him on the nose. An uncomfortable feeling—not exactly jealousy, but close—made me turn away. It was still weird seeing them like that. Not because I hadn't suspected they would end up together—I always had faith—but for the longest time it had been Adam and me who'd been the couple of the group. Seeing their easy affection always reminded me of what I'd lost.

Brady sighed. "Fine. At the pool."

"The house has a pool?" I chuckled at Josh's outrage.

"Yes," Matt said matter-of-factly as he went to discard the bag he'd been using to collect trash from around the kitchen.

"Wait. You *are* going to sort that, aren't you?" Josh chastised. Matt frowned before picking out the cans and bottles from the food waste with two fingers and placing them in the blue bin. While Josh was our resident environmentalist, he seemed to take extra enjoyment in calling Matt out.

Siddharth shook his head at Josh, clearly unbothered but nonplussed by their dynamic. "Thank you, hon."

Matt flashed a toothy grin and kissed Sid. "You're welcome. Always happy to do my part for the planet," he said, then turned to face Josh and Brady with a smirk. "There's also a hot tub, which is why I'm so glad the environmental footprint of my private plane didn't stop you from joining us, Josh."

Josh's jaw dropped, and we all held our breaths to see if Josh would stop stammering to actually respond, but then Brady snorted and everyone dissolved into laughter.

"Oh, ouch, Josh. Did you need some ointment for that burn?" Adam ribbed good-naturedly and high-fived Matt. "Respect. Do you know how long I've waited for Mr. Sierra Club to slip up?"

Josh pouted as we all took our turn piling on until Brady wrapped his arm around his red-faced boyfriend. "C'mere, beautiful. I still love you." It was a good reminder that Adam and I weren't the only two-some in the group with a past. If Josh and Matt could keep a sense of humor about their situation, so could I.

"Fine. My concern for the planet does have its limits, but seriously, dude. How rich are you?"

As he often did, Matt ignored Josh's question. "I've got a car coming at six o'clock, gentlemen." He turned to Siddharth. "I'm going to say good night, babe. You ready?"

"In a minute. I want to get everyone set up."

Matt nodded, said another good night, and headed toward Siddharth's bedroom. The rest of them followed, migrating from the kitchen and lingering where the main living area met with the stairs and hallway leading to the master suite and Sid's office, which was when it hit me that while Matt had a four-bedroom house, Siddharth's was only three.

"Josh and Brady, you can take the room at the top of the stairs. I left fresh towels in the en suite." They nodded, then Siddharth turned to Adam and me. "So, um, there's the king in the third bedroom or one of you can take the pullout couch in the office."

"I'll take the pullout," Adam said.

"What?" I twisted to glare at him, mouth tight as I gave him a face that asked, *Why are you saying stupid things?*

"Awe, baby. You want to share with me?" Adam said, his eyes half-lidded and his breath telling me he'd switched to whiskey after his beer.

"You're six foot two and I'm five feet six. If anyone should take the pullout, it should be me."

Adam held up his hands, palms out, a smile edging his mouth. "Whatever you want."

"Okay," Siddharth said. "I'm sorry. I should have considered the sleeping arrangements earlier."

"We get it. One of us was always single," Adam said.

I gave him a look. When would he realize we were not a *we* and he shouldn't speak for me anymore?

"*I'll* be fine," I said. With Brady and Josh, there might have been an ulterior motive, but Siddharth? There was no way he'd planned this. He and Matt were new. If this had happened a few months ago, I would have slept with him in his bed.

After exhaling a breath of relief, Siddharth kissed me and hugged Brady and Josh before they excused themselves.

There was a beat of silence when Adam's eyes fixed on my face. I cleared my throat, but before I could say anything, Adam spoke first.

"I was going to shower tonight, so just come into my room—"

"I'm not—"

Adam held up his hand for me to stop and rolled his eyes. "As I was saying . . . come up to my room in the morning so you can use the bathroom." He smirked and all I managed to do was nod.

"Good. Glad that's settled," Siddharth said with a sympathetic quirk of his mouth. "Good night." He left Adam and me standing together in the family room.

"So . . ." Adam said, ending my dilemma on where to look.

An odd sensation hit my chest, like my heart skipped a few beats. My eyes ran all over him before I could stop them. "So . . ." I parroted.

"It's good to see you. I've missed you." The low timbre of his voice still did things to me, but as badly as I wanted to, I shouldn't. One nod and he would happily turn me inside out with pleasure. But nothing had changed. We were still the same two people who were fantastic at sex and terrible at everything else. I'd started to work on myself for a reason, and not falling into old patterns with Adam was an essential step in that journey.

I rocked up on my tiptoes and pressed a chaste kiss to his cheek. His arms came around me and my body reacted to his touch, so I pulled away. "Good night, Adam. Sleep well."

Chapter Two

Adam

C ade had taken one Instagram-worthy photo with us and then sequestered himself with noise-canceling headphones in the last row and closed his eyes. His head rested on the headrest, chest rising and falling in slow, even breaths like I didn't remember what the loud damn drooling, mouth-breather looked like when he slept. He'd been avoiding me since shutting me down the night before. If I wanted to feel ignored, I'd have gone to visit my parents.

"How long is this damn flight?"

Brady lifted the silk eye cover they'd handed us when we boarded, retrieved a paper from the seatback pocket in front of him, and shoved it into my hands. I scanned the itinerary and did a double take. "Ten hours?"

Sid tsked at me from across the aisle, unimpressed. "It's *sixteen* hours to India. Relax, you're on a private plane. Have another drink."

Next to Sid, Matt lowered the screen of his laptop. "There's wi-fi, Adam. And every sports channel you can imagine on the entertainment system. The Braves are playing the Rangers."

Oh, man. Baseball wasn't my favorite, but if my hometown team were playing Josh's, it'd be more enjoyable. I searched behind me for Josh, who'd stretched out across from Cade in the last row.

"If you wake him, I'll punch you in the balls," Brady warned. "He hardly slept during finals, and I need him well-rested for this week."

I smirked. "Didn't sound like you cared if he slept last night."

"Shut up." Brady whacked me across the arm. "Liar." Sid barked out a laugh and Brady turned a bright shade of red. "Are you serious?"

"'Fraid so," Sid said. "Josh is, um . . ." He smiled knowingly at Matt.

"Exuberant?" Matt supplied.

Sid nodded with a wry grin. "Yes. Very exuberant and . . . surprisingly detailed."

"I'm going to pretend that this conversation didn't happen. No one better say shit to Josh about it either." Brady pulled his mask back down and covered the rest of his beet-red face with his hands.

As far as I was concerned, he should own pleasing his man with pride. Typically, Josh was big on manners and appearances, so I imagined Brady had to be hitting it right to turn him into a porn star.

"I lived with Cade; I'm used to it," Sid said with a dismissive shrug, then froze. His mortified expression fixated on me. "Adam, I'm—"

I stopped him with a wave. Cade liked sex. After we'd broken up the first time, he'd refused any label that implied monogamy and made it clear I shouldn't ask for more. Sid's revelation was strangely affirming. Unlike Josh, Cade had a mouth on him every day. My specialty involved turning him into a whimpering, trembling mess that couldn't form a complete sentence. Chances were high if he was still coherent enough to bark out orders, the guy wasn't getting invited back. I stole a glance at Cade right as his lip twitched, and wondered if he was pondering the same thing. "No one needs to walk on eggshells this week. You've noticed that we try to keep you guys out of our drama?"

"Excuse me." The flight attendant approached with a smile. "I'll be serving lunch in a few minutes. I wanted to check who gets the vegan meals?"

"Oh, just me." Sid raised his hand.

"No. Cade asked for one too," Matt said.

"He did? Hon, are you sure? Cade's not vegan."

Matt shrugged. "Yeah. I emailed asking about allergies, and he said he wanted whatever you ordered."

"Very well. Should I wake the two in the back?"

Brady pulled off his mask and blinked against the light. "Let Josh sleep."

"I'll get Cade," I offered and answered Sid's face full of apprehension with a shake of my head. "It will be fine, I promise."

As I stood, Brady leveled a concerned expression up at me. I clutched his shoulder and did my best to ignore the conversation his eyeballs were trying to have with mine. There was no way I'd make it through an entire week around our friends like this. Everyone worried about us and afraid to cut loose? No, thank you. By my calculation, there were four hours left in this flight, so Cade and I had two hundred and forty minutes to fast-forward past the eggshell-tension phase of our breakup cycle and get to the let's-be-friends stage. If that meant I needed to cut out all the "who did what to who and why" conversations and own my part, then so be it.

I made my way to the back of the plane, and I slid into the seat next to him. "Hey."

He didn't move.

I leaned in close and blew along the shell of his ear before moving his headphones and whispering, "There's no drool, Goulue. You aren't fooling me with the peaceful-angel bit."

One green eye opened and trained on me. "I do not drool and don't call me that. No one enjoys being called a glutton." He pulled his headphones off and stored them in their case.

I snorted. "You would turn our origin story into something that makes me sound like an asshole."

"If the shoe fits . . ."

"I call you that because the first time I saw your ass you were dancing the can-can in an homage to Louise Weber. I was so inspired by it, I made up a whole fake research paper about her for a whole fake class to have a reason to talk to you."

He sat up, dropped the act, and combed his fingers through his shoulder-length blond hair. Both emerald eyes focused on me. "Yeah. Yeah. And I called you out on your bullshit then too. What do you want, Adam?"

"I want to apologize."

He huffed. "Translation—you realized you're missing a prime opportunity to join the mile-high club and you need me less hostile."

"Don't pretend you weren't running your eyes all over me last night."

Cade sighed, and I realized I was getting off track. That was us—sometimes I couldn't tell if we were flirting or fighting. It all kind of seemed like foreplay. "I'm serious, Cade. I want to apologize. I understand Maura and Hayley need you, and no matter how disappointed I was, I shouldn't have said that shit about fucking other guys. I realize it triggers you, and I have only myself to blame for that, so I'm sorry."

"But . . ." Cade prompted.

"No buts."

"But I broke our plans and I should call first and I'm not making you my priority and why won't I just let it go?" He counted my usual excuses out on his fingers.

My jaw tensed. Hearing them from his mouth, I realized how trite they sounded. Immature, to borrow a favorite description of my behavior from my siblings. "Aren't you tired of fighting? Like bone-deep exhausted?"

Cade checked his imaginary watch. "That line is a few weeks early."

"Cade," I pleaded. "Please, can we call a truce? For Josh and Brady, if not for me."

Cade shifted away and angled his body toward me. He peered over at Josh and smiled. "Is it weird that *we're* the only single ones in the group?"

I followed Cade's wistful gaze to Josh, who still slept soundly across from us. When I turned back to Cade, I mirrored his genuine smile with one of my own. "They make it look easy."

Cade nodded. "Even before they were dating, it's like they always put each other first."

"Like you and Sid."

"Adam, I don't put Sid before—"

"I'm not saying that."

Cade's jaw tensed. "What are you saying?"

"I'm agreeing with you, I guess. In our group it was always you and me, Josh and Brady, and Sid. But Sid was never the odd man out because you and he were best friends."

"Don't be stupid, you're not the odd man out."

I hated when he outright dismissed me. My birthright was being a fifth wheel. I understood what it felt like. "Sorry," I said instead to keep from arguing about whether I was entitled to my own fucking feelings. God knew there was no way to win the "my family sucks more than yours" argument with Cade.

"Adam." Cade touched my arm, reminding me he rarely meant the first thing that popped out of his mouth.

"I realize you don't want to listen to me get into my feelings about my perfect family again. How's Maura?"

Cade's eyelids fluttered, and he glanced at our friends, then back to me. He never liked his sister's issues advertised, but he seemed . . . regretful?

"Is Hayley okay?"

"Yeah. Yeah. She's fine. About to ace the fifth grade and excited for summer."

"What's Mr. Doyle got on her summer reading list?"

Cade flashed a brilliant smile, erasing all my concerns. The way he lit up about books made me miss how we used to be together. In the early days of our relationship, we loved to lie in bed reading to each other from the same book. I was a little uncomfortable when he first asked, but Cade had a deep, soothing James Earl Jones quality to his voice. Relaxing and lying contently in his arms became the best part of my day. I would let him read an instruction manual to me to recapture a tiny piece of that.

"This summer we're diving into Louisa May Alcott."

"*Little Women*?"

Cade nodded. "She's excited about it. I ordered that and *Little Men* for her the other day."

"Did she see the movie?"

Cade groaned. "Yeah. I asked her to wait until she read the book, but you know Maura when she gets her head on something."

"Yeah. I know Maura," I echoed, quickly changing the subject. "How about you? How are your classes going?"

"Awful," Cade deadpanned. "But I had six seniors get a five on the AP English exam, the most of any teacher in the district."

"That's outstanding."

"Thanks. How about you? How's work?"

We paused our conversation as the flight attendant delivered the meals. "Would you like a drink, sir?"

"I'm good with the water," Cade said, gesturing to the small glass in front of him.

"You sure? It's free," I said and raised my tumbler full of whiskey. It wasn't like Cade not to indulge on vacation. "It's afternoon somewhere."

Cade smiled tightly and shook his head. "Water is fine. Thanks."

When the flight attendant left us, Cade surveyed his sizeable Southwestern-style salad and gave my cheeseburger a side-eye.

"You want half?" I offered.

He shook his head again and started deconstructing his salad, pulling off the tortilla strips, then the avocado and placing them on a side plate, which made absolutely no sense because I'd seen Cade pack away the chips and guac.

"Suit yourself." I took a bite of my cheeseburger and struggled to keep from making a mess as the juices ran down my hand. I licked my fingers mindlessly and caught Cade, mouth gaped and eyes narrowed. I extended my tongue and gave him a good show, moaning, because I was just that extra when he was looking at me like that. He shook his head and cut up an already bite-size piece of iceberg lettuce.

"What's with the rabbit food?"

"Nothing." He drew one shoulder up in a half-hearted shrug.

I shook my head. "Still trying to fight nature, huh?" At twenty-six, Cade still resembled the boy I met our first year at school, which, in a way that sometimes made me uncomfortable to admit, turned me the fuck on. Emotionally, mentally, legally, Cade was all man, but our size difference and his compact, practically hairless, lithe body gave me wood every single time. "You won't put on muscle eating lettuce."

"Not everyone wins the genetic lottery." Cade's pursed lips and hardened jaw sent me back to the small bedroom he'd had senior year.

"You're going to the gym again? At least let me go with you. I've barely seen you all week."

"I've been busy student teaching and working. Not everyone has a mommy and daddy to pay their rent. I can't just drop everything because you're horny again. You insisted on this Mexico trip. I have to save for it."

"It's not about sex, Cade, and you know it. No one works out six days a week and doesn't see any results. If you want to bulk up, I can help, and we can spend some time together at least."

"I don't want your help. I like going alone. It's how I clear my head. I'll be back in an hour. Sid will be home soon; you can wait here if you want."

"That's what you said last night, but I woke up in your bed alone."

I sighed. Once again, I found myself with one foot poised above the minefield that was Cade. Having no idea how to defend myself without pissing him off. "You know I think you're sexy as hell, right? It's not like I think you need to put on muscle."

"It's a new program I'm trying," Cade said in a less hostile tone, but still in a way that meant *leave it alone.* I knew better than to take another step. These were old grievances, and there was no way to navigate around them without detonating Cade's temper. In the spirit of peace and harmony, I focused on devouring my lunch.

When I finished my burger and fries, I watched Cade take another bite, this time a single bean from a pile of black beans. He chewed it for what had to be ten seconds longer than necessary. From the looks of it, he'd eaten about half of his salad, but it was hard to tell because he'd cut everything into such small pieces and separated each food into sections in the bowl. Exactly what kind of program was he on?

Cade

My stomach gurgled, and I had a niggling worry there was dressing already mixed in with the vegetables. It shouldn't bother me since I'd removed the avocado just in case. But, damn it, I didn't like when I couldn't calculate the exact number. Away from home, following my program would be harder than I'd expected.

"Are you listening?" Adam asked, snatching me back from whatever twilight zone my mind had wondered into.

I pushed my thoughts aside and refocused on Adam. Lord knew the man couldn't handle me not giving him my rapt attention even for minute. "Of course. I'm proud of you, sounds like a challenging project."

I ignored Adam's doubtful, narrowed brows and opened my shade. "Wow," I said as the airport came into view and the crystal-blue water rose to meet us. The beach looked amazing. I sat back to allow Adam to see, and he placed his hand on my knee and leaned over.

"I can't wait to get out on the water. You remember Aruba?"

We'd spent the entire week dancing, drinking, and fucking. *Yeah. I remember Aruba*, I thought with a smile. It'd been one of the better vacations of our relationship. I'd felt so close to him.

The pressure of Adam's hand shifted, sending a pulse of awareness up my spine. "Um . . . your hand."

"Oh, sorry," Adam said, righting himself with a fluster. That was how it was for us. I'd learned every curve of his muscles and every mark on his skin. The effortless way our bodies sought each other's was as magical as it was maddening.

Brady let out a cheer as the captain announced we'd be landing soon. Then he rushed toward the back to wake Josh by kissing the top of his head and stroking his stomach. The way those two interacted was something to behold, but it was gentler than the way Adam touched me. If Adam and I were fire, Josh and Brady were earth. Their chemistry was rooted in something far more nurturing than primal. As they returned to the front, I watched with envy. A quick peek at Adam's soft, half-lidded eyes said he had as well.

A wave of nostalgia swept over me. "You remember the first time you asked me to hang out in your dorm room?"

He turned toward me and winked. "I remember all our firsts."

I gave him a weak smile, because his smirk told me he was thinking of the second time. "No. The first time. Brady stopped by to say hello and wouldn't leave."

Adam groaned. "Oh god. I forgot about that. I was trying so hard to get you alone."

Brady's crush on Adam had been endearingly obvious. I remembered being so frustrated at first, but after I realized Adam wasn't the type of guy to kick a friend out to get laid, something in my chest had loosened. Adam was careful with his heart. I had believed it meant I could trust him with mine. "So much has changed since then, huh?"

"Yeah, now we'll be on the other side of the nonstop love fest. Suppose it's time for some payback?" Adam jutted his chin to Siddharth and Matt, who were engaged in a kiss that even from a distance promised more. "What do you think? Should we wait until Matt starts moaning and knock on their door to see if they want fro-yo?"

"Or hide their lube like Siddharth did when I accidentally locked him out of your dorm room during finals?" The hairs on my arm stood up as Adam grasped my forearm and tossed his head back and laughed. My heart did a little flip, and I felt his fingertips pulling me into his orbit. So warm and comfortable, like slipping into a hot bubble bath. The familiarity of being like this was too much for my pathetic defenses. Not when Adam stuck to our highlight reel. We'd inscribed all the wonderful memories in our brains; it was the muscle memory that guided all our reactions that were problematic.

"Listen, Gou . . ."

His silly pet name put me on edge. Goulue, Gou, or "my greedy boy" if I was being particularly desperate in bed—all reminders of what a glutton I was for him. That was what my program was all about—ridding myself of that particular deadly sin.

"I'm planning to stay off your dick this week."

Adam's disbelieving grin called bullshit on my declaration, and perspiration beaded on the back of my neck as I withered under his scrutiny. One look and he knew I was lying. To him. To myself. I hated when he read me so easily. It made all the times when he wouldn't or couldn't all the more devastating.

"Let's just keep our distance as best as we can. I'm sure we can both find suitable replacement ass on this island."

The mischievous twinkle in his eye faded. He shifted and pulled his arm away to make room for the barrier he erected whenever I said unnecessarily shitty things. The deep breath he exhaled expressed a weariness that used to annoy me but now filled me with guilt.

"If you'd have let me finish, I was going to say I think it'd be nice to work on our friendship this week."

I smacked my lips. "Oh," I said as the plane touched down.

"Never mind. Let's do it your way." He picked up his phone and scrolled through Instagram, making sure I noticed all the hot guys he was drooling over as we taxied what felt like the entire island to the terminal.

After the plane rolled to a stop, Adam jumped up. He kept his face hidden from me, but the brooding way he picked up his belongings and stuffed them into his bag made my heart literally ache. The weight of memory, regret, and anger crushing down so hard that I had to take a breath to collect myself.

Why did I say that? I should have taken a leisurely stroll down memory lane and let Adam walk off the plane thinking about the fun we used to have together. I gathered my carry-on items, still mulling over how to repair the damage.

When the rest of our friends had deplaned, I tugged Adam's arm to hold him back. "Hey . . ." I said and waited for him to meet my gaze. "I didn't mean it."

"Yep. Got it, Cade. You never do."

"I'm sorry."

"But . . ." Adam supplied.

"No buts. You don't deserve to be my verbal punching bag. I don't understand why I say things I don't mean to you when I don't do it to any of my other friends. You're right about needing to work on our friendship. I'm willing to try it if you are."

Chapter Three

Cade

"Aloha," Brady greeted me cheerfully on the second morning of our trip. "You're up early. I made coffee."

The promise of coffee perked me up. Unfortunately, I'd learned coffee led to temptations like curling up on the couch with a book instead of exercising. So now I did my workout first, then breakfast. "I think I'm still jet-lagged. Where is everyone?"

"Josh is sleeping in. Sid and Matt left to meet with the real estate lady. Don't forget we have the boat trip today. Josh and I are heading over early to have dinner. We'll meet everyone else at the dock. Do not be late. The sunset is at 6:54 tonight. It's important that you get there on time. And don't forget to charge your camera."

"Okay," I said, drawing out the word. Puzzled, I checked the clock. "It's 7:32 in the morning. We have time."

Brady face-palmed. "Sorry. Ignore me. There was already a glitch in the reservation, and now I'm paranoid."

"No worries. I'll make sure everyone is there on time. Where's Adam?" I bent into a stretch, admiring the hardwood floors. This house was adorable. Two huge bedrooms downstairs were intended to both be master bedrooms, and there was a little open loft above the family room with a double bed, where I was sleeping. The low ceiling and décor made it an obvious children's space, but it suited me fine. Adam's room ended up being a small guesthouse on the property that was accessed through the backyard.

When I finished my stretch, the grin plastered across Brady's face looked permanent. "Not sure, haven't seen him. I'm sure he wouldn't mind if you woke him up."

I suppressed a groan. How much longer would everyone be in the cultlike stage of love, where the high was so good you recruited?

"What did you two end up doing last night after Josh and I turned in?"

Brady would be less than amused to learn we'd tried to ignore his and Josh's not-so-hushed reminders to each other they needed to keep it down. "Not much. We put on a movie and I finished grading some papers."

Brady guffawed. "You're working? This is supposed to be a vacation."

"Relax, we're still enjoying ourselves. Low-key is sort of the goal for Adam and me this week. It's going well so far. Over twenty-four hours in and no shots fired. I'm excited about the sailing trip."

Brady made a sound in his throat that I wasn't sure what to make of. "The Na Pali Coast is supposed to be breathtaking."

I nodded. "I've seen pictures. It was two or three on that list Matt sent us of Top Ten must-see sights." I crossed the room to the large window to check out the view. You couldn't see beyond the rolling landscaping full of tropical blooms—red hibiscus, yellow bird of paradise, and at least fifteen plants and flowering trees I couldn't name. Kauai had certainly earned it's Garden Island nickname. I sighed, relaxing into the feeling of being on vacation now that the jet-lag had started to lift. I turned back to Brady. "I forget the number one. Do you remember?"

"Waimea Canyon, but Josh did yoga on the beach yesterday." Brady grinned. "I assure you nothing else comes close."

That got a laugh out of me. I had to admire Brady's taste. Josh and Adam were indisputably the most attractive of our little group. Both were just a shade over six feet with bodies that spoke to their love of the gym and sports. They both had Hollywood-leading-man jawlines and full heads of hair that belonged on shampoo commercials. Going out to the clubs with them made me feel like a troll doll next to two Kens. "Oh, Brady. Never change. I need to work out before I lose motivation and so I can finish my grading before our trip tonight."

"Grading papers, Cade? Is that how you want to spend your time here?" Brady rested his eyes on me as though guilt was transmittable.

"It's a few hours here and there. It's not like I'm glued to my laptop." I knew the words came out defensive, but helping Maura take care of Hayley had put me woefully behind, and grades were due. I could have canceled the entire trip, but I hadn't. I was here, what more did they expect me to do?

Brady winced. "I'm sorry. I get that you and Adam don't need the peanut gallery weighing in, but you have this great opportunity to make things right. It might not be the 'together forever' kind of right, but there's something that keeps bringing you back to each other. I don't want you two to leave this place and regret not tapping into it."

I let out a long exhale, struggling to not dismiss his words as symptoms of acute love indoctrination. Adam had complained when I graded papers before, but we'd been dating then. Still, my commitment to Adam to work on our friendship might have been better served if I'd actually watched the movie with him. Adam took film almost as seriously as I took books, and he had seemed enthusiastic about it when he talked me into it. I tried to remember if he appeared upset when he headed to bed, but I'd been dealing with a text from Maura and barely remembered him leaving. *Great. Now what?*

After considering the options, I determined Adam probably felt a little isolated not being in the main house. "I'll go see if he's up and bring him some coffee. Maybe he'll want to come workout with me."

Brady smiled approvingly as I trudged to the kitchen and poured a mug, then added some milk, before remembering that Adam had bought hazelnut creamer the day before. I glowered at the coffee as though it had screwed up and not me. My first instinct was to add a splash of the creamer. Adam probably wouldn't realize, but I would know.

In one swift motion, I dumped the coffee and fixed a fresh mug and prepared it the way I knew Adam would like it. The sense of achievement was so strong, I grabbed some yogurt, fruit, and granola for him too. I carried the dishes past a smirking Brady and bumped the sliding door that separated the outdoor living space from the indoors out of the way with my hip.

Matt assured us the home was modest by Hawaiian standards, but the elaborate deck and gardens surrounding the small pool and hot tub sure seemed luxurious. I weaved my way around the path to the guesthouse entrance and knocked, splashing a wave of hot coffee onto my hand. I yelped and brought my hand to my lips and slurped away the burning liquid from my skin. "Fuck."

Heavy footsteps proceeded the door flying open. "Are you okay?"

I stumbled back, gasping. "You're naked."

Adam rolled his eyes. "You've seen it before. What's up?"

It seemed unfair to expect him to be modest in his own room, but I stood there irritated while he moved aside and stared at me expectantly. "Are you coming in?"

"Uh, I can't . . . with you like that. Could you . . . just cover him."

Adam peered down his long torso before giving me a smirk. "'Him'?" He laughed.

"Jesus. Yes. Put some goddamn boxers on already. Why are you sleeping naked, anyway?" *Did he have someone with him?* The words almost escaped, but I caught myself.

He retreated into the compact space. "I was getting ready to shower when I heard you scream," he said over his shoulder. Swooping down, he retrieved his underwear from the floor.

I bit back a groan as the muscular globes of his naked rear flexed. Adam's ass still existed in my mind as the standard of perfection. I couldn't understand what he saw in mine.

"Eyes up here, Gou." Adam snapped his fingers and brought my attention to his cocky-ass smirk. "Better?"

I locked my gaze on his face and forbid myself from ogling his body. "Yes. Thank you."

"You're welcome. What's that?" He gestured toward the mug and bowl.

"Breakfast."

"Afraid there's no place to eat in here. Unless you've changed your opinion on eating in bed." He gestured to the queen-size bed. "Kind of weird but be my guest."

"It's not for me. It's for you."

"*You* brought *me* breakfast?" His incredulous stare erased all the satisfaction I had from doing something nice for him.

I set the dishes down on the dresser with a clang. "You act like I never did nice things for you."

"You did all kinds of nice things for me, Goulue."

His lascivious tone was not something I was equipped to deal with when he was nearly naked. I narrowed my eyes and pressed my lips together. *I will not engage in flirting.*

Adam gave me a funny look. "You get that I'm kidding, right?"

"Sure. Yeah." My monotone cadence probably damaged the conviction of that assurance. I searched my memory for one nonsexual thing I'd done in the past year to prove my case. *Had I not done anything? Not one thing? How was that possible?*

Adam took a sip of his coffee, keeping his gaze locked on mine. His Adam's apple convulsed as he swallowed. "This is perfect, Cade. Thank you."

I smiled; at least I'd done one thing right. "Okay. Good. Well, I'll leave you to it."

"Don't leave." Adam's brows knitted together in confusion. "Where's yours?"

"I need to work out first."

"Stay. I'll share. Then we can work out together. What were you going to do?"

"Matt said there was a park about two miles from here. Supposed to be steps and some bars I can do pull-ups on. I'll make the rest up as I go."

"I'm in. These strawberries are delicious." He stabbed one with the fork and held it up for me. The sweet fragrance made my mouth water, and I swallowed hard. I'd already messed up by sipping the coffee off my hand, but that was an accident. If I accepted his offer, I'd be off my program, and that would put me in a foul mood all day. I didn't want to expose my friends to that. If I stuck to my plan, then I'd allow myself an entire cup of strawberries as a reward. Decision made, I stepped back. "No, thanks."

Adam shrugged and leaned against the dresser as he bit into it. "Keep me company then?"

"Sure." I flopped onto his bed and frowned. Adam liked a firm mattress. "This is too soft."

"Yours isn't?"

"No. It's firm. I'd offer to switch, but you'd bang your head every time you got up."

"Got it." He smiled, and by the amusement displayed on his face, I gathered he was holding back another comment. "Sleep okay?"

"Yeah, fine. Hey, can I ask you something?"

"Sure." Adam nodded.

"You all right out here? Really?"

The corners of Adam's mouth turned down at the edges. "I'd prefer to be in the main house. I know it's stupid, but you know . . ." He lifted his shoulders as his voice trailed off. Adam-speak for *I feel left out*.

"If you don't mind the low ceiling, I'm happy to switch with you." It'd be a lot easier to stay on my program without a stocked kitchen anyway. "I don't want you to feel iso—" My heart sped up the way Adam eyed me. "Why are you staring at me like that?"

"I'm surprised. Pleasantly. I'm good where I am, but it means a lot you offered. Truly. Did you finish your grading?"

"Not quite. I have a few more. Did it bother you I graded papers last night during the movie?"

Adam's face screwed up. "Why are asking me all these questions?"

"Just answer it," I huffed in frustration. Why did he act like everything I did was a trap? He gave me shit about overreacting, but Adam's defenses were as entrenched as mine. "Something Brady said got me thinking, I guess. I plan to finish today so it'll be done."

"How was Brady this morning?"

Well, all right. I guess we were changing the subject, then. "Fine. A little oddly concerned about the sailing trip." A grin split Adam's face, and I instantly recognized the conspiratorial glint. He was up to something. "What do you know?"

Adam's eyebrow peaked. "Did he seem nervous?"

I scrunched up my face, trying to decipher what he'd learned that I hadn't. "Why would he be nervous? Does he not like boats or something?"

"You sure you want to hear this one? If I tell you, you have to keep your mouth shut."

All my friends viewed me as a terrible gossip, which . . . granted. I had a gift for relaying observations and speculation with an unwarranted level of confidence from time to time, but that was years ago. Yet I was still the last to learn something juicy or scandalous. Kind of ironic given all the real secrets I'd kept.

"I will," I promised.

"Brady is proposing tonight." Adam's face lit up and, in his expression, I saw only a reminder of what we should have had, unleashing a fresh wave of grief over what we'd lost.

Adam

Sunbeams broke through the overcast sky, illuminating the emerald cliffs of the Na Pali coastline like a spotlight. The magnificent view from the boat was still no match for the sheer joy radiating from Josh and Brady.

"It was perfect," Josh said, gushing at Brady. "So romantic."

"So, come on. Tell us all the details," Sid encouraged.

Josh and Brady shared a meaningful look before Josh launched into the story. "Brady found this place that serves these gourmet picnics right on the beach. Here . . ." Josh pulled out his phone and showed us the white linen table setup and the chilled bucket of wine. "Brady told me we were going to the beach first. I was all flustered because it seemed really important to him, but I didn't want to get sandy before we had dinner."

Brady rolled his eyes. "He was not budging on the sand issue. I almost had to drag him onto the beach."

"Stop. You did not," Josh protested until Brady kissed him on the nose. He beamed, then turned back. "An-y-ways. We get there, and I freeze because I'm sure we've walked into someone else's romantic dinner, so I'm pulling Brady back toward the car by his arm like 'We got to get out of here.' Then this woman approaches and greets us by name and shows us to the table."

"Josh is hyperventilating at this point," Brady interjected, practically radiating pride.

Josh elbowed him playfully. "Only because I was so floored that you pulled off a romantic dinner where Sid and Matt didn't randomly show up."

At that, the entire group cracked up. Josh referenced that story no less than a million times, so I couldn't help but add a sarcastic, "Oh my god, I'd forgotten all about Matt crashing your first date and bringing Sid along for the ride. You hardly mention it."

That Josh kept laughing showed how far he and Matt had come. I caught Brady's eye and winked. He absolutely made the right call proposing here. Josh had put Matt and Brady's history behind him.

Sid shook his head at his boyfriend. "You realize we will pay for your poor judgment that night forever."

"Forever?" Matt blushed, eyebrow raised in challenge, but Josh wasn't having it; he lashed out playfully, landing the back of his hand on Matt's chest.

"I swear to God, Matthew Weston, if you propose to Sid before I get down the aisle, they will never find your body."

Wanting to share a private laugh with Cade, I sought out his reaction, which was unusually muted. I knew that pensive there-but-not-there stare well. Cade would be "on" for hours, but he had an introspective side that sometimes took over. I wasn't used to seeing it when we weren't alone. I nudged him gently, asking with my eyes if he was okay. He shook his head, which pretty much meant it didn't concern me. But whatever it was that had him so in his head, he snapped out of it and refocused on our friends' conversation.

"We're sorry. Finish the story," Sid prompted. Matt's grimace matched Sid's.

"So we had this amazing dinner . . ."

"You suspected nothing?" I asked.

Josh shook his head emphatically. "I totally believed the dinner was the surprise."

"Nice, Brady." I chucked him on the shoulder.

"So we finished dinner and . . ." Josh's voice started quivering with emotion before tears sprung loose. "And . . ." He reached for Brady's hand and leaned against his chest.

"And then I told you I was so proud of you for following your dream to go back to school and how strong I thought you were for persevering through so much. That I loved how no matter what you had going on, you always took care of me and supported me. Then I got down on my knee, took a deep breath, and asked you to let me return the favor for the rest of our lives." Brady brought Josh's hand to his mouth and kissed the ring he'd placed there. "I love you, beautiful. I can't wait to marry you."

"To Josh and Brady," Cade said, offering a toast with his champagne. We all toasted, and then everyone started moving around, giving the couple a semiprivate moment to kiss the living fuck out of each other. Matt began sharing his encouraging news from the real estate agent, the profits of which Matt planned to funnel into an LGBTQ youth shelter.

Sid pulled out his camera and snapped a candid of Cade lost in thought again, before checking the screen and showing it to me. Cade's blond hair was blowing in the breeze, elbow placed behind him and legs crossed, leaning back with the dramatic landscape in the background. "Send that to me," I said. Sid winked before crossing to the other side of the boat and aiming his camera at the coastline.

I held my plastic champagne flute, taking conservative sips and trying to stay in the moment. Everyone was in a celebratory mood, and I didn't want to ruin anything because I was in my feelings about Cade.

"Look a sea turtle," Sid exclaimed. He leaned over the railing just as a swell rocked the boat, and he labored to keep his balance without dropping his camera.

Matt moved in a flash, stepping past Cade to grab his hips and steady him. "Careful, babe," he said in the same moment that Sid cried out.

A second later, Sid became a total damsel, gushing over Matt's heroism like he'd slayed a dragon rather than taken two steps and extended his arm. Instinctively, I sought Cade's reaction again, knowing he'd have an opinion on the over-the-top swooning. His hand was on the railing, his focus out on the sea rather than toward our friends.

A little moment of daydreaming was one thing, but it wasn't like Cade to be this withdrawn. Especially during a celebration. He should be tossing back champagne and asking invasive question after invasive question until he'd extracted every tiny detail of Brady's beach proposal. He should be giving Sid crap about his clumsiness. I moved toward him, sitting my hand gently at his shoulder to get his attention. "Hey, you okay?"

Cade didn't move.

I squeezed his shoulder, mentally preparing myself for him to tug away. When he didn't respond, I dug my thumb in deeper, massaging the small knots below his neck. "You tired, Gou? That was some Rambo-like intensity on your workout today."

Finally, a reaction in the form of a little quirk of his mouth. "I noticed you never came back from that last water break."

"Guilty."

Cade twisted, removing my hand from his shoulder in the process, and met my gaze. His half smile delivered a slight amount of reassurance.

"My legs are longer. I can't stay in a squat like you can," I explained.

Cade's grin blossomed into a full laugh. Damn, I loved that sound. "Yeah, I seem to remember someone told me strengthening my quads and core was an investment in my future." His eyebrow rose and his expression was classic Cade. The version of him that I knew I could tease without reservation and who would happily dish it right back.

I leaned in, rising to the challenge, and whispered, "I seem to remember my tongue paying you dividends on that investment."

Cade's breath hitched, and he shuddered as he pulled away from me. I'd stepped over the line. I hated that I couldn't reliably read his moods anymore.

"Don't." I tugged his shirt. "I'll behave."

Cade stopped but his shoulders stayed tensed as he hesitated, his doubt of my sincerity playing out on his face. "Adam, I can't . . ."

"I will behave. Old habits, you know?"

"Yeah. I know."

I regrouped. Aiming for friendly concern this time. "So seriously, you doing okay? You're not really yourself tonight."

Cade stole a peek at the cheerful couples in our party. "They're so happy. I'd rather not get into it now."

Every cell in my brain was screaming at me to point out the only thing stopping us from being like Brady and Josh was his unwillingness to forgive me. It wasn't fair, and it likely wasn't true. I'd spent years convinced that all our issues boiled down to Cade's stubbornness. If he were only willing to commit to being together like we'd been before I screwed it all up, things would somehow be perfect. Now, I understood that was only part of it. Even if Cade had the will to resolve that hurdle, we had miles of other issues waiting to trip us up. "I understand."

"It's beautiful here," Cade said, leaning on the railing, angled so I no longer saw his face.

"Yeah. It is."

"Would you want to do something tomorrow? Just the two of us?" Cade asked, still directing his focus to the ocean.

My heart leaped. I worked to tamp down my excitement. "Sure. I'd love to. What did you have in mind?"

Cade twisted to look at me, perhaps a bit surprised that I'd agreed to one-on-one time without any sort of sexual innuendo. Which, what the hell? I wanted him in my life, getting off together wasn't the only good times we had together.

"Not sure, but I don't want to put a damper on Josh's and Brady's mood. I need to get out for a while."

"Want to go hiking? There are amazing trails around."

Cade's eyes widened. "Yeah. That sounds good."

"Adam, Cade . . . What are you doing? Get over here." We turned to see our friends grouped together, the setting sun in the background and fresh glasses of champagne. Sid had handed off his camera to one of the crew, and we posed for a ridiculous number of pictures, then turned our attention to the horizon. Cade and I watched the most gorgeous sunset separated by two happy couples, one newly engaged, and the other in the early stages of love. As a dazzling array of pink and orange lit up the sky and the sun slipped into the Pacific Ocean, my heart ached to have Cade in my arms, to lean in and whisper how much I loved him.

All I could think about was how we'd missed out on another moment that should have been perfect. I knew Hawaii would deliver regrets, but nothing like this.

Chapter Four

Adam

Hanakapiai Falls Trail started with a sharp incline that never got easier. Between the crowds, boulders, mud, and tree roots, Cade and I were too busy trying not to fall on our asses to talk much, but I welcomed the quiet. It felt important to prove we could just be together, enjoying an activity that didn't lead to orgasms. The winding path switched back and forth, and every time Cade held out a hand for assistance, my optimism for the day grew.

"Do you want to rest?" Cade asked when we reached Hanakapiai beach. Red rocks, jungle greens, and the striking blue of the ocean created a vivid palette that made me wish I had brought my good camera.

"Sure." We stood there for a long moment, side by side, taking in the sights and drinking water before settling on some large rocks. I pulled two protein bars from my pack and offered one to Cade. He shook his head and took a long gulp of water, so I devoured them both in silence. A few times, Cade glanced over like he expected me to break the awkward tension with some of our usual banter, but I'd committed to behave. Cade and I communicated on three channels— fighting, fucking, and trying to fuck. So, silence it was.

Ever since Cade had arrived at my bedroom door that morning with coffee and a full plate of protein, there'd been this unsettled energy between us.

The sailing trip had created an urgency to make things right, like there was a closing window of opportunity for us to salvage some sort of relationship before we both gave up. My attraction to him would never go away, but I could rein it in. There had to be a channel for friendship; I just had to find it and hope he tuned in too.

"Let's keep going. We can always spend some time here on the way back." I pushed off the rock, brushed my hands off on my shorts, and headed for the trail, with Cade following.

The second half of the hike was less crowded than the first. Anticipation pushed us forward until we arrived at the waterfall. The 3,000-foot thunderous shower seemed to fall out of the sky into the emerald pool below. Yelps and laughter echoed from the brave souls taking the plunge, declaring the water freezing, but it looked invigorating.

"Want to?" I tried to keep my question neutral as I pointed at a man and woman holding hands and jumping. The more I pushed, the higher the likelihood that Cade would resist. Sometimes it felt like he took pleasure in denying me things, other times . . . I wasn't sure if he cared enough to put that much thought into it.

"Nah," Cade said. "I didn't wear a suit."

"Neither did I. Your shorts will dry."

"Adam." Cade tsked. "I said I don't want to."

"Okay. Fine." I did my best to keep disappointment off my face. It wasn't so much that I wanted to freeze my nuts off, but we were missing yet another opportunity to make a memory. We were in Hawaii, at a waterfall, that we'd spent a lot of effort to get to—the old us would have gone skinny-dipping, and more than anything, lately, I missed the old us.

We settled on a slight ledge to the left, snapped some photos with an outstanding perspective, and caught our collective breaths. My question might have dampened our arrival, but Cade didn't seem upset.

"This is amazing," Cade said, his eyes cast skyward at the top of the falls. "It makes me feel so small."

I chuckled. "You are small."

He shook his head, unamused. "You know what I meant."

"Yeah, I do." I stared at him, trying to keep the intensity of my thoughts off my face. There used to be nothing I couldn't say to him. *Why did talking to him now have to be so hard?*

There was more silence as we watched the falls side by side, but without other things to concentrate on, the fact that we were intentionally not talking became impossible to deny. One of us had to say something, or the whole day was going to be a bust. I took a small breath and brought up our friends—the safest topic I could think of. "How are things with you and Sid?"

Cade shot a mistrusting glance in my direction. "Fine. Why?"

Friendship was going to be difficult if neither of us could answer a question from the other without assuming there was subtext. "Just wondering if him and Matt getting more serious is bothering you. He hasn't had a boyfriend in a long time. Since that one guy in college."

Cade huffed. "Matt is way better than that douchebag."

I chuckled, and the earlier tension eased from his shoulders. "Matt seems cool. He's modest, like Sid. You'd never suspect they were both loaded."

"Except for the private plane to Hawaii?" Cade deadpanned.

"Touché." I smiled. "But you know what I mean. He goes out of his way to not throw his money around."

Cade shrugged. "I presume he's like Sid. They put up with a lot of bullshit for that money. Matt isn't out to his family either."

"Isn't Matt's money from his business?" As far as I understood, Matt started his own IT security company that had made a real name for itself. Brady worked in human resources at Weston Security, so he never elaborated on the techy parts.

Cade gave me a pointed look. "Money breeds money."

Reflexively, I sucked in a sharp breath and prepared to defend myself.

Cade's eyebrows snapped together. "That wasn't a cheap shot. I swear."

By the concern on his face, I knew he was sincere, so I nodded and tried to lower my hackles while he explained: "I meant Matt used family money to start a successful company. It doesn't take away from his accomplishments, but it's also not fair to compare the home run count of someone who starts life on third base to someone who's a hundred miles from the nearest ballpark and reliant on public transportation."

I was tempted to ask what base Cade had determined I'd started on. Compared to Matt and Sid, I wasn't even at bat, but admittedly, and unlike Cade, I'd already arrived at the ballpark. "I get that."

"Have you spoken to your parents?"

I nodded. "I'm going to Atlanta this summer. My dad made R.J. a partner. There's a party."

Cade made a face. "Wonderful. So the firm is what now? Smyth, Creedon, and Creedon Jr."

I chuckled because I'd had the exact thought. "I understand they are going with Creedon and Creedon. Smyth is retiring. Oh, and R.J. has decided he's too important to be *R.J.* now, so I'm supposed to call him *Robert Jr.*"

"Ah yes, the Robert and Robert Jr. Creedon law firm. Amazing. And the Drs. Creedon?"

I laughed. "My mother and sister are well. Mom is still keeping Atlanta's housewives perky and wrinkle-free, and Rachel finished her fellowship."

"Impressive," Cade said sympathetically. "It must thrill your parents."

"The twins never disappoint. That's what Adam is for."

"Adam," Cade objected.

I dropped my gaze to the ground. I knew compared to Cade I had no right to complain, and I really hadn't meant to. "Sorry. I realize my family is privileged and I'm lucky. I'll knock off the self-pity."

"You . . ." Cade nibbled on the inside of his lip. "I didn't mean to make you feel like that."

"Huh?"

"I . . . You said something like that on the plane too. Whatever I said that made you believe you didn't have a right to be angry with the way your parents treat you, I'm sorry. Just because you didn't deal with abuse and neglect, doesn't mean what they say doesn't upset you. I've heard your parents lay into you; they're not abusive, but they're also not kind. Not like they should be."

"I, um . . . Thanks."

"You're welcome," Cade said and there was a pregnant pause while I processed what felt like a genuine breakthrough.

"My mom thinks I need to get serious about my career."

Cade chuckled. "What is a serious graphic designer exactly?"

"I don't know—a rich one? They offered to help me start a business. With their connections, I'd have plenty of work."

Cade made an epic *I told you so*, gesture that made me laugh. "You going to do it?"

I shook my head. "I like where I'm at. Law practices and medical offices aren't asking for innovative designs."

"I saw what you did for The Art Stop. The logo was sick and the website—the paint splashes. I loved it."

"How did you figure out it was mine?"

"Hayley attended a birthday party there last month. I searched for the address at Siddharth's before I picked her up. He mentioned you had worked on it, but I would have recognized your style. You're really talented, Adam." I must have looked flabbergasted, because he shoved me. "Shut up. You know I think your work is amazing."

"Thanks, Gou." We exchanged a glance full of nostalgia for the talks we used to have. Long, drawn-out conversations about everything and nothing. Cade had been my biggest supporter, but after I fucked up . . . Let's say if it was my choice, I'd have rather had him withdraw sex than support. When the silence stretched on, I stood and pulled out my phone. "Take a picture with me?"

"I'll take one of you. I'm disgusting." He swatted at the mud streaks on his ankle and tugged on his clothes. Some fussiness was firmly in Cade's wheelhouse, but he wasn't any sweatier or dirtier than I was, so I wasn't about to indulge him.

"We'll do faces with the waterfall behind."

Cade huffed but took my hand and let me pull him to his feet. He dumped some water on his head and smoothed the strands back away from his face. Huddled close and smiling, I captured some spectacular selfies. "See, stunning as always." I extended my phone to him.

Cade studied the pictures with a contemplative eye and a creased brow line. The rare glimpse of his serious, analytical side sent ripples of longing through me. When Cade caught me staring, he blushed and handed back my phone.

"Can we . . ." Cade began, and the slight shake in his voice had me reaching for him, but before I touched him, I caught myself.

"What's wrong?"

Cade frowned, his voice slightly wet. He shook his head. "Are you *really* happy for them? Not that you're unhappy, but . . ." His voice trailed off, leaving me to fill in the blanks.

I'd been conflicted about Josh and Brady too, and it was a relief to learn I wasn't alone. Seeing them make it when Cade and I hadn't had stirred up a lot of unexpected feelings. Not quite bitterness, but regret, maybe? Or nostalgia? I didn't know, and I doubted Cade did either. But it dampened the excitement, which sucked, because I wanted to be excited for them. I loved them both and was beyond thrilled they were happy. "I know what you mean. It's hard. You want to talk about it?" I asked, twisting my hands into my clothes.

Cade cast his eyes up to me, and the wariness on his face gave me my answer. I wasn't surprised. Even in better times, Cade hadn't confided in me in years. Wanting to talk about it was probably selfish on my part anyway. Cade had Maura; I didn't have anyone but the guys on this trip.

Cade stepped forward to allow a sizable group to pass. His feet planted, his chest leaned in my direction, and I stood there, holding my breath, as his hand rose to my shoulder for support, his fingers curling around the back of my neck, igniting tingles down my spine. I diverted my gaze, eyes seeking out anywhere but him, reminding myself that today was about friendship. But eventually that mysterious force between us became impossible to ignore.

As our eyes met, my heart pounded in my chest. I wanted to touch him, taste him, remind him of how good we were together. But more than that, I wanted to understand what was going on inside of him. Overwhelming need forced my eyes closed just as a bump from the crowd behind sent him stumbling into my arms.

"Adam," Cade said, his deep but soft voice summoning my attention. His lower lip compressed between his teeth and his eyes lifted up to me. Two green pools of want I'd gladly drown in. He rocked up, bringing his lips within inches of mine. Our magnetic pull as strong as ever.

How many times had I started this free climb toward a relationship he didn't want—at least not with me? I wanted him so much, I always settled for what he gave me, but—I swallowed hard—this was a terrible idea.

"I want to go swim." My words broke the spell, and the roar of the waterfall rushed back into my consciousness.

Cade rocked back on his heels. "Yeah, um, sure. I'll come with you."

His easy acquiescence astonished me. But as I took his hand and led him down to the base of the waterfall, I couldn't figure out why. Cade's first reaction had always been contrary. When we reached the bottom, I stripped down to my shorts and stashed my shirt and phone in my pack. Cade eyed me silently, curiosity etched on his face. No doubt expecting me to change my mind. With each skeptical glance toward the water, the more determined I became.

I knew working on our friendship meant I would need to get a handle on my feelings and respect his boundaries, but now I realized it also meant establishing some limitations of my own. I craved a relationship like Brady and Josh—one built on mutual respect and trust and a desire to take care of each other. Cade might not want that with me—in fact, he'd been clear he didn't. But I did. I wanted more. And it was time to stop letting my fear of losing Cade stop me from getting it. I took a deep breath and jumped in, hollering at the rush of icy water. When I surfaced, Cade was starting at me—amused and fighting himself over it.

I held out my hand to him, beckoning him to join me. "Come on."

Then, to my utter surprise, he jumped.

Cade

Insomnia was the last thing I expected after our eight-mile hike, but I'd been in bed almost two hours and sleep had eluded me. When my stomach gurgled for the millionth time, I picked up my phone and flipped through the pictures Aislinn had sent of her and Hayley from their trip to the zoo. They'd arrived before we left for our hike, but I'd spaced the time difference and by the time we made it back, it was too late to call. I checked the clock app. They'd probably be up by now.

Cade: *How's Maura?*

Aislinn: *She seems okay. Sleepy. Probably the increased dose.*

Cade: *Is she following her schedule?*

Aislinn: *Not really. I'm sorry. I'm doing my best. Tried to get her to go with Hayley and me to the zoo, but she refused.*

I sighed. *Try making her at least take a shower before nine. Even if she goes back to bed.*

Aislinn: *Will do.*

Cade: *Is Hayley okay?*

Aislinn: *Yeah. We're having a wonderful time.*

Well, good.

Cade: *Thanks for doing this. Remind Maura that Hayley has a math test on Friday. She'll be tempted to let her stay home if you're not there. Hayley's counselor is making waves with Maura about her attendance.*

Aislinn: *Do you want me to call in and move my flight till Saturday?*

Cade: *No, you shouldn't call in to a new job. Maura can pull it together for a day, even with the side effects.*

Aislinn: *Will do. How's Hawaii?*

I sorted through my phone camera, searching for some pictures to send, but I'd only taken a few. I attached the single photo I took at the falls, then added, *Good. Josh and Brady got engaged.*

Aislinn: *That's awesome. Tell them congrats for me.*

I texted the thumbs-up emoji. *Going to go back to sleep now.*

Aislinn: *Okay. Love you, Bro.*

Cade: *Love you too.*

I opened Instagram, unsurprised to find a feed full of Hawaiian landscapes. Siddharth and Adam were both consummate users, but Brady and Josh had upped their game with matching engagement announcements and a multitude of other candid photos from our trip.

There was one of me on the boat. I stared at it for a long time, knowing the exact thoughts that were rolling through my mind at the moment. It should have been us who got engaged. Hell, five years ago, I would have said Adam and I would be hitched by now. No part of me questioned our path back then. I had dealt with my issues and I was ready to move on, finish college, and start my life. He was everything I wanted in a partner—beautiful, supportive, kind. He didn't drink excessively or fly off the handle. We'd already decided the exact breed and name of our future fur baby.

Brady's proposal had left a heaviness in my chest, and I hadn't taken a carefree breath since. The weight of lost potential, I supposed.

I scrolled through my feed, liking and commenting on most of the images. I stopped on the one Adam had taken of him and me at the falls. It clashed with the ones of us on the boat trip. Today, on our own, we seemed happier. Well, I looked annoyed because I didn't love having pictures taken. And why did my cheeks always puff out like I had marshmallows stuffed inside? My arms resembled limp twigs next to Adam's. But Adam remained all smiles, and when his light shone like that, it was hard not to get caught in the glow.

I sighed and scrolled through the comments, wondering if others noticed as well. Adam had a lot of followers, and there was already a slew of comments.

BradynotTom: *Gorgeous. @Josh_Meyer is bitter we didn't get an invitation.*

Josh_Meyer: *Cuties*

JambaJoe13: *Such a cute couple! Where is that?*

RJCreeden: *Bro. Work. It's a thing. Life isn't a vacation.*

DrRachelC: *Not again.*

BryGuy223: *Reported. Reason for reporting: You deserve better.*

The flare of possessiveness hit me hard. I snapped off a quick text to Adam.

Who the fuck is BryGuy?

My thumb hovered over the Send button. There was a good chance Adam was asleep, and an even higher chance I would go insane wondering why he hadn't responded to me. Alternatively, he would answer and tell me to mind my business, which would piss me off. If he responded that BryGuy was no one, could I believe him?

I sighed. There remained no scenario where I got the reassurance I needed. *And that right there was the problem.* That was why Adam and I didn't work. I wouldn't trust him enough to be monogamous, and remaining uncommitted ensured he would never prove me wrong. The last four years had been a lose-lose proposition, and we wondered why it never worked.

I exhaled a lengthy breath and deleted the text.

If I remained true to my program, I'd have put my phone away. Instead, I stalked BryGuy. After thirty minutes of concentrated searching, all I'd determined was that he'd turned thirty-two in March, was definitely gay, and his thirst seemed directed solely at my boyfriend—*wait, not boyfriend*—friend.

But did he know Adam? If so, from where? I continued to search until I found the answer.

There was a picture of him with Adam at what appeared to be a poker game. I cringed at the cigars in their hands. Adam only smoked when he drank. They weren't touching, but judging by the lopsided quirk to Adam's mouth, he had more than a little buzz going. *Since when did Adam play poker? Who was this guy?*

I'd met all of Adam's friends. Or at least I assumed I had. I inspected the guy's picture. He wasn't Adam's usual type. The guy appeared to be on the petite side, sure, but . . . well, okay, he was also blond, but other than that, he wasn't Adam's type. Adam didn't go for older guys. I closed my apps and put my phone down with a huff. I twisted to lie on my side, slid my arm between my two pillows, and tried to get comfortable. Thirty seconds later, I was back on my phone flipping through BryGuy's profile and reading every comment he'd ever posted to Adam. Adam had never responded. Not to validate his rude comments about me, nor to chastise them, so it was possible he just didn't read his comments anymore. I couldn't process all the emotions I had about that, but the feeling wasn't good.

My stomach growled again, and I tried to switch my brain to focus on healthier things. Small successes where I'd followed my program. We'd left too early to work out before the hike, but it turned out to be way more strenuous than we imagined, so I regarded that as a win. I'd gotten in a decent workout and watched my diet today. Adam and I had made it back without losing our shit, so also a success. Not sending that text counted as an accomplishment, but when I factored in almost kissing Adam, I had to consider that a wash.

How did I manage to make the same mistakes with Adam? I should have walked away when he returned from Mexico and confessed. That's what most people did with cheating exes. They cut off all ties and moved the fuck on.

I hadn't. I pushed away all thoughts of why, focusing on the narrative everyone had accepted: my friends were tied up with Adam and it was nearly graduation. I'd been adamant I would not miss out because he didn't keep his dick in his pants. Our friends had dished out a lot of atta-boys for being so mature about the situation, but the truth was I'd been unable to cut him off. My desire for him hadn't faded at all, and it hadn't taken long for us to wind up in bed again. I'd managed okay until . . .

I swallowed hard, recalling the night I'd couldn't keep pretending.

Adam's hot breath hit the back of my neck. "Fuck," he murmured and dropped kisses along my shoulder in between low moans of pleasure. Adam loved to pin me to the bed, force sweet endearments into my ear, hold me close. That was so not on the menu anymore. I pushed up with my hips, straining to get the show on the road.

"Up." I arched my back and pushed until I was on my hands and knees and Adam was kneeling behind me. Adam's breathing changed, and I didn't need to see him to sense his hesitation. "Go hard."

Adam jerked my hips toward him. "My greedy boy." Adam laughed and thrust into me hard. "Is that what you want?"

I whined my assent, whimpering. "Hard—oh, fuck." I held on to the sheets for dear life, letting Adam erase my knowledge of the English language. "Gah," I panted as he nailed my prostate.

Adam groaned low in his throat and didn't stop. He smiled against my shoulder, his wet lips leaving a damp trail over my skin. He thrust into me again, giving me what I'd asked for and stealing my breath. I rocked back on his cock, smiling to myself at his predictable reaction.

"Yeah. Just like that. Fuck, Cade. You're amazing. God. I missed this. I missed you. Need to come."

"Yeah, do it."

"You first," he begged, his voice strained as he reached for my cock and started tight, quick strokes over the head.

My orgasm rocketed through me, spilling out onto the sheets below. I clenched around him in tight pulses. He clamped his hands on my hips and came with a tortured groan. "Fuck. I love you so much, Cade."

His words sent an arctic blast over my sweat-drenched skin.

I lurched forward, not caring that I landed in the mess. The hard plane of Adam's chest collapsed against my back, and my arms buckled as his weight settled on me. "Stop."

"What's the matter?" Adam panted against my neck.

"Get the fuck off me."

Adam's body stiffened as I attempted to crawl out from under him. "Jesus, Cade. Give me a second to pull—"

I jabbed my elbow back and rolled his weight off me, grunting with the abrupt withdrawal.

Adam landed with an oomph and scrambled to keep from falling off the bed. He made an undignified dismount and switched on the light. His hand dropped to keep the filled condom from falling off his softened erection.

He opened his mouth to say something, but when I lifted my chin, ready to go ten rounds, he sighed and ran his other hand through his ridiculously soft, beautiful hair. "Are you okay?" His eyes cast down my body, and the flood of concern made me twitchy.

I gathered the blanket to me. "You need to go."

"Cade—" Adam protested. "I'm sorry."

"I warned you."

"Gou . . . please. Can we talk about—"

I shook my head. My world tunneled until all I focused on was Adam's baby blues begging me for forgiveness. Telling me he was sorry for the umpteenth time. Lies, all lies. He didn't even understand how he'd broken me.

His apology ripped off the scab over my heart that never seemed to heal. I battled with the part of me that wanted him to stay there and watch me bleed.

"Cade, please. I don't want to do this tonight. Graduation's tomorrow. We can start over. A new chapter."

Why didn't he see the begging made it worse? I wanted him in pain. Needed him to suffer for not seeing what I was hiding from him. For breaking me instead of fixing me. I wrapped the blanket tight around me, walked to the small bathroom, and shut the door with a slam. The bedframe squeaked, and I pictured Adam sitting on the edge of the bed, running his hands through his hair in indecision. Waiting for me to come out. To be reasonable. To talk to him.

"It's just fucking. You agreed," I shouted.

Adam's footsteps neared the door. I heard it in his breathing: the exasperation, the despair. He knocked. "Cade, can I at least get some tissue to throw away the condom?"

"Kleenex. In the kitchen." The crack in my voice betrayed me.

"Damn it," Adam yelled. "I only said what you already know. Fuck these theatrics, Cade. I love you and I'm so damn sorry. You love me. I know you do. Why can't we be happy again?" He begged and pleaded over and over, but I said nothing because what could I say? I'd tried to forgive him; I couldn't. He'd tried being fuck buddies; he couldn't. Finally he walked away, the door slamming as his last words cut through me.

"It was one mistake."

There it was again. That fucking, wholly inadequate word—*mistake*. Thoughts of the word stirred resentment in me. I rubbed my belly, feeling the edges of the hurt and anger grumbling inside.

When Adam and I had made plans to move in together after graduation, every dream I had for my future was about to come true. I'd proved my mother wrong—every time she called me worthless or told me no one would want me. It wasn't true, because Adam did. Adam valued me. I did really hard things to be better for him. To be worthy of him. Part of me grasped that was why I kept letting him back into my bed. No matter how rude or cruel I was to him, he wanted me when I couldn't stand myself.

Maybe BryGuy was right. If my poor self-esteem was all we had left, I didn't deserve him. The honorable thing to do was let him go for real.

There was only one problem with that plan—I didn't know how.

Adam

I was up early, hoping to have some time alone with Cade before the rest of the guys woke up, but no such luck. The house was buzzing with activity, so I stayed on the patio, swaying in the hammock and staring at my tablet, but mostly reliving moments with Cade, trying to remember better times.

My initial attraction to Cade was his outrageous personality. Everything about him screamed trouble, which, after a lifetime of walking in the twins' shadows, was what I'd been gunning for. He put so much effort into feeding the stereotypical twink image—always some biting or innuendo-laced comment at the ready, always down for a good time, never wanting the mood to get too serious, but it didn't take long to learn there was more depth to him.

"Breakfast is ready."

Josh's bellowing voice pulled me out of my thoughts. I clicked off my tablet and headed inside to help.

"Inside or out?" I asked Matt as I grabbed the stack of plates from the cupboard.

The way Matt glanced at Sid for the answer made me smile. In a few quick days, Sid had taken to his role as cohost quite well.

"Outside," Sid said. Matt turned to me with a face that read, *You heard my man.*

Chuckling, I led the way to the patio. Brady and Matt trailed behind me with silverware and glasses.

"So what's the plan for the day?" Brady asked.

"Unfortunately, I need to meet with the agent again and fill out some paperwork. Someone will be by later to take pictures for the listing, but Sid was talking about seeing Waimea Canyon, perhaps doing a hike."

"You sure you want to sell this place? Sid is ready to move here," Josh said, carrying a casserole dish that smelled like blueberry goodness. He set it down and turned toward the door, waiting for Sid to appear with his other creation. "Okay. So this is a French toast casserole made with vegan egg." He smiled at Sid as Sid placed the second platter on the table. "And this is an asparagus and tofu scramble."

Brady groaned and Josh shushed him. "I also made a side of bacon for the carnivores of the group. I'll be right back with it."

"You need help?" I rose to my feet, but Josh waved me off. "No, sit. I'll get it. Everyone dig— Wait, where's Cade?"

"He left for a run," Sid said.

"Yeah, but that was well before we started cooking."

"Maybe he snuck back in and fell back asleep. I'll go check." Two steps from the stairs, the front door opened. Cade's skin was so pale it was practically translucent.

I gasped. "Jesus Christ. Are you okay?" Cade's eyes, sunken and unfocused, weren't quite tracking to my voice.

"I'm—" Cade listed and stumbled.

"Cade!" I scrambled toward him, catching him before he hit the ground. The rest of the group rushed inside, gawking at me with matching perplexed faces and cries of concern.

"His skin is so clammy. Someone call 911. Cade. Cade." I smacked his cheeks and got no reaction. "What's wrong with him?"

"Does he have low blood sugar? That happens to me sometimes," Matt said.

"No." I shook my head. "What do we do? Shit. Cade, c'mon. Wake up."

"Get your sugar tablets, babe," Sid barked. "Josh call 911. Brady get me that water." He pointed to the counter.

Brady handed over the glass, and Sid splashed some ice water on Cade's face.

Cade stirred, fighting against my efforts to keep him from trying to get up. "What the fuck, Adam?" Cade flailed, hitting me across the cheek, but in my relief, I barely noticed it.

"Here are the tablets." Matt popped one out of the blister pack and placed it in my palm. "They dissolve under the tongue."

I tried to place it in his mouth, but Cade shoved my hand away. "I'm fine. Get off me!"

My fear dissolved into anger. I'd shove it down his throat if need be. "You fainted, asshole. Now, stop fighting me and take this goddamn tablet."

Cade stilled and heaved a sigh. "Would you at least let me sit up?"

I relinquished my hold, keeping a hand on his skin, which was getting some color back. "Go slow."

"Here's some water." Sid handed him a glass, and we all stood, freaked out, watching intently as he popped the tablet into his mouth, then sipped from the glass.

"Oh my God. Everyone quit staring at me like that. I'm fine." Cade took another drink of water.

"The operator asked if we want an ambulance."

"No!" Cade barked at the same time Sid and I said, "Yes."

Josh, never one to go against anyone's wishes, gave Cade a sympathetic smile before turning to Brady with a pained expression. Brady cast the tie-breaking vote with a shake of his head.

"Thank you, operator. No, I think he's okay now. Yes, perhaps just dehydrated." We all gawked at Josh as he finished his call. "Okay. We will. Okay. Thanks."

Josh ended the call and kneeled in front of Cade. "She said you were probably dehydrated and that you should drink fluids and take it easy and follow up with your doctor."

"Okay. I will when I get home." Cade glowered at me. "Can I get off the ground now?"

"Let's help him up," Sid said. He and Matt took a step toward Cade.

"I got him." I didn't plan to growl at them, but whatever, it worked because they stopped. I slid my arm under Cade's knees.

Cade rolled his eyes at me but handed the water glass back to Sid. "For fuck's sake, Adam. You don't nee—"

I hoisted him up and carried him to the small loveseat that had the best air flow. As soon as I sat him down, he tried to stand. "Don't."

"I'm disgusting and I'll get the couch dirty. I need a shower."

My heart was still pumping with adrenaline. "Sit there and don't move. I'll get you more water and some food."

"This whole Neanderthal vibe isn't working for me, babe."

"Gou." I took a deep breath and exhaled, willing the fear out of my body as I kneeled down to meet him face to face. His color was back to normal, and he was well enough to give me grief, so I tried to dial it back. Bossing Cade around was above my paygrade now. "Please. You scared the hell out of me." I didn't intend it to be a guilt trip, but something flashed in Cade's eyes that looked suspiciously like surrender.

He slumped back and crossed his arms over his chest. "Let me sit at the table and stop making a fuss. I promise to eat and drink like a good boy."

"Adam." Sid's soft voice floated above us. His gentle hand rested on my shoulder, encouraging me to stop pushing.

I cast my eyes up at him and swallowed the lump in my throat, then returned my focus to Cade with a contrite smile. "Okay. Get up slowly."

Cade nodded and accepted Sid's and my help to walk to the table. No one protested when I moved seats to take the one next to Cade, while Sid handed him a plate. Matt set a banana down next to him. "Some potassium might help."

Cade glanced up with a grateful smile. "I'm sorry, guys. I must have overdone it on my run."

"Did you go to the park again?" Brady asked.

"No, it was gorgeous out and I just started running. Before I knew it, I'd been gone more than an hour. Then I made a wrong turn coming back, so . . . I honestly didn't mean to worry anyone."

"Didn't you take any water?" Josh asked.

Cade shook his head. "I don't like to carry anything. I didn't think I'd go that far."

"Well, no wonder you fainted," Josh said. "You need about eight ounces of fluid for every twenty minutes."

Cade nodded and took a long drink of his water. "I'm better, honestly. Let's change the subject. Please. Stop with the worry. Eat. Seriously." Cade scooped a healthy portion of the French toast casserole onto his plate and passed the dish to Josh, who seemed eager to move past the conflict. Cade took a small taste and patted my hand, like he finally realized how freaked out I was. "It's okay, Adam. I'm okay."

"Eat some protein." I put two slices of bacon on his plate. He opened his mouth, ready to fight me, but changed his mind and nibbled the bacon, then switched to peeling the banana.

"Perhaps we should do something a little lower key than Waimea today," Sid said to a chorus of nods.

"No. I don't want to change our plans. I'm fine."

Brady shrugged. "I'm a little tired, anyway. We haven't gotten in the pool much; we can hang here today."

Josh nodded. "Yay. I still haven't seen the speedo."

"I'll call the real estate agent and have them take the pictures after we leave."

"Are you sure, babe?" Sid asked.

"It'll be easier for everyone. Let's just relax today."

"Absolutely not. No one is changing plans because I'm an idiot." Cade's alarmed eyes flashed to me and essentially begged for my support.

Our eyeballs held a silent negotiation on the matter, and when I sensed he understood my terms, he gave a slight nod. "Cade's right. You guys go. I'll stay here."

"Are you sure?" Sid asked, soliciting Matt and Josh for their thoughts. "Perhaps we can go to the lookout and skip the hike so you can go."

"It's a really winding road," Matt said. "Even when you're healthy, the drive can make people sick to their stomach."

"It's fine," Cade answered firmly. "You all take pictures for me. I'll stay here, read, and relax. I'm sure Adam will club me over the head and drag me back to the cave if I step out of line." Cade laughed, but the anxiety in his voice was undeniable. It almost seemed like embarrassment, which wasn't like Cade at all.

Cade spent the rest of breakfast alternating between reassuring everyone and chastising us for our concern. In the end, the guys went, leaving me to clean up and Cade to shower. He returned as I pushed the Start button on the dishwasher.

His hair was still dripping as he walked into the kitchen carrying a book. He wore some loose-fitting shorts and an old college sweatshirt of mine that must have stretched out, because it was swimming on him. My stomach flipped, and I recleaned the counter just to keep my hands from touching him. "Haven't seen that in a while." I tried to keep my tone neutral, but surely his choice meant something.

Cade shrugged. "I'm always afraid you'll steal it back."

I met his gaze, searching for reasons to not give up. "It's yours. Besides, you look sexy in my clothes."

Cade smiled but didn't respond.

"Feeling better?"

"Yes, much. Is there coffee?"

I wasn't sure if the caffeine would be good for him, but I wasn't brave enough to deny him. I pulled a mug down and poured him a cup, then retrieved the milk.

"No, thanks," he said.

I cocked my head, but he answered my unasked question. "Working on eliminating dairy."

His smile blossomed a bit as I slid the coffee across the counter to him. The sleeves of my sweatshirt covered his palms as he gripped it with both hands and brought it to his lips. He exhaled like he'd just tasted heaven. "Thank you."

I had to close my eyes for a moment to keep the image from imprinting in my head. "So what are you reading these days?"

"*At Swim, Two Boys.*" I opened my eyes to see Cade smile. "You'd like it. O'Neill writes in a stream-of-consciousness style, similar to Joyce."

I nodded. "I still love *Portrait of an Artist as a Young Man.*"

Cade nodded enthusiastically. "We read that together, right?"

"Yeah," I said. A warmth spread through my chest. "I miss it."

"Me forcing you to listen to classic books from my classes?"

"You never forced me. I loved it."

"I distinctly recall you ripping Steinbeck out of my hands and throwing it across the room."

I guffawed. "George killed Lennie, Cade. He shot him in the back of the head. That was not okay."

Cade broke into laughter. "It was out of mercy. Curley would have tortured him."

"I don't care. Steinbeck is an asshole."

Cade shook his head, still struggling to contain his laughter. "I forgot how passionate you can get about literary character justice."

Thoughts of lying in bed naked on Sunday mornings, debating some aspect of literary analysis with him made my chest ache. *If only I could recapture that connection with him.* I pushed the thought aside. "The hammock outside is perfect for reading."

Cade glanced over his shoulder, then back to me, his eyes twinkling. "I believe you called dibs. Am I allowed?"

I shoved his shoulder in the patio's direction. "Just stay off the ground, would ya?"

The levity got caught in something between us. He didn't move, assessing me like he was seeing me for the first time. "I'm sorry I scared you, Adam. I shouldn't have . . . I know you were only trying to take care of me."

The sincerity in his voice shook something loose that I hadn't felt in a long damn time.

Hope.

I was fantastic at loving Cade. That's what I wanted back. The ability to see more than lust in his eyes. I needed to understand what he was thinking. It wasn't only a want—it was past time to admit I needed that connection with my lover.

"I'm glad you're okay."

Chapter Five

Cade

"You have got to be kidding me." I rolled my eyes as Sid and I approached the beach. Kicking off my flip-flops, I scooped down to pick them up, loving the sensation of sand between my toes. "I thought this was a small bonfire for our last night."

"Matt's excited to do something for Brady and Josh. He wants to put the past jealousy behind them."

"There's so much food."

"Just enjoy it. It means a lot to him."

"Fine," I said. When we arrived at the buffet, I stared at the array of dishes as Sid handed me a plate. A tide of anxiety rose in my chest. I hadn't prepared for such an enormous meal and didn't have any way to track calorie counts. I bit my lip, unsure of what to do. Sid was heaping some rice dish with pineapple onto his plate.

"I'm so glad you came, Cade. This week wouldn't have been the same without you."

"It's been fun." It was mostly true. Even if the week had taken a toll, the guilt of disappointing everyone would have been much worse. "Um, I'm going to go down by the water for a minute." I put the plate back and walked down to the shore, staring at the waves rolling onto the sandy beach, trying to summon some gratitude. The day had been hard. Aislinn had left Maura's, so I'd spent a fair amount of time worried about Hayley. At least Maura had gotten her to school for her test.

I ran my hands along my biceps, rubbing my arms to warm myself against the wind.

"Are you cold?" Adam's incredulous voice asked from behind me. I turned, meeting his gaze as he stepped toward me. "You all right, Gou?" he asked, tone laced with concern.

"Yeah. My stomach is a little off." It wasn't a lie. Nausea had hit as soon as I'd seen the buffet.

Adam stood there for a few minutes, his hand resting on my shoulder. I shivered again, and Adam chuckled, opening his arms for me. "It's at least seventy degrees," he said in disbelief. I moved closer toward him, and his arms collapsed around me. He rubbed along my back as I tucked myself into him. I loved how Adam's body molded against mine, my head just at the right height to lean on his solid chest. When the tug on my heart grew, tormenting me with doubts, I pulled away. I'd been faithful to my program all week. One more night and I'd get off this island and away from near constant reminders of how sweet and caring he could be. I'd survived sunset sails, romantic waterfall swims, and his Florence Nightingale routine; I could manage bonfires on the beach—despite the other four of us relentlessly making the case for boyfriends.

He followed my gaze toward the two couples sitting around the fire. Josh was on Brady's lap, his arm thrown around his fiancé's neck, eating from a shared plate. I watched as Josh scooped up something and fed it to Brady, who struggled to cram it all in. I wrinkled my nose at them, slightly disgusted by how cute they were. "He'll gain all that weight back if he eats like that."

Adam's mouth gaped. "Cade," he chastised. "Why would you say something like that?"

"Sorry," I snapped, frustrated by how they made it seem like it was all so easy. They decided to be together less than a year ago and now they were engaged. No drama. No breakups. They never fought, at least not in front of us. But it wasn't only their relationship that bothered me. Brady wanted to lose weight, so he did. He worked out and dieted and changed his body without going overboard. He took a day off without blinking an eye.

"You shouldn't have thought it. Brady's worked so hard to lose weight."

"I know," I said. "You have to be so careful or it comes right back." My words came out bitter. All the effort I was putting into my program. Food, Adam, my family . . . I was so sick of repeating the same mistakes.

Adam shook off his confusion and removed his hoodie, handing it to me. "Here. Put this on. I want it back, though. Come on. We're getting a look from Sid."

I slipped on his sweatshirt and followed Adam back to the group, then took a seat as far from him as the arrangement allowed. A small voice in my head reminded me I'd been kind of shitty about Brady, who was basically the nicest guy in the world. Not only did I not deserve Adam, but I also didn't deserve any of my friends. Not when their happiness was making me so sad. So I sat there, staring vacantly as they laughed and ate a ton of delicious food. It was so strange being surrounded by people I loved and feeling so alone. I wanted nothing more than to go back to the house and wallow, but that would invite a lot of unwanted scrutiny, so I did my best to join in the conversation and tried not to rain on Josh and Brady's parade.

I picked at the plate Sid handed me, mindlessly separating some pasta salad into its parts. When I had everything separated, the notion of eating it made me queasy. I took a sip of my drink, stood, and grabbed empty plates, stacking them on top of mine, before throwing them away.

Josh's voice yanked me out of my thoughts, and when I glanced up, his grin moved me out of my agonizing. "I need to grab my jacket from the car and Matt's got Brady strategizing about some work thing. Come with me?"

I nodded, following Josh toward the public parking area.

"You've been quiet."

"Just tired. The week is catching up to me."

Josh flashed an appreciative smile. "I'm thrilled you were all here for this week. Not that I realized it would be such a special occasion, but I can't imagine it was easy for you."

"It was fun."

"Did you and Adam have time to talk yesterday?"

"Yeah. The cease fire is in place."

"A cease fire, but not peace talks?"

I shook my head. There was a moment when Adam sent me to read in the hammock, I'd almost brought up the topic of our relationship, wanting a status check of sorts, but I didn't trust myself not to bring up BryGuy's comments, and I didn't trust Adam to not break my heart by revealing he was fucking him.

Josh cracked his knuckles as we approached the car. He slowed, working up the nerve to say something else. Josh and I were complete opposite in that regard. I'd always admired how carefully he chose his words. The car lights flashed as Josh pushed the unlock button. I remained on the sidewalk, hands shoved deep in Adam's pockets, waiting for Josh to get what he needed.

Josh opened the door, reached inside, and closed it. Turning, he leaned against the car, facing me. "It's so pretty here." He gazed around at the palm trees and the tropical plants.

I nodded. "You ready?"

"Um . . ." Josh said, hemming and hawing, his jacket clutched tightly with both hands.

I shook my head, growing weary of his stalling. "Josh, for fuck's sake. I love you, man, but spit it out."

Josh barked out a laugh with a slight shake of his head, like he was chastising himself for being so wishy-washy. He exhaled a breath and smiled. "Okay, so here goes—I've been in love with Brady for a long time."

I rolled my eyes, with a sarcastic "Yeah. I know. We all knew."

"Brady didn't."

"True, but Brady can be sort of clueless."

Josh heaved a frustrated sigh that might just as easily have been aimed at me as his husband-to-be, but his smile flattened and he took a deep breath and finally, the point of inviting me on this little errand became clear. My pulse raced and the hairs on the back of my neck stood up.

"It took Matt coming into the picture for me to see that if I let my fear of ruining our friendship keep me from acting on my feelings, I might lose my shot. I had to let go of so much crap from my past to be with him. To be who he deserved." Josh chewed his lip, staring at me for a reaction to that bit of well-told history. When I didn't respond, Josh continued. "I don't want you to let your past stop you from having what you want."

"Josh—"

"No, Cade. Listen. I get Adam hurt you."

Every muscle in my body tensed. "Yeah. He did."

"But he's not the same guy who—"

"With all due respect, Josh, that's because you're in love. I'm happy for you and Brady. Sincerely. I know you both mean well, but you need to butt out." Josh recoiled, and I instantly felt like shit again. "I'm sorry for yelling, but we keep you out of our issues for a reason. Why does everyone suddenly have an opinion on me and Adam breaking up? It's not the first time and let's face it—it won't be the last."

"We love you and we love him."

"Yeah, so you don't love us if we're not together?"

"No, of course we do. We want you guys to be happy and this time seems so final. You're not yourself. You spent all week . . . We all thought yesterday, with the way he cared for you . . . But you two didn't makeup. It's so obvious you love him."

"Josh. That's not the problem."

"Then why? We don't understand why you can't forgive him."

I gasped. Our friends had never taken sides before, but I never imagined if they did it would be to support Adam. "Because he broke my heart, okay? He yanked it out of my chest and stomped on it and it doesn't fucking fit right anymore. So now I'm just a fucking asshole who doesn't know how to love, I guess."

"Cade—" Josh's eyes went wide. He hated confrontation, but fuck it—I couldn't have stopped my mouth in that moment if I tried.

"No, Josh. You asked. Do you realize he never apologized for cheating? He says he's sorry he hurt me—that he made a mistake. Like he tripped and his dick fell into some asshole's mouth. He never says the word 'cheated.' Ever. How can I forgive him when he won't acknowledge what he did?"

"Josh." Adam's soft voice broke through the darkness. I whirled around, and Adam stepped out of the shadows under the streetlight. He cleared his throat, and his body was so rigid his jaw barely moved. "Will you give us a moment?"

"Adam, I'm—" Josh stuttered, clearly mortified.

"It's fine. Please just give us some space."

Josh pulled me into a hug that my body refused to accept. "I'm so sorry, Cade. You're not an asshole. We love you both, and I shouldn't have said anything." He sprinted past me, leaving Adam and his apparent confusion.

"Adam—"

"Don't," he barked, putting his hand out. "Don't talk, I need to get this out."

"But I—"

"You meant it. Clearly you meant it. And you're right or I guess . . . I've apologized for that night so many times, I'm not sure what exact words I've used, but if you were waiting for me to say it a certain way, then I trust you would remember."

"Adam—"

"I cheated on you. There. Is that what you needed me to say? I did it. It wasn't an accident. I was drunk, but not so drunk that I wasn't responsible for my behavior. I was frustrated because my parents were going to my sister's medical school graduation instead of mine and there was this distance between us. That trip was the only thing I was looking forward to, and you canceled on me. Your reasons for canceling didn't matter. It triggered every insecurity I had, so when I met someone who showed me a little of the attention I was missing, I decided to be unfaithful. I asked him to leave the bar with me, I pushed him to his knees, and I told him to suck my dick. There was no confusion on my part that it was wrong. I wasn't unaware that it would hurt you. I did it *because* it would hurt you. It was my petty and immature way of hurting you back after you hurt me, and it obliterated your ability to trust me. I am one hundred percent accountable for my decision to cheat on you. It was the stupidest decision of my life, and if I had any way of undoing it or minimizing the damage I caused, I would."

I stared at him, blinking rapidly in stunned silence. For so long, I'd convinced myself Adam didn't get it. He didn't understand what he'd done, so how could I trust him to not do it again. Hearing him admit he'd intentionally hurt me, validating my every suspicion, didn't bring the peace I hoped it would, but it did . . . something. Like a splash of icy water or a smack across the face, it jarred me out of the past and into the present.

"But I'm not that guy anymore, Cade. I'm just not. The day after, I realized I had to tell you the truth because lying about it would make it that much worse. For four years I've tried to make it right."

"I know."

Adam was weeping now. He always cried when we talked about that night. I always believed it was his way of scoring sympathy points, something my mother used to do. But this was different—he wasn't demanding I forgive him, but he wouldn't keep hanging on, not when we had Brady and Josh showing us what we might have. He swiped his hand under both eyes, but more tears kept coming. "But you can't forgive me?"

Memories raced down my spine, uncurling fresh reminders of a period in my life I'd worked ridiculously hard to forget. Every time I'd pushed him away and made him think I didn't want him reminded me why this was so hard. I couldn't trust him enough to be together, but I couldn't hate him enough to cut him off. Not completely. "I've tried. Adam, fuck . . . I've tried to."

"It's really over this time, isn't it?" His words came out in choking gasps.

I closed my eyes to block out his pain . . . The same pain he'd caused me. I couldn't do it. It shouldn't end like this. I wanted what Josh and Brady had too, but I wanted those things with Adam. No one else. I wanted to stop punishing him. I wanted to trust him. If I could only explain why . . . "I . . . Fuck. I don't want it to be," I breathed, and a little of the weight eased off my chest.

Adam

I'd imagined I'd seen every side of Cade there was, but it'd been years since I'd seen the unguarded, vulnerable side. Unfamiliar laughter resounded from the pathway that led up from the beach, and I heard a small group of women approach the foot wash station I'd passed about fifty yards back. A powerful need to protect whatever was happening between us from the outside world overcame me.

"Can we walk?" I sniffled.

Cade stiffened.

"Please," I begged.

He nodded, a quick bob of his chin, and started back toward the beach. He followed the sidewalk away from the section of the beach the guys were at, staying four or five steps ahead of me the entire time. I slowed my stride to give him the space he so obviously wanted. Afraid he'd walk back his words if I pushed too hard. I'd have walked around the full island just to keep from extinguishing the slight spark of hope he'd given me. I wiped my eyes, removing the tears before Cade could accuse me of trying to garner sympathy I didn't deserve.

When he arrived at the short wooden bridge that crossed over to the sand, he stopped and waited, looking back at me. It was too dark to see him, but I heard the hesitation in his breath.

We walked down to the shore where the sand was compact and wet. I kicked off my shoes and carried them, and Cade did the same, holding his flip-flops between his fingers, soles out and aimed toward me. It seemed no matter how flimsy, he needed a physical barrier between us. Through the crash of the waves, my ears kept finding his breaths. At first, labored and shallow, then slowing and deepening after about ten minutes of silence. He switched his shoes to his opposite hand and walked closer to me, so close the cotton sweatshirt I'd loaned him brushed against my bare arm.

The silence, like the beach, stretched on. His fingers brushed against mine, unfurling pent-up emotions I couldn't classify. We continued down the dark beach toward a well-lit hotel area. We'd walked miles and gotten nowhere. When his furtive glances became more brazen, I suspected he was waiting for me to take the lead.

"Should we sit?" I said when we crossed over from the public beach to the property of a resort. There were lights up by the pool deck, and I made out the shapes of a few people sitting at the bar closer to the lobby, but the cabana beds on the beach were unattended.

Cade startled, staring up at the property. "Are we allowed?"

I shrugged. "The worst they can do is ask us to leave."

I led Cade by the small of his back to the cabana bed and took the spot on the opposite side. He seemed so scared sitting there, doing his best to not make eye contact. My heart hadn't slowed since Cade's confession, and I worked to temper my optimism. A part of me—an enormous part—worried this was some apparition born out of our collective envy. Which seemed like a safe topic and a reasonable thing to rule out.

"Are you jealous of Josh and Brady?"

Cade lifted his head, his eyes finding mine in the near darkness. "Are you?"

"I mean . . . It's good to see them as happy as they are, but yeah. It's hard not to be envious."

"Yeah."

I bit my lip, trying to interpret Cade's vague agreement. "Josh shouldn't have cornered you like that."

"Right?" Cade said, then shrugged. "Brady has too. All of a sudden, everyone is Team Adam."

I cringed. "They're not taking sides. If anything they're Team Adde." My attempt to force our names together made Cade laugh, so I tried again. "Team Caam?"

"We don't have a suitable ship name." Cade sighed, like that fact was an indictment on our chances. His chin was down, gaze fixed on where his toes were digging into the sand.

"Do we still need one?" I asked guardedly.

Finally, Cade's eyes rose to meet mine. "I honestly don't know."

"We can't make this work because it's easier on our friends or because we're jealous of their happiness."

"I know," Cade snapped, the defensive jut of his chin threatening to end the conversation before it began, but before I tempered my statement, he softened. "Sorry. I . . . Everything about this week is bittersweet. You and me . . . it's been good, but that's not why I said it."

"Things between us—is it just me, or are they different?"

"It's not just you."

"You're being . . ."

"Less bitchy?"

I laughed. "I would say 'thoughtful,' but sure. You brought me breakfast and offered to give me your room. That was . . ." I searched for a word that wasn't *nice* because I knew it would set him off. "Sweet?"

"You act like I've been an asshole to you. I mean, if that's true . . . why do you even want me?" I detected the anxiety in Cade's voice.

"Cade, that's not what I'm saying. I just . . . Since I made a mis—" Cade leveled a warning glare that dared me to use any euphemistic language for what I'd done. I sighed because I got then what he meant. It sounded like I was trying to avoid responsibility when I labeled it a mistake. "Since I cheated, we spend a lot of time keeping score, and we never used to be like that."

"So, I guess this is where you tell me to forgive you so we can be happy."

I took a deep breath. "I recognize I can't demand forgiveness."

"Fucking finally."

"Cade," I pleaded, resisting the urge to surface any of the lines I'd learned didn't make a bit of difference to him. "Maybe this would be easier if we lay all the cards on the table? Forget what happened for a minute and focus on what we want to happen next."

Cade huffed, and the cushion shifted. He twisted to face me, resting his knee on the bed between us, creating a new barrier. "I'm listening."

"You want me to go first?"

"This was your idea."

"Can you promise to let me finish without getting angry?"

Cade rolled his head like he was forcing the tension from his neck, shook his shoulders, and released a breath. "Yeah."

I smiled nervously. "I've never stopped loving you, and I don't think I ever will, not totally." Cade's smile sent a rush of acid in the back of my throat. I'd spoken those words so many times but gotten back only sarcasm or a dismissive gesture. Now, Cade sat there, leaning in with a tender, almost empathetic countenance, instead of crossing his arms and listening for a reason to go off. But we had to get to the fresh stuff if anything would ever change. After a deep breath, I laid the rest of my hand down. "I can't keep getting on this roller coaster with you. I need an actual shot at making this work. I want what Josh and Brady have—love and commitment."

Cade stoically shook his head, but I couldn't stop.

"I want us to stop keeping score—we don't have to erase the record, but I want a new game. A fresh start where I call you my boyfriend and we say we love each other because we do, Cade. It's still there for us."

Cade's earnest eyes found mine in the darkness and his mouth gaped, but he was listening. No, not only listening. For the first time in a long time, he was hearing me. I fought back the anxiety I had about pushing too hard and losing him for good. If it meant getting off the path to nowhere, I had to say it.

"If you can't do that with me, I'll understand . . . honestly." I choked on my words. "We can keep working on being friends because no matter what, I want you in my life, but if you don't want love and commitment—or if you just don't want it with me—then I need to get off this ride."

Cade's head bowed, his blond hair falling like a curtain around his face and obscuring my view of his reaction. "Adam, I've—"

The moment his voice broke, pain shot through my chest. For a heart-wrenching second, I thought I'd lost him for good, but then he lifted his hand and wiped under his eyes. I froze.

Cade rarely cried. My instinct was to comfort him, but he'd made it clear that was not my role anymore. I watched him struggle, unsure of what to do, of how to console him without crossing lines. His wet breaths came louder without answer. I slid as far as his barrier leg allowed, moving with sloth-like speed, giving him time to back away. When he dropped his foot to the ground, I took it as permission. Shifting so we were hip to hip, I wrapped my arm over his shoulder and left it there as Cade stiffened, then relaxed. After what seemed like an eternity, he rested his hand over mine and peered up at me. "I want to try."

We stared at each other. Breaths synchronous and heavy. Cade's eyelids fluttered and his lips parted. As he leaned in closer, a sound erupted from the back of my throat, a surprised gasp that didn't quite break free. My neck heated, and the only thing I needed in the world was for him to kiss me and make this real. Cade stroked his hand down my cheek, his uncertain touch loosening my tongue. "Cade . . ." My shaky voice sounded like a plea for mercy. "Does this mean . . . Are we going to try? For real?"

"I want to," Cade whispered. My heart pounded. The heat flashed in his eyes as he straddled me. Before I caught my breath, his lips were on mine, palms enclosing my face. My tongue licked the seam of his lips, flicking forward, sliding into his mouth until it danced with his, a slow reacquainting. No matter how long it had been, my body recognized Cade's. His smell. His taste. All my senses reacted to him, and I was hard in seconds.

He yielded to me, and I cupped the back of his neck and took control, kissing him until I was sure our lips would bruise.

"Fuck," Cade moaned, his fingertips digging into the back of my scalp as I kissed down his neck.

"Tell me you want me," I whispered in his ear.

Cade pressed himself against me. The evidence of his desire slid against mine, triggering a deep groan from both of us. "Can't you tell?"

I shook my head. "I need to know, Goulue. I want to hear it."

Cade's breath warmed the shell of my ear as he nibbled my earlobe. "Adam, fuck. Yes, I want *this*." He writhed against me, angling his hips to intensify the pressure. His hand slipped under my shirt, caressing along my spine, as he kissed me silent.

We pressed together every inch of us, and I was so turned on I struggled to breathe, but still, he understood what I needed to hear and he wasn't saying it, and my mind refused to let that go. I groaned, knowing what I was about to do risked ending this reunion before it even got started. I leaned away from him, bracing one hand on his shoulder to prevent him from chasing me. "Cade," I said in a somber voice, "tell me."

Cade retreated like I'd pushed him. His eyes narrowed and his jaw tightened as he scrambled to his feet. "Are you kidding me?"

My head dipped. "I'm not starting a fight, Gou. I want to be sure we're on the same page."

"Well, I was on the page where we have mind-blowing makeup sex on the beach in Hawaii, and you're apparently on the page where we both have blue balls and keep talking."

I couldn't help it, I laughed. "Will you come back here, please?" I reached for him.

Cade hesitated, but he allowed me to pull him toward me until he again straddled my lap. When the weight of him settled back onto my knees, I cupped his face and kissed him, a slow, reassuring nibble of his lips that always drove him crazy. He groaned when I pulled back. "It has to be different this time."

"I'm going to hate the next thing out of your mouth, aren't I?"

"I'm going to suggest we don't fuck tonight."

Cade shook his head. "That sounds like a horrible—" He stopped and met my sober expression with a curious one. He swallowed whatever sarcastic retort he had queued up and heaved a resigned sighed. "Fuck . . . Really?"

I nodded. "I want this time to be real, Cade. Let's start by not repeating the same mistakes."

Cade shifted out of my lap and adjusted his erection. Lying back on the bed, he exhaled a lengthy breath and covered his face with his hands. He stayed like that for a few minutes, before sitting up and meeting my gaze. "So, now what?"

I shrugged. "What do we normally do when we get back together?"

Cade snorted. "We fuck and then you blow up my phone wanting to come over and hang out so we can do it again and again until we have another fight."

I shook my head, laughing at his unflattering, but reasonably accurate, portrait of our pattern. "Well, then maybe we should go out."

He sputtered, like the idea was ludicrous. "Like dates?"

"Yeah, Cade. Like dates. We used to date from time to time."

"Except for the first one, our dates included sex."

"True. I'm not suggesting we table sex forever, Gou."

"So, we date until when?"

"I guess until you fall in love with me again."

Cade grabbed my hand, brought it to his lips, and kissed my palm. "Adam, I already love you," he whispered. "I never stopped."

Chapter Six

Cade

Two days later, I was still processing Hawaii. Adam and I agreed to play it cool on the plane since neither of us wanted to do whatever we were doing with four sets of heart eyes staring at us. Other than clearing the air with Josh when we got back to the house, I left Adam to do the usual "game on" announcement in the group chat.

"Uncle Cade!" Hayley raced out of their first-floor apartment and barreled toward me.

"Oomph," I cried out with her impact. Her bony arms wrapped around me so tight I had to grasp the car door to keep from falling backward and taking her with me.

"I missed you." She squeezed tighter. "*Little Women* came yesterday, and you said we could start it as soon as you got back from your trip."

"I missed you too, kiddo." I patted her head, which seemed to get higher every time I saw her. It was becoming obvious she would take after her sperm donor in the height department. Shane had towered over Maura. If memory served, he was around six foot four, so at least Hayley would escape the Doyle genes that kept Maura, Aislinn, and me forever asking for help to reach the top shelf. "I have a T-shirt for you from Hawaii."

"Cool. It's not pink, is it?"

I gave her an eye roll. "Of course it's pink. I went all the way to Hawaii and forgot that my niece loathes pink."

Hayley smiled. "What color is it?"

"It's rainbow. You can have it as soon as you name the colors of the rainbow in the correct order."

"Red . . ." She contemplated that for a minute, green eyes drifting toward the sky. "Yellow?"

"Ehht," I made a buzzing noise and poked her in the belly. I reached into my trunk and retrieved the plastic bag that contained gifts for Hayley and Maura.

"Give me a hint."

"Roy G Biv."

Her face scrunched up adorably, and she put her hands on her hips, looking so much like her mother I had to laugh. "What kind of a hint is that?"

"It's an acronym. A-C-R-O-N-Y-M. Go search for that word in your dictionary and then see if you can figure out the hint."

"It means opposite. Like up and down," she sassed.

"Wrong. Up and down are antonyms, so now you also get to tell me what the suffix '-nym' means."

She planted her palm to her forehead. "Why can't you just hand over my T-shirt like a normal uncle?"

"It's the curse of being a teacher. I can't give away the good stuff without making you think." We walked together up the sidewalk that led to a common area between her building and the parking lot.

"Hayley." Maura appeared at her back patio that faced the courtyard, still in her bathrobe and unwashed. "Oh, hey, Cade."

"Hi, Sis." I wrapped my arm around my niece. Maura pushed open the screen and stepped out.

"What have I told you about running out of the house?" She grabbed Hayley's arm and yanked her inside.

"Sorry, Mama. I saw Uncle Cade pull up."

"Chill, Maura. I was with her the entire time. Hayley, go look up that word in your dictionary."

I waited for Hayley to leave the room before I addressed my sister. "How do you feel today?"

"I'm fine, Cade. Tired. Hayley's been bouncing off the walls since Aislinn left. Wanting to go here and there like money grows on trees. She needs new shoes."

"Aislinn said she took her shopping."

"She let Hayley pick out ones that she can't wear to school."

"What did she get her?"

Maura walked into her bedroom and returned with blue Converse shoes that had unicorns all over them.

"I thought you were going to bring out stilettos. Those are cute. Why can't she wear those?"

"Because, Cade. They have to be solid colors."

"Did you tell Aislinn that?"

"Hayley knew."

"Well, I'll get her a cheap pair that will cover her the last few weeks of school, and she can wear those over the summer."

"She yelled at me when she couldn't wear them Friday. The other ones hurt her feet." My sister slumped into her chair, appearing far older than her thirty years. A shopping trip was so not part of the plan for my day.

Hayley came racing out of her room and stopped short in the doorway. "Red-orange-yellow-green-blue-idiot-violet," she said in one breath.

I laughed. "Indigo, not 'idiot.'" I grabbed the bag from the table and held it out. "What about the suffix?"

"Um . . . '-nym' means 'word.' Like an acronym stands for words and antonym is opposite words."

"Close enough." When I let go of the bag, she tore open the ties, yanked out the shirt, and thrust it into Maura's hands.

"Eek," she squealed. "Mama, it matches my new shoooeeesss." She held the shirt up to her and grabbed the shoes, jumping.

"Hayley," Maura chastised, rubbing her temples. "Good God. It's just a T-shirt. We have neighbors."

"Thank you, Uncle Cade." She thrust her arms around my waist and hugged me tight.

"You're welcome, hon."

"Can we read my book now?"

"Soon. Give me some time to catch up with your mom. Then we need to get new shoes for school tomorrow."

Hayley frowned. "Mama, you said you would take me."

"Hayley, I'm tired. Uncle Cade can take you."

"But that's not fair," she yelled.

"Hayley, I swear if you don't knock off that shrill voice of yours, I will duct tape your mouth closed. Now go to your room and watch television so I can talk to Cade."

Hayley looked at me for help. I hated getting stuck in the middle, but as a teacher, I knew what it felt like when others undermined my authority in the classroom. Maura needed support. "Listen to your mother, hon."

Affronted, Hayley stomped out of the room.

Maura shook her head, and I wished I could hear the tiniest bit of regret in her exhausted scoff.

"Did you promise to take her?"

"Cade, don't start. I got it all day from her."

"Maura, you can't break promises to your daughter. At least come with us. We can go to the Target by my place. You like that one."

"No. Please. I've been up since this morning. I made Hayley get dressed and brush her teeth. She ate breakfast and lunch. This medication is awful."

I surveyed my sister's kitchen, distracting myself by tidying up. I put the lukewarm milk back in the fridge and cleaned up the chocolate powder that was spilled on the counter. The dishes hadn't been washed since Aislinn left, so I stacked them in the sink and tossed wrappers in the trash, then removed the spoon and resealed the open jar of peanut butter. "It's almost eight. Did she eat dinner?"

"She made herself a sandwich. The better question, little brother, is did *you* eat dinner?"

I sighed, not wanting to justify my program to her again. "I have things under control."

"Will you at least talk to Sid?"

I swallowed hard. We'd been down this road before. I'd been tempted more than once to come clean with Sid about the past, but I couldn't. It wasn't fair to ask him to keep something like that from Adam, and now that we'd agreed on a fresh start . . . Besides, Maura couldn't bring up my issues to avoid her own, not when she had a daughter to take care off. "Why didn't you take her to get shoes today?"

"Cade—"

"I'm jet-lagged, and I need to finish prepping for tomorrow. If I take her to the store, we won't have time to read before she needs to get to bed."

"She doesn't need to read. She needs shoes. I'm begging you. I need sleep." The weariness in my sister's face took me back to high school. Nights when she'd come in after her waitressing shift—offering to stay late whenever they let her. Sometimes she wouldn't even pull out the sofa bed she slept on. I'd wake up for school and find her, still in her uniform, crashed on the couch we'd picked up from the Goodwill. *Fuck.* Here I was back from vacation and bitching about one little errand. "Fine."

"Thank you."

I smiled warmly, still irritated, but her obvious relief helped. "Are you going to open your gift?"

She pulled the bag off her lap and retrieved the small box from the bottom. Her eyes widened as she pried the lid open and smiled, admiring the silver bangle engraved with *Kaikuahine*. "This is beautiful, Cade. What does this word mean?"

"The jeweler said it means 'sister' in Hawaiian. I got Aislinn one too."

Maura made a tsking sound. "As a thank-you for babysitting me?"

"No, because she's our sister too. And I didn't think you needed a babysitter, just some help."

She pursed her lips and replaced the lid without trying on the bracelet. "Did you have a good time at least?"

"I did. Adam and I got back together."

She rolled her eyes. "I knew it. Aislinn owes me twenty bucks. So how long did you last before Adam sweet-talked you back into bed?"

"Actually, he didn't." She leveled a *bitch, please* expression at me so fierce I snickered. "I am as blown away as you are. Apparently, there is this new-fangled concept out there that you're supposed to learn from your mistakes."

"If only. You're so much like Mom."

"Maura—" I warned.

"Well, how many times did she relapse? How many times did she let Tim back into the house?"

"I'm not an addict. And don't compare Adam to that loser."

"Maybe you're not an addict, but your so-called program and getting back with Adam without telling him about Meadowbrook?

Sorry, kid, but that's Colleen 'just one little taste to get right' Doyle if I ever heard it."

"I'm backing off of the program, okay?"

"Well that's a fucking relief. What about Adam?"

"He wants a clean start and I do too. It's different this time. I don't see what good it does to drag up the past."

"Ah, yes. The past. I hear it's not at all helpful in predicting future behavior."

"Maura," I warned again. "This is different."

"Once a cheater, always a cheater," she mumbled. Maura rivaled my mother in the *people who dole out advice they don't follow* category. Unlike Adam, Shane was a serial philander and as much as Maura liked to pretend that she'd kicked him out because of his infidelity, the truth was he'd had one foot out the door once Maura announced her pregnancy. She might have told him to go, but he was already halfway up the road and down the altar with his other girlfriend when she said it. "Mom was right. Men are scum. You should try harder to be straight."

I dropped both fists to the table harsher than I intended. "All right, well as much as I love to recount the many profound insights of Colleen Doyle, I will scrape Hayley off her bed and take her to get some shoes."

Maura laughed. "Do you remember when she tried to light Tim's golf clubs on fire?"

I closed my eyes. Tim was one of our mother's many, many boyfriends, so it was hard to keep them all straight. He was memorable only because he'd been gainfully employed, so the months he was around we'd eaten more regularly, and our mother had tried a little harder. I think I was around eleven when she discovered he had another woman on the side. Or maybe our mother was his sidepiece. Who the fuck knew? Whatever happened, she let the crazy flag fly at full staff when she found out. Maura had a way of remembering our mom's drunken antics with far more fondness than they deserved. That particular stunt had summoned both the cops and child protective services, and Aislinn's father was back in court the next week, seeking to further limit our mother's visitation.

"Hayley," I called out. "Let's go, hon."

Hayley appeared a short time later wearing her new shirt and shoes, her hair in an off-center ponytail. There was sparkly blue eyeshadow smeared above her puffy red eyes and pink lip gloss well outside the lines of her thin lips. I stared at her face, searching for other signs of distress. I still saw her as a little girl, but the makeup, no matter how poorly applied, made it clear she was getting older now. As old as I was when CPS first entered my life, which meant she was old enough to understand that other moms didn't sleep most of the day or need help to get through the week.

"What in the world. Jesus Christ, did Aislinn buy you makeup?" Maura asked.

Hayley nodded.

"Go wash that crap off your face, you look like a child prostitute."

"Maura," I gasped.

"Cade, I told Aislinn she's too young for makeup. I don't need her coming in here and treating my daughter like she's on *Gossip Girl*."

Hayley frowned. No child her age should have brow creases that deep. "What's a prosti—"

"It's not a word you need to learn. Go wash your face, hon," I said, exasperated.

"But Aunt Aislinn said it will make me pretty."

"You're already gorgeous, hon. Wash your face and we'll get your shoes."

She opened her mouth to protest, but when I trained my best Mr. Doyle classroom stare on her, she snapped her jaw shut and obeyed.

I never wanted Hayley to grow up in the same dysfunction we had. But here we were. Maura was bipolar with limited patience, Aislinn had no respect for boundaries, and I couldn't control my mouth or manage a healthy relationship—the Colleen Doyle DNA lived on in us all.

Adam

My second first date with Cade was roughly a week after we returned from Hawaii. Work obligations had swamped both of us upon our return. The end of the school year was a busy time for all teachers, but Cade had been voted by the seniors as one of their favorite teachers, so he now had to participate in the graduation ceremony on top of everything else.

I left my office early, hoping to have some time to prepare before Cade came over, but I pulled into the parking lot and noticed Cade sitting in his car, speaking to someone on the phone with animated gestures. When I hopped out and waved, he turned off his ignition and opened the door. I approached, catching the end of his conversation.

"Yeah. Okay. I've got to go, Sis. Yep. Tomorrow. Will do. Love you too. Tell Hayley I will. Sunday. Yep. Got to go. Okay. Bye."

Cade dropped his head and exhaled as soon as he disconnected.

"Hi," I said, unable to erase the smile on my face from seeing him. I leaned down to kiss his cheek through his open car door. "You're early."

"I realized there was no point in going home since you moved two blocks from my school. I still have some clothes here, right?" There was no acknowledgment I'd purchased my condo because of its location, hoping to sway Cade to move in, only to learn teachers were loath to live amongst their students.

"Yeah. I have a few of your things. You could have called me. I would have given you the new code."

"Do your neighbors realize you hand out their building's code to a first date?"

I chuckled, but Cade's come-at-me grin was making me want to move us out of public. "Come on, Mr. Doyle. Let me usher you in before you see a parent or student lurking about."

"Sure thing, Mr. . . . Oh, my bad—what was your last name again? In my phone I labeled you 'Grindr Adam big dick.'" Cade laughed.

I rolled my eyes and held out my hand to assist him out of his car. When he accepted it with a playful smile, I yanked him up and into my arms, crowding him against the body of his car. "You do not understand how excited I've been about seeing you this week."

Cade gazed up at me and wet his lips. They were so perfect—pink and full, softening before my very eyes. "I've been looking forward to tonight too."

I loved how he rose to his toes when we were close, involuntarily seeking more contact. Always my greedy boy. And who was I to disappoint? I pressed my lips to his, keeping the pressure light while licking and nibbling in a slow, continual tease. When he pulled away, he swallowed hard, wide eyes blazing up at me, and touched his mouth, like he was just as surprised by how good it felt.

"That was . . ." I chuckled. "A hell of a second first kiss."

Cade nodded and I could almost sense us retreating into old patterns. The goal of the night was to relax and have fun together, not to end up in bed. I wanted Cade to see how committed I was to this new plan. "Let's go inside. I need to change."

Cade followed me up the path to my condo building, and I punched in the code to let him inside. Once I had him in my unit, I forgot what I was doing. "You want a drink or a snack?"

"I thought we were going out?"

"Yeah, I mean first. Um, I can put together something."

Cade laughed. "Adam, go shower. We've been joking around about starting over, but I don't think we need to pretend I've never been here before, or that we don't know each other. I've probably made more meals in your kitchen than you have."

I exhaled a lengthy breath. "Sorry."

"It's kind of cute you're nervous. Reminds me of our actual first date."

"And the next five or six. I had it so bad for you. Oh my god. I cringe just thinking about it. I had no game back then."

Cade's smile unleashed a warmth in me. "I think you had more than you give yourself credit for."

We exchanged a look that under different circumstances would have ended with my dick in his mouth. Fuck, this no-sex thing would be hard. No, not hard—difficult. *Don't get hard.*

"I'm gonna grab a change of clothes from the spare room." Cade motioned to the hallway that led to my second bedroom and the closet he used to store the stuff he left here. Because, by his logic, if it wasn't in my room, there'd be no temptation for me to consider us in an actual relationship.

Oh, boy. Here we go. I took a deep breath. "Actually, your stuff is in my bedroom."

Cade's teeth caught the corner of his lip, and he ran his fingers through his hair. "Your bedroom?" he repeated, as though trying on the words for size.

"I . . ." I swallowed. "Okay, don't freak out, but I sort of did a thing. I was planning to show you the night we . . . the last night we got into it."

Flashing red sirens were less effective than the warning sign plastered on his face.

"This will be easier if I show you."

"Yeah. Okay."

Cade followed me into my second bedroom. I glanced back during the quick walk, not once, but twice, certain he was planning to hightail it out the front door. When we crossed the threshold, I turned on the lights, and he gasped.

"*What* did you do?" His eyes darted around at the space that used to house junk, the desktop computer I never used, and an old box spring and mattress. The walls were now a light lavender, and there was a twin-size daybed with a colorful quilt, a bookshelf, and a small dresser on one side. The other side had a new child-size corner desk with my computer. He picked up a few of the books and stared at me, wide-eyed.

"I mostly got everything at garage sales except the mattress and desk. It's not exactly rainbows, because . . . well, I thought a gay man with a little girl rainbow room was a bridge too far, but I made sure there was no pink, because I remembered how Hayley feels about pink. A lady from work gave me the books and toys. Her daughters are in high school now, so I figured Hayley might like them. You can remove the ones you think are trash or inappropriate. I wiped the computer and I thought she could use it for games or schoolwork, or whatever." I was rambling. How was it possible to be this cold and this hot at the same time?

"Adam." Cade pinched the bridge of his nose. "Why?"

"You said you couldn't move in with me because Hayley wouldn't have anywhere to stay when she came over. So I fixed that."

"I meant a spare bed or a pull-out couch. You understand that's what I meant, right? Hayley doesn't even have a bedroom at my place. You do too much. It's too much pressure. It's the same thing as demanding I forgive you. You make it impossible not to . . ."

"I know." A tightness squeezed my airway. I choked on regret. It had started with just getting the bed, but then something else took over and . . . Damn it, I'd been thinking it would make Cade happy, but there was no denying I also thought Hayley would love it so much Cade would have to move in. I clenched my hands, trying to calm the shaky feeling inside of me. "I'm sorry."

"Come here." Cade pulled me into his arms, surprising me with the comfort he'd too long withheld. His embrace released a tingling warmth through my veins. I closed my eyes, savoring the sensation of his arms around me, his hands rubbing my neck. He released me and brushed some hair off my forehead. "We need to talk about this."

I nodded, bracing myself for the fallout. Instead, he sat on the bed and patted the spot next to him. When I joined him, any relief about his lack of anger was overshadowed by flashbacks of being sent to the principal's office.

"Okay. This is a new game, right? That's what we're calling it. You wanted a clean slate."

I met his softened gaze. "Yeah. Clean slate."

"Well if that's the framework I'm using to evaluate how I feel about this, then having you show me you are making space for me in your life and that you understand my sister and niece are important to me is a sweet, thoughtful gesture and not a means to guilt trip me."

"But—" I interjected, and the corner of Cade's eyebrow quirked up "—also a little smothering."

Cade smiled patiently. "Perhaps a bit much . . . for a first date."

"I understand. Cade, everything I do is meant to show you I want this." I gestured between him and me. "But I will be more mindful of the pressure it creates for you."

He nodded. "So, you wouldn't happen to have any of your ex-boyfriend's clothes hanging around, because I don't want to go out wearing my Mr. Doyle khakis."

"Funny thing. My ex was exactly your size." I got off the bed and led him back to my room and retrieved some of his pants and jeans from my dresser and shirts from my closet.

"Your ex had great taste . . . in clothes," he teased.

"Yeah, well, we can't all shop in the junior section." I held up the shirt to my chest.

"Give me those." He yanked his extra-small, slim-fit shirts from my hand. "Where are we going, anyway?"

I grinned. I had a few options for our evening planned. "That depends—this is a choose-your-own-adventure situation. Do you want to keep the new us, adult vibe going; relive some serious, classic Cade and Adam better-time moments; or a mixture of both?"

Cade's immediate response and grin filled me with pride. "Mixture of both."

"Okay, then we have a reservation at that new Italian cafe and tickets to see *The Time Traveler's Wife* at the rooftop cinema."

"Oh," Cade said, sounding pleasantly surprised. "I love that book."

"I recall," I said, shaking my head. "Aruba, remember?"

"Fuck, I forgot about that." Cade blushed. "It was an interesting book."

"Must have been since it was more enjoyable than the blowjob I was giving you."

"I was only going to finish the chapter, but you kept trying harder to get me to put it down, and the entire thing got me hot."

"Now the truth comes out. Ignoring me turns you on." I was going for a chastising tone, because there were few things I detested more than feeling ignored, but the brief noises of arousal that had kept escaping as he turned pages had been more than worth it.

"No, having you desperate for me turns me on."

We shared a knowing smile. "Same, Gou. Same." I dropped my gaze down his body. Desperation was my default setting with him.

Cade shook his head and shoved me in the direction of my bathroom. "You promised me a date. Go shower, Adam."

Cade

"It's a metaphor for failed relationships," I explained. "The time travel is just a mechanism that shows how two people in a relationship can experience it in completely different ways."

"So Claire knows Henry from her childhood, but he only knows her when he drops in from the future, but he can't bring anything with him or change anything that happens. Wait, is this one of those cases for soul mates, like you're destined to love one person, or is it more a statement that everything is random and ultimately meaningless?"

The waiter, an adorable redhead, cleared her throat, and Adam and I glanced up. "Sorry to interrupt you guys when you're so deep in conversation, but I thought I'd check in to see if you'd like dessert or coffee."

Adam peeked at his watch and frowned. "Shit. We have to go if we're going to make the movie, Gou."

"Okay. Can I get you a to-go box, sir?"

Adam's eyes sized up my nearly full bowl of pasta with almost as much regret as I had felt after ordering it. "Cade, you barely ate anything. We can stay so you can finish."

"It's fine. I'm not that hungry, anyway. Can you wrap this up for me?"

She nodded, a shy smile playing on her face. "I hope it's not inappropriate to say this, but you guys make me so jealous. I'd love it if my boyfriend would talk to me about books."

"Date an English teacher," Adam snorted.

"Wait until you graduate," I cautioned because I wasn't sure she was older than my students.

She giggled and it was apparent she'd been hoping we'd confirm her suspicions we were more than two straight bro bibliophiles. "How long have you two been together?"

Adam and I exchanged an amused grin. "Actually," I said, placing my napkin on the table. "Would you believe this is our first date?"

"You're kidding?" She gawked. "I would have guessed you two had been together for years."

Adam winked at me. "Yeah. Me too. It's going pretty well."

"I'll say." She nodded approvingly and snatched my plate. "I'll get this wrapped up and be back with your check."

"Thank you," Adam said without removing his eyes from me. His intense stare sent a shiver up my spine.

"I like your question," I said, trying to bring the conversation back to the book. "Let's talk about it more after the movie."

"You know I believe in soul mates."

"Yeah. I remember."

The server returned and set the bag on the table. "I added a piece of cheesecake in here and two forks. Figured a first date this good needed to end with something sweet."

Adam paid the check with cash. "Keep the change." He handed the leather folder back to the server and grabbed my takeout container. "Should we go?"

"Yeah," I agreed. "Thank you," I said to the server, who was still gawking at us like we were the cutest thing she'd ever seen—which okay. I had to admit when things were good between us, we were. I'd missed the admiration on people's faces that acknowledged it, after a lifetime of being pitied. Poor Cade with the shitty mom, the absent father, and the crazy sister. It was nice to have people look at me like I was lucky for a change. It would be more helpful to *feel* like I was lucky, so I tried to remember how it'd felt to have a boyfriend I loved and trusted. How special it felt knowing that someone like Adam loved me before . . . I sighed, forcing myself to stay in the present.

"You okay, Gou?" Adam's light touch on my lower back unleashed a wave of goosebumps.

I gazed up at him, his baby blues fixated on my lips so intently, I pushed up to my toes to kiss him. "Yeah, I'm good." And in that moment, I was.

The evening was amazing. We watched the movie and talked about determinism versus free will as we walked hand in hand back to the car. After so much time and so many failures, it felt like a real accomplishment to pull off such a pleasant date. The smooth, effortless way Adam engaged my passion for books had me half-hard and so full of optimism that my empty stomach stopped growling.

Adam pulled into the parking lot of his condo next to my car and, with a happy sigh, shut off the engine.

"Should I come up?" I asked with thoughts of Aruba in my head. I touched my chest over my rapidly beating heart.

Adam arched a brow at me. "If you come up, I won't be able to keep my hands off you."

I laughed. "Did you hear me asking you to?"

He gripped my hand, and when his remorseful eyes found mine again, I knew he wasn't kidding.

"Still?" I asked, disappointed, but not exactly surprised. There'd been plenty of changes in Adam the last few years, but the most obvious was his determination when he really set his mind to something.

"I know we agreed to leave the past in the past, but this fresh start . . . it kind of only works if we're being completely honest with each other, right?"

My chest clenched uncomfortably. "Yeah."

"I think I need this for a little bit before we have sex again." He gestured between us, then clarified, "I need to prove to myself that this is different."

"This is different."

"What you were saying earlier about the book—that you could be in a relationship and living a slightly different love story than your partner. It got me thinking. I don't want that for us. More than anything else, I want us to get back to a place where we tell each other everything. Isn't that what you want?"

Adam's expectant stare, like honesty was a tangible thing that I'd taken from him after our breakup and should now return, turned the handful of movie popcorn I'd eaten into a solid mass. "Of course," I lied.

Adam nodded and his hand slipped from mine as he reached for the door handle. "You ready?" Adam asked, but the click of the door opening seemed to say my answer didn't matter very much, so I nodded and exited my side of the car.

I kept the maelstrom of emotions off my face as he walked me to my car, kissed me good night, and disappeared inside his condo. On the drive home, though, I felt everything—desire, disappointment, fear, guilt. They sort of mixed with all the anxieties Maura stirred up. Was I making the same mistakes over and over? If I wanted things to be different with Adam, did I owe him the truth?

The thought alone filled me with an ominous sense of dread—like the one I'd get halfway through a book when I knew some devastating twist was coming and that it was going to hurt. Only Adam wasn't some character in a novel I'd gotten too invested in. He'd been clear in

Hawaii: This was his last ride on the roller coaster. If we didn't make it this time . . . Well, I didn't want to think about that.

We had to put the past behind us. Both our pasts. Which meant . . . I was going to have to let Mexico go once and for all.

Chapter Seven

Adam

"That's a throwback," Cade said as he lowered himself into my car.

I smiled, shifting my attention from his ass to the radio.

"Arctic Monkeys?" he guessed.

I nodded and wondered if he recognized it as anything other than a song I'd once played in heavy rotation. The particular track was about obsessing over a lover and not knowing if they felt the same way. You could say it resonated with me.

My day had been particularly trying, but as soon as he pressed his lips to mine and smiled, the world was right again. I patted his knee while he fastened his seat belt. Although we'd kept to our "no sex" rule, I found myself mindlessly reaching for him now more often than not.

We chatted off and on about nothing for a significant portion of the drive until Cade's focus turned to the passing scenery.

"How was your morning?" I asked, squeezing his thigh to draw him out of his quiet rumination.

Cade flashed a smile at me. Sweet, but still a little in his head over something. "Good. Went to the gym and did a little cleaning. I've been spending so much time at your place, I had a ton of stuff that was about to expire, so I took it over to Maura's and she made breakfast."

"Cade," I laughed, "we're on our way to meet the guys for brunch."

"Oh. I know. I'll have a Bloody Mary or something and hang out. Have you heard from Brady? How are the wedding plans coming along?"

I tensed at the mention of the wedding, then navigated around a slower vehicle to buy myself some time on how to approach the subject. "Yeah. I wanted to talk to you about that, actually. Brady asked me to be his best man."

"Really? That's so sweet." Cade sounded surprised, but not unhappy.

I took my eyes off the road long enough to make sure his body language matched his tone. "You think?"

"You can use some of our epic awkward moments in college for the best man speech, but maybe don't use the ones where Brady openly pined over you."

"So I should accept?" I still wasn't sure it was such a good idea, but I wasn't sure how to say that without sounding like I expected us to break up. I was confident things were different this time. Mostly confident. But if something did happen . . . I couldn't imagine how awful a best man I would be.

"Of course. Why wouldn't you accept?"

"I just— Hawaii was hard on both of us."

"Oh," Cade said, and I didn't need to see him to know he finally understood my hesitation.

"The wedding is months away and—"

"I think you should do it," Cade interrupted.

His certainty surprised me. "Really?"

"Yeah, because it's not about us. It's about Brady and Josh. Brady asked you because he trusts you and wants you to stand up for him."

"But what if . . ." I couldn't bring myself to say it.

"Then we keep our shit between us like we always do, and we'll go together as friends."

"So no matter what, we're going to the wedding together?"

"Yeah." He smiled reassuringly. "It's a date."

Cade's willingness to make a commitment that far in the future bolstered my confidence. "Wow! Look at us making plans for the end of the year. Here I was debating asking you to my brother's party next month."

Cade frowned. "Do you really not think we'll make it a month?"

"I wouldn't be doing this if I didn't think it would work. I'm trying to be mindful of the pressure thing. You don't like my parents, and if we consider that our do-over began a few weeks ago—"

"Oh yeah, I guess it would be early for a meet-the-parents trip." Cade laughed. "Although, do you think we could come up with a new identity? 'Cause I'd love to *not* be the guy who knocked over the giant swan ice sculpture at your grandparents' fiftieth anniversary party and doused your grandfather with cocktail sauce."

"Oh, Jesus." I barked out a laugh. "I will never forget my mother's face."

"I didn't know it would fall over."

"I've told you a million times it was not your fault, the caterer put the chafing dishes too close to it and the heat melted the bottom faster than the top, so the entire structure was unstable. My mother had noticed it was listing and was trying to get someone to move it when you walked up. It was rotten luck that it hit that shrimp cocktail tray at the exact angle to launch it into the air."

Cade shook his head, burying his face in mortification.

"So . . ." I prompted. "Did you want to go, or is it too soon?"

"When is it?"

Even with my eyes on the road, I felt the mood shift and I stole a glance to see Cade pull out his phone, lips pressed together.

"First Saturday in June. You're out of school before Memorial Day, right?"

His head was down as he thumbed through his calendar app. "The students are out. I still have to break down my classroom. They're painting over the summer."

"Do you want help?" I turned into the restaurant parking lot and caught another peek at his face, but still couldn't nail down where his head was at. Since we were about to walk into a crowded restaurant, I kept it safe and lighthearted. "I can take down the tall stuff," I teased.

"Those jokes never get old," Cade deadpanned.

After parking, I reached over and squeezed his knee, but the best view I got was his profile. "You know I love your size."

Cade's eyelids fluttered, and he turned away with a tight smile. *Shit. Now what did I do wrong?* "Cade . . ."

He met my puzzled expression with a sardonic one. "Yeah. I'm aware you like your men pocket-sized."

Chuckling, I responded to his teasing like I always did: I doubled down, grateful for the levity. Anything to move him back to a smile. "Not exactly. More hobbit-sized."

"Fuck you."

"Elfin?"

"Adam, do you remember what happened the last time someone called me that?"

"No. Why? What did you do to Brady?"

"When did Brady call me a fucking elf?"

I broke out my best Will Ferrell impression. "Oh. He's an angry elf."

Cade huffed and grabbed the car door, but I couldn't stop laughing. "Cade—" When he twisted back, I sobered at his red eyes.

"Are you upset? You are, aren't you? Fuck, Gou." I shifted to groveling. "I'm sorry. I didn't know the teasing upset you."

"It's fine. Can we please just go inside now?"

"Not until we clear this up. Listen, seriously, Brady didn't call you an elf. We were talking about the types of guys we date. He said something about my type being elfin. He also called my former brunch dates the Sunday Parade of Twinks. Brady was teasing me, not you."

Cade scowled, but the emotion on his face seemed more hurt than anger. "You think I missed the pattern, Adam? Do you realize how often I get comments about my size, like my body type makes me less of a man? Meanwhile for guys like you, there are endless numbers of men out there competing for your attention."

"What are you—" I willed myself not to react, not to fall into old patterns. To listen to what he was saying without getting defensive. "I'm trying to follow you here, but I don't understand."

Cade rolled his eyes. "I got the message, okay. You had endless options for more attractive guys, and I was the idiot who ended shit over one blowjob."

Panic rose like bile in the back of my throat. "Gou. No. That wasn't why. All those guys—they served one purpose."

Cade's eyebrow shot up.

"God. Not *that*. Cade, to make you jealous—yes, but not to say you couldn't do better than me. Not to put you down or make you feel you had to take me back because no one else would want you. I swear."

"Please. Don't bother denying you slept with them. I could tell by how they looked at you."

"How did they look at me?"

"Like they thought they hit the jackpot because they found themselves a real sweetheart with a steady job and an enormous dick."

I didn't know how to respond to that, so I didn't. "What about you?"

"You're not that sweet to me."

I cringed, diverting my gaze. The closer his tone edged toward hateful, the harder I had to bite my tongue. He never meant it, but it still hurt.

"Fuck, Adam—I didn't mean it."

I sighed. "I know."

"Just forget it."

"No, Cade. I can't just forget it. That's the old way. There's some truth in there, and I want to understand what it is."

Cade crossed his arms and pursed his lips. "It was always me pushing for us to fuck around, but you can't act surprised. You knew *why*."

"Because I was supposed to watch you with other guys, but never—" I bit back my words. That's what he expected me to do. As my punishment for breaking his heart. "Yeah. I do know why, and I'm sorry."

"Me too," Cade mumbled.

It'd be so easy to end it there, but I needed to understand what else I was missing. What else had we been experiencing in different ways? "There were a few guys you brought around acting like they wanted a shot with you. You give any of them a genuine chance?"

The softness in his eyes told me I'd touched a nerve. I hated the idea of another man being with him, but I had only myself to blame for putting us in that position. Cade's head tilted to one side, white knuckles curled around the door handle. "Spencer, maybe."

"Spencer? Is that the guy who spent all of brunch talking about his vitamin routine?"

The corner of Cade's lip quirked up. "That was Brent. Spencer was the book editor. About two years ago."

The image of the guy hit me. He was like a better version of me. Slightly taller, more muscular. I remembered thinking he treated Cade like a prince. I also recalled feeling inferior to him. Shit. *Is that how Cade felt every time?* No wonder my attempts to make him jealous didn't work. "What happened?"

"We had incompatibilities . . . in the bedroom."

I didn't want to go back to old arguments and insecurities, so I tried not to focus on the fact that if Spencer knew how to fuck or had a bigger dick, I'd be having brunch with Mr. and Mr. Spencer Whatever-his-last-name-was right now. This was a clean slate, a last chance to get it right, and nothing else mattered. I took in a breath and let it out. "Well, I'm grateful it didn't work out."

Cade laughed joylessly. With a mixture of fear and reluctance in his eyes, he dropped his gaze to the floor. "So you never considered getting serious with any of them? I mean, no matter what you say, I know you didn't use them all for sex, that's not like you."

I shook my head. "It never felt right with anyone else."

"So was it . . . to hurt me back . . . like in Mexico?"

His words stung. I rubbed my thumb over his brow to smooth the furrow and cupped his cheek. "Cade, no, baby. From the moment I lost you, all I've done is volley between attempts to get you back and trying to survive losing you. I've fucked up in so many ways when it comes to us, but I promise you, whatever happens, I'm done playing games. This—us being able to have heartfelt and honest conversations about where we went wrong and what we want from our future—I think that's the way we make it different this time."

He bit his lip, letting everything hang in the air between us. My knee trembled, waiting for him to say something, but he merely nodded, like he was still a little suspicious of my words. It killed me, and I wished it weren't necessary, but I had to be upfront with him about everything this time. Not leave anything open for misinterpretation, starting with the topic that got us off on this tangent in the first place.

"I have to go to Atlanta next month for my brother's party. It would mean a lot if you would go with me, because I want to spend time with you, but if it's too soon or if you don't want to go, I will understand."

Cade batted his eyelashes, mouth gaped, as though he hadn't quite discerned what to make of my direct approach to communication. After a long moment of silence, he nodded. "I'll think about it."

Cade

Adam's words were still echoing in my mind, perhaps a little louder since I was sucking down my second Bloody Mary on an empty stomach. I'd tuned out Matt and Sid's updates on their plans for the LGBT shelter to reconsider how I felt about our conversation.

Humiliated. Angry at myself. Adam was right: I used to make jokes right along with everyone else. But that was back when I used humor to mask embarrassment pretty effectively. *Why did I bring up Mexico?*

I'd promised myself I would do things differently. Meadowbrook? Mexico? A fresh start meant it didn't matter anymore. The past needed to stay in the past. That was the way we moved on.

I was so distracted I consumed the second drink I'd ordered. A steady drumbeat of guilt and regret hit me hard.

You only exercised enough to have one.

My hands started shaking, and no matter how much I tried, I couldn't get the uneasy feeling to go away. Some days it felt I was incapable of learning.

How did anyone trust me to educate their children?

Maybe you need to put your drink down and get a little more serious about your program.

"Cade, what do you think?" Josh asked.

I pushed away my glass, feigning attention. "Yeah. Sure."

"Great. The kids really need some GED prep help."

Huh?

Adam's mischievous grin grew. He knew I had zoned out and let me walk directly into that one. I tried to pay better attention, sipping water in an attempt to dilute the effects of the alcohol. By the time everyone's plates arrived, my stomach gurgled, and I couldn't stop staring at their food.

For most of the meal, I tried to make the best of the extra alcohol, doling out fake smiles to my friends. Adam seemed to notice my efforts, since he rested his hand on my upper thigh and rubbed his thumb back and forth along the inside seam of my shorts, casting a heated gaze at me whenever he brushed against my balls.

Was he teasing me? I arched an eyebrow at him and stilled his hand. *Did this mean?*

In response, he brought my hand to his lap and pressed it against his obvious erection with a smirk. Had we made enough progress to put sex back into the picture? I shot him a dubious look and he leaned in to whisper in my ear.

"You got me feeling some kind of way, Gou."

He only cares about you because you let him fuck you.

The floating, slightly horny feeling I'd been holding on to came crashing down, along with my water glass. Thankfully, it was nearly empty.

The table laughed, and I smiled sheepishly as I scrambled to redirect the water flow with my hand. I felt stupid and clumsy, but I laughed anyway.

No one here likes you. You're ugly and fat.

"Maybe you should slow down on those Bloody Marys," Siddharth said.

You can't follow simple rules. Don't bring up Mexico. How hard is it to be a little disciplined?

"He only had two." Adam touched my lap with his napkin, dabbing much higher than he needed to be to get at the wet spots. "Maybe you need to eat some food." He wore his fake concern well, but my entire body seized up in panic at the mention of eating and I . . . *Shit.*

I broke into a cold sweat, eyeing the exit. I needed to get out of there. "Would you mind if we take off? I'm not feeling well."

Adam's filthy grin was clouded by actual confusion and worry. "Uh, sure. Let me pay our check."

Siddharth waved Adam off when he went to retrieve his wallet. "Take him home. We'll cover it."

"Thanks, guys," I said, clutching the ballooning swell of my belly.

By the time we made it to the car, Adam was in full caretaker mode, even going so far as to buckle my seat belt.

"I'm sorry," I said.

"What's wrong? You were fine, then suddenly you kind of looked like you wanted to puke. Are you nauseated? Would it help to have the windows down? I'll take you home and then run to the store and get you some Sprite."

"Adam, for fuck's sake, I'm not dying. My stomach is upset." *Stay calm or it'll only invite more questions. We can fix this. We won't eat the rest of the day.* "Maura's cooking isn't sitting right. Sorry if this ruins your plans."

He exhaled with an uncomfortable smile. "It's not . . . There was no plan. I started thinking about you and how grateful I am that we're doing this. Our talk felt like a breakthrough and . . . well, anyway I got turned on and you used to like when I teased you in public."

"I'm sorry."

"It's fine. Let's get you home. So, um, my place or yours?"

"Would you be upset if I wanted to go to my place?"

"No," Adam answered, but I didn't think he heard the implied *alone* in my question.

I remained silent on our drive home, and for some reason, it either didn't ping Adam's *figure out what's wrong with Cade* radar or my earlier reaction had him hesitating to start another fight; neither seemed good for this fresh start we were striving for.

His hand rested on my knee. With my eyes, I followed the length of his arm to where his neck and shoulder met, the place he carried all his tension. Without thinking, I reached for him, hoping it would somehow calm me down to touch him. Adam tilted his head, making room for me to slip my hand between his collar and warm skin.

I rubbed his neck all the way home like one of those stress balls. Redirecting my attention to literally anything I could.

I hadn't noticed earlier he'd worn a collared shirt. Adam used to be the king of expensive—T-shirts and sweatpants that had the nerve to cost hundreds of dollars. He'd really stepped up his wardrobe in the last year, still preferring designer labels but always proud to recount the bargains he used in their acquisition. Teaching Adam that thrift stores exist was one of my better memories. The look on his face when I explained pawn shops and consignments—like I'd basically revealed the secrets of the universe to him. I concentrated on that. Fuck, it made my heart beat fast when he discovered how the other half lived and embraced it.

"You sure I can't get you anything?" He reached for the ignition button to turn off his car, and I realized we were home.

"No, I'm good. Thanks for driving."

"Anytime." He stared at me for a long minute. "You don't want me to come up, do you?"

I bit my lip. "I think I'm going to lie down and sleep."

"Cade, do you really not feel well, or is something else going on? Is this about my parents?"

"No," I said emphatically. I didn't want him to blame himself. "It really is my stomach. I will think about Atlanta. I'd like to go to support you, but Maura..."

"I thought she was better."

"She is, but Hayley will be out of school for the first week, and it's a lot for her to have her all day."

"What if Hayley came with us?"

"Are you serious?"

"Yeah. Atlanta has a lot of cool things for kids to do."

"But your brother's party..."

"Don't eleven-year-olds stay by themselves for a few hours?"

I wrinkled my nose. Maura left Hayley alone sometimes to run to the store or for quick errands, but I didn't think she was ready. Not with all the addicts rummaging around their complex. Maybe where Adam's parents lived, but god willing we wouldn't be staying there. "In a hotel where she wouldn't know anyone? No, I don't think so."

"I can try to get a babysitter or ..." Adam paused. "I'm getting ahead of myself. First, you decide if you *want* to go. Then, talk to Maura about Hayley joining us. If both things are a go, we can work on a solution for the party. Worst case, I'll go alone to the party, but we can still get away and show Hayley a good time."

"Will I see you tomorrow?" I asked cautiously.

"Do you want to?"

"Yeah. Come over when you get off work."

"Okay. Hope you feel better." He leaned in and kissed my cheek.

"Thanks, Adam."

"I'll call you later to say good night."

Adam peered at me through his long lashes. His lips softened and his tongue ran across his upper lip. I wished I could give in. But I couldn't. Not when I finally recognized that the past was back to haunt me and I needed some time to figure out what to do about it. The window to act would close soon enough. The fact that I was already considering letting it indicated how little time I had left before that voice in my head assumed all control.

Chapter Eight

Cade

I awoke cold and clammy. My head ached, and everything had a floaty, distorted appearance. I closed my eyes and the small voice—the old friend I'd ghosted but who'd refused to take the hint—told me to take off my shirt and run to the mirror.

I felt out of control and angry that instead of coming home to rest the day before, I'd forced myself to exercise away the second Bloody Mary, then binge-watched shows about food. When I stumbled upon an old favorite of mine, I jumped down the rabbit hole, watching an obese man shamed for his weekly food intake—chips, cookies, ice cream, pasta, and bread laid out on a table for everyone to gasp over. Every time the show's host picked up the food and called it bad, I felt calmer. I went to bed hungry, obsessing about food, and bargaining with myself on when I should actually eat. *Later* was the best answer I had in me.

I breathed deeply and reminded myself it was a new day. Today I would follow my recovery plan. Pinching my stomach, I told myself I didn't care. That it wasn't a new fat deposit. It was skin. Normal. Totally healthy. Today I would get back on track. I covered my bathroom mirror with a towel.

I arranged for a substitute teacher and went to the grocery store. When I came home and eyed the various food choices to decide what I would eat, I couldn't. Not yet. Not with the mysterious substance splashed on the shelf of my fridge.

As I scrubbed, my thoughts drifted back to Adam's good-night call. Adam had suggested we have a quiet night in just the two of us. He'd used words like snuggle and relax, but for all intents and purposes, that meant sex. But not just any sex—boyfriend sex. The "hold me close and whisper sweet endearments into my ear while I turn into a boneless, spineless whimpering mess" sex. In another time and place, the term *making love* applied to what Adam would do to me tonight. He wanted to start over, but I felt stuck, reliving the very nightmare that broke us to begin with. The more guilt I had over lying to Adam, the more powerful the voice in my head became, until it was a constant, unrelenting itch under my skin.

I dedicated the next six hours to cleaning my apartment. Everything needed to be spotless. I could do this. I wouldn't push him away again. Not this time. I owed him that much. I owed myself that much.

From the sheets to every stitch of machine-washable clothing, I spared nothing. I scrubbed the baseboards under the kitchen and bathroom counter, pulled everything out of drawers and scoured every pot and pan, even the cheap plastic container that held my cooking utensils couldn't escape boiling-hot water and Dawn. I removed the contents from my closets and organized, folded, and repacked. Every windowsill, pane of glass, corner, and crevice sparkled. It still wasn't enough. Like a horse with a carrot dangling a foot in front of my face, I couldn't achieve the calmness I sought.

So, I sucked it up and pulled the box out from its hiding spot and abstracted the folder from the Meadowbrook Center. I carried it to my bed, biting my lip so hard I could taste blood. Desperate to exorcise the self-destructive demon in my head that now returned in the quiet of my immaculate apartment. Louder and more persistent than it had been in the restaurant the day before. *Don't open it, Cade. Remember our program. It's going so well, just keep going. Try harder and you'll be so much better.*

Defiance set in. I sprang from the bed and stormed my way to the kitchen, retrieved a bowl, and set it on the sanitized-within-an-inch-of-its-life countertop with a clang. I paced the small galley-style space, palms shaking, psyching myself up like a boxer going into the fight of his career. *That's right, Cade. You're a fighter. You got this.*

I pulled the cereal box from the pantry and dumped the contents into the bowl. *Good.* I retrieved the almond milk from my fridge, opened it, and poured a generous portion over the cereal, letting the small splash on the counter serve as my battle cry. *You can do this.* Hands shaking, I reached for a spoon and then slammed the drawer shut, satisfied with the angry rattle of its contents.

"Good. Get mad!" I yelled at the drawer. A general rallying his troops to the cause. "We're doing this."

Don't, Cade. You'll ruin everything.

I took a victorious bite. Crunching and crunching until I knew it was time. I summoned as much saliva as I could and forced my throat to swallow. The rough texture scraped all the way down my esophagus, but I confirmed I could do it. I closed my eyes and took another bite because I had to prove that voice did not control me.

Today, I was fixing things with Adam and having long overdue sex. "You want to see a glutton," I mumbled at myself with my mouth full. I decreed tonight I would be the most well-fucked and well-fed bastard I could be. *What do you say about that?* I scooped a larger spoonful, laughing at how good it tasted.

I finished the entire bowl of cereal and drank the milk left in the bowl, and then, because I wasn't a total Neanderthal and appreciated a clean kitchen, I rinsed my dishes and wiped the spilled milk off the counter.

For a moment, I sat on my couch, taking inventory of my options. *Call Maura.* It'd be the prudent thing to do. She's seen me though so much, and I knew Dr. McNamara would encourage me to use my support system, but Maura had warned me starting any diet and exercise program was a slippery slope, and she had her own problems right now.

I pursed my lips, weighing how catastrophic doing this alone would be. Even though I won this battle, I knew that voice in my head wouldn't disappear after one bowl of cereal. I picked up my phone and called Aislinn.

"Hello." Her voice sounded agitated, and I aborted my mission.

"Hey, Sis."

"Hey. I got your bracelet last night. Thank you. I love it."

"Good. I'm glad. So you busy?"

"Um . . . sort of. I didn't get a break today, so I'm scarfing down dinner and trying to finish my charting before the late shift arrives. What about you?"

"Dinner?" I checked my phone. Holy shit. Adam would be here in less than an hour, and I was a sweaty mess. "Well, I don't want to keep you."

"Hey. Before you go, I wanted to ask if you thought Hayley seemed okay?"

"Yeah. She's fine. Why?"

"She's been calling me a lot since I left. It's odd for her to call me and not you. I don't mind, it's just . . . I worry because she seems a little anxious about things. You think I should tell Maura she's calling?"

Worry flared in me. "I'll see if I can take her next weekend for a few days, give her a chance to open up. She's more aware of her mom's issues now; maybe we need to encourage her to talk about it."

"Okay. That's good. Maura never talks about anything. My dad was wondering if she'd heard anything about her dad and she lost her shit. Keep me posted, would you?"

"Aislinn, do me a favor and leave your father out of this," I warned. The last thing I needed was Aislinn's father and stepmother sticking their nose into our family business. I was too young to remember how James was as a stepfather, but Maura still blamed the guy for taking her baby sister away. No good could come of adding him into the mix.

"All right. I'm sorry."

"Never mention Larry to Hayley either. Hayley thinks both her grandparents are dead, and Maura wants it that way."

"I won't say a word."

"Thanks. I'm glad you like your bracelet, now get back to work. Save people from their dangerous decisions and poor life choices. Heal the sick or whatever your mission is."

"I'm an ER nurse, Cade, not a miracle worker. My only mission is to keep people alive with all their organs and limbs attached long enough to discharge them or send them to the floor. Oh and finish my paperwork before the end of my shift."

"Well, carry on, Ace."

Aislinn laughed at her childhood nickname. "Love you, Cade."

I hung up the phone just as there came a firm knock. *Fuck.* I checked the clock. Adam was early. I was steps from opening the door when I remembered my folder. I rushed to the bedroom and yanked it off the comforter and shoved it back into the box in the closet. Another knock sounded, and I hurried to the door to answer it.

"Hey . . ." Adam's bright smiled dimmed. "Are you still sick?"

I glanced down at the same grubby clothes I'd used to clean my place. I'd meant to change into work clothes so there'd be no reason for him to question me about it. "No. I took a mental health day to take care of stuff."

There. Not a lie. I stood aside and let him into my apartment.

"Wow, your place looks great."

"Thanks. Have a seat. I'm just going to take a quick shower."

His hand reached out to stop me, and heat rushed up my neck as he crowded into me.

"Are you feeling some kind of way again, Mr. Creedon?" My back hit the wall.

His hands came up to rest on either side of mine, trapping me. I stopped breathing as his searing gaze tracked down my body, inspecting me in a way that made my heart race. I closed my eyes, reminding myself that Adam found me attractive. Even when I drove him crazy, he always appeared ready to devour me. I kept my focus on that.

"I'm always feeling some kind of way around you, Gou. Been thinking about you all day."

"Oh yeah?" I bit my lip. The only thing I could control about my deep voice was the volume, but Adam's could fluctuate from sultry and teasing to demanding and toppy. Tonight, as expected, he came to make me beg, and I was here for it. "What were you thinking about?"

"I'm thinking about how good you're going to taste when I put my mouth on you. Those sweet sounds you'll make for me."

I swallowed. Adam leaned closer, our hot breaths comingling in the narrow space between us. He hovered there, waiting for me to rise and close the gap. When I did, he pulled back just enough to drive me crazy.

"Nuh-uh," he teased. "Tell me what I need to hear."

"Adam—" I whined.

"Yes, baby."

"I love you."

His smile—*How was it possible to be so endearing and so fucking filthy at the same time?*

"I love you too. You want to feel how much?"

"Yeah," I keened. Fuck, what he did to me.

He rubbed the prominent bulge between his legs. "You've been missing it, haven't you?"

"So much." I nodded, batting my eyes up at him. Letting him see how much he turned me on. I needed to hold it, wrap my hand around the silky soft skin, but that wasn't on the menu tonight and fuck if I wasn't starving for what he was dishing out.

Adam zeroed his attention to the curve of my neck, trailing up. Fine baby hairs standing at attention. I held my breath, anticipating his lips and yelping when his teeth found my earlobe, biting sharply enough to sting. "Touch yourself, Gou."

I moaned, scrambling to comply.

"That's it, baby. Show me how hard you are for me." I stroked faster at his command, jerking in tight, quick strokes to his approving smile. "How good is it going to feel when my tongue is inside you?"

I choked on my answer, and only a strangled noise escaped.

"I'm going to stretch out that hole of yours. Lick inside you, baby. That's it. Keep stroking for me." He wet his fingers and my hole clenched, more than ready to have something filling it.

"Adam—" My voice inched dangerously close to begging already.

"Are you dripping for me, baby?" His finger found my slit, and I cried out as he smeared pre-come over the head and brought his finger back up to his lips and tasted me.

"Fuck, Gou. Seeing you like this gets me so hot. Look at that gorgeous cock. Doesn't it feel good to touch yourself? That's it, baby. Make yourself feel good. You're turning me on so much."

I closed my eyes and the hot pants of Adam's breath came closer. He blew across the shell of my ear. "My sexy boy. I missed you so much. There hasn't been one night I didn't go to bed with this sweet face on my mind and my hand on my cock."

"Fuck, I'm getting close," I groaned.

"Damn, baby. You're so perfect like this. You know what you need to do."

"Please," I begged. Adam groaned.

"If you get off now, you'll be too sensitive to take my cock later."

"No." I rocked my head.

"What's it going to be, Gou? Show me how hot this makes you, turning me on like this, teasing me? Or do you want to stop now? Tell me, Gou. Come now with your own hand or wait and let me fill you so full. I love when you come on my cock, all desperate for it. Your clenching that ass, aren't you, baby? Thinking about how good it will be to have my cock inside you."

"Adam— Fuck."

"Harder, baby. Show me how good it feels. I want you to feel good, baby, but you can't have both. What's it going to be?"

"Both," I begged.

"Ask nicely."

"Please, can I come and still get fucked later?"

"My greedy boy wants both, doesn't he?"

"Yes," I moaned. My balls pulled close to my body.

"It will be my way, Cade. I have a lot of time to make up for. Stroke that cock, Cade. If you want it, show me. Let me hear how badly you need it, Goulue."

"I will. Please, Adam."

"There it is. Good boy. You're so hard for me. Is it throbbing, baby? Get that spot right under your head I love to flick with my tongue. Makes you all needy. You feel it yet? Tell me."

I nodded. "I'm so close."

"There you go, baby. So perfect. Come for me. Now. Cade."

"*Fuuuck,*" I breathed as I came and slumped against him to keep from falling. "Jesus Christ."

Adam laughed and pressed a gentle kiss to my forehead. "Couldn't have you jacking off in the shower alone."

I reached for the button of his pants. "Let me suck you."

Adam covered my hand and shook his head. "That was just for you. I want to take my time with you tonight. Thai food should be here soon. Go shower, then we eat. You will definitely want to fuel up, because I am going to take you apart."

I sucked in a breath, doubling down on my promise to myself. I was going to let go of everything other than this right here.

Adam

Cade returned from the shower wearing gray sweatpants slung low on his thin hips and the same sweatshirt of mine he'd brought to Hawaii. No one should look so cute in such baggy clothes.

"Smells good," Cade said, toweling his hair dry. "What did you get me?"

I placed the last of the Thai containers on the coffee table and dug out two sets of chopsticks from the plastic bag. "I got our usual, and then I also got the tofu shit Siddharth likes in case you were still doing your weird program."

Cade froze for a second, an odd grimace on his face. "Why do you think vegan is weird for me and not Siddharth?"

"Uh, because you've never been vegan, I guess. I don't get the whole separate out all the foods thing either. What's that about?"

"It's nothing. I'm not doing it anymore."

Thank God. "Okay. So you want your usual?"

"Please," he said.

I patted the cushion next to me and smiled as he pulled his legs up to the couch and sunk into the back cushions and sighed contentedly. I handed him the container and his chopsticks. "Relaxed?" I asked, trying hard to restrain my smirk.

"Yeah." He peered into the box, and his smiled dimmed and his nose wrinkled.

"What's wrong? Is it not chicken with basil?"

"It is. Thanks, it's good." He pinched a piece of chicken and brought it to his mouth. "Thank you for getting dinner."

"You're welcome." I dug into my laab and toed my shoes off. "How was your mental health day?"

"It was productive. I got a lot accomplished.

"That's good. So were Maura and Hayley okay?"

Cade tilted his head, his mouth gaped and eyes narrowed in question.

"You know," I prompted, but got back no sense of recognition. "From the spoiled food. I figure if it upset your stomach, they were probably sick too."

Cade jolted a bit. "Oh, um. No. They were fine. How was work?"

Having someone who cared about my day was something that never got old for me. "It's good. I'm working on a rebrand and CMS design project for this bike share company called Greenspoke."

Cade smiled. "What's that?"

I launched into the finer points of my project and my recent client, which was a pretty cool organization. The director of sales and marketing was easy to work with, which wasn't always the case. "So this company has multiple city contracts, but each location sets up their web presence, which was all over the place in terms of content and branding. None of them had enough information on their mobile app to explain pricing and let people easily purchase a monthly pass. So, we're building a content management system, which gives every location a predefined website structure and UI/UX so they can spin up a new website and mobile app about ten times faster."

"That sounds way more involved than some other stuff you've worked on."

"I'm not the new guy anymore, so I get better projects. We compete for the UI/UX stuff. My firm doesn't get a lot of that work, but there's good money in it, so I'm hoping to get more experienced."

Cade frowned. "Your mom still giving you shit?"

I shook my head. "Yes, actually. But it is something I'm interested in."

"Because it's more money or because you like the work?"

"I don't know. Both, I guess. You have to admit traveling on private planes was pretty sweet. It'd be nice to make more. You think that's wrong?"

"Adam, I'm a public high school English teacher. Clearly I care shit all about income potential." He snorted. "I like you passionate about work. If UI/UX is your jam, go for it, but it doesn't sound as creative as what you were doing before, and I know you love to get creative."

That was all it took for my mind to dive into the gutter. I winked. "I do love to get creative." Cade's mouth gaped and I couldn't wait any longer to wreck him. "You done eating, baby?" I took his container and chopsticks and moved them out of my way.

Cade's teeth sank into his lower lip and he nodded.

"Bedroom?" I asked.

He nodded again and rose to his feet. I led him by the hand to his room and switched on the small lamp next to his bed. Opening the bedside table, I retrieved the lube and condoms he stored there. I held one up to him. "You want this?"

Cade's eyes went wide. We hadn't used them when we were together in college, but hadn't *not* used them in years. Physically I didn't care, it felt amazing to me either way, but Cade liked it messy and I hated that he denied himself, even if I understood why.

He bobbed his head, so I laid it on the bed next to the lube and beckoned him closer. Getting him off at the door had been a spontaneous decision. Something to take the edge off and play a game I knew he liked. But I was going to be a little selfish this time and take him apart the way I wanted to do it—slow and tender. If he'd let me.

"Take off my sweatshirt."

Cade wrinkled his nose, and I laughed. "Don't worry. You still get to keep it."

He reached for the hem and pulled it free from his body, revealing a T-shirt underneath. This pulled tight across his small frame, so I wanted it to stay. "Come here."

When he was within reach, I spun him so his back was against my chest, facing the bed his knees were touching. I ran my hands down his sides to his prominent hip bones and nibbled on his ear. He groaned, trying to lift higher and push his ass back toward me.

My hips canted forward of their own will, but I held him at bay. The more he struggled to put pressure on my filling dick, the more determined I was not to let him. "Put your hands flat on the bed."

Cade did as I asked, parting his legs to get into position. He was so goddamn perfect. I slid his sweatpants down, just over the curve of his ass, and shoved his shirt up his back, momentarily startled by the visible outline of his spine. I traced a finger down the bony protrusions, not sure what to make of the change.

At my touch, Cade's eyes whipped back toward me, all heat and lust and desperation, with an edge of warning I knew too well.

I smiled reassurance. *So, he'd lost some weight.* With all that Maura had put him through, that was to be expected. "Arch your back for me."

Cade beamed, flexing his spine and lifting his ass for me.

I took my dick in my hand, stroking myself until my body remembered what the hell it was supposed to be doing.

Cade's booty was small and round. But, my God, he was the most responsive bottom I'd ever had the pleasure to touch. I slid down to my knees and kissed each hip and traced my lips along the upper globes of his ass with featherlight pressure. When he moved, I nipped him.

Cade canted forward, humping the mattress. I let him undulate as I made my way to all my favorite spots, ending at the small freckle where his ass met his left thigh. I flicked it, tracing along the lower curve toward his exposed taint, removing the pressure as soon as I arrived.

"Adam—" Cade groaned in frustration.

"Show me that hole, Gou."

Cade reached back and spread his cheeks with his hands, revealing the absolute star of the most perfect, hairless, blemish-free ass God ever created. It fluttered in anticipation, and my cock throbbed.

"Fuck," I tapped it so it would do it again.

Cade didn't need a lot of prep. Sometimes he didn't even want lube, but the thought of damaging something so perfect always had me taking my time. I dipped down, taking a long slow lick of his rim, then pulling back to admire the glistening coat of my saliva. Fuck. I had to take a deep breath to calm myself before I went in again. Using a little more pressure, I circled his rim with the tip, alternating with stronger laps of the entire opening. When that little jewel relaxed for me, I pushed inside and ate him out until sweet gasps poured out of him.

"Fuck, babe." He let go of his cheeks and grabbed the back of my head, dragging me by my hair closer still. I chuckled against the sensitive rim, and he keened. Since his fingers hadn't released the chunk of hair he'd grasped, I stuck out my tongue as far as it would go, grabbed his hips, and let him ride my face.

Moaning loudly, Cade's ass bounced up and down, grinding and yanking my hair where he needed me to be. I had to let go of him to squeeze the base of my cock to stay my rising orgasm.

Cade buried his face in the mattress and released a long groan, part frustration, part desperation, before declaring he was done being patient. "Fuck me, Adam."

Laughing at the needy quality of his baritone voice, I pried the fingers loose from my hair and sat back on my ankles. His hole, slicked and winking, invited me to put something, anything, inside of him. I smacked him, an upward thrust right on the sensitive area nearest his thigh. "On the bed, Gou. I told you we're going at my speed tonight."

He scrambled onto the bed, settling on his back with his long hair spread out like a halo behind him. His sweatpants had rucked down, exposing the base of his cock surrounded by a fine strip of trimmed blond hair. The outline of the tip was tucked inside, pressed against the wet spot.

I jutted my chin toward it. "Show me."

Eye's half-lidded, Cade rolled the waistband down inch by inch, revealing himself to me. When his cock sprung free, it smacked against his abdomen, leaving a stringy stand of pre-come behind. Cade lifted his shirt above his nipples and trailed his fingers over his lean torso. When he closed in on his dick, he swiped up the pre-come and held it out for me like a present.

This is what I had missed. The slow give and take. Sex was so much better when we weren't racing to get off before some emotional bomb detonated and covered us in actual feelings.

I leaned down and opened my mouth to taste him. Savoring him because I could now.

"So sweet," I said in response to how docile he was being. Waiting wasn't a skill that came easily to Cade.

I lifted from him and freed us both of our shirts and him of his sweatpants. I settled myself at his side, rolled him toward me, and rested my hand on his waist. My palm slid into place, nestled in the inward curve, and I could tell by the unfamiliar angle of my wrist that he'd lost inches since the last time I'd touched him.

"Kiss me," Cade demanded, and my heart leaped, pushing aside my concerns again. We kissed languidly for a long time, bringing the temperature down by unspoken agreement. Just touching and kissing, more out of need than excitement. He was still so beautiful.

I brushed a strand of hair out of his eyes. "The things you do to me," I breathed.

Cade's eyelids fluttered closed. His voice shaky, he whispered, "I've missed this part," and snuggled into me as I wrapped myself around him.

"What else have you missed?" I grinded my cock against his.

Cade's eyes flew open, and the excited little gasp he let loose was everything. "Is it my turn?"

"There are no turns. There's just making each other feel good."

"I want to make *you* feel good."

"You've been doing that all evening, Gou."

"Then I'll make me feel good more."

"Tell me how."

"Adam—" Cade complained, but I smiled wider and pushed against him again. He knew I could keep this going all night. I loved when he asked for it. When he told me that my body gave him as much pleasure as his gave me. "With your dick, jackass."

Laughing, I rolled onto my back and rested my hands behind my head. "Okay, take whatever you need."

Cade scrambled to arrange himself between my knees and pulled on the waistband of my unbuttoned jeans. Chuckling at his enthusiasm, I planted my feet and lifted my ass so he could pull them off. I had on black briefs underneath; they were tight, but also a favorite of Cade's and I hadn't expected to be wearing them long when I picked them.

His hand rubbed my erection, first over the fabric, but after a few seconds he moved it out of his way.

His hand wrapped around my dick created some sort of optical illusion. This was where his size really impacted my ego. My cock appeared twice as big in his hand than in my own, and I had the pictures to prove it. I tossed my head back as Cade touched me, not jacking me off so much as just trying to make sure I was as rigid and engorged as I could be before he put his mouth on me and took me into his throat.

I'd watched him play with my cock like it was his favorite toy a million times, often admiring it like he wanted to worship it, revere it, so much so that in my less evolved days, it made me feel like that was the only thing he needed me for. Tonight, the way he touched and sucked me, was more subdued. Almost wistful. The mood shifted when Cade slowed his pace, and I wanted to find out what was going on without overreacting or calling attention to it.

"Feels good," I said benignly. "Is that what you wanted, baby? To touch me."

Cade nodded.

"You see how much I want you?" I stroked a hand through his hair.

He nodded again.

"You're so beautiful. I want you so, so much."

"I want you too."

With tentative eyes, he moved up to kiss me softly. My thumb traced his swollen lips, swiping at the plump flesh. He kissed it and eased away.

"How do you want me?" I asked.

Cade tilted his head, analyzing me like one of his books until he found a deeper meaning to my question. "I want back what we had. So damn much. I don't want to deny myself anymore."

Emotion welled in his eyes as I yanked him toward me. I kissed him, years' worth of guilt and remorse and unspoken confessions consumed in a fiery passion. "I'm sorry. We will get there. We will. God, Cade. I need you. Please."

"Yeah." Cade settled on his back again, grasping my bicep firmly. He was scared. Afraid of trusting me again, but not nearly as terrified as I was to mess this up. "Missionary, like we used to."

I nodded, knowing this was a huge milestone. I broke speed records getting the condom on and lubing up for fear he'd change his mind. Cade spread his thighs and brought his legs around me as I slid inside him.

"Adam," he breathed.

I clung to him like I did our past, lowering myself so there was no part of my upper body not touching his. "Let me see those green eyes, Gou," I whispered. When he obliged, I braced my forearm on the mattress above his head, rocked inside of him, and stared into his eyes until the sensations overwhelmed us. The grip of his tight heat almost an afterthought until his mouth gaped and his breath stuttered. I moved faster, propelling us both over the edge in an intense silence broken only by the final grunt of my climax.

My head dropped to his shoulder and his fingers combed through my hair, the lub-dub of his heart racing beneath me.

Chapter Nine

Cade

I'd promised myself I would not skip meals, but the voice was making it difficult to eat in front of people, and the one chance I had to eat alone I'd spent trying to find out why Hayley's school recorded her absent . . . again.

Exhausted and hungry, I jumped into the car, shoved a meal replacement bar into my mouth, chugged an Ensure Plus, and sped toward Maura's, prepared to be mildly annoyed by whatever prompted the message from Hayley's school. When no one answered the door, I could barely hold my keys steady long enough to let myself in. The heavy smell of paint fumes and cigarettes permeated the air and panic set in. "Sis," I called out and slid open the patio door to air the place out. "Hayley."

There was no answer. I checked my watch. It was well after the time Hayley would be home from school. I moved past the family room to Maura's bedroom and flipped on the light.

"Well that explains the paint smell," I said, surveying the multiple stripes of slightly distinct shades of blue on the wall. There were small paint sample cans left open on her dresser, and a paint tray and paintbrush sitting on the tan carpet with no barrier. I lifted the tray and, sure enough, a rectangular outline remained on the carpet. Fuck, there went the security deposit. "Goddamn it, Maura." I hung my head and blew out a breath as I carried the materials to the bathtub of her en suite.

The medicine cabinet was open, and inside were three bottles. I found the Risperdal, her antipsychotic, nearly full, quickly enough. The other two—the mood stabilizer she took all the time and the antidepressant she took when she was having a low period—were both half-empty. I checked the dates. She'd filled them all on the same day three weeks before. I counted the pills and worked the math. She'd been off her antipsychotic for ten days already, but she'd been missing doses of all of them.

The front door opened. "I'm positive I locked this door," Maura announced. "Hayley, go change your clothes. Your hair is dripping all over the floor."

I walked out of the bedroom. "Maura," I said from the doorway.

She jumped. "Fucking Christ, Cade. You damn near gave me a heart attack."

"Uncle Cade." Hayley ran to me, arms extended for a hug before crashing into my side, soaking my pant leg.

I patted her head before coaxing her off me. "Why are you wet?"

"Mama and I played hockey and went to the lake. It was so much fun. Mama taught me how to do a flip."

"Hooky," I corrected, trying to keep my anger from boiling over in front of Hayley. "Go change, hon. I need to talk to your mother." She nodded and I cringed at her nearly blue legs as she scurried into her bedroom.

Although we were the same height, Maura drew up taller and jutted her chin out. Her defensive stance. Before I could say a word, she launched in. "She's got straight As. She's not missing anything."

I hated when she made it sound like I was the unreasonable one. "It's barely eighty degrees today; the water had to be freezing."

"It was fine. We needed a little break. You're always bitching that I don't spend enough time with her. I can't do anything right, I guess."

"Maura, you could have at least brought her a change of clothes."

"I forgot. What are you doing here? You and Adam break up again?"

I ignored her jab. She always insinuated I didn't spend enough time with them when Adam and I were together, which was one of the reasons Adam insisting I spent too much time with them was so infuriating. I could not win. "The counselor called me. Again."

"That nosy asshole. What did you say?"

"What could I say, Maura? I thought she was in school."

"Well, she wasn't." Maura sulked to the kitchen table and plopped down into a chair.

"She needs to be in school. You couldn't wait until the weekend to go to the lake?"

"Would you quit harping on this? It's done. Get off my ass." She grabbed her purse and began searching through it.

I sighed. "Called you today. Multiple times."

She shrugged and pulled a pack of Marlboros from her purse, extracted a cigarette, and lit it. Sucking on the end of her cancer stick like she hadn't quit years ago because Hayley had gotten bronchitis when she was seven. "I forgot my phone was in my pocket when I jumped in."

I pressed my lips together and smacked them. This discussion was futile. "Okay. Well, I see you have life by the balls here, so I think I'll just go ask if Hayley wants to have a sleepover this weekend."

"No," Maura said, blowing a cloud of smoke in my face.

I waved it away. "No? Seriously? After all the times you've begged me to take her because you needed a break."

"I don't like this attitude you're giving me."

"You want to see attitude?" I set the medication bottle down in front of me. "Take your goddamn medicine. How's that for attitude?"

"I'm not taking that. They make me too tired."

I did my best to keep my frustration off my face, but I sucked at it. "You know the fatigue wears off."

"Yeah. When I stopped taking them."

I heaved a sigh and worked to find a more supportive tone. It wasn't her fault, I reminded myself. This was part of her illness, and me getting frustrated wasn't going to solve a damn thing. "You know you'll get manic if you take the antidepressant without the antipsychotic. Do you want Hayley to have to deal with that again?"

"Hayley is fine. She deserves a mother that can get out of bed, Cade. You should have seen how happy she was today. We had fun."

"She deserves a mother who can take care of her, which you won't be able to do if you don't take your pills. It's always fun until it's not. She's getting older now—don't you remember when Colleen went off the deep end? How it felt to come home and not know what mood she would be in? Do you want that for Hayley?"

Maura grabbed a small plate and snuffed out her cigarette. I could tell I was getting through to her, so I let the silence stretch on.

"Fine. I'll take it later, after she goes to bed."

"How about you take it now so you don't forget?" She pouted, but before she could object, I reminded her of why. "You told me to hold you accountable. Would you have accepted, 'I'll eat it later' from me when I was trying to get better?"

"I'll be in bed for days again."

I moved behind her and rubbed her shoulders. "Then she'll stay with me and I'll bring you food."

"Cade—"

"Maura . . ." I poured her a glass of water and set it next to the medicine bottle. "I love you. Hayley and I need you to be okay."

Hayley returned to the room, her nose wrinkling. "Yuck." She stuck her tongue out and waved her hand around, dispersing the smoke. "Can we read more of my book tonight, Uncle Cade?"

"Yeah, hon. If your mom says it's okay, maybe you can have a sleepover with me tonight."

"Yay! Can I?" Hayley asked.

Maura's shoulders slumped, but she sighed, grabbed the medicine bottle, and unscrewed the lid, eyes broadcasting enough disdain to serve as a passable substitute for the *fuck you* I knew she wanted to say.

"Did you hang your swimsuit up like I told you?"

The grin slid off Hayley's face. "Uh. I forgot."

"Go hang up your suit and pack a bag."

Hayley clapped her hands and skipped off.

"Don't forget socks and underwear," Maura yelled after her, then put the full weight of her disapproval on me. "You suck."

"I know. But at least this way you can go to sleep if you want."

"I'm not Colleen, Cade. I love my daughter, and I hate not being able to do things with her."

"I understand, Sis."

She placed the pill on her tongue like it was poison. When she brought the water to her lips and swallowed, I recognized she did it for Hayley, which alone made her a better mom than our own.

I handed her my cell phone. "Call Mr. Bach. Tell him Hayley had a slight fever today and your phone broke so you couldn't call the attendance line."

I picked up the landline we had installed when Hayley started staying home alone. "This bill caught up?" I asked.

She nodded.

"Okay, good. I'll see if I can find you a new cell. In the meantime, keep mine."

"What will you use?"

"Don't worry about me."

"Cade, that's stupid. I'll be sleeping. You can keep the phone, that way I can check on Hayley when I want to."

"Fine. Mr. Bach mentioned Field Day and I got the strong impression one of us should volunteer. Do you think you can manage going to that? I can't take off this close to the end of the year."

She nodded and set her head down on the table. "I don't understand. Why me?"

"It will get better, Sis." I stroked her hair. "I promise. You went a year without a major episode. We just need to get you stable, and then you'll be back down to one medication again."

She lifted her head, the usual light in her hazel eyes succumbing to the dark shadows surrounding them. My heart ached for her. She deserved so much more out of life.

"I'm ready." Hayley arrived dragging her child-size roller suitcase Aislinn had bought her for Christmas last year. I grabbed the bag and set it on the table, unzipping the top to examine the contents. She had two pairs of shorts, some matching T-shirts, a few pairs of underwear and a . . . "What is this?" I held up the training bra.

"Aunt Aislinn bought it for me."

Maura sat up and shrugged. Shaking my head, I put it back. I was so not prepared for that conversation. "I don't see any pajamas."

Hayley's eyeballs bugged out. "Oh, yeah. Mama, I couldn't find any."

"There might be some in my room. Cade, can you check the dryer?" Maura asked as she stood up.

I made my way to the small laundry closet in the hallway between the bedrooms. Rummaging through the dryer, I pulled out more of my sister's panties than I cared to see and a pair of men's boxer briefs?

"I found them—" Maura froze, her eyes widening as they narrowed in on my hands.

I held up them up, dangling the briefs on one finger, and mouthed, *Oh my god.*

She yanked them out of my hands, wadded them up and threw them back into the dryer. I stifled my laugh. "Thanks for coming over, Cade." She shut the dryer and handed me Hayley's pajamas.

"Who are you fucking?"

She shoved me toward the kitchen. "No one."

"Maura Kay," I teased her. "You little tramp. How did I not know you're getting some action?"

She scowled. "It's not going to happen again."

"Why? No good?"

"Nope," she said, popping the *P* sound.

"The sex or the man?"

"The man. He's a snake."

"You okay?" I asked around tight lips.

Maura's expression softened. "Yeah. I was just lonely, Cade, and a little desperate."

"Hey, trust me. I get it. Lonely and desperate explains a lot of my life choices too. Focus on getting healthy, and we'll find you a good one, okay?"

"Speaking of good ones. How are things going with Adam? Do we love to hate him or hate to love him these days?"

"Love to love him?"

She laughed. "Is that a question?"

"It's a little confusing right now. The sex got pretty intense the other night, but things are progressing."

"Ew," she said. "Spare me the details please."

I chuckled. "I'm not going to review the mechanics with you. Maybe I should have said 'emotionally intense.' Feelings were shared, barriers were breached."

"So, are you going to tell him? I really think you should."

I shook my head. "We want to move on. It's all very adult and functional. I'm out of my element."

"*Adam* is adult and functional?"

"I know. It's like he grew the fuck up when I was busy trying to convince myself he was too immature to commit to me. We talked about some guys we dated over the last few years. Turns out they meant nothing."

"He knows he couldn't do better than you. Besides, you weren't exactly a monk either."

"Aww, thanks, Sis. Any guy would be lucky to have you too."

She rolled her eyes. "Yeah, they're just lining up to date a bipolar, high school dropout, single mother."

"Uncle Cade." Hayley cocked her hip to the side and gestured wildly. "Move your fine ass. We're burning daylight."

Maura and I exchanged an amused look and cracked up.

"Where in the world did you hear that?" I asked my niece.

"Daddy said it to Mama the other day."

I gasped, and one glance at Maura's face, I knew exactly who had slithered his way into her bed.

Adam

Something came up with Maura. I'm sorry.

I'd gotten so used to spending the evenings with Cade, that I'd forgotten the disappointment that came from having our plans canceled at the last minute because of Cade's sister. Before I responded to his message, I waited for the feeling to pass.

Everything okay?

His quick reply helped.

Yeah. But it will probably consume my weekend.

I stared at his message. This was undefined territory of our new dynamic. A few years ago, I'd have interpreted his message as a *Fuck off, I'm busy with someone that isn't you*, and inevitably responded accordingly. A few months ago, I might have offered to join them and gotten an angry text back that we were not in a relationship. Now, I didn't know what the deal was, but I couldn't risk jumping to conclusions.

Cade answered on the first ring. "Please don't be mad. I couldn't help it." Hayley sang badly in the background.

Calling had been the absolute right decision. "Hi. Hello, dear. How was your day?"

The anxiety in his voice lifted. "Terrible. Then good. Then terrible again. Now back to good. Please don't send me back to terrible. I can't take it."

"I won't. Just wanted to check in. Were you wanting to spend time with your niece alone or should I grab a pizza and come teach Hayley how to stay on key?"

"You want to hang out with an eleven-year-old girl?"

"No, I want to hang out with you. I don't mind spending time with Hayley, but if I'm intruding, then I'll call Brady and see if he wants to game."

"You'll have more fun with Brady."

I paused, pursing my lips as I considered if his response was a subtle *fuck off* or he really was attempting to care about my preference. "Is this a test? I feel like it's a test."

"What do you mean?"

"I mean, I'm offering to come over and spend time with you, and I'm asking if you'd like that or if I should make other plans for the evening. Forget which one is more fun for me for a minute; which do you prefer?"

"Oh. Um. I'd like to see you."

I smiled, giving myself a small pat on the back for navigating the situation without setting off any landmines. "Okay, then what does Miss Hayley like on her pizza?"

"Adam, you'll be bored. We can't do anything while she's here, and she can't watch the movies you like. I appreciate you don't like kids."

I shook my head as he spoke because he was wrong. I was never bored around Cade, and I kind of liked having the chance to spend time with him when sex wasn't on the table. It felt like progress. "Gou. First, I may not want to have kids, but I *like* kids fine. Second, I understand how children work, and I'm still coming over. Now, I suspect green pepper and sausage will not work, so what should I get?"

"Half cheese, half green pepper and sausage."

"Very good. Is she allowed to have soda?"

"She can have caffeine-free stuff—Sprite or Hi-C."

"Okay, I'll see you in about an hour. Bye."

"Babe," Cade called before I disconnected our call.

"Yeah?"

"You might want to bring some pajamas and your pillow."

A grin split my face. "Really?"

"We're building a blanket fort. We may need to saw your legs off, but I think we can squeeze you in."

"Mm. I don't know, I kind of like my legs. How about I bring more blankets instead?"

"Maybe that quilt from the daybed in the spare bedroom."

"Will do. Anything else?"

"Nope. Just, um, I love you."

"I love you too."

Chapter Ten

Cade

"Hayley drools like you do," Adam said, peering over my exhausted niece. He looked fuckable as hell, all messy hair and bulging biceps.

"I do not drool."

"Pfft. Please. I used to wake up in your dorm bed with my shoulder soaked."

The pain of nostalgia squeezed my chest. "Thanks for hanging out with us and for dinner."

"Thanks for having me. You want to talk about your terrible day?"

I shook my head and rolled onto my back, arms tucked under my head. I stared at the purple quilt ceiling. "This is some fort."

Adam mirrored my position. "It was fun. I never got to build forts when I was a kid. You're fantastic with her. Her and Maura are lucky to have you."

"But . . ." I prompted.

He rolled toward me again and propped himself up with a bent elbow. His eyebrow lifted. "But nothing. That's the entirety of my thought."

"You used to say Maura was a bitch and insist if I kept helping her, she'd never learn to take care of herself."

Adam sighed. "I used to say a lot of stupid things."

Hayley stirred, and I didn't want to take a chance that she would overhear us talking about her mother. I pulled a blanket over her shoulders and gestured for Adam to take our conversation to another place. We ambled to my bedroom, which was the only room out of her earshot. When he stepped inside, I closed the door with a soft *click*.

"What changed?" I whispered.

Adam shifted uncomfortably. "Me? I don't know, honestly. Maura has problems that I didn't understand, and it's fair to say I didn't try very hard to. I still think she takes advantage of you sometimes, but I was wrong to frame it as a choice you had to make. I shouldn't have tried to lay guilt trips on you about it."

"You realize Maura and I . . ." I ran my fingers through my hair, trying to find the best way to explain how much I owed my sister without getting into details I'd rather not get into. "There were a lot of years when Maura was the rock, and I was the one who needed help. You didn't see what she was like before her bipolar. She's three years older than me, Adam, and she practically raised me. She dropped out of high school to waitress full-time because we needed the money, and my mother would disappear for days and weeks at a time. Maura is not taking advantage of me, Adam. I owe her. There will never be a time I will not make her and Hayley a priority. You need to understand that."

"I don't want to get you upset, Cade. I trust your judgment, and it's not my place to interfere in your relationship with your family. This"—he gestured vaguely between us—"is what I should have done all along. I should have been trying to lighten your load, not add to it. I want to be there for you, so you can be there for her."

Maura had been the catalyst for so many arguments, I'd lost count of how many variations I'd heard of Adam's *I'll be more understanding* speech, but this was different. For the first time, he'd tied those words to actions. "I wish you could have known her before . . ." I closed my eyes briefly to picture Maura before she was sick. "She was so cool and fun and spontaneous." Like skipping school to take a lake trip. I wished I could let her have that. Allow her to show that part of herself to her daughter, but I'd seen first-hand how quickly impulsive turned dangerous with our mother. I never wanted Hayley to feel afraid of Maura.

"The doctors called it hypomania. It's this sort of endless energy and extra creativity. But Maura's episodes sometimes progress to 'haven't slept in days and I think I can fly off this building' kind of mania. Then the depression would hit."

Adam's eyes softened, and there was a glimpse of genuine empathy for my sister. "God. I know I blew off how sick she was in college and that's why you don't like to talk about Maura much with me, but I want you to know you can—good stuff and bad. I'll be here to listen."

His earnestness made me wish I could tell him everything. What Maura had been through. How it had impacted me, but there was no way to explain it without dredging up our past. And no way to talk about the past honestly without ruining what we were building. "She was the coolest older sister—smart and vibrant. She used to make me play school with her. I was like four or five, but Maura would bring home books from her school library and read them to me."

Adam smiled. "The twins played school too, but they expelled me . . . multiple times. Once Rachel wrote report cards, gave me all *F*s and R.J. all *A*s, and my mom thought it was hysterical. That shit was on the refrigerator for a month."

"I guess that explains your reaction when I decided to be a teacher."

"If I had teachers that looked like you, I would have cared a hell of a lot more about class."

"You did fine in college."

"Yeah. High school was another story."

"Maura was the same way. She never liked school the way I did. For her, it was a way to get out of the house and get some proper food, but I loved it."

Adam shook his head, amused. "Nerd."

I smiled acknowledgment. I'd seen childhood pictures of Adam, so I knew he'd always been a good-looking, stylish kid, whereas my bookworm nature, stringy blond bowl cut, and closet of worn-thin hand-me-downs hadn't exactly won me a seat at the popular table. "So much so. Do you ever wonder if we'd met in high school if we'd have clicked?"

"Sometimes. I mean, I was still dating girls through senior year, so I'm guessing I would have stayed clear of you just to hide my attraction. But do you remember that Mandy Moore movie, *A Walk to Remember*?"

"Yeah and it's a book, actually."

"Of course it is." Adam huffed. "I used to have this nerdy tutor who I was fairly sure was gay. It was like eighth or ninth grade. He was older, maybe a senior, but built like you. I had such a crush on him. Anyway, I used to daydream that he and I would have this magical opposites-attract love affair and I'd tell my friends we were in love and I didn't care what they think, then I'd find out his bucket list and we'd do all these crazy things like get married to check off everything on the list."

I burst out in a loud squawk, then remembered Hayley was sleeping in the next room and quickly quieted myself. "Adam, she has cancer. She's dying in the movie. That's why they get married."

"Yeah, but he doesn't know at the beginning. He's brave and tells all his friends to fuck off, and I wanted to do that for that hot little twink. It's romantic."

"If you say so," I said, still chuckling. "It's kind of sweet, though. How come you never asked for my bucket list?"

He shrugged. "I think I know most of it."

"Oh, really? What would be on it?" I put my hands on my hips, genuinely curious if Adam did know me as well as he thought.

Adam said nothing as he seemed to mull my question over for a second. When he spoke, the smile on his face looked pretty damn confident. "Well there are the simple things like having a Goldendoodle and a house with a big yard. The gay things like drag and making that trip to Stonewall. The more adventurous things like visiting New Zealand and that crazy cliff-diving shit you saw on YouTube. Then there are the sexual things like getting fist—"

I waved my hand. "Okay that's enough. You didn't mention the number one thing on my list though."

"Write and publish a novel," Adam said without hesitation. "I was still getting to the actual goals."

My heart thumped in my chest with all the feels. This was always the part of being my boyfriend Adam excelled in: he paid attention. *Except when* . . . I sighed, shaking my head, forcing memories that threatened to surface out of my mind. "Yeah. Writing would be number one for me."

"Did I miss any?"

"See Hayley graduate college."

"Um . . . what about your own kids?"

"Kids?"

"I mean, I watched you build a pretty kick-ass fort tonight. You'd be a wonderful dad."

I wasn't sure if he was teasing, but the thought of raising a kid with that particular grin of Adam's almost made me reconsider my views on parenthood. Almost. "I'm pretty happy being an uncle. I spend all day with teenagers; if I weren't gay, it'd be pretty decent birth control. Plus, I wouldn't wish my family genetics on anyone."

"Okay. Just checking. I think you could talk me into substituting a Goldendoodle for a kid if you ever changed your mind."

"Really?" I laughed. "You with kids?"

Adam seemed affronted, so I backpedaled. "Not that you aren't able to change your mind, but I kind of thought we agreed about that."

The line of Adam's frown broke when his lip quirked. I breathed relief that this wasn't really a change of heart, merely a momentary flirtation. I could entertain a little what-if scenario if it kept us talking about the future and not the past. Adam would make pretty babies.

"I wonder if Rachel or R.J. will have kids? I want to be an uncle."

The offer to share Hayley was on the tip of my tongue, but I couldn't let her form a bond with a man who might disappear on her. Adam and I had a long way to go before I'd trust him fully with my heart, let alone hers. "Rachel probably. Robert Creedon Jr. doesn't strike me as the parenting type. Just as well. It'd be really confusing to have another Robert Creedon join the practice."

Adam shivered. "Never mind. I had an image of my parents as grandparents. Maybe it's best we let my family line die too."

I shook my head, suppressing my laughter. A snowman had more warmth than Adam's parents. They weren't terrible people, necessarily. Other than being insanely pretentious, they seemed like decent humans in that they provided for their children, gave money to charitable causes, and treated their household staff well, better than they'd treated Adam, I thought. Even thinking about their visits to see Adam stressed us both out. Luckily, the visits were pretty rare. I knew I needed to manage my stress level to get my eating under control, but it'd be the perfect opportunity to join him in this whole mature-adult relationship thing we were striving for.

"Speaking of your parents, I thought about it, and I do want to go with you to your brother's party. I need to discuss it with Maura, but I think we can make it work."

Adam's smile was the only confirmation I needed that I'd made the right decision, but Adam smothered me in a bear hug.

"Okay, okay," I said, struggling, but not struggling, to break free. It felt good making him happy again. I took a deep breath, trying to savor the feeling for when I'd inevitably fuck it up. "So, it's all of nine o'clock. You want to find a movie or something?"

"Won't that wake Hayley up?"

"She's a heavy sleeper."

"We can chill in your room."

I shook my head. "I told you—"

"Not to fuck." Adam smirked. "Jesus. You've got to stop thinking I'm trying to bang you every time I open my mouth."

"Aren't you?" I teased.

He grinned. "It's difficult, but I can control myself around you." He shimmied up to me and grabbed my hips before kissing the tip of my nose. "I do like doing other things with you, you know?"

"I know . . ." My mouth stretched into a yawn, and Adam laughed. "Sorry. I'm tired. It was a long day. I kind of want to get pajamas on and read?"

Adam's eyebrow peaked. "You want to get in bed and read . . . with me?"

"Oh. Um. I meant I would read, and you could do whatever, but you want to, um, like before?"

"Yeah. I mean, I would love that. But I also have my laptop, so if you don't want to, you can read, and I can watch a movie on Netflix or something."

All the pleasurable feelings evaporated. Reading together had been such a special thing for us. I'd drawn a lot of red lines in the sand since our initial breakup.

No sex.

Okay, yes to sex, but never face-to-face.

Okay, yes to face-to-face, but no sleepovers.

Okay, yes to sleepovers, but no monogamy.

The lines had been breached as fast as I could draw them, but not that one. I hadn't laid in bed and read with Adam from the same book since the night before he left for Mexico. It seemed like a silly barrier to erect, but I did it precisely because of what it meant to him. In a lot of ways, reading together was a reminder of what had deepened our intimacy. It was the only card I held back to remind him of what he did to us, and I wasn't ready to play it. Not yet. I bit my lip. "Let's watch something together in my room, then. You pick."

And there it was. I'd undone Adam's smile in less than five minutes. A record.

Adam

Cade was snoring less than forty minutes into the movie. My arm was asleep, my shoulder was wet, and my brain was active. The film was a dud—some documentary that sounded more interesting than it was, but I let it play to distract myself. There was no reason to be upset, but I was. Cade and I were doing great and pretending that him not wanting to read didn't hurt like hell was a small sacrifice to keep the evening on track. He'd agreed to go to Atlanta. That was a monumental step in the right direction.

With that focus, I staved off the sense of failure long enough to fall asleep.

I woke in the morning to an empty bed and the sound of Hayley and Cade carrying on about something in the front room. For as deep as Cade's voice was, his laugh was a rapid fire *he-he-he* that ended in a *ha-yeh-yeh*. If something was hilarious, it had a lengthy sigh at the end. I'd always loved it, and hearing the same pattern echoed in Hayley's sweet giggle made me smile. I indulged a few minutes while finding the will power to start my day.

After a stop in the bathroom, I found only Hayley in Cade's kitchen, moving pancakes from a stack on the counter to plates on the small kitchen table.

"Adam, look!" She pushed the top of the whipped cream canister and drew a curved line. "Do you want blueberry or raspberry eyes? Mama lets me use chocolate chips, but Uncle Cade didn't have any."

"Um . . . blueberry."

She nodded like I'd made a smart choice and added a dollop of whip cream to place the nose and eyes on her smiley face.

"Where is your uncle?"

She pointed to the small balcony. "He's calling Mama, but he went outside because he doesn't want me to hear that she's not taking her medicine."

My gaze whipped from the balcony back to Hayley. "She's not?"

"They make her be a zombie."

"How about I help you with the pancakes. Did you make these?" I pointed to the five or six already on the plate.

"I made the batter and scooped them up and Uncle Cade flipped them, but I can do it by myself. Watch . . ." She reached for the measuring cup.

My face scrunched up. Should I let her? I glanced nervously over my shoulder at Cade. "I'll tell you what. Why don't you sit down and eat that one, and I'll check with Cade on the plan for the rest?"

"Okay," she said. I waited for her to settle at the table, before turning off the griddle and checking on Cade.

Morning, he mouthed as soon as I opened the sliding door. He spoke into the phone with a furrowed brow. "Yes, I'll check on her today. Yes. I promise that I will keep you updated. I got to go, Sis." He disconnected the phone and pressed a kiss to my lips.

"Good morning," I said. "Hayley said you were talking to Maura. Everything okay?"

"Yeah," he said before wavering. "Well, maybe. Maura's phone broke and she wasn't answering her landline, but she called me a few minutes ago. I was updating Aislinn since she spoke to her last night and Maura was, um, energetic."

"That's good, right? Wasn't the problem she was sleeping all the time?"

"Well," Cade hedged, then lowered his voice. "It could also mean she's becoming manic."

"Oh. The nonscary kind or the scary kind? Hayley said she stopped taking her medicine."

The cringe on Cade's face confirmed that he wasn't aware Hayley knew. "Damn, she must have heard me and Maura talking. So far, nothing scary. If she takes her medicine, her moods should stabilize."

I shook my head. "She said Maura told her they made her a zombie."

Cade frowned. "I wish she wouldn't talk to Hayley like she's an adult. Maura needs some girlfriends."

"Do you want me to stay with Hayley while you go check on her?"

"No. If I go over there this early, she'll think I don't trust her. She seemed okay this morning. I was calling to remind her to take her morning dose. Hayley and I will run by later after she eats breakfast. I have to go drop some money I don't have on a new phone for her."

I was tempted ask why he felt responsible for replacing his sister's phone, but I held my tongue. That was the sort of unhelpful shit that only added to his stress, and I'd promised myself I wouldn't do that anymore. "If it helps, I have an old phone Maura can use. It's still good."

Cade peered up at me, and there was a meaningful exchange that acknowledged the significance of my offer. "It helps. A lot. Thank you," he said sincerely.

Feeling awkward about how proud it made me to do something so simple, I gestured over my shoulder toward Hayley. "She's eating. I wasn't sure if she's allowed to cook, so I turned off the griddle."

"Yeah. Hayley likes to help cook, but I don't let her use the hot stuff unsupervised."

"Okay, good to know. Should we go eat?"

"Sure." Cade followed me into the apartment, where Hayley was still working on decorating pancakes.

"Finally," she said. "Is Mama coming to pick me up today?"

"Later," Cade said, but the uncertainty in his voice made me think she might be staying another night. Hayley set the Happy Face pancakes in front of us. I kept an eye on Cade while Hayley decorated a third pancake, then ate, unbothered by her uncle's quiet demeanor.

"You okay, Gou?" I gestured to his barely touched plate.

"Yeah. Not hungry."

The taste of my pancakes turned to ash in my mouth as Cade pushed his plate away, body stiffening like he smelled sour milk instead of maple syrup and berries. "Are you sick?"

"No. I must have snacked too much while I was cooking." Without thinking, I cast a glance to the kitchen, but there was only coffee, the pancake mess, and some berries. I shrugged off the question in my mind about what he'd eaten. Cade never had been much of a breakfast guy.

After we ate, I tidied up the kitchen while Hayley and Cade returned the living room to its standard configuration. We lounged around for a while, watching some animated movie that Hayley picked out. The entire domestic scene had my brain churning. I'd maybe underplayed my interest last night in having kids someday. In college, it was a hard no, but I'd thought about it, mainly when Cade and I had been on the outs. Wondered what it'd be like to have a family with him—if that was something he saw us doing. Now I had my answer, I guess. Which was fine with me. It wasn't like I was ready to hire a surrogate or anything; it was simply a pleasant daydream.

"Your phone is buzzing," Cade said, leaning forward to free up space for me to reach my pocket.

I fished it out, and Cade resumed his position, propped up against my side with his head tucked under my arm. I finagled a hand free so I could read the reminder. "Oh shit."

Cade peered up. "Everything okay?"

"Yeah. I'm supposed to go with Brady and Josh today to check out wedding venues at one."

"What time is it?"

"Almost noon."

Cade shifted away from me. "Go shower, you have time."

I heaved myself out from the cozy nest we'd created and rushed to his bedroom to get ready. When I reemerged, Hayley and Cade were stretched out on his couch, her head resting on his shoulder as they read from *Little Women*. Hayley read the dialog for all the girls and Cade read the rest. I sucked in a breath and refused to feel jealous of a little girl.

Cade dropped the open book to his chest. "You ready?"

"Are you sure you don't mind?" I asked, feeling slightly guilty for leaving Cade to deal with Hayley on his own.

"Of course not. You're Brady's best man." He bumped Hayley so he could stand and handed her the book.

"I can help tomorrow or this week," I said as he hugged me goodbye.

The eye roll told me he was getting annoyed. Which, okay, they'd managed without me for years. Still, I needed him to know he didn't have to do this sort of thing alone anymore.

"We have it. I'll drop Hayley at her before-school program Monday morning. She has field day all day, so hopefully Maura makes it, but if not, then she'll pick her up, because there is no afterschool during the last week. I have to attend a faculty meeting about the building upgrades, then graduation practice, and I hope to get my grades done so all I'll need to do is their final exams."

"Last week, huh?" I'd learned from experience Cade was not a fan.

"Between graduation and this remodel they're planning, I'm so done. You know they're making us take everything down. We can't leave one thing in the room. Some of the foreign language teachers think it's a conspiracy to move them out of the language wing to the portables because they're adding new contemporary and popular literature electives next year, which will need their own classroom."

"Wow. That's right up your alley. Are you going to teach one of them?"

"I doubt it. There are three of us under consideration, but I don't have my master's so . . ." He shrugged. "My only hope is that not enough kids take AP English, and I hate to wish for that."

"You'd be great at it."

"Thanks. I'm still pretty junior compared to my colleagues. I'm glad I got some input into building the curriculum, though. They wouldn't go for an entire section devoted to LGBT literature, but I got some quality stuff added to the Gender and Relationships module and *Middlesex* is on the required reading list . . . Oh, damn, I forgot I was going to pull a list of the LGBT-themed books to add to the summer reading list this weekend."

"Can't you do that off the top of your head?"

"Yes, but they have to have administrative approval, so there's an entire form I have to fill out for each one. Damn, I can't believe I forgot." Cade's brow furrowed. It wasn't like him to drop the ball like that, and I knew he'd beat himself up if he didn't get it done.

"Tell me how I can help."

"Adam—"

"Seriously, I can't do your forms for you, but I told you I have an extra phone sitting in my drawer. I can drop it off to Maura."

"You're going to go by Maura's?"

"Sure. Text me the directions and I'll stop by on my way home from work Monday with an active cell phone. I can bring her and Hayley dinner so you don't need to worry about it. Stay and finish your work."

"I don't . . ." Cade's eyes cast over to Hayley, and I knew he'd accept help if he thought it was best for Hayley. "Fine. Thank you. I can check on Maura tomorrow morning and get my forms done. That will be an enormous help."

I gathered the few things I'd brought to Cade's but left the quilt, pleased to see Hayley had taken to wrapping herself in it while she read. "Call me if you need me."

"Tell the boys I said hello. Don't let them pick anything tacky." I smiled as Cade play-shoved me toward the door and kissed me goodbye.

I took a few reluctant steps down the walkway toward the parking lot. "Text me the address," I called over my shoulder.

"I will," he answered before heading back inside.

Chapter Eleven

Adam

I wasn't sure what to expect from Maura's apartment complex. Other than the peeling siding, the building pretty much resembled Cade's. Well, except for the common areas that were littered with cigarette butts and other trash and the somewhat neglected grounds. But I'd never had an instantaneous sense of alertness when I exited the car at his place.

I strolled up the path toward Maura's, following the route Cade had described. Music, heavy on percussion, grew louder as I approached the building. A group of three rough-looking men—not much older than myself—congregated on one patio facing the courtyard, drinking beer, and laughing. Their eyes weighed heavy on me as I neared them. Every designer label I wore announced my foreigner status like a beacon. Swallowing hard, I sped up as I rounded the corner of the covered breezeway and came face-to-face with the faded gold numbers marking the door apartment 151. *Shit*.

The only thing that drew my fist to the door was the thought that Hayley was in there. When the door opened, I stepped back. Holy shit, one of the men from the balcony was a lot fucking bigger when standing.

He surveyed me up and down, lip curled in disgust. "Who the fuck are you?"

I cleared the frog from my throat. "Is, um, Maura around?"

He crossed his arms over his broad chest, revealing some seriously intimidating ink. I glanced at my phone. Apartment 151. Was this the set of *Sons of Anarchy* or Maura's apartment?

"Maura," he barked. "Get your ass out here."

"Wait a minute." I recognized the sound of her voice before she appeared from the bedroom. Her blonde hair was longer than I remembered and styled to compliment her face full of makeup. She sure as fuck wasn't dressed like she'd attended her daughter's field day that day.

"What the fuck," Maura said, eyes narrowed. "Adam?"

"Hi, Maura. Good to see you." I gave her a little wave and the most confident smile I could muster.

"You throw your cooch at the country club boys these days, Maura?" He opened the door wider and stepped back.

My hands clenched into fists, and I worked to calm myself enough to step inside. "Where's Hayley?" I directed my question to Maura, but the instant flash of concern in her eyes silenced me.

"He's no one, baby. I'll deal with this." She grabbed a can of beer from the fridge and handed it to him. "I'll bring out some snacks in a minute."

I waited until Mr. Sons of Anarchy rejoined his friends on the patio. "Where's Hayley?" I asked again, taking the time to assess her condition now that I wasn't worried about getting jumped.

"Did you bring my phone?"

"Yes. Where's Hayley?"

"I don't believe that's any of your business." Her body stiffened and there was something wrong with her speech. Not only the usual slur associated with drunkenness, something else was off. I took a deep breath and closed the gap toward her.

"Maura, I want to help."

She huffed, and the overwhelming smell of marijuana and beer saturated the air between us. "God, you're as obnoxious as I remember. Hand me my phone and get out of here. I don't need you starting some shit with them." She tilted her head toward the patio door.

"Does Cade realize you use his money to entertain guys like that?"

"Does he *realize* you're a pretentious asshole that looks down on other people?"

I sighed. "I'm not looking down on anyone. Here's your phone," I said, handing her the bag. "Can I please say hello to Hayley?"

"Thank you. She isn't here." She picked up some chips from the table and popped one into her mouth, moaning obnoxiously like it was the best thing she'd ever tasted, then laughing for no discernable reason. I'd never seen Maura manic, but it was either that or she was doing a lot more than smoking pot and drinking beer this afternoon.

"Maybe I'll hang out until she gets home."

Maura stumbled, and my hand shot out to catch her. She laughed like it was the funniest thing that'd ever happened. "My little brother was right. You are sexy. He tells me all about you, you know." She cast her eyes downward and trailed a fingernail over my shirt. It took my brain a few milliseconds to realize where she was headed.

"Oww," she cried as I squeezed her wrist.

"Yeah. That's not going to happen." I softened my grip, and she cackled loud enough I was sure I hadn't hurt her. "Where is your daughter, Maura? Tell me, or I'm calling Cade."

"Fuck. You're awfully sanctimonious for a guy who enjoys getting sucked off in alleys by little Mexican boys. Relax, I pick her up from afterschool at six and the guys will be gone, so don't go tattling on me to my little brother."

My heart leaped into my throat. "Today was field day. Cade said there was no afterschool."

"No . . ." She walked to the fridge, stumbling all over the place. *Maybe she was intoxicated?* I wasn't sure if that was better or worse. She pulled a paper down from the magnet. "See . . ." She handed it to me, and I attempted to decode the symbols around the school calendar.

"Yeah. This says there is no afterschool." I handed it back, already springing into action. I checked my watch. Cade would be in his meetings, so I doubted he'd answer his phone right away. Maura was in no shape to drive, but I sincerely doubted the school would release Hayley to me. "Maybe she got the bus?"

Maura was still staring at the calendar, eyes unfocused.

"Maura," I snapped, unsure what to make of the confusion clouding her hazel eyes.

"But it's Monday. There's always afterschool on Monday. I told her not to take the bus home and I'd get her from afterschool."

I huffed a breath and did my best to stay focused on the problem. "Get your purse. We're not that late. Maybe she's still at the school."

She nodded. "Wait. What about them?"

I turned to see the outline of the three large men on the patio through the plastic, horizontal blinds. *Oh, yeah.* "Can you ask them to leave?"

She shook her head, seemingly regretful. "Not without starting something."

"Then fuck it. We can walk around the other side of the building. If it's a problem, I can take you and Hayley to my place. Let's go." I grabbed her by the upper arm and tried to edge her toward the door.

"Wait," she said, slipping her arm out from me. She slid open the patio door. Music and laughter flooded inside. "Um, I'm going on a beer run. You need anything?"

A chorus of chatter resounded that basically sounded like no one cared. Good. That was probably for the best.

I escorted Maura out of her apartment and took the alternate, safer route toward my car. "Which way to her school?" I asked.

She pointed west, and my tires squealed as we turned out of the parking lot. Other than the nervous tapping of her cherry red-painted nails and her bouncing leg, we drove in silence about three miles.

"It's on the left up here."

I turned at the sign for Dawson Elementary, grateful there were still a sufficient number of cars. At least Hayley wasn't alone.

Maura sucked in a breath when she saw two police officers immediately inside the glass entrance talking to a balding man. "I can't go in like this. You have to do it."

"Maura," I said as I pulled into a visitor parking space. I threw the car into Park and turned off the engine. "They're not going to hand her over to a random guy off the street."

Maura's gaze shifted back to the door, before returning to me. A dab of bright red lipstick stuck to her teeth where she'd bitten her lip. "That's Mr. Bach, Hayley's counselor. He hates me. Call Cade to come get her." She slunk down in her seat, fidgeting like I was making her go on my personal errands instead of claiming her offspring.

"Let's make sure she's in there first."

"Where else would she be?" Again, the agitation in her voice was disturbing enough to push me past annoyed into concerned. I never had a great impression of Maura, but her demeanor was so odd I had trouble attributing it solely to alcohol.

Before I could answer, the glass door in the front of the school opened and the police strolled out with the counselor and Hayley. "Get out of the car," I ordered.

I opened the door, still completely unsure of how much trouble Maura was in. Surely, she could explain it. Parents ran late, didn't they?

"Mama," Hayley cried and broke out in a sprint toward Maura. Maura pulled the hem of her dress down to midthigh, which only served to further show off her cleavage. She rushed forward, boobs bouncing out of the top.

All the adults gawked as Maura and I closed the gap to them.

"Miss Doyle, we'd nearly given up on you."

"I'm sorry. Baby, are you okay?" She smooched Hayley's cheeks together and placed a big kiss to her forehead, then swung Hayley's braid around like a jump rope. Without prompting, she rushed into an explanation speaking so fast, my head spun. "My car broke down and I don't have a phone. I had to get a friend to drive me."

I tried to keep my face neutral, nodding along as Maura played with Hayley's hair and whipped up a barely coherent story that even Hayley didn't seem to believe. The few questions the police directed to me, I answered without overtly lying or conflicting with Maura's story by being vague as fuck. In the end, Hayley's counselor released Hayley to Maura and hurried inside with the police officers, presumably to ask each other *What the actual fuck is wrong with her?*

I was so in over my head. Cade was going to be pissed I hadn't called him.

In the car, I turned to Maura, who was still talking a mile a minute to Hayley, and reached for my phone. "I'll call Cade."

Maura snatched the phone from my hands and tossed it into the cupholder on her side of the car. "Do not call Cade. He'll just worry. Can't we keep this between you and me?"

"You and Hayley can come back to my place, and we can talk to Cade together."

"But he's—"

I didn't need her explanation. She knew how shaky Cade's trust in me was, and while I didn't think she'd intentionally set me up, I wasn't going to risk it. "Cade and I don't keep secrets."

Her mouth snapped shut. I didn't need to be a detective to see she knew something about Cade I didn't, but that was for another time. "I can't keep this from him. You and Hayley can come back to my place, and we can talk to Cade together." I started the car and backed out of the spot.

"What about Shane?"

Hayley sat up when I pressed the gas. "Can we visit Daddy again?"

Daddy? I slammed on my brakes and jerked around so suddenly I pulled a muscle in my neck. My hand shot up to rub at the twinge. Oh, fuck. Cade was going to murder me. "Put your seat belt on," I barked, this time waiting for Hayley to comply. Reaching over Maura, I retrieved my phone and handed it to her. "Call your brother and tell him to meet us at his place."

Cade

"What the fuck, Maura?" Vacillating between angry and freaked out, I watched her pace back and forth. The way she had dressed, her mannerisms . . . everything about her from her pressured speech to her wild eyes to the French tips on her new pedicure announced she'd been lying to me all weekend.

"I'm allowed to have fun. You never let me do anything fun. I thought there was aftercare, so I had a little me day, then Shane showed up with friends . . . This isn't my fault."

"Whose fault is it? Mine? Adam's? He brought you a free phone and you had him lie to the police?"

"He didn't lie. He just . . . He's actually a good non-liar. Cagey. Like Shane." She tossed her head back and laughed maniacally. "He was totally checking out my tits, by the way. I don't think he's quite as gay as you think he is."

I pinched the bridge of my nose and exhaled a long breath. No wonder Adam was so eager to take Hayley to get a snack. Manic Maura thought every guy was after her. "Maura, I can't deal with this. You need to take your medicine. You promised." She walked by me again. I fought my last nerve to keep from demanding she sit down.

"What's wrong with Mama?"

"She's fine. Stay there so you don't cut yourself." I didn't care that it was all a lie. Hayley was old enough to recognize her mother was not okay, but a confident command of the situation gave me a sense of control I desperately needed to ward off my own meltdown. She would have one adult in her life capable of being emotionally stable during a crisis.

Maura re-entered the family room, a bandage around her finger. She fiddled with her phone, and loud pop music began playing as she pulled Hayley up from the couch to dance. Adam seemed utterly freaked out. I'd told him about Maura, but hearing about and witnessing mania were entirely two different things. I should have never sent Adam to Maura's. I should have never left her alone. I should have stayed with her and Hayley. *How could I do something so goddamn stupid?*

My entire childhood, Maura had always gone above and beyond to keep Colleen's crazy off the radar of anyone who might be in a position to stick their nose where they didn't belong—teachers, neighbors, Aislinn's father, fucking child protective services. When Maura got sick, I promised myself I'd do the same for Hayley, but I'd fucked up. What if Adam hadn't been there? What if the school had called CPS? What if the police showed up today and found Shane there and who knows what illegal substances? This whole day could have gone so badly. A well of panic started to build inside me. I needed to think, so I moved to the kitchen.

Adam followed me, worry lines etched deep on his face. "Cade, you okay?"

To his credit, Adam let me move around the kitchen uninterrupted, wiping away the blood and bagging the trash with the broken glass. "Yeah, I'm getting this glass cleaned up."

"What can I do to help?"

"Can you, um, go dance. You know. So Hayley isn't worried."

He nodded. "Of course."

Adam, Maura, and Hayley had a dance party while I tried and failed to scrub, sweep, and sanitize away the deep vulnerability the day had exposed. I didn't know how much time had passed before a hand dropped to my shoulder.

"Babe, I think that dish is clean." Adam reached over me and turned off the steaming water, then pulled the plate I'd been washing out of my hand and placed it in the rack. Gently, he gathered my bright red hands in a kitchen towel, stilling them as they trembled, and dried them.

"It's getting late. Maura asked me to take her home," Adam whispered, moving a strand of hair from my face and tucking it behind my ear.

My mind returned to the shit-show happening in my apartment, and I found the sound of Maura laughing. She was still dancing around the living room with Hayley, but it was all wrong—Maura's laughter too agitated. Hayley's too hesitant. I followed Adam out of the kitchen, and the second Hayley's frightened eyes found mine, I choked on a breath. My mind went to a grim night.

"Cade, baby. Where are you?" Colleen's sing-song voice woke me from a deep sleep.

"Get in here," Maura hushed at me, waving me into the closet we shared. That wasn't good. Maura only put me in the closet on the really bad nights. I stood from the bed, fighting a yawn as I tucked myself into the back corner behind the laundry hamper. Maura handed me her favorite teddy bear and shut the door.

There was a lot of muffled commotion, but the sounds drew closer and I could hear Maura clearly. "Go to bed. Cade has school in the morning."

"We're going for ice cream."

I was already eleven. Too old for stuffed animals, but my mother's laugh made me hug the bear tighter.

"No, Mom. Let me help—" A loud thud reverberated in the apartment.

"Don't tell me what to do, you little bitch. I'm the mother. Give me my fucking keys, Maura."

"You can't, Mom. Cade's asleep. The ice cream place is closed."

"Get out of my goddamn way." The cheap closet door rattled as a loud crash banged against my bedroom door. Then another. Then smack. Smack. Smack. Maura screaming. I closed my eyes. I wanted it all to go away. To be better.

"She can't be alone with Hayley."

"Okay," Adam said, yanking me into a hug I couldn't handle. I pulled away from the place he'd made for me to let go. To be vulnerable. *Too old for teddy bears.*

"Don't fucking say 'okay' like that. You don't know us."

Adam's hands shot into the air as he stepped back. His jaw hardened, and there was a moment where his eyes seemed to debate if I were worth all this. "Cade—" he said, sadly. The silent question stuck with me though. Why would he want any part of this?

You're not worth it. You can't do anything right. You know what will make it better.

The voice was louder, more insistent this time . . . and not wrong. It *would* make it better. That was the problem. Restricting, exercising, losing weight—I fucking loved the strength it gave me. The control. *Maybe you should do it . . . just for a little while. Just long enough to see Maura past this episode.*

"Ahh," Hayley cried out. I saw her fall in slow motion, hitting her arm along the side of the coffee table as I lurched toward her.

"Are you okay?" I asked as she rubbed her arm.

"Yeah," she sniffled. Maura turned up the music, so Hayley had to yell. "Mama was spinning me and I lost my balance."

"Here." I handed her my tablet and headphones from the coffee table. "Go into my bedroom and watch something? Shut the door."

"Maura," Adam said sharply as soon as Hayley was out of sight. He lowered the volume of the music. "Come sit for a bit. I doubt Cade's neighbors appreciate all this stomping around."

Maura kept right on dancing, and Adam's expression was every person in my life who looked down on my family.

"Don't fucking look at my sister like she's a low-life."

Adam flashed an apologetic smile, but the pity didn't quite disappear. "I'm not. It's . . . I know you told me what her mania was like, but I didn't really understand. I'm sorry, Cade. Do you want me to stay with Hayley so you can take Maura to the hospital?"

"You think I'm going to hand Hayley over to Shane?" I seethed. "'Cause if Maura gets admitted, and they take her—"

His hands flew up in protest, and he cocked his head. "Whoa. No one is trying to take anyone's daughter. Maura is not well. She's clearly in some sort of crisis. We don't know if Shane is still at Maura's place, and I don't think the two of you need to be going over there by yourselves. Maybe we take them both home and stay with them."

"No, Adam. I'll take the girls home and stay with them. You go home."

Adam made a frustrated noise, and he tossed his hands in the air, clearly exasperated. "I want to help."

"I appreciate that, and you did. Thank you for taking Hayley to get something to eat and for giving Maura a phone."

"What if Shane comes back?" His furrowed forehead reflected genuine concern, and while it was nice that Adam cared, I didn't have the energy to help him and Hayley and Maura and myself. I pushed a long breath through my nose as Maura barely avoided crashing into the table. Why couldn't he do what I asked without me having to explain shit?

"If he can't fuck her, he'll disappear again soon enough. She'll get back on her meds and feel better in a few weeks."

His shoulders stiffened, and a tight mouth formed his response: "We're supposed to leave for Atlanta in a few weeks."

Was he serious right now? "I'm not going to Atlanta, Adam."

His face fell and he sighed. "Yeah, of course."

"You say 'of course' like you knew I wasn't going to make it. I didn't plan this." I gestured to Maura. Frustration bubbling hot enough now I knew it was going to spill over soon. My only choice was who would take the hit—Maura or Adam? I didn't need to think about it, because I already knew it wouldn't be Maura.

"No. I said 'of course' because I see that your hands are going to be full and I get that you can't go now."

"Yeah. Right. That's why you have that same *hurt little Adam* look on your face like your mommy and daddy didn't give you what you wanted. It's a fucking party. Do you grasp how much I wish my biggest problem was that my boyfriend couldn't go to a fucking party with me?"

"I know, Cade. But fuck . . . Am I allowed to be fucking disappointed for a second? Christ, why am I never allowed to feel anything you don't approve of?"

The response my brain delivered to my mouth was as predictable as if he'd pulled the string on one of those talking dolls. "Maybe because you get your feelings hurt easier than a ten-year-old and every time you do, I have to worry you'll go out searching for a pick-me-up blowjob."

Adam recoiled, but he crossed his arms and stared at me like I was the one dancing around my living room by myself.

"What?" I asked, lifting my chin to meet his defensive stance. The pressure I'd carried in my chest all evening squeezed tighter.

"If you don't want my help, fine, but you don't get to be a dick about it."

"I don't need you to take care of my family. I need you to stop asking dumb questions."

Adam huffed. "No one said *need*, Gou. I said *want*. What Josh and Brady have that we both envy? This is it. They stick it out and they fucking lean on each other. Can't you trust me when I say I'm trying to help you?"

Trust him? How? I didn't even trust myself right now. "You can't help me."

I expected an explosion. A twisted part of me probably hoped for one. But Adam raked his hand through his hair and let his gaze drift toward the ceiling, pausing for a minute. He returned his attention to me, staring at me in a standoff of sorts, long enough for me to see the flash of dark intensity in his eyes and rigid jaw as he made his decision. Then he snatched his wallet and keys from the table, sniffled, and heaved a resigned sigh. "I'm going to go."

His words were so final. Panic rocketed through me as the bone-deep fear I'd carried since college sprung from my lips. "So that's it. I can't go to your party so you're leaving? Gonna walk out the door? Fucking brilliant."

He flinched and tension tightened in his body. "Cade, what the hell do you want from me? I don't know what I'm doing here. You don't want me to stay. I can't ask questions. My advice is apparently total shit. I have no idea what you need from me." He took a step toward me, but I couldn't. If he touched me, I'd completely fall apart. I was too drained on every imaginable level to offer him any reassurances.

"Please, don't," I said, shaking my head. He froze and cast a glimpse at Maura, who continued to spin, spin, spin, siphoning all the energy from me like a tornado. "This is her illness, Adam. It's not her."

There was so much skepticism in his weak smile, but I needed him to understand Maura was not my mother. I was not my mother. *There is no way he'll stick around.* "It's not her fault."

Adam's eyebrows shot up, but his voice stayed even. "Yeah, Cade. I know that. I promised you that I won't add to your burden anymore, but I'm not going to be your punching bag either. I want to help, but if you aren't ready to accept it from me, then the only thing that's going to happen is you saying a bunch of things you don't mean and us fighting. You have enough on your plate right now without worrying about me. I'm here if you need me. Anything. Call, okay?"

I stood silently, a little shell-shocked by his words and the absolute lack of anger in them. *Fuck.* Why did I never learn? He'd stepped up for me today. So why wasn't I leaning into that . . . leaning into his strength instead of taking cheap shots? Even as I thought the question, I knew the answer. I wanted him to feel weak like me. To feel helpless and powerless. Because admitting Adam was strong enough to handle Maura meant he was strong to handle my anorexia. Which meant if I had just told him why I couldn't go to Mexico, none of this would have happened. The realization rubbed the blister of guilt in my chest into a festering wound.

"Adam—" I cried as he reached for the door.

He turned to meet my gaze. His features softened. I let myself really look at him, at the slight quiver of his lower lip—he wasn't holding in anger. Far from it, actually. He was disappointed in himself. In us. For failing this test. "Yeah?"

We only fail if I let him go. "Please don't leave."

Chapter Twelve

Adam

"A re you sure?" Cade asked for the millionth time since he started talking to Aislinn. "Okay. Yeah. We'll get her a ticket . . . Yeah . . . She'll love it. Thanks, Sis." He smiled wide and flashed a thumbs-up sign. "Love you too. I'll text you the confirmation."

Cade sighed. His relief evident as he hung up the phone.

"So . . ." I prompted.

"You were right. She's thrilled to get to show Hayley around Boston, and she knows someone who can stay with Hayley when she's at work."

I laughed. "And?"

"And she's happy to help."

I pulled him against me and kissed the top of his head. He wrapped an arm around my waist and rested his head on my chest before exhaling. There was so much exhaustion loaded in a single huff; the last few weeks had taken their toll.

"You okay?" I asked.

He pulled back and peered up at me. "Yeah. I'm glad we figured out something for Hayley. She needs a break from all this."

The warmth I found in Cade's eyes was something I'd never tire of. We were still a work-in-progress, but there was definitely leaning happening over the last few weeks. Cade had asked me to stay with Hayley while he took Maura to her doctor's appointment and again for him to attend graduation, and I helped him take down his classroom. It felt like we'd turned a corner, and I dreaded leaving, but my parents would lose their shit if I didn't show up to R.J.'s party.

"Are you sure you don't want me to fly with her? I can trade my ticket to Atlanta in."

"I appreciate the offer, but please don't. Now that Maura is cooperating with her treatment again and school's out, I think I can get back to something resembling a routine. At least with Hayley at Aislinn's, I'll get to sleep in a proper bed."

I glanced over Cade's head at the old sofa Cade had been crashing on and cringed. The middle cushion dipped so severely I knew it was at least partially responsible for the wincing Cade had been doing all day. I ran my finger down Cade's rough cheeks. His ability to grow facial hair had improved little since we were eighteen, but the recent stress had aged him a few years. He'd lost more weight, and his pale skin and sunken eyes weren't doing much to assuage my concern. "Promise me you'll start taking care of yourself."

The corner of his mouth turned down in a frown. "What? You don't like the acne?" He laughed, scratching over his chin where his usually unblemished skin had broken out. "I thought you liked the barely legal look?"

"Cade—" I chastised.

"Don't play all innocent. You're following a fair number of models from that porn studio—Boys Next Door—on Instagram."

I blushed, because okay, Cade was well aware that lithe, smooth-bodied, big-dicked twinks were my weakness. They were giving me an outlet for the sudden interruption to our recently revived sex life. "Does it bother you?"

Cade shook his head. "No, not really. Does it bother you I'm here and not in your bed?"

I shook my head. "This works fine." I lifted my right hand.

He raised his palm and interlaced his fingers with mine before kissing my knuckles. "I was thinking…" A coy little smile accompanied a small bite of his bottom lip. I couldn't imagine what was on his mind, but my cock voted yes.

"Yeah," I whispered and stepped closer to him, my crotch coming in contact with his for the first time all week.

"What would you think about going to the clinic with me when you get back? We could get tested together."

I gasped, truly having expected his suggestion to be something quick and insignificant. This felt huge. "Really?"

"I mean, going bare is one of the major perks of being in a relationship."

"Yeah, but . . ." *Wait, why would I dream of talking him out of this?* "Yes. I would love to." I grabbed his ass and drew him closer to me, leaning down to kiss him. His lips parted at the slide of my tongue, and we rolled into an intimate connection I'd missed more than the sex. Comforting and full of promise. The more he relaxed against me, the more confirmation I had that we'd found a new normal.

"I love you," I said, breathlessly.

"I love you too. Thanks for being here for me."

"Anytime, baby."

He rocked up to his toes, his body creating a long stroke of sweet pressure that took my chub to fully erect, and kissed me again so hard I groaned into his mouth.

"Mama," Hayley called from her bedroom. "Come here. Quick."

Cade chuckled against my lips and whispered, "If I pull away, are you gonna be able to hide your wood?"

Before I could answer, Hayley stormed into the living room on her way to her mother's room. "Oof," I cried as Cade pushed me into the old recliner and tossed a throw pillow on my lap. He stepped in front of me, blocking prying eyes from my tenting pants and barely constrained laughter.

"Keep your voice down," Cade whispered.

She eyed us suspiciously. "What are you doing?"

"Nothing. Adam was . . . tickling me and fell over." He glanced at me over his shoulder, and I grimaced. I had no idea how naïve Hayley was, but it wasn't a convincing lie.

She rolled her eyes. "Where's Mama?"

"She's taking a nap."

"Again?"

"Yeah, but I'm here. What's up?"

"I'm bored."

"Do you want to read some more of your book?"

"No. I want to go outside. Can I ride my bike?"

"Um, your bike is at my apartment."

"Can we go get it?"

"Oh, Hayley. I'm sorry, hon, but I need to stay here in case your mom wakes up."

"It's booorriiing here."

Cade rubbed her head. "I know, sweetheart, but I talked to Aunt Aislinn. We thought you'd like to go visit her for a little while this summer."

"In Boston," she squealed.

I shushed her. "Yes, but I still need to talk to your mom."

"When am I going?"

"Soon, okay. I will look at tickets tonight."

"Can I pack my makeup?"

"Um, that's up to your mom. Let's—"

"I'm going to go pack right now."

Cade's face fell as soon as she ran from the room. I pulled him into my lap, but instead of feeling his solid, warm body relax against me, I felt sharp edges dig into my thighs. "Damn." I shifted him to a more comfortable place.

"You okay? Am I too heavy?"

I laughed. "Yeah. That's it." When he scrambled to move, I gripped him tighter. "No, you're too skinny. You've got to eat more."

Cade sat up suddenly. "I ate the entire sandwich you bought me like an hour ago."

I was quick to quiet the defensive edge to Cade's voice. "I know. I was kidding, babe. I don't remember your ass being so bony. It was digging into me. It's fine now."

His face etched with doubt, Cade shifted sideways more until his ass was on the arm of the chair. I pulled his legs across my lap and he settled down.

"I should have talked to Maura first before I told Hayley about Boston."

"You don't think Maura would really say no, do you?" It didn't seem like Maura should have much of a say in the matter since she could barely take care of herself.

"No," Cade said, still wearing his regret. "But . . . she won't be happy about it."

"Do you want me to stay? I can take Hayley out for a bike ride."

"No. Sid, Josh, and Brady are expecting you in what . . ." He checked his watch. "An hour?"

I nodded. "I wish you could come with us."

"Me too."

"Should I bring you back some cake? The way Brady is talking about this bakery, you'd think he's more excited about the cake-tasting than the wedding."

Cade laughed. "I have the utmost confidence in Brady's ability to find the good cake. Remember that ice cream place he made us walk to all the time by my and Sid's apartment? We passed like three other ice cream shops and the campus dining hall. What was it called?"

"Rollies. That shit was so good."

"Yeah, that's it."

"Brady wants them to do an ice cream sundae bar for the reception."

"You're kidding? That doesn't sound like something Josh would go for. I thought he wanted an elegant affair."

I shrugged, because as soon as Josh and Brady disagreed on something, they were quick to move the conversation to a private setting. "I had Josh pegged as the groomzilla, but I actually think Brady's going to be the higher maintenance groom."

Cade chuckled. "I could have told you that. Josh would probably elope, but Brady's getting used to the spotlight now that he's lost the weight. Sid told me he changes at the gym now."

I shifted, still uncomfortable with the way Cade talked about Brady's weight loss. Somewhere between envious and bitter, his tone reminded me of the way we'd felt about their engagement at first. But Cade had never been overweight, so I couldn't understand why. "I don't think it's all about the weight. He wants everything to be perfect for Josh. It's kind of cute how focused he is on the details. I never pictured Brady so . . . mushy."

Cade bit his lip. "Do you ever wish . . ." He trailed off and his eyes flicked up to me.

"What? Me and Brady?"

"I mean, he gave you plenty of opportunities. If Josh weren't in the picture, would you have ever pursued him?"

"Before I met you?"

"Sure." Cade shrugged.

"Probably not."

"Even if he looked then like he does now?"

I frowned. Before he and Josh got together, Brady had thought his weight was the reason I hadn't been interested in him, too. "It's not his weight. I just . . . Okay, I'll admit I was pretty stoked by his attention at first. He certainly knew how to boost my ego, but he never made me work for it, you know? Like, we met and he decided he wanted me before he learned anything about me. I don't know how to explain it, but Brady wouldn't push me to be better."

"But I did?"

"Fuck, Gou. You're always challenging me. To be a better man. Like the way you questioned me about that work project? Made me realize if I take the money out of it, I prefer the creative parts."

Cade nodded, clearly pleased with himself.

"Do you remember our third date? I was trying to impress you—I suggested we go for sushi."

Cade's face split into a grin, and he nodded. "I've never seen a grown man pout like that before."

"I told you I could put it on my credit card."

Cade laughed, and it was so close to sounding like the actual first time I suggested letting my parents' credit card pay for our date, that a wave of nostalgia hit me right in the chest. Every one I'd dated to that point would have had zero issues with that. "We ended up walking around campus and saw that guy dumpster diving."

Cade aww'd like he missed the guy, which he probably did. "His name was Charlie. He was a sweetheart. You got so freaked out by him."

"Well, all I remember was I'd spent the entire evening running through my favorite comic book movies and trying to impress you with my movie knowledge, and then we run into Charlie and the next thing I know, I'm involved in a long discussion about homelessness and the severe shortage of affordable housing in the area. It blew me away. If I wanted to impress you, I was going to have to work at it. I started reading the paper after that so I wouldn't sound like an idiot."

"For what it's worth, your cinematic knowledge impressed me. It came in clutch on trivia night at Chester's."

I beamed because the five of us had made for a pretty balanced trivia team. "I miss trivia night. We need to pull the team back together when Maura's better."

Cade made a disagreeable noise. "Some of my former students go there now. I'm not about to hit up college bars in this town."

"Fine. Maybe we can find another trivia night, then? We haven't been out as couples since we got back together. I don't think we've ever all been coupled up at the same time before."

"Sure. After things are a little calmer, I'd be down for that. We might as well admit we've become *those* kinds of gay men."

I laughed. "What do you mean?"

"I mean . . ." Cade counted off with one hand. "Josh and Brady. Matt and Brady. Matt and Sid. You and me. Sid and both of us." He laughed. "Remember when we all thought Josh was the promiscuous one?"

"Ah, yeah. I guess if you count the one drunken twenty-first birthday threesome with Sid, we have all sort of made the rounds. Whatever . . . we ended up with the right people. Everyone is happy. Who cares?"

"I don't. It's simply an observation."

"Cade," Maura called from her bedroom.

Cade and I exchanged a worried look. She didn't sound happy. "Yeah?" he responded over his shoulder.

Maura's door opened. She stood in the doorway, wearing a T-shirt and panties, rubbing the sleep out of her eyes. "What the fuck did you give me? It's the middle of the afternoon." She glowered at me and pulled her shirt down to cover herself. "Oh. Great. You're still here." Just as quickly she sighed, turned back into her room, and shut the door.

Cade grimaced. "You should go. It doesn't sound like she's going to be up for company."

I was disappointed, but not terribly so. I'd spent more time with Maura in the last few weeks than I had during my entire relationship with Cade. At present, her company definitely left a lot to be desired. "I have some errands to run before meeting the guys for the cake-tasting, anyway." I leaned down to kiss him goodbye. "Call if you need anything."

Cade

After saying goodbye to Adam, I found Maura lying on her bed, staring at the ceiling. She had zoned out, eyes wild and her lips were moving, but she wasn't saying anything. All things I associated with her manic states.

"Scooch." I lay down next to her, following her gaze to the insignificant dots of texture on the ceiling. She'd told me before that she used to count things to slow her thoughts, so I grabbed her hand and let her until her lips stilled.

"How ya feeling?"

"Wonderful," she snapped. "My head is all foggy. It'd be nice if I could walk around my apartment once in a while."

I sat up and played with her hair. I wasn't about to apologize again. We'd had enough apologies over the past few weeks. She was sorry. I was sorry. Maura and I were both too experienced at *this fucking sucks but it's no one's fault* situations to hold grudges with each other. "Adam brought Hayley some lunch and some groceries. You want anything?"

"No. Did *you* eat?"

She shifted on the bed, turning toward me. I appreciated she was on to me, but admitting it . . . . Letting her down gave me way too much anxiety.

"I've learned the signs," she continued. "Even on this shit, I've seen your body-checking. I know you're restricting again."

Not wanting to lie, I didn't say anything, but soon cracked under her scrutiny. "I am eating."

"Yeah. You ate one egg this morning. I saw you remove the cheese from your burger yesterday. You had one bite of an ice cream scoop with Hayley last night. If you're not eating when you're hungry, you're restricting. Are you eating when you're hungry?"

"No," I confessed. "Not really."

"Be honest with me, how bad this time?"

"Um, not terrible, but not great. I'm getting in my minimum daily intake at least a few days a week, but it's a struggle. I made an appointment."

"Cade, your relapse plan calls for no exercise. I heard you doing sit-ups and pushups this morning."

I cringed. "Yeah. I knew Adam was coming by with food, so . . ."

She sighed. "So it was either not eat in front of him or do enough exercise to earn your calories before he got here? You have other rules?"

Full of shame, I nodded. "Um, some of my blacklisted foods are back too—meat, at first. Now bread and pasta."

Her face fell. "Oh, Cade. I'm so sorry. This is my fault, isn't it? Because I went off my meds."

"No, Sis. We don't do that. You're not anymore responsible for my problems than I am for yours. You warned me about trying to do that stupid program, and I didn't listen. I thought it would help me feel better about being alone and fucking things up with Adam again. I thought I could do the vegan thing, but then the anorexia voice came back, and it happened really fast."

"When is your appointment?"

"Next week."

"I'll go with you. Hayley will be okay for an hour or so."

I took a deep breath. "About that. I called Aislinn."

Maura jerked upward and gawked at me. "Cade. No. Why would you get her involved?"

"Because Hayley shouldn't have to suffer because we're both such a mess."

"Did you tell her you relapsed?"

"Not in so many words."

"Did you tell her I went off my meds?"

"No, only that they were tweaking your meds and you were having some mania."

"Why would you do that?"

"Mau, I didn't have a choice. She talked to you. You were all over the place, and your speech is pressured. She knew what was up."

Maura heaved a resigned sigh, rubbing her temples. "When?"

"We can look at tickets when you're up for it."

"I don't want Brenda or James anywhere near Hayley."

"She knows. She's going to take some days off, and she promised me she'd keep her dad and stepmom away. They adore Hayley though. They wouldn't do anything to hurt her."

"I hate this idea, but I'm so tired and you need to focus on your recovery." She threw herself back onto the mattress, rolled into me, and buried her face in my shirt.

"I know. Me too." I smoothed her hair.

"At least you have friends and Adam. I have no one."

"You have me. You always have me. And I'm not sure how much longer I'll have Adam." Although I'd been thinking it for several days, it still hurt to say out loud.

"What happened?"

"I'm going to wait until after he gets back from his trip, but I can't pretend this shit is in the past anymore. I already know I can't hide it. He knows I've lost weight. He's going to hate me."

"It's an illness, Cade. You didn't ask for it."

"Mom had an illness and I hated her."

"That's different."

"No, Maura. It's not. Even when you're suffering, you don't get to hurt people and walk away from all the responsibility. All this time, I've been blaming Adam for everything, and I think it's warped his perception of our relationship. He keeps idealizing college like everything was perfect until he fucked it up by cheating. I lied to him to keep this secret. More than I realized. It's going to hurt him so much."

Chapter Thirteen

Adam

"Chocolate cake on the bottom and lemon on the top with buttercream frosting," I said definitively. "That's the one."

Josh smiled. "I agree."

Brady took another bite of the red velvet. "Are you sure, beautiful? This cream cheese frosting is amazing. And you loved the coconut."

"Babe, I think the chocolate and buttercream combo is more universally appealing."

"It's not about pleasing everyone. You get what you want. It's your day."

"It's our day." Josh tsked.

"Fine, but if you want the coconut, we should get another tier for the coconut."

"That's such a waste. We don't need three tiers for such a small wedding. We're only getting the second tier because you want something we can stick in the freezer for a year."

"It's a tradition. Adam, tell him it's a tradition."

I glanced at Sid, who was clearly already thinking the same thing as me. "I feel like I'm in some parallel universe. Is Brady advocating for spending more money?"

"I suggested the vegan carrot cake, but I was overruled because it was more expensive." Sid shrugged.

"Okay, how about a compromise?" I suggested. "Chocolate on the bottom and coconut for the top tier. You can buy a lemon cupcake to freeze for your first anniversary."

Brady and Josh exchanged gooey smiles. "Yeah?" Brady asked Josh.

"That works," Josh responded. My heart went sideways as I watched their excited smiles melt into a sweet kiss. They were so adorably in love and so fucking happy, I couldn't stand the sugar rush any longer.

"Adam," a familiar voice gushed from the doorway.

I turned my head to see a familiar face. "Hey, Bryan." I stood, cleared the frog from my throat, and intercepted his attempted hug with a handshake. "What are you doing here?"

My friends' heads popped up as their attention turned from cake to the man who had used his small body to box me between the table and the large window in front of the bakery.

"Guys, this is Bryan Crandall. He lives in my building. Bryan, these are my best friends: Josh Meyer, Brady Whittington, and Sid Srivastava. Josh and Brady are getting married. We're doing a tasting."

Bryan flashed his toothy white smile at the guys. "Oh, congrats. When is the big day?"

"December sixteenth," Josh and Brady said in unison. "At the Colonnade."

"Oh, I know that place. My work had a party there last Christmas. The ballroom is gorgeous."

"We're using the smaller room next to the ballroom. It's the one with the fireplace and the piano."

"Oh. An intimate affair. Even better. Much more romantic." Bryan nudged me with a wink. "Holler if you need a plus-one. I love a Christmas wedding."

Sid choked on his water, and my friends' stares had me shifting uncomfortably. "Well don't let me keep you," I said. Brady shook his head at me. Apparently, I'd given the wrong response.

"I'm here picking up a cake. My boss's secretary is leaving, so we're throwing a little bon voyage."

I nodded. "That's nice. Their cake is delicious."

"Why don't I stop by tonight and bring you a slice?" The tone in his voice was undeniably flirtatious.

"Aren't you going out with Cade tonight, Adam?" I turned to stare at Josh, a little perplexed since he knew Cade was staying at Maura's. Josh turned to Bryan. "Have you met Cade, Adam's boyfriend?"

Oh, fuck. That's why I was getting the stink eye.

"Boyfriend?" Bryan's hand rose to his chest and his amused smile reminded me of how much I overshared at the last poker night. "Well, you naughty boy."

After a few seconds of confusion, his meaning struck me with the subtly of lightening. Our last poker night. I'd stayed to help him clean up, and he'd made his interest known. I'd only remembered turning him down with a long soliloquy of angst over Cade followed by a lot more whiskey. But then . . . Yeah. I smacked my lips, tasting the cigar we'd smoked that night and something else. My tongue had definitely been in his mouth before I'd stumbled home.

Josh's guffaw didn't do much to hide his outrage. I shifted from one foot to the other, before finally pulling my seat out and resting one knee on it to create some space.

"Yeah, I guess I haven't seen you in a month or so." Sid's and Brady's eyebrows came down once I emphasized the timing. "Cade and I got back together in Hawaii."

"Well, I'll have to meet him soon. Maybe he can join us for poker Monday night?"

What was the friendly way of saying I would rather douse myself in honey and roll around on a fire ant mound? "Oh, darn. I'm going out of town. To Atlanta. On Tuesday. My flight is super early, so I'll probably just go to bed. With Cade. You know, my boyfriend, because I'm sure he'll take me to the airport."

Bryan's grin blossomed into something resembling the Cheshire cat. "No kidding. I'm going to Charlotte for work on Tuesday. I connect through Atlanta. How wild would it be if we were on the same flight? I was going to call an Uber to the airport, but if you have a ride, perhaps I could tag along. I'd love to meet Cade."

The table rattled, and I turned to see Brady's arm stretch out and firmly cup the back of Josh's neck. "Um, Adam, I think we'll finish up our order and wait outside for you." Brady yanked Josh up and shuffled him toward the counter.

Sid stared for a moment before shaking his head. "I think I'll use the restroom before we leave."

"Wait," I said. The heat flared up my neck. "I need to go too. See you around maybe, Bryan."

"Ok, no worries. I need to run. Don't be a stranger. Nice to meet you, Sid. Toodles." He waved each long, thin finger in quick succession, then blew an air kiss near my cheek.

I busied myself clearing the plates of cake from the table when Sid spoke. "Does Cade know about that?"

My heart was beating so hard my chest hurt. Cade and I were finally in a good place. If he found out . . . I instantly went into damage control. "There's nothing to know. I swear. He invited me to poker a few times. We made out one time—it was before Cade and I got back together."

"Whoa. Calm down." Sid touched my arm. "I'm not saying you did anything wrong, but if you have that—" he gestured toward the counter where Bryan was waiting in line "—living next door, you've got to tell him."

"I haven't spoken to Bryan since before we went to Hawaii."

"Hey." Sid held his hands up. "I know what Cade means to you and I know you. This isn't judgment. Even if you are hanging out and playing cards with him on the regular, there is nothing wrong with it. But you can't have it be a secret. All you have to do is mention you ran into him with us and that the guy was flirting pretty hard, so you got nervous. Don't make it be a big deal, because it's not."

"I got nervous because you guys all acted like I was doing something wrong."

Sid shook his head. "Adam, we didn't know what to think. I think it surprised us you were acting so guilty."

"I would never hurt Cade like that again."

"Adam, we know, okay? You need to forgive yourself. We all have."

I wasn't so sure Cade had. Not completely. "Sorry, I . . . Everyone was getting angry with me."

"Josh and Brady aren't angry. They want you and Cade to work out as much as I do. I understand you both try to keep us out of it, but we've all been affected. It hurts us when you guys are unhappy, and it's been difficult to get our hopes up, then dashed over and over."

"If it doesn't work this time . . ." I sighed.

"It will. If you want it to. If you trust each other."

"I do trust him."

"Good. Then there should be no reason to not tell him about Bryan."

"You don't think it'll hurt him and make him worry?"

"I think finding out your neighbor is pretty obviously interested in you and is apparently the type of person who thinks a boyfriend is a fun challenge to overcome will probably make him worry. Finding out you hid that from him? Now, that will hurt him."

"He's got a lot going on right now with Maura. What if I tell him when I get back?"

"Isn't he taking you to the airport?"

"No." I laughed. "My flight isn't at the crack of dawn. I made that up."

"You could have told him to fuck off. That's what Cade would have done."

Clutching my chest, I smiled, doing my best impression of my mother. "Well, bless your heart. I was raised in the South, darling. That is simply not the way things are done."

Sid shook his head at me.

"I'm joking. And thank you. You're right. I should talk to him. It's good advice."

Chapter Fourteen

Cade

I shifted on the worn leather coach, unfolding and refolding a single sheet of loose-leaf paper that had served as my security blanket the last few days. After twelve years, the creases were wafer-thin, and my words were barely legible along the worn seams. The greeting made me chuckle.

dear cade

My teenaged self wasn't so hot on punctuation or capitalization.

A door clicked opened. I turned to see a young, waiflike girl, no more than late teens, step into the waiting room. When our eyes met, I recognized her fear and offered a slight smile she didn't return. She surveyed the sparse furnishings. Her jet-black hair brushed across her shoulder, each wispy strand lifeless, much like her affect. A furious rush of stomach acid licked at my throat.

Reflexively, I touched my scalp, rubbing a thick blond lock between my thumb and forefinger. *Keratin.* There was a time my body didn't have the energy for nonessential functions like growing hair. So many proteins dedicated to such a frivolous activity.

I lowered my chin, partly to give her privacy as she checked in at the glass-enclosed reception desk, but mostly because seeing her triggered me.

I scanned my letter, reminding myself how far I'd come.

Im sorry for blaming you and wishing you were different. Im sorry I tried to starve you away.

I cringed. Thank God for spell check or I might never have made it through college.

Tucking the bottom of my foot along my inner thigh, I sat up straighter and stretched my hips, but it didn't ease the throbbing in my head or the dull ache in what was left of my glutes.

The glass slid open and Jill, Dr. McNamara's receptionist, acknowledged the girl with a nod. "Here's some paperwork. Take a seat, dear. It will be a few minutes."

The girl pulled her jacket tight around her and took the seat next to me on the couch. There was other furniture across the room, but few who walked through the doors of Meadowbrook Center had the body fat to deal with the wicked draft between the door and the windows. I observed her reflection in the window. Staring without staring, while she finished her paperwork, and set it back on the counter for Jill.

When she returned to the couch, she pulled her knees up to her chest, folding her arms around them. The sleeve of her jacket slid up, momentarily revealing a jarringly thin wrist before she tugged it down and jerked her gaze to me.

Once again, I gave her a weak smile, slightly embarrassed by my rudeness. She dropped her knees and angled away from me, reading something on her phone. More than once, a tear slid down her cheek, and I clenched my fingers into a fist to avoid taking her hand. A year ago, I would have, but today, it'd have been the blind leading the blind.

"Cade," Jill said from her window. "We're ready for you."

I stood, taking a moment to gather my belongings and tuck the letter into my messenger bag. Sam, my favorite nurse, led me down the hallway to an exam room.

"School out?" he asked and shut the door behind us.

I nodded and took a seat on the paper-lined table, glancing around at nothing in particular as Sam took my vital signs with a practiced proficiency. "Your heart rate is good." Sam smiled at me, taking pride in my accomplishment as he ripped the Velcro from the blood pressure cuff from my arm.

I nodded again and concentrated on breathing. This part of Meadowbrook looked like any other medical office, with standard rooms containing your basic equipment—an exam table, a computer, some chairs, that little machine that took your blood pressure. But there was one thing that was glaringly different. I swallowed the lump in my throat, knowing what came next.

The encouraging smile on Sam's face widened. "You ready?" he asked and gestured to the raised platform.

I took a deep breath and closed my eyes to let the tidal wave of unease retreat. Toeing off my shoes, I stripped down to my underwear, blushing as Sam gave me a quick once-over. I hated being naked, but I knew enough anorexics that had strapped weights to their body that I no longer questioned the rationale. My heart pounded as I approached the scale with no display screen. With another deep breath, I stepped up. A second later, a completely unreadable Sam said, "Okay. You can step down now."

I hurried to replace my clothes. Exhaling, I released the tension from my shoulders, and rolled my neck. "What's the verdict?"

In recovery, getting my weight taken was like a game of Russian Roulette where every chamber was loaded; instead of a bullet, it was like an electric shock to the disordered part of my brain. If I gained weight, I failed my anorexia. If I stayed the same or lost weight, it was never enough. But knowing my weight was out there, in some part of my record, where other people could see it and judge me by it, well, that drove me all kinds of crazy too.

Sam shook his head. "You know Dr. M. decides who gets told their weight." I watched him as he jotted notes on his tablet. He flipped the screen toward me and offered it to me. "Survey time."

I read the first question. *In the last month, how many times have you had a definite fear of losing control over eating?*

I scanned across the numbers. I'd been so confident in my recovery when I'd started my program, I'd have clicked *no days* and moved on. Fighting back a wave of disappointment, I checked the box next to *16-20 days*. The screen slid to the right, and a new question appeared.

In the last month, how many times has thinking about food, eating, or calories made it very difficult to concentrate on things you are interested in?

I hovered over *no days* for a second, but hesitated. Chewing on my bottom lip, I relived how many conversations I'd tuned out of with my friends. I selected *10-15 days* instead.

Question after question slipped across my screen, forcing me to confront my behaviors and quantify my thoughts into electronic bubbles. I breezed through the ones meant for bingers and bulimics. I rolled my eyes as some questions reappeared, asking the same questions differently, which always felt like a trap to see if people were lying. When I got to the end, my stomach twisted, but I handed Sam back the tablet knowing I'd answered them as honestly as I could. "All done."

Sam smiled at me. "Outstanding. It'll be a moment before Dr. McNamara is ready for you."

"Hey, Sam," I said as he was exiting the room.

He turned back toward me.

"That girl in the waiting room . . ."

"What about her?"

"She's new, right?"

"I can't talk about other patients with you."

"Don't scare her away."

Sam frowned. "We don't scare people away."

"The first time I came here, Dr. M. told me I was thirty pounds underweight and threatened me with a feeding tube. If you tell her she has to gain weight, you'll never see her again. She's not ready."

"When you are as underweight as you were, your brain isn't capable of rational thinking. We don't threaten our patients and, if I recall, you didn't get a feeding tube."

"Because it was the only way to avoid foster care."

"Still. You got help because you had a reason to get better. If she's here, she does too."

"Cade." Dr. McNamara breezed into the room, and Sam handed her my chart and ducked out, shutting the door behind him. In no hurry, she glanced at Sam's notes and the tablet I'd used to take my survey. When she was finished, she washed her hands and approached the exam table, stethoscope at the ready.

I took a few deep breaths while she listened to my heart and lungs. She checked my mouth, eyes, and ears. "Lie down for me."

I leaned back so she could finish the examination. "How are your bowel movements?" she asked, pushing on my stomach.

"I've been a little constipated and lots of bloating."

She pushed on my belly a few more times. "Are you having pain?"

"No, not really. Some leg cramps at night."

"Okay. You can sit up now." She stepped back, and I immediately yanked my shirt down to cover myself.

She grabbed her stool and wheeled herself over to me and patted my knee supportively. "So your survey has me concerned. You've been in recovery for how long now?"

"A little over eleven years. My last relapse was four years ago last March."

Dr. McNamara flipped through my chart. "That's right. We did intensive outpatient then to get you back on track, but you withdrew from the program after a week."

"I was student teaching then and could only attend over spring break, but it was enough to get back on track." Until Adam came back from Mexico and I realized what my eating disorder had done to us.

"Okay, well the important thing to remember is relapse is not failure. We want to get you out of these restrictive behaviors right away. I'll have Sam come back and review the Minnie Maud plan. You're over twenty-five now, so that's 3,000 calories daily minimum, but eat when you're hungry—no exercise, no measuring, no weighing. I want to recheck your bloodwork and weight next week, and I want to see you at group."

I nodded, the sheer thought of going back to eating like that was enough to make me lightheaded. Eating disorder recovery was a full-time job of stuffing your face and forcing yourself to do things that made you sick to your stomach. I drew a deep breath, reminding myself that everything the voice told me was a lie. "How much this time?"

She wheeled over to the computer and clicked a few keys. "Your BMI is not too worrisome. I'd like to see you gain about sixteen pounds to get back to your set point. Remember your weight is not the key indicator. You've never gone below target since you left the hospital. Now your sisters are your principal support, right? Are they aware of this relapse?"

I nodded. "But Aislinn moved to Boston and Maura's having some issues right now."

"Oh? I'm sorry to hear that. Do you have others who can step up?"

"Um, no one who knows about my anorexia."

"Well, I suggest you reach out to friends who can support you. Group is good, but recovery is much more successful with support from people who love you. Are you still seeing a therapist?"

I shook my head. "I stopped going when my sister got sick."

She flipped through my records, and the worry lines on her forehead deepened. "Cade, I can't stress enough how important it is for you to have a solid foundation of support to maintain your recovery. That means a therapist and friends and family."

I nodded. It was the same advice my therapist always gave me, but I couldn't tell my friends if I hadn't told Adam, and I'd never been able to tell Adam. "I plan to tell my boyfriend."

My chest clenched with the reality of that statement. I had to tell him, and soon, but telling him because I needed his support felt both selfish and woefully optimistic. More likely, telling Adam was going to make things a million times more stressful.

Dr. McNamara nodded approvingly and finished my appointment. Sam returned, and I half listened as he stressed elements of the recovery plan I'd already reviewed multiple times on my own. I knew what to do. I knew how to eat and how fucking stupid it had been to think I could do some sort of controlled program after Adam and I had had our last big fight. *Just enough to feel better about how shitty I'd been.* What a joke. That was the thing people didn't get about eating disorders. Healthy people think starving yourself is a form of punishment, but to me it was the opposite. Anorexia was a reward. It made me numb. A numbness I needed to replace the guilt.

Every time I thought of Mexico—of Adam's cheating. How I'd been beating him up for what he did, refusing to forgive him, refusing to acknowledge my role in things, and the secret that made me pull away from him. Smug and self-righteous, I screamed and hurled accusations at him . . .

"Cade are you listening?" Sam said, gently tapping my knee.

"Yeah. Sorry." I grimaced.

"So, here are the calorie-dense foods we want you to incorporate during this week. Are any of these fear foods?"

I surveyed the list. "Avocados are hit or miss. But, um, pasta and cheese are a struggle. I can eat cheese by itself sometimes, but not melted or on things."

"Okay, so you need to eat both this week at least once. Add olive oil or butter to your pasta and try a cheeseburger or pizza. Chips and guacamole make a great snack. Challenge your food rules every day."

"Yeah, I remember."

"Have any questions?" He handed me the papers.

I opened my bag and shoved the papers inside. "Nope, I get what I'm supposed to do, it's just doing it."

Sam nodded sympathetically. "Hang in there, Cade. You've done it before, and you can do it again. Jill will get you booked for a return visit and with one of the therapists here. Don't forget to pick up the group schedule too."

"Thank god it's the summer, I guess."

Sam smiled. "Yep, nothing to do but focus on recovery."

Yeah, and a tenuous relationship, a mentally ill sister, a niece hurtling toward puberty, paying two apartments' worth of bills. I forced a smile as I walked with Sam to the hallway leading toward the entrance. "Jill will get you checked out," he said, offering me a shoulder pat before walking away.

The glass window slid open. "Your copay is one hundred today, Cade."

And a shitload of medical bills.

"A hundred? No, that's not right. My copays are forty."

"Oh? Let me check." Jill clicked on her keyboard, making small indecipherable noises. "Yes, I see the reason. Dr. McNamara is out of network for you now."

"Fuck!" Jill frowned at me and I muttered a hasty, "Sorry."

"Do you want to see the financial counselor before I set your appointments?"

While she clicked her long fingernails on her keyboard, I pulled up my banking app and checked my balance. "Um . . . No. Can I pay half today and the rest when I come back next week?"

Jill's lips flattened. "Sure," she said, taking my debit card. "The insurance covers therapy visits at sixty percent, so that will be about one twenty a week."

Damn it. After the last-minute airfare for Hayley, I was blowing through my paycheck at a record pace, and I hadn't paid my car payment. Two hundred and twenty a week, plus Maura's visits were sixty, and her new medicine had been two hundred for the month since insurance wouldn't cover replacing the flushed medication. It would be cheaper when we could go to mail order, but I didn't want to do a ninety-day supply before we knew it would work. It had been impossible to get into see an eating disorder specialist the first time, and I liked Dr. McNamara. The thought of switching made me want to puke. "Thanks, yeah. I'll keep my appointment with Dr. M., but can you cancel the therapy appointment for me? I'll find someone in my network."

"Of course. I can send you some recommendations."

"Thanks, Jill. See you next week." I walked out of the office, still ruminating over how I could pay for my bills and Maura's. Maybe Aislinn . . . but Aislinn was too likely to go to Brenda and James for the money. The logical choice was Siddharth . . . but that meant coming clean and putting him in an awkward place between me and Adam, which I promised I would never do. Maybe I could go without therapy a little longer, only until Maura could cover a little more of her bills? It wasn't ideal, but nothing in my life ever was.

Chapter Fifteen

Adam

"Adam, for goodness sakes. Watch the wheels, darling, you're scuffing the floor."

"Hi, Mom," I said, lifting my carry-on up over the black-and-white checkered floor to set it on the rug-covered hard wood curved staircase. Every time I returned to my parents' Buckhead home, it felt like going to one of those stores full of glass and china when I was a kid. The ones where they put the fear of God in me to not touch anything. It didn't help that I hadn't grown up here. No. While other parents downsized when their youngest left the nest, my parents decided it was time to buy their dream home.

Set on multiple acres with hand-carved marble mantles, barrel-vaulted ceilings, and paneling from some chateau in France, it was an eight-bedroom, ten-bath ostentatious gated country estate in the middle of the city. There was an impressive swimming pool sparkling through the French doors on the other side of the foyer. The last few times I'd been home for the holidays, it had been too cold for swimming, but this week I planned to spend some quality time there avoiding my parents, neither of whom swam.

"Did you have a pleasant flight?"

"Yes, it was fine."

"Well, lovely dear." She stared at me, her lips puckered. "Your hair is too long. Your brother and father go to a lovely barber. I'll make you an appointment before the party. Did you bring your tux?"

"Mother, I don't have a tux. I brought my black Armani suit."

"I'm sure I told you to bring a tuxedo."

I guarded my body language against anything my mother could use to accuse me of being difficult and laid out the facts as I saw them. "Well, since you didn't send me twenty-five hundred dollars to purchase it and I told you I couldn't afford to buy one and you forbid me from renting one, I brought my Armani suit."

"Adam, why must you always be so difficult? Even before you were born. I missed a chance at the Berghoff—"

"Endowed Chair because you were on bedrest with me for preeclampsia. Yes. I'm aware," I deadpanned.

My mother placed a hand on her hip and shook her head. "Well, I worked hard for that. I was the only woman up for consideration and I already had the twins."

"Yes, Mother. I believe I've apologized multiple times for my inconsiderate behavior in utero."

"Oh, Adam. Must you be so dramatic? I don't understand where you get that from. Neither your father nor I are the least bit dramatic."

"She says dramatically," I muttered under my breath. When her eyes widened, I gave up both on the conversation and civility. "It's been a long day, Mother. Can you print me directions to where I'll be staying?"

She heaved a sigh. "You'll be in the blue room."

I glanced up the staircase. "That upstairs?"

"Yes, dear. It's the third room on the right. Next to Rachel's."

"Rachel has her own room? What happened to her townhome near the hospital?"

"She stays with us sometimes. She likes to use the pool."

"What about R.J.?"

"Robert Jr., please, Adam."

"Fine, what about Robert Jr.?"

"Your brother has his own pool. In Lenox Park. You would know that if you bothered to speak to your siblings once in a while. Or us."

A sinking feeling descended and washed away even the small glimmer of optimism for this visit going well. My mother's love language was guilt trips. I didn't know why I had expected she'd miraculously change. "Okay, well we have plenty of time to catch up this week, won't we?"

"Well, not really, dear. You chose to come on a Tuesday, and we all work. If you'd come in on Saturday, we could have arranged something."

"The flights are cheaper during the week, and it's fine. I have some work I can do this week."

"Ah, yes. Well, I'll wait for your father to get home before we broach your little art job."

I sighed. "Oh good. Something to look forward to. I'm going to find my room and maybe the kitchen to grab a snack." I took a few steps up the stairs.

"I'll have Angelo make you something."

Turning, I didn't risk masking my irritation with sarcasm my mother might ignore as inconsequential. "Who the hell is Angelo?"

She waved a dismissive hand at me. "The chef, silly."

"You said you weren't going to hire new staff. Why couldn't you have kept Ms. Sandra?"

"Adam, I have explained this to you a million times: Ms. Sandra was perfect when we needed full-time childcare and housekeeping, but she wasn't happy living here after you decided to go out of state for college and never return. She was too hard-working to be satisfied with cooking and cleaning for two adults who are rarely home. We didn't fire her; she wanted to find a family with young children. Angelo comes in the afternoon and shops for us and prepares our evening meal, cleans the kitchen up and leaves. He's lovely. I'm sure he won't mind preparing a small snack for you."

"Don't bother. I'm going to call Cade and take a nap. We can have dinner tonight and if the twins can't make it, fine." I was actively pouting now over my nanny. Regressed eight years in ten minutes. Wonderful.

"Fine, but don't get in the way. Angelo isn't Ms. Sandra; he doesn't want to hear about your problems. Lord, how she spoiled you."

"Sure thing, Mom." I grabbed my suitcase and stomped up the stairs. How was this house I'd never lived in like a time machine to my adolescence? I wished Cade had been able to come. It would have been the perfect excuse to stay in a hotel.

At the top of the stairs, there was a long hallway with eight doors. Most led to bedrooms, but there was a gym at the end of the hall and a bathroom. I sulked down to the third door and tossed it open. The blue room was actually the least-decorated room in the house. It had a four-poster bed, draped in high-end linens ,and a fancy rug, but the other furnishings had come from the old house. I swung my luggage up onto the small bench under the window and peeked out of the curtains. At least there was a decent view of the pool from here.

I lay on the bed, rethinking my strategy for getting through the week. The key had been to not let them get under my skin, but unfortunately that key was not in my possession, so the backup plan was to avoid them at all costs. Plan made, I calmed down enough to check in with Cade. I navigated to my favorites and pushed the icon for FaceTime next to his name.

"Hey, you made it." Cade yawned and stretched from Hayley's bedroom, and it gave me a brief rush to know he answered my call when he was clearly resting.

"Yeah, just a bit ago. Sorry I woke you."

"It's okay. I've been dozing off and on."

"How are you and the girls?"

Cade straightened his spine and attempted to smile. It didn't do much to mask his weariness, but he'd been trying to stay positive. "Maura is feeling okay. She's going back to the doctor tomorrow to get her blood checked. Aislinn called last night to report Hayley is in love with Boston. I guess she had her first lobster roll and has declared all other food inferior." He chuckled.

"They are pretty good."

"Yeah, tell that to Maura."

"Shit. I'm sorry."

Cade cocked his head. "Why are you sorry?"

"Because I don't think about things like that. I hear lobster roll and think 'Good for Hayley getting to experience some quality things in life' instead of how hard it would be to see your kid enjoy things you can't give them. That would suck."

"Yeah." He blinked rapidly, surprise melting into a smile. "I think that's the first time you've tried to put yourself in Maura's shoes. I'm impressed."

"Don't be. I had a tantrum over the fact that we have a new chef."

Cade laughed. "You've been home like five minutes?"

"More like thirty, but yeah. You should have come with me; then you could keep me from losing my mind."

Cade's jaw tensed, and I was quick to reassure him. "Gou, relax. I understand why you couldn't come. I want to be able to say I wish you were here without it meaning anything other than that."

He relaxed, his lips turning down in what looked to be sincere regret, and nodded. "Sorry I couldn't be there."

"I know. I'm getting better at being patient."

"Is that a reference to the fact that we haven't had sex in two weeks?" Cade made a face that I'd learned was a sign of both insecurity and irritation because he didn't like admitting to his insecurity. I hated that he even had to ask, but I was grateful for a chance to show him I'd changed.

"No. It's a reference to me growing the fuck up and realizing you have a lot of other things going on and it's not all about me. I'm serious, Cade. I'm really working on it."

"Me too. I'm working on things to make us better."

"Like what?"

"Um, like trusting you more and remembering that we're not the same people we were four years ago."

Forgetting the camera for a second, I closed my eyes and sighed. It was the perfect opening. Sid was right, I needed to tell him about Bryan. "About that."

"What?" Cade's eyes went wide, and I tried to remember Sid's advice. I'd done nothing wrong and acting like I had would only make Cade more anxious.

"It's nothing big, but the guys and I ran into my neighbor at the bakery and he sort of came on to me."

Cade's face went stoic, unreadable. "Should I be concerned?"

"No, but we hung out a few times before Hawaii and one of those nights we messed around a little, so he may have gotten the impression I was interested."

"Are you?"

"No, babe. I set him straight that I have a man."

Cade swallowed and a slight uptick in his voice eased the tension I carried in my shoulders. "Okay, well, I guess that's all I can ask you to do. It's not like either of us were monks before."

"Really?"

"Yeah. Should I be more upset about this?"

"No, I kind of dreaded telling you."

"I haven't exactly been reasonable about the subject in the past, but this is a clean slate, right? So we both get a chance to be better."

"Fuck. I love you." I smiled, letting myself exhale fully.

"I love you too."

Cade and I talked for almost an hour, until Maura woke up and Cade said he needed to go eat dinner. By the time I hung up the phone, there was enough noise in the house, I suspected my father or the twins were home. I drew out of bed, taking the time to unpack and store my luggage, which I knew my mother would do for me if I didn't. I again reconsidered my avoidance strategy, in light of my conversation with Cade. Maybe what I needed was a little less avoidance and a little more maturity with my family too. After all, I was an adult, same as them. If I still sulked upstairs and back-talked them like a teenager, it stood to reason they would still treat me like a child. I paid my own bills— there wasn't so much as an emergency credit card with my father's name on it in my wallet—my condo and car were bought with my income and credit score, no cosigner needed. They couldn't exactly demand a refund on my college tuition. I had no reason to give them as much power over me as I did.

I bounded down the stairs and ran into Rachel. She was in blue hospital scrubs, her long, dark hair in a ponytail. "Adam!" She pulled me into a hug. "It's good to see you."

"Hi, Rach. Good to see you too. How's work?"

"Meh." She made a dismissive hand gesture. "I was going to go for a swim. You want to join me?"

"Yeah. Robert Jr. here?"

She huffed. "Not you too. R.J. will always be R.J. You don't get to change your name at thirty unless you're changing genders or something."

I laughed. "I'd pay good money to see R.J. come out to Mom and Dad as trans."

She burst into laughter. "They'd find a way to use it to their advantage. You should hear Mom talk about her gay son when she's around the chief medical officer and his husband."

"You're kidding."

"Nope. Sorry, kiddo. You're like her rainbow passport."

"Well, at least I'm contributing," I deadpanned.

"Speaking of . . . I'm supposed to encourage you to bring a date to the party."

I shook my head, once again wishing Cade could have made the trip. My parents were way better behaved with an audience. "Cade couldn't come. He had some family issues."

She shook her head. "I'm not talking about Cade. I have a colleague, Max—"

"Nope. Thanks, but I'm good going solo."

She eyed me suspiciously. "I thought you and Cade were—what do you call it?—open."

"Not anymore. We're committed. He's the only one I want to be with."

She sighed, peering over her shoulder toward the study where our parents were fussing over something. "You sure? Max is hot and a radiologist."

I nodded and added an emphatic, "Not interested."

Rachel once again checked behind her with a nervous glance. "Do Mom and Dad realize that Cade is back in the picture?"

I nodded. "He was going to come with me."

"It's not going to go over well."

I shrugged. "I don't care if it goes over well. It's my decision."

"All right, little brother. I don't understand the attraction to a guy you've literally spent your entire adult life trying to make love you. He's such a train wreck and that family of his . . ." She shuddered. "If you ask me, if you have to work that hard to stay together, it's not worth pissing off your family for him. Think about it, at least."

Rachel walked past me toward the stairs, but I rechanneled my urge to storm off into something resembling a mature response. "Hey, Rachel."

She twirled around. "Yeah?"

"I don't need to think about it. I don't have to make Cade love me. He loves me. I cheated on him in college and it's taken a while for him to forgive me, but we're doing good now and I'd appreciate it if you'd keep your opinions about him and his family to yourself from now on."

She smiled, almost as through I'd impressed her. "Get your suit on. I'll grab you a towel and meet you by the pool."

By dinnertime, I thought I'd hit my stride. I'd solidified my defenses and not even my father's disapproval was landing a punch. As usual, dinner conversation was a whole lot of shoptalk held at a level of detail that ensured I didn't have the slightest thing to contribute. My mother and sister engaged in a debate about diffusion tensor imaging, whatever that was, and my father and brother were discussing whether adding *.com* to the end of website made a difference to intellectual property. I somewhat followed the argument, but then they began starting every sentence with *what about blah versus blah* and throwing out names and cases, so I tuned it out. The only information of interest was the news that my brother had started dating an intellectual property attorney named Catherine, who I immediately liked because her views were causing the vein on my father's forehead to bulge.

I had plenty of time to think as I ate silently and nodded occasionally. I listened, growing increasingly irritated by my exclusion. My parents and siblings navigated conversations seamlessly, talking fast by usual standards, but practically at lightning speed for the native Georgians we were. When the meal was nearing the end, I realized no one in my family had bothered to ask me one question other than a *How are you?* since I'd arrived home. *Fuck this.*

"So," I shouted over the chatter, "would anyone like to hear about the project I'm working on?"

Four sets of brown eyes landed on me, and the room fell silent.

I cleared my throat. "If not, I'll excuse myself."

"Well, by all means, Adam. Your sister and I were discussing lifesaving technology . . . but please do go on."

"Thank you, Mother." I launched into the specifics of my latest project with Greenspoke, tossing out as many terms of art as I could manage. By the time I wrapped up a pretty convincing argument on the science behind font design, I thought I'd gotten my point across.

"Well," my father said, dabbing the corner of his mouth with his napkin before placing it across his plate. "That sounds like an interesting project, Son."

"It is. Thank you. Now, Rachel. Explain to me exactly what diffusion tensor imaging is and why I should care about it?"

Rachel did her best to hide her smile behind a sip of her wine. "Well, Adam. Thanks for asking. Diffusion tensor imaging is a technique that shows the contrast based on the diffusion of water molecules in the brain. So researchers can see things like brain connectivity and brain development and learn more about diseases that affect the white matter, like stroke and dementia. They asked me to be a co-investigator on an interesting study that's using DTI to examine the brains of people with depression and mood disorders."

"So, like a clinical trial, right?"

My mother's mouth gaped, but before she could correct me, Rachel chimed in, "Exactly."

"That's great, Sis. Congrats."

My mother clucked her tongue. "Occasional research is fine, Rachel, but the academic route is nothing but headaches—grant writing, institutional review boards. Stick to the plan." My mother continued to rant about the headaches of academia. By Rachel's indulgent smile, I sensed she'd heard it all numerous times.

When my mother took a sip of wine, I dived in again. "R.J., tell me more about this woman with the questionable law credentials. Is it serious?"

R.J. chuckled, looking nervously at both our parents. "Yeah. We've only been seeing each other for a few months, but she's different."

"Cool. That's how I felt when I met Cade. When you know, you know." I took the last bite of my perfectly al dente linguine. "This is amazing, Angelo," I hollered, loud enough for the man I had yet to meet to hear me in the kitchen and my mother to wince at my poor table manners. "Cade wishes he could have joined me. His sister was not doing well, so he stayed to help take care of her."

R.J. nodded, then shared a few more details about Catherine. She graduated from John Marshall instead of Emory and seemed decent and down to earth, which explained why my father was not enthusiastic about their relationship.

"I assume you're bringing her to the party?"

"Oh, I don't think—" My father started before R.J. nodded.

"That's great. I can't wait to meet her." I stood, grabbing my plate and my mother's and sister's.

"Adam, what on earth are you doing?"

"I'm clearing the table, Mother."

"Angelo clears the table."

"Well, I'm going to walk into the kitchen to say thank you for the meal, so I'll save him one trip."

She clucked her tongue again, gaping at my father as though he should do something to stop me from assisting the help, but neither of them said a word as I carried the dishes out of the room, victorious.

I stayed in the kitchen, chatting up Angelo as well as I could with the language barrier, until it became clear the man simply wanted to do his job and get home. On my way back to my room, my luck ran out.

"Adam, your mother and I would like a word, please." The sole of my shoe squeaked to a stop, and I twisted to meet the narrowed eyes of my father. He retreated to his office without waiting for my response.

Cade

"It's like I have two voices in my head. The rational one that tells me to eat and the irrational one that tells me that if I don't follow these stupid rules my brain comes up with, I'm worthless." I paused, peering up at Maura expectantly.

Her mouth gaped like she wanted to say something, but nothing came out. She probably couldn't fathom what kind of an idiot doesn't know how to talk to his boyfriend.

"Sis. Come on."

She took a deep breath. "Okay, so I think if you're going to do this, you need to use the word 'anorexia' somewhere. Just get it out of the way. Adam, isn't exactly the sharpest tool in the shed, and without it, the whole thing sounds a little mental."

"Hey, don't insult him, he's trying. Not all of us took childhood immersion courses in mental illness. What about if I say the thing about the voices, but call it my anorexia voice? That way I can put it out there without being all, 'Hi, I'm Cade and I'm an anorexic. Sorry, I should have told you years ago.'"

"You're not *an* anorexic, you suffer from anorexia. Language is important, Cade. And you would have told him, except he sprung his whole south-of-the-border-sodomy saga on you. It's not like you owed him an explanation after that."

I frowned. "Maura. Come on. I have to tell him something to explain why I'm eating like a pig and can't go for a fucking walk around the block, not to mention some way to explain my whereabouts two nights a week for group and therapy, plus why I have no money. He's really trying to be straightforward with me, I can't keep this a secret and recover; I know either my recovery or my relationship will suffer."

"But 'anorexia voice' sounds like you're hearing hallucinations."

Forget it. Talking about my anorexia made the voice louder anyway. "Never mind, I'll figure it out. I need to eat." *Again.*

"Cade, don't get pissy with me. I'm trying to help."

"I can't deal with this right now. It's six o'clock and I'm a thousand calories short of my minimum daily intake and I was going to try to eat pasta." My heart rate sped up—all day I'd been trying to psych myself up for it. *Yay, tonight we conquer super-scary pasta.*

Maura cringed. "All right. Calm down."

"I'm calm. Fuck. No, I'm not. I can't do it, Maura." I started pacing, letting go of the anxiety by hopping and jumping around, like I could shake the feeling of doom out through my toes.

"Stop. You're exercising. Sit down. Let's start with ordering the food. Will seeing the pictures help?"

"No."

"Is there any particular pasta that might be better than others?"

Pasta had been on my blacklisted food since the night Adam and I went out on our first date. "Um, nothing stuffed. No ravioli or cannelloni."

Maura frowned, but kept scrolling through the online ordering app. "Okay, I'm going to give you two choices, and you tell me which one sounds better. Choice one is plain old spaghetti with meatballs, choice two is fettucine with Alfredo sauce, no meat."

I swallowed the lump in my throat. *Cream sauce is all fat. Fat covering carbs with virtually no nutritional value. You will immediately gain five pounds and you won't stop there. You will keep eating and eating and . . .*

"Cade," Maura said sternly.

"Spaghetti, but—"

"It's good to eat it the way it comes."

"Can you ask them not to put parmesan on the top, please?"

"No, but I will open it and if I see parmesan on top, I can stir it for you, so you won't see it's there."

I exhaled through my nose as she typed the order into the app. She kissed my forehead.

"It'll be here in thirty minutes. This will not get you quite to a thousand, so would you like a salad as well or we can have ice cream for dessert?"

"A salad, but I should probably eat the pasta first."

"Okay. You're doing great, Cade. It's only been a week and you know it gets easier. Do you want to talk about the voice?"

I rolled my eyes comically. She was right, *the voice* sounded a bit mental, but it was the only way I'd figured out to describe it to people who didn't understand. "You mean my hallucinations?"

"Stop. You know I get it, but I don't think Adam will. I kind of have a voice with my depression; it basically lies constantly and tells me I'm better off dead." The words jarred me, but she carried on so matter-of-factly, I wasn't sure if I should interrupt. "I remember one time I was driving home from work and it'd been an okay day, nothing too upsetting happened, but this idea got in my head that I could totally drive my car into a tree. Once it was there, I couldn't let it go. The whole way home I sort of fantasized about it, like what it would be like to not be here anymore and not have any problems. I kept looking at trees as I was passing them and thinking, 'Would that one work?'"

"Jesus, Maura. How can you be so cavalier about that?"

"Because, Cade. When I got home, I saw you and Hayley. The voice doesn't really go away, but I know not to listen to it."

I took a deep breath, exhaling loudly as the panic subsided. "I'm glad you don't listen to your voice. I couldn't survive without you and neither would Hayley."

"Well, I won't listen to my voice if you don't listen to yours." She patted my hand. "You sure you don't want to talk about it?"

"Adam took me out when we first got back together. We had been reminiscing about our trip to Aruba."

"You loved that trip."

I nodded. "I got to the restaurant and things felt so right between us, like they had on that trip, and I wanted it to be okay like that again. They sat this big plate of pasta in front of me, and there it was. It was this whole cascade of thoughts I know are irrational. First, it was reminding me how happy Adam made me, then it was how awful I've been to him and how he deserved someone so much better. Someone thinner and sexier and more fucking together. Then somehow my entire future happiness became tied to me not eating one bite of that pasta. If that isn't fucked up enough, I made myself stare at it the whole meal and take it home so I could stare at it some more. Then I ate and spit out an entire slice of cheesecake bite by bite. I haven't been able to eat pasta since."

"Oh, honey. I wish I'd been in a better place to help you. The meds are working and I'm feeling more normal. I slept a full night last night without sleeping pills. I miss Hayley though."

"Me too. Listen, the pasta is making me really anxious, can we do something besides talk? I need you to distract me."

"Want to play cards or something?"

"Whatever. Just . . . Yeah."

She hurried to her room and returned with a deck of playing cards and a bag of Hershey Kisses. She dumped the kisses on the table, and I reminded myself there were no bad foods during recovery, before unwrapping one and popping it into my mouth. "Gin Rummy or Double Solitaire?" she asked as she shuffled the cards.

"Gin Rummy."

She nodded, dealing out ten cards a piece. We started the game, and before long she brought up Shane. Apparently, he wasn't thrilled she'd never returned from her supposed beer run, especially since he'd handed her a twenty for it.

The knock at the door took a sledgehammer to my ability to avoid thinking about food. The voice screeched, and the tomatoey-meaty smell wafting from the hall turned my stomach acids up to a boil.

Maura brought in our meals and set them on the coffee table. "Do you want the television on?" she asked, arranging the plate in front of me along with a slice of garlic bread dripping with butter.

I leaned my head back, gut twisting on itself. *It's too much food. I can't do it.* My throat tight, I ignored the heaviness pushing against my chest and the taste of bile and grabbed my fork. Maura took her seat and switched on the television, nodded encouragement, and dug in. She knew better than to stare at me. It was easier without an audience. I tried some tips I'd learned before. Positive thinking. *My body needs this food to function. Anorexia does not control me. I'll feel better. My skin will clear up. My sex drive will be higher.*

For whatever reason, that was the winning affirmation tonight. I twirled the pasta around my fork. I knew from experience I had to get the first bite down. That was the hardest. So I stuck the fork in my mouth and pulled off the noodles, focusing the whole of my mind on what I needed to do. I would try to enjoy it later, but after the first bite. *Food is pleasurable. Pasta tastes good. The sauce is fantastic.* I repeated those phrases in my head as I chewed and swallowed.

"Is that your phone?" Maura asked, drawing my attention the faint buzzing noise. I lifted the couch pillows until I uncovered the lit screen of my cell.

"Shit. It's Adam. I wasn't expecting him to call again. Should I answer it?"

Maura shook her head. "If you stop now it's going to be that much harder. Finish first, then call him back."

I took a deep breath. "I should at least text him."

She wrinkled her nose, but this was part of the change I was trying to make. I fired off a quick message. *Sorry, in the middle of something important. I'll call you back.*

Satisfied, I silenced my phone and went back to eating. It wasn't easy, but I kept going, dipping the bread in the sauce when I needed a break from the pasta. My stomach felt too full, but a distended and bloated belly was typical for recovery. I reminded myself of all the reasons eating, really overeating, was necessary, countering the voice with logic and affirmations the best I could.

My free hand I kept on the table. I'd slipped a few times during the week, touching, and scrutinizing the convex shape of my abdomen as I ate. Letting the voice tell me how gross and disgusting it was. I fought images of it filling with a solid, indigestible mass, contorting my body in grotesque ways.

"Well, I did it," I declared when I finished the plate without body-checking. "Now for the salad."

I walked to the kitchen with Maura following to grab the container. When I opened the refrigerator door, one of the magnets holding Hayley's drawing slipped, revealing a distinct blue envelope underneath, the words *final notice* stamped on the outside.

"What's this?" I asked, pulling it from the fridge. Maura had given me access to her accounts years ago, so I already knew she'd need more than the usual amount of help to make bills this month, but final notice implied she was already behind in something.

I opened the envelope, horror growing at the words I was reading. "The rent!"

"I'm sorry." Her shoulders collapsed forward and her gaze stayed on the floor.

"Food to eat, place to live, a way to get to work—those are your words, Maura." We always prioritized bills in a certain order when money was tight. No exceptions. "This is two months. Why didn't you tell me?"

"I didn't want you to worry. I'll go back to work, and I have some things to return to the store I bought when I was manic." She took the letter from my hand and stuck it on top of the fridge.

"I don't want you to go back before you're ready."

"I won't. I'm going to talk to my boss about going back part-time, but I wanted to make sure you felt well enough for Hayley to stay with you over the summer some first. When school starts, I'll try full-time and I can bartend on the weekends. I'm not about to try to get child support from Shane. He'll make our lives hell, and if he pays one dime, he'll expect to have input. I'd rather move to a one-bedroom again."

"You don't need to move. My apartment lease is up at the end of the summer; if it's still an issue, I can move to a cheaper place."

"Maybe I can see about getting a three-bedroom here? It'll be cheaper than paying for two places, and I don't think they'd hassle me about my lease if I swap apartments."

"Um, depending on what happens with Adam, I thought maybe . . ."

Maura's eyes grew enormous. "Really . . . That's wow."

"I don't know. Maybe it's too soon, but I know he wants to move in together, and I'll need to do something after I tell him . . ."

"I know you aren't thinking of moving in with him to stop him from breaking up with you. If he doesn't take things well, then fuck him. And you're not doing it because of money either. We'll figure it out. If I have to, I'll apply for benefits."

"I'd rather live together before we go that route." There wasn't anything wrong with people needing help, but we both knew that asking for things from the government had a way of inviting scrutiny into your lives and was best avoided if possible. I grabbed the envelope and sighed. "How much of this can you cover?"

"I've got most of it, but they'll only accept the full amount now. After I do the returns I need to do, I'll be short about three hundred."

The car payment I still hadn't paid was three fifty, and the late fee was nominal. If I was careful, I could pay it with my next check before it hit my credit report, but I'd have to get way more creative about how I paid for my therapy and all the calories I'd need to consume. "I'll transfer the money to you."

"Cade, are you sure?"

"Yeah. We'll take care of it tomorrow."

"Thanks." She hugged me fiercely. When we parted, she took the small salad container from the fridge that we definitely could have made at home for a fraction of the price, pushed it into my hands, and pointed to the table. "Now, go eat."

Three thousand-plus calories in, Maura and I played cards for the rest of the evening. I made sure she took her medicine. She made sure I didn't give into my urge to do sit-ups all night. I went to bed and, without the numbness of starvation and exercise, the possibility that I had failed Maura yet again weighed on me until I couldn't fight it anymore. I crossed my hands over my chest and hauled my upper body off the bed, again and again until the feeling settled, and new guilt arrived to keep me company. If I lived with Adam, I couldn't do sit-ups in the middle of the night. Before I could decide if that was a positive or a negative thing, I remembered I'd never returned his call.

"Fuck." I scrambled to see the clock. It was three in the morning in Atlanta. I went in search of my cell phone, finding it in the living room under the throw pillow. Adam had texted me back.

Bad night. Call me when you can.

Adam

"What's your problem?" Rachel stripped off her cover-up and tossed it onto the lounge nearest the tanning shelf at the far end of the pool.

"Nothing," I grumbled.

She dove in, clearing the width of the pool in a few strokes and broke the surface an arm's length from me. She ran a hand over her face to clear the water, opened her eyes, and continued our conversation. "Whatever. You're slamming doors and skipping meals like you're in high school, and now you're hiding in the pool."

"I'm not hiding."

Wordlessly, she grabbed my hand and presented the pruned digits to my face as evidence.

I sighed. "Dad wants me to start my own company."

Rachel nodded like this wasn't news to her. "So, what's the problem?"

"I don't want to." Since I sounded like a sullen child, I tried again. "He wants me to start my own company *in Atlanta.*"

"Makes sense. Going away to college was one thing. They want you home."

"They want to control me."

She rolled her eyes before dipping her head back in the water to slick back her hair. "Get a grip. They're not trying to control you; they are trying to fix a problem the only way they know how."

"Yeah, it's a problem where I live and what I do and who I want to spend my life with. My entire existence is a problem to them."

She shook her head. "This poor-Adam schtick is getting fucking tired." With that, she ducked under the water and pushed off the wall. I pouted, watching her swim laps back and forth as I considered her sentiments were close enough to Cade's that maybe she had a small point. After all, I'd been sulking all morning because Cade hadn't called me back the night before. Because he was in the middle of something important. *More important than me.*

I groaned inwardly. Had I really thought my parents trying to hand me a large sum of money was a problem worth whining about to Cade? *Thank God he didn't call me back.* I'd have sounded like a complete spoiled brat. This wasn't a real problem. It wasn't even a minor annoyance in the grand scheme of things. All I had to do was say, "Thanks, but no thanks," which I had. So what if my parents acted like I was ungrateful. Their opinion mattered a lot less to me than Cade's anyway.

Still, was it too much to ask that my boyfriend return a call after I had a bad day? That didn't seem too unreasonable. I couldn't imagine Brady not calling Josh or vice versa if they asked for it.

My sister swam by again.

"Rachel," I yelled to get her attention.

She stopped mid-stroke and floundered a bit navigating to a spot where she could touch the bottom. "What?"

"If you asked your boyfriend to call you and he didn't, would you be upset?"

Her face scrunched up. "Were you being a childish ass about it?"

"No." I huffed, regretting my decision already. "Never mind," I grumbled.

"Adam, what is it you want me to say?"

"I don't know. Maybe something supportive for a change. Is that too much to ask in this goddamn family?"

"Support isn't exactly a one-way street, baby brother. I've barely heard from you since you left for college."

"Fine." I turned, bracing my hands on the side of the pool to lift myself out of the water.

"Adam, don't leave."

Twisting, I sat on the edge and stared at her expectantly.

"I want to help. Tell me what's really going on with you and Cade and I'll try to."

I explained what had happened after Mexico, how Cade and I had been stuck in the endless cycle of fighting over the same shit and that we were supposed to be starting over. Rachel nodded sympathetically. I wrapped it up with, "I know Cade had a lot going on, and I'm trying to be supportive, but I don't want to be in a relationship where I feel discarded all the time."

"It doesn't sound unreasonable to expect a return call, Adam, but you have to see it from Cade's perspective. Maybe he figured if it were important or you were truly upset, you'd tell him that or call back."

"I did."

"I thought you texted him that he should call you when he could? 'Call me when you can' means 'call me when you have a minute,' not 'drop everything and call me.'"

"I said I had a bad night too."

"True, but from what you've told me, I'm guessing Cade's definition of a bad night and your definition of a bad night are pretty far apart. He said he was in the middle of something important. Maybe he was dealing with actual bad shit, not your kind of bad shit. Did you ask what was so important?"

I pouted because, fuck, she was right. "So I'm being selfish?"

"Not selfish. Maybe not clear enough about what you need."

"How can I make myself clear without coming off demanding?"

Rachel thought on that for a second. "It's like when I see patients: I have to listen to their complaint and rapidly identify if I'm dealing with something urgent or something more routine, right?" I nodded and she continued. "If a patient says they have abdominal pain, I can't assume that all abdominal pain is urgent. I can't link the amount of pain someone seems to be in to their diagnosis either, because there are a lot of factors that impact someone's pain tolerance. It could be the guy screaming for narcotics has gas pain, but the quiet woman wincing subtly has an appendix about to rupture. I have to use labs and vitals and other things to make decisions and prioritize. Cade's life sounds like constant triage."

"I'm not following."

"If you need Cade to prioritize your bad day above whatever other crap is going on in his life, you're going to need to stop screaming in pain and start giving him some details. Why did you have a bad day—were you in a near-fatal car wreck? Did your dog die? Or did Dad yell at you? Because with you, he probably assumes it's a Dad-yelled-at-you kind of situation unless you give him something else to work with."

"It was a Dad-yelled-at-me kind of thing."

She laughed. "I figured."

"So, I should let it go? Even if I really needed to talk to him?"

"Do you believe Cade loves you?"

"Yes," I answered without hesitation.

"Then you should probably call him and find out about his ruptured appendix and go from there."

Chapter Sixteen

Adam

"Finally," I said as I flung open the front door, excited beyond reason to score some time with Cade alone. "Oh, hey . . ." I scowled.

"Wow. Way to make a man feel special." Bryan laughed.

I clung to the door jamb enough to ward off any inadvertent invitations. "Sorry. I thought you were Cade. What's up?"

"Ah, yes. The mysterious boyfriend."

"He's not mysterious."

Bryan winked and I had no clue what to make of that. He extended a plastic container toward me. "Cake. As promised."

I stared at it, then him. "Why?"

"Because I'm a sweetheart. I'm also very forgiving." His bottom lip pouted as he held the container toward me, joggling it. When I didn't reach for it, his lip lifted in a slight smirk. Was everything a game to him? "There's two slices in here. They're fresh."

"Bryan, don't take this the wrong way, but I don't want your cakes."

"Well, that's a first." His smirk swept from his mouth to his full face, and I realized what I'd said. "That's— I don't— Like I said: I have a boyfriend. I'm sorry if I gave you the wrong idea . . ."

"Oh, sweetie. Calm down. It's just some dessert. Call it a neighborly gesture if you want." He thrust it at me. "Seriously. Share it with Cade."

"Fine," I said, letting go of the door to accept the container.

"Is that yours?" Bryan pushed past me, making his way to the table to pick up a sketch book I'd left open. "Oh, wow." He picked it up, admiring the bicycle-themed iconography I'd been experimenting with for my project. "I love the bicycle handlebar clocks and this one—using the tires and frame to make an infinity sign. Very cool."

"Thanks. Yeah, that's for the unlimited monthly pass."

"I can't believe you drew these. You're really talented."

"Thanks," I said, taking the sketch pad back from him. To my bewilderment, he took a seat.

"So how was your trip? What was it for again? A wedding?"

"Um . . ." I cast an eye toward the door. A small voice in my head told me I should absolutely get rid of Bryan before Cade arrived, but then I remembered what Sid had said. I wasn't doing anything wrong, so there was no reason to act guilty. Bryan was a neighbor, maybe a little too friendly, but Cade was aware of the situation. I needed to relax and stop acting like I couldn't trust myself around him. "It was good. My brother's promotion, actually. There was a party," I said, shutting the door and taking a seat across from him.

"You have other siblings?" Bryan casually toed his shoes off and tucked his foot under his other thigh, settling in like we were old friends.

"Yeah, my brother has a twin sister." An uncomfortable silence descended as I tried to suss out what was happening. Was he really going to make himself at home?

"Me?" He pressed a palm to his chest, his eyes twinkling playfully. "Thank you for asking. I'm an only child."

I smiled nervously. "That figures."

"Oh yeah? Why do you say that?"

"I don't know. You strike me as someone used to getting a lot of attention. Isn't that an only-child trait?"

"You wound me. Are you saying you don't get enough attention?"

"I didn't say that."

"You did actually. The last time we hung out. You mentioned you were tired of Cade icing you out for his family, before you jammed your tongue in my mouth."

I shifted to the edge of my seat. "Listen, about that . . ."

"It's fine," Bryan said with a dismissive wave. He slunk back into the seat at the same time, like a child who'd been stripped of his video game controller.

Cade often said one thing when his body language was saying something else—nine times out of ten, the body language won. Surely some drunken kissing didn't issue any promises, but what had I said? I'd thought over that night, but the conversation was hazy enough, I couldn't be sure. *Shit.* Had I led him on? Did I owe him an apology? "Look, I'm sorry for giving you the impression I was interested in more than friendship."

Bryan's laugh came out in one loud bellow. "Oh, honey. You are so freaking adorable." Heat flared up my neck while I watched him delight in my confusion. Okay, so he wasn't expecting a marriage proposal, that was good.

"I'm not hurt you don't want to go steady. I confess I am a little disappointed I sent your drunk ass home that night. If I knew there was such a brief window of opportunity . . . You did sort of lead me to believe Cade was an asshole, so I thought I had more time, but I get it. First loves are hard to let go of. My college boyfriend and I did the whole break-up-and-get-back-together thing a few times too. I'm a patient man."

"Cade isn't an asshole. We were in a difficult place, but we figured it out."

"Uh-huh." Bryan's voice pitched higher as he added a mocking tilt to his smile.

"Speaking of Cade, he's going to be here soon. So, thanks for the cake but you should go."

"Wow, he's that touchy, huh?" Bryan stood. If he expected a response to his question, he was going to be disappointed. I stared at him, lips pursed as he slowly shuffled his feet back into his loafers. "What time is he supposed to be here?"

"Seven."

Bryan checked his watch, a rueful grin on his face. "He's late. It's ten after now."

"I don't make him clock in and out," I deadpanned.

"Well, since he's already late, I can keep you company until he gets here. Tell me more about this." He picked up the sketch pad and thumbed through it as he plopped down again.

I hesitated, still annoyed and fighting off doubts that this was all kosher.

"It's fine, Adam. We're neighbors and I'm hoping friends. He allows you to have friends, right? Those guys at the bakery, for example."

"Yeah. It's not . . . Of course, I can have friends."

"Good. So tell me about your trip. Wait. Do you have pictures? I have to know if your brother is as hot as you."

I laughed uncomfortably and pulled up a picture from R.J.'s party: the one of my siblings, Catherine, and I—Rachel in her stunning black sleeveless Versace gown, R.J. in his Tom Ford tux with his arm around Catherine, who was in an emerald-jeweled floor-length gown, and me in the Armani tux that had arrived in my room the morning of the party. I sighed, reliving the defeated feeling I'd had putting it on, but it made my mother happy and Rachel convinced me it was more appropriate attire than my suit.

"Damn. You look amazing," Bryan said. "And what a pity. The hot brother is straight."

"He is." I huffed amusement at the thought of my brother being considered hot, but I guessed R.J. was handsome. "Trust me. His straightness isn't the only part of his personality that you'd find objectionable."

Bryan seemed to have a million and one questions about me, my job, my family and my friends. After a while I realized two things: The first was that Bryan was incorrigible. He flirted, but there didn't seem to be any actual goal behind it other than pushing my boundaries to get a response. The second was how ridiculous I'd been thinking he was a threat. No one, no matter what they said or did, could tempt me to do anything that would put my future with Cade in jeopardy.

Now, if he would hurry up and get here, I could tell him that.

Cade

I fussed with my hair again, although the mirror time I had allowed myself to get ready had already expired. I was late. So late, but the one fucking strand of hair refused to lie flat. Adam deserved the truth. Not merely about my anorexia, but everything else. Honesty was essential to our recovery, but like eating, I wasn't sure I could do it.

Maura knocked. "Cade, it's time."

A fresh jolt of panic rocked me, and I picked up the gel with shaky hands and tried one last time to tame it into submission, before the door opened.

"You look great," she said and promptly turned out the bathroom lights.

"Are you sure you're okay to stay? I can cancel," I said as I left the bathroom.

"I'm actually doing good today. I'm here to use your wi-fi to Skype with Hayley, not because I need a sitter. My mood is stable. No racing thoughts. I slept a full eight hours. The new medicine is working, Cade. You can go out for an evening with your boyfriend. After Hayley calls, I'm going to watch some trashy Lifetime movies."

Maura reassured me she was fine and started talking about arrangements to get Hayley home, but I couldn't concentrate on anything other than the hair on my head taunting me. Calling me ugly. I did my best to ignore it, but in the end, I would not be able to function. I walked back into the bathroom and turned on the lights and the faucet.

"Cade, no," Maura said, but it was too late. I lowered my head into the sink, restarting the entire hair-styling routine from scratch.

"Hand me the shampoo." I twisted to see Maura's disappointment pressed between tight lips. She retrieved the bottle, placing it on the counter with a sigh as she walked from the room. Palming exactly a quarter-size amount between my hands, I scrubbed my scalp. This was the part that always made me want to cry. I would rather go days without eating than see my mother's compulsive behaviors reflected in the mirror.

When I finished washing and drying, the product seemed to do the trick and all the strands on my head lay the way I needed them to. Since I had already failed miserably and my shirt was wet, I undressed in front of the mirror. I touched my arms. *Too gangly.* Turning, I pinched the skin that rolled over my pants. Inhaling a sharp breath, I then exhaled slowly. *It's not fat. It's skin.* I closed my eyes and forced myself to stop.

I found Maura sitting on my bed with my laptop. She said nothing, but the empathetic smile she gave me expressed her considerable concern.

"As much therapy as I've had, you'd think I would understand why my stupid brain uses the food I cram into my mouth each day to fuel my obsessive thoughts."

"It'll get better. You were like this before too. The first time. Remember, I took the mirrors down?"

"I'm having second thoughts about telling him." *Second* seemed conservative. I was well over a million if I counted the actual thoughts.

"You don't have to."

"I think I kind of do. I mean, I was talking about moving in with him. What was I thinking? There's no way I can hide this from him. Look what happened last time."

"Do you . . . Never mind."

"What?"

Maura chewed on her lip for a second before answering. "Do you think if you'd told Adam about your relapse senior year he wouldn't have cheated?"

Wasn't that obvious? "Whenever he mentioned wanting to spend time alone, I avoided him and blamed it on stress and student teaching, but the more I tried to hide it . . ."

"I know. But, Cade, he . . . Just because someone is busy, doesn't mean they deserve to be cheated on. I'm not saying don't forgive him or whatever, but don't blame yourself. Every time you relapse or get a little stressed out, you can't be worried he's going to fuck around on you."

"No. It was more than that. I avoided him so he wouldn't see me like . . ." I pointed to the bathroom. "That." I sat next to her on the bed and hung my head in my hands. I couldn't hide it from Adam. He deserved to hear what he was hitching his wagon to. I was working so hard to stop, but the only thing that made me feel better was restricting and that . . . Well, I'd learned from experience I couldn't hide both things. "Adam not knowing means having to lie to him or avoid him, and I don't want to risk making the same mistakes again."

"If you're sure you can trust him to be supportive. I worry he's going to turn this around on you. Try to blame his cheating on your illness. When he should have known—" Maura's voice cracked as a familiar anguish rose to the surface.

I wrapped my arm around her. "He didn't know because I didn't want him to. Just like you didn't see it because I didn't want you to. I was fifteen: old enough to keep a secret."

She shook her head. "All those times I told you how we needed to watch the food budget. Teased you. I fed that voice in your head."

I sighed and lifted her chin so I could look her in the eyes. "Maura, we've been over this. You didn't trigger my anorexia. You were working two jobs and paying all the bills at eighteen; we barely saw each other, and when we did, I hid myself under baggy clothes because I knew you would make me stop. Okay? Telling you meant I would get help that I wasn't ready for."

"Still . . . it took CPS showing up for me to see my own brother was starving himself to death."

I closed my eyes. To this day the hardest thing I'd ever had to do was admit it wasn't the lack of food in my home that had caused my weight to drop dangerously low. After they tried to blame Maura, I'd had no choice. If I didn't get treatment, they'd put me into the system.

But telling Adam?

I might not be a kid anymore, but confessing the truth to him didn't feel any more voluntary.

My anxiety level dialed up to ten on the drive to Adam's condo, and by the time I pulled into the lot, I was pretty sure it had obliterated the scale I used to assess my fear level.

I turned off the car, grimacing at the wet spots on my steering wheel. How was it possible for hands to be so sweaty? With a deep sigh and a racing heart, I exited the car and set my feet toward the door. A mixture of excitement and dread swam in my belly. For all my mental rehearsing, I needed to see Adam before I could be sure if I could do it. I had to stare into his eyes and well—maybe him wrapping me in his arms and telling me he completely understood wasn't realistic, but I had to at least know he wouldn't get angry, and trust that this wouldn't be the end of whatever we were starting.

Still, that fantasy danced in my head as I approached the door and pressed the buzzer. Once I'd been let in, I climbed the stairs, one at a time, a little tempted to turn around so I could race up and down them until the uncomfortable feeling inside me subsided a little.

"Hey," I breathed as the door opened. "Who the fuck are you?" came out before I realized I recognized him.

BryGuy laughed. "I'm Bryan." He stuck his hand out. "I live next door. You must be the boyfriend. Cade, right?" He tossed out my name like I was a distant aunt who'd been mentioned once in passing conversation between them.

"Yes. Adam mentioned you." *It was my stupid fault for not asking more questions about the flirtatious neighbor, like what his Instagram profile was.*

"It's nice to meet you finally. Adam's in the bathroom, but I promised I'd skedaddle when you arrived, so tell him I said goodbye."

"Sure thing," I said sharply as Adam emerged from the bathroom and hurried toward us.

His smile quickly blossoming, he nudged Bryan out of the way to get to me. "You're here. Fuck, I missed you."

I tried not to stiffen as Adam lifted me off the ground in a hug. There was no way I was giving Bryan the satisfaction of knowing his presence caused me a moment of doubt.

"I missed you too," I said, my eyes drifting closed as Adam pressed my back against the hallway outside his apartment door and lifted my legs around his waist. All right, then. Apparently, we were giving Bryan a little show.

"Well," Bryan said with a chuckle. "I'll leave you two lovebirds alone."

"Bye, Bryan," I called, my voice a little unsteady as Adam worked his way down my neck. Bryan turned back and gave me a face I could only describe as *undeterred.*

When Bryan's door shut, Adam pulled back enough for me to slide my legs down to the floor.

"Bye, Bryan," Adam repeated breathlessly against my lips.

"So, that was Bryan?" I tried to keep concern out of my voice.

He cast a quick glance over his shoulder at Bryan's door. "Let's go inside."

Adam yanked me out of the hallway and shut the door behind us. Licking his lips, he stared at me like it'd been months instead of days since we'd seen each other.

"Damn," Adam said, beaming at me like he didn't have a care in the world. The way his face lit up with a combination of admiration and desire eased some doubt from my mind. I could trust that Adam loved me. There wasn't going to be a better time to say what I needed to say. But before I could signal my desire to talk, Adam announced he had other plans.

"Cade." My name released on a raspy breath as his hands rose to my buckle. "Fuck, I missed you, Gou." His intentions were as evident as his erection—an erection I couldn't help wondering had something to do with Bryan.

"I missed you too, but . . ." I gripped his hips, but the tension in my arms slacked as soon as his mouth found that spot on my neck. He pressed against me, smelling of cologne and sex, slamming the snooze button on my plans for a very unsexy conversation. He brought our lower halves together, and my body felt the moan before it came out of my mouth. I couldn't be expected to stop this. After all the pressure of the week, a chance to forget my problems for a bit sounded terrific. And when it came to sex, I trusted Adam to get me out of my head.

"But what, Gou?" He made quick work of my zipper and pushed the fabric out of his way. His expression managed to be both concerned and determined as he lowered to his knees.

Fuck it. The conversation could wait. "Nothing. Carry on."

He grinned brightly. The first tease of his tongue nearly made my knees buckle. Adam peered up, eyes framed by long lashes, finding mine. He drew his hand up to my chest, holding me still as he took me deep.

"Shit," I moaned as my chest heaved against his palm. On instinct, I rocked forward, chasing the pleasure. "Yeah. Like that."

Adam pulled off. "Don't come," he breathed and resumed his work, running his tongue over the head before swallowing me again and again.

I nodded, with no thought given to my ability to actually comply. It felt too good. I leaned over, needing to touch him. To explore the hard planes of his body. I gripped the cotton clinging to his back and lifted, quickly meeting an obstacle.

He laughed with his mouth full, the vibration reverberating down to my balls and up my spine. Amused, he gave a tiny shake of his head and a wicked brush of his tongue at the sensitive spot under the head as he refused to stop so I could get him naked.

"C'mon. Lose the shirt."

He pulled off and huffed, the cool air hitting my spit-slicked member as Adam ripped his T-shirt over his head. Before I realized he was indulging me, I was inside him again, enveloped in warmth and wet. I licked my upper lip and peered down at the unobstructed view revealed to me. Every muscle tensed and flexed. "Fuck." My cock throbbed as I reached for him again.

Adam slurped and sucked harder. I gave in to the need to hold his hair, pulling him toward me and fucking deeper into his mouth, dancing along the edge between good and too good.

"Oh, fuck. Babe, I want . . . Stop." I gasped and pushed his head away, breathing heavy, toes and fingers curled as though they were the only thing keeping me from falling over.

Adam's lean, muscular body rose before me. Defined pecs and built arms. His body was so incredibly different from mine. That awareness momentarily chased away the happy, lust-drunk space in my brain, and the doubts flooded back as Adam peeled my shirt free and caressed my soft doughy skin. *Why couldn't I have been built like him?*

"Let's go to bed." Adam kissed me, hands searching out the globes of my ass. He massaged them, squeezing hard while my pants fluttered to the floor. One slight kick and I was untethered from the fabric.

Adam wasted no time, lifting me up again, manhandling me to his room, kissing the entire way. We crashed onto the bed, and I rubbed a hand over my aching cock while Adam finished stripping. He flicked open the button of his shorts and removed them.

"Lift your legs up," Adam ordered in the authoritative tone that always made me shiver. He kneeled on the bed. His long, hard torso loomed over me as he slid his thighs under my parted knees. He lowered his head and drew his tongue across my right nipple before scraping his teeth along the same path.

"Jesus," I whimpered. I pushed my worries beneath the surface and kissed my way up his neck and nipped at his earlobe.

One hand braced him as he stretched over me; the other he shoved roughly between me and the mattress, reaching until his fingers slid closer to their target.

"*Ahh*, Adam. Fuck."

"Feel good, baby? Let me hear you."

A strained sound escaped my lips as Adam slid a long finger into me and rocked against me. His head crashed to my shoulder, long, wet kisses pressed to my neck and jawline as he thrust one digit inside me, teasing me open.

Adam's erection pressed against my belly. "I want it," I groaned and struggled to carve enough space to reach it. Adam chuckled but removed his finger and lifted to make room for my hand. My fingers curved around his thick shaft, and his blazing stare sent tingles up my spine as I stroked the velvet rod already slicked with his pre-come.

"Mm-hmm." Adam hummed approvingly, flicking his hips forward, fucking into my fist more urgently.

"Yeah, baby. Take us both." Adam shifted upward, clenching one hand on top of his headboard so I could grasp his cock and mine. He rocked forward. "Oh God. Fuck."

For all my English studies, he reduced my vocabulary to grunts and moans to describe how good it felt.

"Yeah, get there. Baby, come all over me." Adam's demanding, strained voice was so hot, I had no choice but to comply. Two more strokes and I was done for.

Adam's upper body lurched forward, his muscled arm shooting out to brace himself as his cock throbbed in my hand and his orgasm spilled out onto my belly. I barely pulled my hand free, before Adam fell in a boneless heap on top of me.

"Oomph," I cried as I accepted his full weight. Every inch of him pressed against me, I lifted my legs to cradle his hips and rested my feet on his back. Holding him like that—all sleepy and satiated, skin flushed red from exertion, made my chest feel like it couldn't expand. But the heaviness had nothing to do with Adam's dead weight. How could I tell him? It would ruin everything.

"You okay?" Adam said, lifting his head to kiss my cheek. He tapped my thigh and rolled off of me. I grabbed his hand and held it against my chest.

"Yeah," I lied.

"You sure? You went all emo on me for a second. Not upset about Bryan, are you?"

I bit my lip. This was my chance. If I were going to deflect, I could bring up the Instagram comments, make it an entire thing about him not defending me, defending us. Probably work myself up until I was convinced that's why I was pissed off. Turn it into a hell of a fight, and then I wouldn't have to feel all this guilt. That was what I always did. I avoided dealing with my behavior by turning everything around on him. God, I was such a shitty person. "No. I'm glad you told me about him so I knew what was going on, and I'm not sure you could have made a stronger 'I'm not interested' play if you tried."

Adam rolled onto his side and gasped. "You mean to say, I actually did something fucking right for a change? What day is it?" He grabbed his phone. "I need to mark this date down for history books."

When I shoved his shoulder, he fell back to the mattress laughing, but I wasn't happy. Bryan was right: Adam could absolutely do better. *Why had I let him believe it was all his fault?* He wasn't perfect, but he wasn't a horrible boyfriend. I mean all he wanted to do was be close to me and spend time together. He'd proven he wanted me over and over, and I . . . "Hey, come here. I want to hold you."

Adam rolled back, flashing a sleepy smile, and tucked himself under my arm, resting his head on my chest. Without thinking, I combed my fingers through his hair.

"It's good, right?" Adam asked, peeking up at me. "Us? We're doing good."

"Yeah," I agreed. My heart rate sped up to match the pace of my thoughts, fear cascading through my body down to shaky hands.

"So, you still want to do that thing?"

I inclined my head, thoughts too consumed by what I had to do, to even guess what he was talking about. "What thing?"

"The clinic. Getting tested."

I swallowed around my dry mouth. *What if?* He wouldn't cheat on me as long as we were like this: naked and not fighting. But what happened if I couldn't get back to recovery? Or if I didn't want to have sex? If I told him and . . . Would it be Mexico all over again?

"Cade, look at me."

Adam pulled my chin toward him, and I couldn't do it. I couldn't lie to him. But I couldn't tell him either. Not yet. Not when we were still so fragile. When my recovery was so precarious. The anxiety took over and suddenly my eyes were burning.

"You still don't trust me, do you?"

Adam's vulnerability was so genuine, I resented him for it. "I didn't say that," I snapped.

Adam sat up suddenly, the old familiar wall slamming down between us. "But you don't?"

I felt his hurt, his devastation. He wielded it over me like a sword, the tip poking the surface, puncturing me. Guilt spilled out, flowing from a wound too exposed to hide and too personal to show. I wasn't ready. "Why do you have to push?"

"I'm not pushing. You suggested getting tested before I left for Atlanta. Why are you acting like I'm an asshole all of a sudden?"

"Don't put words in my mouth. I came over here and found you with another guy. I'm allowed to change my mind."

Adam sighed. "I just . . ." He took a deep breath, and his eyes welled red. His voice was shaky but decisive. "I asked you if it upset you. Why didn't you tell me it was bothering you? We could have talked about it first."

The words flew out of my mouth: angry, hateful, and altogether the opposite of what I wanted to be saying. "Maybe because you molested me the second I walked in the door." I stood up, searching for clothes that weren't in the room. The wounded quiver of Adam's lip pierced me again. "I need to go. Where the fuck are my pants?" *Later. I would try again later.*

Adam stood and came to my side of the bed, sitting with a sad, exhausted sigh. "Please don't leave like this. I want to understand what's happening. Please talk to me. Gou—"

"I've asked you a million times not to call me that. I'm not . . ." Of course, my pants were by the front door. I zipped past him into the hallway.

"Cade, please. Stop." Adam's footsteps trailed me.

I lifted one leg to slide into my pants and nearly fell over. My balance wasn't great on an average day, but the woozy feeling had me stumbling naked toward the side table. Adam shot a hand out to steady me. "Are you okay?"

Even in my worst moments, he cared. *Why would he care about you? You're a piece of shit. You don't deserve him.* "I'm fine."

"Cade, don't lie to me. You're not fine. Talk to me." Adam pushed himself against the door to keep me from leaving.

"I need to think, okay? Can I please have some goddamn space to think? You always do this. I tell you not to push and you keep doing it."

Adam tossed his head back, hitting the back of the door with a thud. "Cade. This is not pushing. This is me trying to communicate. I don't understand what the fuck is happening right now. We had amazing sex and you're storming out of here because . . . Why? Stop treating me like I'm some fucking guy you met on Grindr instead of your boyfriend. It's like I can hear the *clank, clank, clank* of the goddamn roller coaster climbing the track, but this time, I don't understand how I got on the damn ride."

"Then move out of the way, so one of us can get off."

"You don't mean that."

I shrugged, my eyes hot with tears.

"Please tell me why?"

"It's like Bryan said, you deserve better."

Confusion clouded his face. "What are you talking about? Did he say something to you?"

"Like you don't know. Now, move." I reached for the doorknob, but Adam swatted away my hand.

"Cade, I seriously do not understand what you are talking about. I've done nothing wrong and you're not leaving until you explain where your head is at."

"Adam. Please—"

The buzzer to the outer door interrupted me. While Adam was staring at me, it rang again.

"You going to get that?" I asked.

"Are you going to bolt the second I step away?"

The buzzer rang again, and this time it sounded like someone was leaning on it. Adam's eyebrows drew together in concern, but he wasn't moving from the door. I sighed, walking over to the window to see who was at the building's front door.

I gasped, my heart slamming against my chest. "Oh, fuck. It's Maura. Let her in."

Without hesitation, Adam scrambled to the intercom and pushed the button.

Chapter Seventeen

Cade

"I'll get some pants on," Adam said, rushing toward his bedroom as the outside door clicked shut. I nodded, a little surprised at how Adam's concern seemed to match mine. Even manic, Maura wasn't one to come over to his place, not without calling.

I opened the door, and waited for Maura. She rushed up the stairs, eyes red and tears streaming down her face. "She's not coming back."

She dissolved into my arms and Adam rushed back into the room and helped me get her inside. When he released her to shut the door, I struggled under her full weight.

"Maura." I sunk with her to the floor. "Calm down. Who's not coming back? What happened?"

"Aislinn." She heaved out each word between loud sobs. "Call. Hayley."

"What happened?" I repeated.

Adam glared at me, giving me my own *why are you saying stupid things* look. "Let her calm down first. She can't answer questions when she's hyperventilating. Let's get her to the couch." Adam picked her up and assisted her. I kneeled in front of her, smoothing the hair out of her face and imagining the worst.

"Not. My. Fault," she gasped out.

"Okay, Sis. Calm down. Breathe."

Adam soothed her back and encouraged her to calm down, something she'd always done for me when I was a kid. Why? Why did he have to be so perfect now? "I'll get you some water," I offered. I didn't know if it would work, but at least it made me feel useful and gave me a minute to catch my breath.

It took at least twenty minutes to get Maura to stop sobbing, then another few minutes of deep breaths before she could speak. Adam and I worked together, but it was Adam who took the lead. Asking gentle questions until I'd pieced together a few things. The primary one being that Aislinn had threatened to call CPS on her. The second being that Adam was a rock in a crisis, which rubbed salt in the festering guilt wound.

"Better?" I asked as I handed Maura the water cup.

She sipped it and forced a grateful smile. "Thank you. I'm sorry, I didn't know what to do. She can't do this, can she? She can't keep my daughter without my permission."

"Not without a court order," Adam said. "Tell us what happened from the beginning."

Maura nodded and took a small breath to regain her composure. "Hayley didn't call me tonight like she was supposed to, so I called Aislinn and she was being all cagey. She wouldn't let me talk to Hayley. I heard James's voice." At the mention of Aislinn's father, Maura's voice went cold. She turned toward me. "Aislinn promised me Hayley wouldn't be around them. I told her she needed to put Hayley on the next flight home or I was coming to get her."

"Maura, I know how you feel about James, but Hayley is perfectly safe there."

"No, James hated Mom and he hates me too. He's trying to take her away from me."

I sighed. Although it wasn't true in the slightest, it's what she believed. James would always be the man who took away her baby sister. She could never let it go, no matter how Aislinn had benefited because he had. "What did Aislinn say?"

"She said that Hayley would be better off staying with her until we were healthy. But I told her you had your anorexia under control, and it wasn't as bad as the last time. You probably don't need inpatient treatment again or even that day program. And I was taking my medicine and my moods were better. She kept saying we weren't capable of taking care of ourselves let alone Hayley and that she was sure child protective services would agree. Cade, if she calls them, and they call the school. Do you think? Is she right? This can't happen, can it?"

"No, of course not. Can we talk to your dad?" I looked over at Adam, instantly alarmed by his pale color and the trench of horizontal lines across the center of his forehead. "What's the matter?"

"What is she talking about?" There was an alarm to his voice that set every hair on my body on end.

I glanced back at Maura. Her eyes grew wide as she clasped a hand over her mouth. "Oh, fuck. Cade, I'm so sorry. I didn't mean to—"

"What is she talking about, Cade? What . . ." He threw his hands up and bolted from the couch. My panic boiled over as I scrambled to my feet, as if getting to him could stop him from putting together the pieces.

"Adam, I'm sorry." He fought my attempts to touch him, but the second he'd put it together, his face was so ice cold a chill ran down my spine.

"When, Cade?" His face contorted from betrayal. Every decision, every mistake boomeranged back toward me. *This is karma for keeping him longer than you deserved.*

"Adam . . ." I begged, my heart slamming against my chest.

"When?" he demanded in an anguish cry. "When were you in the hospital? What is she talking about?" His hand flew to his hair, and he raked it over his head and began to pace. I tried again to reach him, but he recoiled like the touch of my skin burned him. "Goddamn it, Cade. When?"

I forced myself to face the daggers darting from his eyes and his quivering jaw, but then I couldn't find the words, so I did the only thing I could do. Eyes cast down in shame, I nodded to confirm his suspicions. Tell him exactly who he'd wasted time loving all these years. I owed him that much. "I'm so sorry."

He made a strangled noise. "You sent me to Mexico thinking you didn't want me when you were sick and you're sorry? You fucking lied. How long did I miss it? Huh? How long have you kept this from me? Does Sid know? Does everyone know?"

I shook my head, desperate to stop him from thinking the worst. "No. No one knows other than my sisters. I wanted to tell you. I swear. I thought I was better. I'll explain everything, I promise." I reached for his shirt. If he would only look at me. I could stop the voice. Adam always wanted me. He valued me. I was worth something to him, and if I lost that . . . "Please let me explain. I'm so sorry." I fell to my knees, begging.

Maura gasped, rising to stand beside me. "Adam, it's not Cade's fault."

Adam backed away, glaring at Maura as she pulled me back to my feet. "Like hell it's not. Jesus. You two. Do you ever take responsibility for anything?"

"I do," I said. "It was my decision. Blame me. I take responsibility."

"You . . ." Adam shook his head. "I can't. Wow. I just can't." Adam ran his hands through his hair again, tugging at the ends, face beet red. He shook his head again, then moved, like he was searching for something. I followed him, still pleading for a chance to make it right. When he snatched his keys from his dresser, an angry scrape across the wood, my fight-or-flight response kicked in and I jumped in front of him. Fuck not having the perfect words, I had to do something. I had to stop him from leaving.

"Move," Adam yelled.

"I can't. Not until you give me a chance to explain. You said I could trust you. Communication. Leaning in. You promised no matter what I could trust you this time."

Maura made a disagreeable noise from the hallway behind me. "Cade, I need you to call Aislinn."

Adam's gaze shifted over my head to Maura, and he huffed. "She's right. You should deal with this first." He extended his arm to move me out of his way, but I caught it and held on to it as tight as I could.

"No," I cried. "You're important to me. Hayley is safe. Aislinn would never hurt her. I really wanted to tell you. I've been trying. I swear. I didn't know how. I never meant to hurt you. Please. Please don't leave like this. I don't think I can take it. Please give me a chance to make it right. You said I can trust you, and I need you to listen. That's it, okay. Please listen."

Adam rocked back on his heels. I appreciated the exact words he was biting his lips to keep from saying. I had some nerve. All the times I'd accused him of emotional manipulation, but here I was willing to say and do whatever to make him stay. "Please." The tears started with no warning. I was desperate, I had to show him. "Maura, you need to go home. Nothing is going to happen tonight, okay? I'll call Aislinn once Adam and I talk."

She glared at me for a minute, tapping her finger on her lip, like she was trying to decide how serious I was. The determined tilt of her chin didn't diminish in the slightest. "This is about Hayley. We need to figure it out now."

"No, Maura," I said, a surge of courage and determination coursing through me. I locked my eyes on Adam's, unconcerned with anything except making sure he knew I could change. "You're my priority. Do you hear me? You. I should never have made you feel otherwise." Praying he knew me well enough to believe me, because it was all true, I turned to face my sister. "I can't do this alone, Maura. I'm not like you. I need him. If you need me to help with Hayley, then I need him. I can't be strong for you and Hayley without him."

She stared at me for a minute, but slowly the big sister I'd been missing for years—the one who worked double shifts to buy me shoes and put me in the closet when our mother was drunk—returned. She nodded, her eyes full of understanding and compassion. "Okay."

"Maura, are you sure?" Adam asked.

She nodded as she spoke to him. "Cade's right. You two should talk first."

When Adam didn't argue, I exhaled relief. "Adam and I are going to take a walk, then I'll come back to help figure it out."

"We both will."

My head whipped back toward Adam, hope swelling. "Are you sure?"

His eyes softened. "Yeah. I care about Hayley. If I can help, I will."

"Thank you." I launched up to my toes to kiss him, but he stopped me with a hand to my chest and shook his head.

"I'll hear you out. That's all I'm promising right now."

I fell back to my feet and let that sink in. We weren't yelling anymore, but in his eyes . . . there was so much confusion and pain. So much betrayal. "Okay."

"Maura?" Adam asked. "You sure you'll be okay for a few minutes?"

"Yeah. Go on. I'll wait."

Adam led me outside. We walked down the path that led to the middle school adjacent to my high school. Past a playground, tennis courts, and several benches. I struggled to keep up with Adam's stride, but he'd said nothing, and since I had no idea how to begin, I followed silently. My heart rate was fast, so fast that I felt the sensation of missing beats and my breaths were shallow and quick. When the path gave way to the blacktop of the parking lot. I stopped him with a tug on his arm, using the other to grip the fence post. "Adam, can we sit? I'm not really supposed to be exercising."

His eyes narrowed. "You're not? You go to the gym all the time. Or is that a lie too?"

"No," I said. "It's not a lie. I . . . There's a lot I need to tell you. When it all started—"

"Which was when exactly?"

"Probably birth," I said glibly, but my attempt at levity was met with a scoff, so I regrouped. "Maura and I experienced some things with my mother that I haven't told you, but as for my eating disorder, that started when I was in high school."

"High school? Jesus, Cade. So, the entire time we were together. All those nights. I thought we talked about everything. I told you everything and you were keeping something this big from me?"

"No," I said, but flinched at the way his eyes narrowed. "Well, yes. But my symptoms weren't active when we met. It didn't start out as a secret. I had put it behind me. I tried to put it all behind me, but . . . it's painful, okay? Who wants to talk about their mom taking off? The first time, I was thirteen. She left us for five days. We had no money, no way to eat, no means to get to the store. Maura and I had no idea when or if she'd come back."

"But you were sick when we were together too. How could you keep that from me?"

"I didn't want to—"

Before I could even attempt to justify my behavior, Adam's dubious eyes narrowed on me again, stopping my words cold. The cloud of his suspicion was every bit as thick as the one we'd stood under the day he got back from Mexico. *Was this how he felt?* Would anything I say about this ever be enough? I closed my eyes, trying to remember what I'd needed from him the night he confessed his infidelity. What had I wanted to hear? *Why? Why had he done it?* I opened my eyes and took a deep breath. For him to fully understand, I couldn't hold anything back, which meant explaining things I'd never been strong enough to explain to anyone.

"Can we please sit? I'll tell you everything."

Adam nodded and when I lowered to the ground with my back to the fence, he sat next to me. It was easier that way, side-by-side, not having to look at the hurt in his eyes.

"It started as a way to help. Maura got a job, but I was too young, so . . . I created a sort of game to see how little I could eat, but the less I ate, the better I felt. I could go days without eating, and it gave me this sense of control. I don't know the best way to explain it other than it made me proud. When my mom came back and moved in her new boyfriend, we had plenty of food again, but I didn't want to stop. It was this thing I had for myself."

"Cade," Adam breathed. I peered up, and already the doubt lines had eased. There was so much tenderness in his expression. Sympathy I in no way deserved.

"Don't do that. I don't want forgiveness because you pity me. You should be furious."

Adam's jaw hardened and his spine went rigid. "Why don't you stick to telling me what you have to tell me and then let me decide how I feel about it for a change?"

Like it'd done a million times before, my body kicked into overdrive and readied itself for defense. To fight back. To say something so cruel and hateful that I wouldn't have to face my own culpability. But there was no point. The truth was out. My heightened senses zeroed in on Adam, and when I searched his eyes, I found only a hard stare and the truth. I'd never respected Adam's feelings as much as he'd deserved. If I had, we never would have broken up in the first place. I had an unnatural, almost painful, awareness of my throat muscles as they worked to gulp down my harsh response. "I don't deserve your pity," I whispered.

"All you're getting from me is a willingness to listen. Because I do owe you that much. After all these years, all we've shared. I'm not . . . Just because I didn't storm out on you like you've done to me a million times, don't think we're all good. You said you could explain, now is your chance."

I nodded, again swallowing painfully around the lump in my throat. "When Maura turned eighteen, my mom took off for good. It didn't matter at that point, really. She wasn't around much and when she was, she took more than she gave. Her heroin addiction was all that mattered to her. Financially, Maura had things under control. She worked out a deal with the landlord, told him that mom and I had moved, but she would finish the lease if he let her change to a one bedroom. We did okay for a few months and flew under the radar. Maura was waitressing full-time, so I was alone a lot and figuring out I was gay. I'd see these guys in videos or what have you. Their bodies were so perfect, so I started working out. Then it was like this whole extra thing. Some guys at school would give me pointers. Eat this food or that, try these exercises. Everything they said became like the gospel to me. One of them told me I needed to add more lean meat and fewer carbs if I wanted to put on muscle, so I stopped eating red meat and all carbs. Another told me that burpees were a great exercise, so I woke up in the middle of the night to do more and more. Before long, I couldn't stop. Maura noticed I was losing weight, but I couldn't see it. I didn't look like the guys on the internet, the sexy guys, the guys who seemed happy."

I braved a glance at Adam, who nodded for me to continue.

"I screwed up. I skipped school to go see Aislinn. Her school called her dad, then he called to talk to my mother. We put him off as long as we could, but once he realized she'd taken off, we were busted. He got his lawyer to end my mother's visitation, even though she hadn't exercised it in over a year. He hired some investigator, who told us she'd died from an overdose weeks before. Child protective services came and took me."

"Cade," Adam gasped, but I kept going, sure that if I stopped, I wouldn't be able to finish.

"They tried to say Maura starved me, but it wasn't true. She brought home food for me every night and I had free meals at school, I simply couldn't eat. The social worker said if I cooperated with treatment, then she would help Maura petition to be my guardian. I was nearly sixteen at that point. We'd been taking care of ourselves for more than a year. So, that's how I got diagnosed and how I recovered initially. When I got out of the hospital, Maura was still blaming herself, and then she got pregnant, so I had to be better. For her. For Hayley. And I was. I felt like it was over. Until senior year . . ." I stopped to catch my breath and readied myself to explain what had made complete sense to me at the time, but now? That was the thing about anorexia: my thinking was so distorted by it.

Adam's pale face had turned practically green. "You cut me off at the knees, Cade. You hid all this from me. I don't understand why you couldn't tell me. Did you think I wouldn't understand?"

"Adam, it wasn't that. I . . . I don't really have a good handle on when the negative thoughts start to become a problem. Maura was depressed. Hayley was starting school. Student teaching hadn't started off well. I'd embarrassed myself at your grandparents' party. There were all kinds of moments, but I remember one right at the start of the year. We were leaving the gym. This kid—a freshman, he came up to you and asked you for directions, so fresh-faced and pretty. I felt so ugly and gross. The way you gawked at him, like a shiny object. I thought I would lose you, and you were the best thing in my life."

"So it's my fault?"

"God, no. Adam, that was one straw, there were a million of them. Okay? What I'm saying is I don't know which one finally broke me. I was stressed and I didn't like who I was. When I got out of the hospital, I'd learned I couldn't have the athletic build I wanted, so I thought I had embraced my body type. Twinks were sexy, so I . . . You saw how I tried to fit that stereotype in college, but it never felt like me. It was all an act. With you, I'd stopped pretending. I could just be me, but anorexia . . . sometimes it's like this voice in my head. That year it kept telling me I'd feel stronger if I lost a few inches off my waist, then it became something I had to do, or all these bad things would happen. I had to look more like that guy. I didn't want to be naked around you because the voice told me I'd disgust you if I didn't lose weight."

"I begged you for attention, not for sex. I wanted to be let in. This doesn't make any sense. I never told you to lose weight. Why couldn't you tell me?"

"The thing about anorexia is it doesn't make any sense. The entire disorder is irrational, and the more you starve yourself, the less capable you are of rational thought. I can't explain it any better. I wish I could. I wish I could explain every decision, but I can't because I don't even understand them. By the spring semester, I couldn't keep it up. Maura was on to me over Christmas break and I didn't want to go back to the hospital, so I tried to stop. We made plans for Mexico, and I told myself I would get better and we'd be back on track, but I couldn't do it on my own. When I told my therapist what was happening, she recommended intensive outpatient, which is this all-day program, but I had to finish my student teaching or I wouldn't graduate, so I bailed on our trip. I planned to tell you when you got back, after I was better, but well . . . you know."

"And now?"

"Now? Now I'm back in recovery and getting treatment again."

"Would you have told me? If Maura hadn't."

"I was planning to tell you tonight. That's why I was late. I . . . When I'm not restricting, sometimes I deal with the voice in other ways. Tonight, it was my hair not lying flat. Other times it's my clothes or my face or my environment. I get a little obsessed with one imperfection or another."

"But in Hawaii. You were sick, weren't you? That's why you fainted. God, Cade . . . I missed all the signs." He dropped his head into his hands.

"Hey, don't, okay?" I rose to my knees, forcing myself into his space as I pulled his arms apart and straddled his lap. "You missed nothing. I hid them from you. From everyone. Maura, Sid . . . I'm good at hiding it. I'm good at changing the subject. I've learned how to eat enough to keep people from noticing. You didn't see it because I didn't want you to. That's it."

"But you passed out. Don't tell me I shouldn't have known."

"Adam, it's not your fault. I promise you. Baby, I . . . Blame me, okay? Don't put this on you. I can't live with the guilt anymore. I blamed you for everything, but it wasn't you and I'm so sorry."

"Cade, you don't understand. I'm not blaming. I feel like a complete idiot. I was supposed to be good at this. You. This is what I was good at. Loving you and I didn't even know? I thought we were special. I thought I fucked up this amazing relationship, but it was never amazing. You didn't stop trusting me when I cheated—you never trusted me. How can we have a relationship if you can't trust me with something like this?"

"Adam, no. Please don't say that. I'm trying."

"Are you, Cade? Because I can't help thinking before Maura came over you were going to leave and let me believe it was because of Bryan."

"I know." The words came with stabbing pain in my heart. Because he was right. I'd been so afraid of me, I'd been willing to hurt him intentionally.

"So explain that to me. How do you love me and let me continuously beat myself up about something that's not real? God, Cade . . . do you realize how fucked up that is? How fucked up we are?"

"I'm the one who fucked up." We'd made so many mistakes, but Adam and I . . . we weren't fucked up. I refused to accept it. The love I felt for him, it was real. It was solid. As solid as the pavement under my feet. I could trust it. "I'm sorry. I know I hurt you, but I didn't know how to tell you, and I was afraid of losing you. We were doing so much better at first, and I didn't want to ruin what we were building. You deserved better from me, but please give me a chance. I'll be better. I'll lean in this time, I promise."

Adam wiped under his eyes, and I didn't know what to say when he didn't respond. After a long stretch of silence, both of us sniffling and wiping away tears as fast as they arrived, Adam's breath stuttered. My eyes lifted to find his quivering upper lip had stiffened. His eyes hardened like he was determined to feel no more emotion. "Is there more?"

"More?" I repeated, terrified that after voicing all these memories I hardly let myself think about, it still wasn't enough. *What more could I say? What more did he need to hear?* His body language stayed unreadable. I didn't buy the coldness he was trying to project, but he'd never attempted to hide his emotions from me before, and I didn't take it as a good sign. "Tell me what you need. I'll do it," I begged.

He shook his head, seemingly unhappy with my comment. When he spoke, his voice was full of ache. "I need to process all this, but is there anything else? Because I don't think I can handle any more surprises. You're in recovery now, right? That's what you said, so you're getting help."

"Um, I'm seeing my doctor, but I haven't started therapy quite yet. I will though. Soon."

"Cade . . ." His voice was firm but kind, and I found hope in his exasperation. At least it was a sign he still cared.

"I'll call one tomorrow," I said. "I want to get better, Adam. I swear I do."

He glanced away, but not before I saw the guilt written all over his face. It was the same look Maura always had when we discussed my anorexia. I slipped a hand over his cheek to make certain he'd heard me earlier. "None of this is your fault. You didn't know because I kept it from you."

He shook his head in a clear but unspoken declaration that he wasn't prepared to discuss it anymore. The desire to stop him from blaming himself was overwhelming. I didn't want him to feel guilty, but I couldn't demand it. No more than he could demand that I forgive him. Adam got to feel however he wanted to feel about my lies; all I could do was let him process everything in his own time and pray he'd forgive me. "I'm truly sorry that I couldn't tell you. You were . . . are the most important person in my life, Adam. I should have leaned into that. I don't know why I didn't."

Adam's concerned eyes found mine. "Whatever happens, I want you to be healthy. If your doctor tells you to do something, I need you to do that."

"I will," I promised.

He nodded, then pushed on my hips, easing me off his lap so he could stand. He brushed the dust from his shorts and, extending a hand, he helped me to my feet and started walking back toward the building. When we got to the entrance, he used his key and pushed the door open.

I hesitated. "So are we . . . Are we . . . okay? We've never talked through a fight before, and I don't understand what you need from me. Am I supposed to leave now or stay?"

He raked a hand through his hair. "Honestly, Cade, I don't know where we go from here, but Maura is waiting for us, so let's deal with that."

"I . . . That thing you said in Hawaii. About our last ride on the roller coaster." I bit my lip. "Did you mean that . . . or . . ." I couldn't even say the words. "Do you still love me?"

Adam sighed. "I wouldn't be here if I didn't, Cade. I . . . It's not like before, okay? I'm not going to run out and sleep with someone else. I'll help with your sister the best I can. But I . . . I'm fucking hurt and angry and worried. And I need time to sort everything out and figure out what I want."

"So like a time-out?"

Adam's lips quirked up slightly as his face searched for a lighthearted smile and came up short. He shifted his weight to his other foot and played with his keys, avoiding my eye contact. "Yeah. I'm asking for a time-out."

My breath caught. "How long?"

He sighed, his patience clearly wearing thin. "I wish I knew. Can we please go deal with your sister right now?"

Unsure of what else to say and unwilling to push any more, I nodded and followed him inside.

Adam

"Maura," Cade called as we walked back into my condo. For a brief moment, I allowed myself to consider she had worked everything out on her own and had gone home. My head was spinning, and I discovered a guilty conscience was one hell of a DJ. *How did I not know? How could I have not seen how thin he was?*

Peace and quiet sounded awfully fucking fantastic right about now.

Cade walked back into the living room, the color drained from his face, but all I could focus on was his appearance. *Were his cheeks always that gaunt?* I sighed. "Now what?"

"Did you . . . You didn't by any chance knock over the bookshelf in the room you made for Hayley did you?"

"What? No. Why?"

Grimacing, he bit his lip. "I think Maura might have misinterpreted the gesture and, um, left."

I closed my eyes and massaged my temples, where the cadence and intensity of the throbs ratcheted up to nausea-inducing levels. "Misinterpreted how?"

"Well, considering she came over here tonight thinking Aislinn was trying to take her daughter and found a room in your condo made up for an eleven-year-old girl, I imagine she thinks we're somehow trying to take her daughter away too."

"Jesus Christ. So she, what, trashed it and took off? How did she know that wasn't for one of my nieces?"

Cade pouted briefly, and as always, defended Maura without hesitation. "She didn't trash it. She knocked over the bookshelf. I'll clean it up. You don't have a niece."

"Well, Maura doesn't know that, does she?"

"Of course she does. You think I don't talk to my sister about you? I've been in love with you since I was eighteen. Just because you two didn't exactly hang out, doesn't mean she doesn't knows who you are. I tell her everything."

By the edge to his voice, I could tell Cade had no idea how much that hurt me. I shook my head, trying to keep the frustration off my face. Toes curling, clinging to the edge of the slippery slope that was Cade's sister. I needed to focus on the situation at hand. Triage, as Rachel called it, but I couldn't let it go. The words exploded from me. "Yeah, her, but not me. Don't you think that's part of our problem?"

Cade stared at the floor. I couldn't see his face, but there was plenty of answer in his silence. With every second that ticked by, I grew more defensive. I was quite sure he was going to blow me off. Tell me I was wrong, or stupid for thinking we could ever have that kind of relationship. But he didn't. He stayed silent. When he met my gaze, I recognized we were in an unfamiliar place. A more honest place and I might finally get an answer to the question that had haunted me. *Would he ever truly forgive me?*

"Well, don't you? I mean, I thought we were in love and I'm apparently not trustworthy enough to hear you had an eating disorder in high school, so—"

He cleared his throat and his neck turned splotchy red. "I thought I didn't have to choose." His voice was so pained, it cracked under the pressure. Pressure I was applying.

I tossed my hands in the air as frustrated by his lack of an answer as I was at myself for not being able to let the conversation die. At least for tonight. "You don't. I'm grateful Maura was there for you. I guess what I'm really asking is . . . Maura's lied to you, she's unreliable, she makes these huge fucking messes. Hell, she comes over tonight and spills this enormous secret, dropped a bomb into the middle of our relationship, and you still trust her implicitly. You defend her. Why her? Why does she get this ginormous benefit of the doubt about everything and I don't? Why does she get your trust back so easily every fucking time and I don't?"

Cade's face fell and I braced myself for the blowback. It maybe wasn't even a fair question to ask. He was sick and his family was in a crisis, but I was so tired of not knowing. Why? *Why didn't he trust me enough? Why couldn't he forgive me? Why couldn't we get this right?*

Cade's whole body tensed, but there no anger in his response. "Because I know she won't leave. She'll never leave me. Ever. No matter what I say or do."

His words were so honest, so unexpected that they took a few seconds to fully process. When they did, it took the temperature out of mine, leaving only dismay. "But you think I will?"

When his chin finally lifted, there were tears tracks down his cheeks. He shrugged. "I don't deserve to be loved like you love me, Adam. Don't you get that?"

My heart ached for the child inside of Cade that I knew believed that, but I had no idea where that left us. No matter how many times we'd tried, we'd never been able to figure it out. If I ended things, it'd only feed that voice telling him he wasn't worthy of love, which of course he was. But how could I make a relationship work with someone who couldn't trust my love for them? How could we go on like that? "That doesn't answer my question."

"Yes. Okay? Eventually. My life is messy and complicated, but yours doesn't have to be. Why would anyone want this? You could have so much better—"

"Stop," I shouted, fed up with the gaslighting. If Cade couldn't trust me, then I'd have to accept that, but he didn't get to turn this around and make this some sort of noble act on his part. "You don't get to tell me what I want or need. All I ever wanted was you."

"You have me. I swear."

But I didn't have him. At least, not like I wanted. Not like Brady and Josh. Maybe I never had, but I loved him. "Cade, come here."

He came toward me, looking every bit as emotionally wrung out as I felt. The entire thing was completely untenable.

"I don't think—" With uncertain eyes, he lowered himself next to me on the couch, and I grabbed his hands in mine. My chest clenched with what I needed to say. "We've been trying to make this work for so long—"

"Adam, no. Please. You're angry. I get it, but we can fix it. I know we can."

I shook my head, but the desperation in his voice was something I hadn't exactly expected. It was more than that, too. We'd never made it this far into a fight without him saying something hateful. Usually, one of us would have stormed away hours ago. But we hadn't done that, and that had to mean something. He'd actually prioritized my hurt ahead of Maura for once, and while it had made me feel better in the moment, Rachel was right about Cade's life being constant triage.

Cade was sick and Hayley was in limbo; this wasn't the time to talk about our relationship. I forced a smile, knowing I was probably delaying the inevitable but making the right decision. "Don't worry about that for now. Do what you need to do to get healthy. Okay?"

"I can do that. I am doing that."

"I know," I said and squeezed his arm supportively. "I want you to get better."

Chapter Eighteen

Cade

My hands were shaking, and for once it had nothing to do with the bowl of ravioli I was eating. It was the phone in Maura's hand. She cradled it to her ear, pacing back and forth and smoking her ninth or tenth cigarette for the day. I was dying to hear the other side of the conversation, but Maura had been adamant. I'd explained the bedroom at Adam's place and that it didn't mean what she thought. But something about it scared her. She insisted her baby brother and his boyfriend were no longer needed to solve her problems, which was true but untested. The whole situation was making me relate a little too strongly to a mother bird watching their baby try to fly for the first time. You think they're ready, but my God, what if you're wrong?

"Okay, Aislinn. I know you're sorry. Yes, I'll be there." Maura hung up the phone and exhaled a relieved breath.

"So . . ." I gestured, gulping down the bite I was working on and taking a sip of my water. "What did she say?"

"We agreed Hayley will come home on Monday."

"Great, but what was all that about Mr. Bach?"

Maura took a long drag of her cigarette, then snuffed it out. Her hands trembled, and I wasn't sure if it was the situation or the drugs giving her the shakes. "Hayley told Aislinn about Shane coming around again. So when she said it scared her to go home, Aislinn thought she meant she was scared of being around him . . . or me, I guess. Yesterday, Aislinn told Hayley she didn't have to leave, and Hayley seemed relieved, so that was what prompted Aislinn to lose her ever-loving mind and try to keep my daughter from me. She called

Mr. Bach, who, being the massive prick that he is, told her I had forgotten to pick Hayley up."

I smiled uncomfortably. "She shouldn't be around Shane. You shouldn't either."

"Yes, Cade. I am aware that I have terrible taste in men. Do you want to hear the rest of the story about my daughter or shall we take a moment to review all our appalling life choices?"

"Sorry," I said, grimacing.

"So Hayley got upset that Aislinn was trying to kidnap her."

"Maura, 'kidnap'? Really? You shouldn't think like that; she was only trying to protect Hayley."

"My daughter does not need protection from me. You know who needed protection from their mother? We did. But did James think for one second maybe he should step up there? No, he did not. He took his own kid and ran and to hell with us. God, you're annoying sometimes. Stop thinking you get to control everyone else's opinions and thoughts. You need to focus on you." She pointed to the bowl of ravioli.

"Jesus, fine." I laughed, taking another bite. "You sound like Adam, you know?"

"As-I-was-saying . . ." She gave a long-suffering sigh. "It turns out Hayley feared the actual flight and not coming home. She thought Aislinn told her I was coming to get her, and when I didn't show, she thought I forgot her again."

"Oh, poor baby. Is she okay now?"

"Yeah. Aislinn will fly with her, which before you tell me is a nice gesture, is the very least she can do."

"Can Aislinn afford that?"

"James is paying for the ticket."

"That's great."

"No, it's not great, Cade. My own sister and brother don't think I can take care of my daughter."

"We don't think that. You need help sometimes, but we all need help, Maura. It's okay to lean on someone. That's what family is for."

She shrugged. "I guess. I'm glad she's coming home."

"This is yummy. Do you want a bite?"

She shook her head. "I'm going to go lay down. I didn't sleep much last night. You have to be exhausted too."

"No, I'm okay, actually. Strangely optimistic about things. Is it weird I'm glad he wanted a time-out?"

She tilted her head and summoned a borderline enthusiastic "You didn't break up. That's progress, right?"

"It's more than that. I don't think I could have trusted it if he forgave me on the spot. He's angry. He has a right to be angry, what I did was—"

"Understandable. Don't forget he cheated."

"I'm not talking about forgetting, Maura. I'm talking about forgiving. Learning. Growing as a person and as a couple. I don't know. Now that he knows about my anorexia, I can't help feeling like we will come through this stronger. I told him in Hawaii that we'd wipe the slate clean, but I wasn't ready then. Now, I feel like . . . I don't really know how to say it. I know he loves me, and I love him."

"Oh my God, Cade. You trust him, don't you? Like for real."

I'd been struggling to put words to what I was feeling after leaving Adam's, but Maura had nailed it. Trust. I trusted him and I trusted in what we had, which filled me with this completely foreign sense of hopefulness. About my recovery. My ability to help Maura. My friendships and, most importantly, about my and Adam's future. "Yeah, I guess I do."

"Are you going to see him today?"

"No. He asked for time, so I'm going to give it to him. He said he'd call me when he's ready to talk some more. Besides, I've got my follow up with Dr. M. and group. I will talk to Siddharth today and tell him what's been going on with me. Then I need to find a new therapist."

"Wow. Productive. Maybe I should get some stuff done instead of taking a nap."

"Like what?"

"I don't know. With Hayley coming home, I need to quit smoking again. It'll be better if I stay busy. I could call my boss about coming back to work. Or finish painting the bedroom. I spent all that money on paint and left six blue stripes on the wall."

"You want some help to paint? I can get it done tomorrow."

"No. I started it and I should clean it up. Thanks, though. Put all this new optimism into finishing your ravioli."

I laughed, taking another healthy bite. I kept going—biting, chewing, swallowing—all things most people do mindlessly, but for some reason I continued to struggle with. When I finished the pasta, I used bread to soak up the remaining sauce, because it was *that* good. I left for my appointments knowing I'd made a ton of mistakes and there were plenty of things for me to feel guilty about, but eating that ravioli wasn't going to be one of them.

Amy's Coffee Shop was a small, six-table hole-in-the-wall less than a block from the Meadowbrook Center. It wasn't uncommon for patients to congregate there before group, since Dr. M. was a stickler for not using the therapy room as a hangout. But after a session, everyone typically scattered. So when I invited Siddharth to meet me for coffee there, I hadn't expected the place to be full of familiar faces I'd spent an hour exchanging profoundly personal information with.

"Hey." Siddharth waved to me, already holding my favorite chai tea drink next to his soy latte. I approached, giving him a side hug as to not disturb the cups. "Wow, this place is packed." I accepted my drink, searching for an empty table.

"I think there might be some benches nearby. Want to walk?"

"Sure."

I followed Siddharth out of the store, grateful for the escape, to a courtyard that had an open bench. "This good?"

I nodded, taking a seat next to him and a few cautious sips of my tea. "So, what's new? I feel like I haven't spoken to you much since Hawaii."

"Oh, I'm good. Matt has been busy with the shelter, but things are going well for us and the job is good. How are you? How's your sister feeling? Adam told me Hayley is in Boston."

"Maura is better. Hayley will be home next week. She had a good visit, but Aislinn pulled some shit and, well, the last twenty-four hours have been a little crazy."

Siddharth smiled knowingly. "And things with Adam?"

"Actually, that was what I wanted to talk to you about." I could see the objection forming on his lips, so I cut him off. "It's not bad. I . . . God, it feels like I'm coming out again." I laughed nervously as Siddharth's brows straightened in a flash of worry. Drawing in a deep breath, I recalled the topic of today's therapy session: *feel the fear and do it anyway.* "So the thing is, I have an eating disorder."

Siddharth's concerned reaction was far less daunting than Adam's had been. He took a sip of his coffee, as though gathering his thoughts. "Are you telling me because you're getting help?"

"It's not a new thing, but yeah. I recently relapsed and I'm getting help. Adam found out yesterday."

"'Found out'? You didn't tell him?"

My teeth dug into my lower lip as I shook my head. "Maura" was all the explanation he needed.

Siddharth nodded. "How did he take it?"

"Not well at first, but we talked some. He's taking some time to process everything."

"I see." Siddharth pressed his already thin lips together.

"You don't seem surprised."

Siddharth sighed softly. "If I'm honest, I'm not."

"How come you never said anything?"

"Well, I was never sure. There've been a few times where you would meet us and say you'd already eaten when I knew that wasn't true. I thought you didn't want to eat what everyone else was eating but didn't want to make a big deal about it. People comment on my veganism all the time, so I've done that too. I figured as long as you didn't look like that girl in the coffee shop, it wasn't an issue."

I knew precisely which girl he was referencing. Jayne was the type of jarringly emaciated girl the media used when they needed a picture of anorexia.

"It's a misconception that people with eating disorders are all thin. I have anorexia, but you can still be sick and not underweight."

Siddharth listened while I recounted my experience, not as much as I'd shared with Adam, but enough that he understood my disorder and me a little better. Then I explained planning to tell Adam that night, finding him with Bryan, and the fight Maura interrupted.

As expected, it took a while to get it out because he stopped to hug me whenever I got emotional.

One of the things I loved about Siddharth was his objectivity. He was never trying to assign blame or find fault, so when our conversation came to Adam's response, it shouldn't have surprised me he didn't choose sides.

"I think you're right to give Adam time, but not too much okay?"

"Don't you think I should listen to him when he tells me what he needs?"

"It's really none of my business."

"No, please. We try to keep you out of the middle of us, but you get us both so well, so if you have advice, I'd like to hear it."

Siddharth thought for a moment, his eyes drifting up as he considered what to say. "I've noticed over the years Adam's deeply affected when you're unhappy, more than I think most would consider normal. It's almost as if he takes your unhappiness as rejection or failure, even when it's not about him. I know he hurt you when he cheated, and I'm not excusing what he did, but I guess I've always understood how it happened. How his insecurity led him to such a self-destructive act. We all felt you pulling away from him that year, from everyone, really. We saw you were going through a lot, but Adam . . . he was pretty wrecked and confused before that trip. It hurt him to not know how to help you. If Adam is asking for a time-out and you give it to him, I worry he's going to use it to beat himself up for not knowing you were struggling. All I'm saying is make sure he knows you're okay and that you need him. You've always had your pride, but you should let him help you as much as you can, because I think he needs to do that for you."

"So, if I was going to ask you for a loan to help with some medical bills . . ."

"I'll give you whatever you need, but letting Adam help you would be better. I'm telling you, Cade, he would be so happy."

"I'm not so sure I can do that. I don't want to put money into the pot of things we have to deal with. I know Adam wants to be supportive, but my recovery is something I have to do alone."

"It is your decision." A rare glimpse of disappointment appeared on Sid's face, causing me to reconsider his advice and my first instinct to reject it. Dr. M. expressly said I shouldn't do my recovery alone. That using my support system was essential. I wanted that system to include Adam.

"Any other insights? I want to be better for him."

"Well, as long as I'm meddling, can I talk to you about what happened at the cake-tasting?"

I laughed. Sid could teach a class on how to give constructive feedback. "Just know I am in a fragile state right now."

"I'll be gentle."

"Okay. Is this about the neighbor?"

"Sort of. It's more about the way Adam reacted to the neighbor coming on to him. All it took was me mentioning it, and you should have seen how defensive and well, frankly, scared he was that we were judging him. He's really afraid to talk to you about stuff because he doesn't want to set you off, and that's not good."

"I don't want him to feel like that. Honestly. I'm really trying to not say things I don't mean, at least Adam isn't taking it so personal anymore."

"I understand it scares you to be vulnerable with all of us, but when you feel like that, you can't let your heart get out in front of your head. You guys need to talk about it so you can get out of this cycle and . . ." He paused, and I finished his sentence.

"And I need to forgive him."

Sid nodded. "Yeah. You do."

I took a deep breath and finished my tea in one long gulp. "In group today we did this exercise. There was a long strip of tape on the floor, and the therapist asked us to stand on it and talk about our biggest fear. She asked us what the line represented for us. Most people said things like getting healthy or gaining weight, but when I got up there, you know what the first thing that popped into my head?"

Siddharth shook his head.

"Finally trusting Adam again and having it not be enough. I put all my eggs in this basket, and I think I'm finally at a place where I trust him. But what if it still doesn't fix us?"

"Then tell him that. This was a gigantic step for you, Cade. If you actually forgive him and trust him, other problems get way easier to solve."

I nodded, embracing my best friend in a tight hug. "I'm so glad I have you."

"I'm sorry if I've been preoccupied with Matt. It's weird having a boyfriend."

Smiling, I nodded. "He seems great. I'm so happy for you."

"He is. We have our issues too, though."

"You need to talk about it?"

"I'm still trying to figure out how I feel about it. Playing house in Hawaii was fun, but I'm not sure about the long term. I think we might want different things."

"Well, I'm here if you want to talk it out."

"I know. And thank you. So do we need to stop at the bank?"

Biting my lip, I closed my eyes and pictured Adam's face when I'd asked him to stay and help me with Maura. Not only accepted his help, but actually asked for it. He'd been so amazing that week, and Sid was right, it would make him feel more secure. "I'll think about it some more."

Siddharth smiled. "Okay, sounds good. As far as your anorexia goes, I'm here to support you. If there is anything I can do or not do, you can tell me."

"I will. This was perfect though. I would have told you a long time ago, but ..."

"No, I get it. Adam needed to know first. But we're here for you. All of us. Are you going to tell Brady and Josh?"

"Eventually."

"After the wedding?"

"Yeah. I know I'm not a part of the wedding party or anything, but I don't want to be a distraction."

Sid's face scrunched in confusion. "You know they plan to ask you to marry them?"

"Huh?"

"Yeah, well, Adam and I are their best men, but you're the best writer and speaker in the group, so they wanted you to get ordained on the internet and perform the ceremony. You didn't think they'd exclude you, do you?"

"I, well ..." I chuckled at myself. "Yeah. I did. I'm not always the most reliable when it comes to showing up for friends."

Sid waved me off. "They want to get you alone, so you won't feel pressured to say yes. But with all that was happening with Maura, they decided to wait until things calm down."

I smiled. "I would love to help them write the ceremony. Hey, that's it."

"What is?"

"I think I figured out how I can give Adam space but still let him know I'm okay and not say things I don't mean. I can write him a love letter. Is that too corny?"

"Not at all," Sid said, little lines fanning around his eyes. "I think he'd really love it."

Chapter Nineteen

Adam

"Hey, neighbor." Keys in hand, Bryan pushed open the outer door to our building before I got my keys out of my pocket. "You look a little wrecked. Rough day at work?"

"I'm fine," I said, trying to keep any sign that I was totally not fine off my face. I waited for Bryan to finish up at the shared mailbox located inside the door. He grabbed his and moved aside, hovering behind me as I stepped forward to check my box.

It took a minute to un-wedge the not-inconsequential stack of bills, flyers, and junk mail the mail carrier had crammed inside. It'd been at least a week since I'd checked it. Or left the condo, really. I'd been pretty much working only as much as I needed to contain my drinking to the evening hours.

"Haven't seen you around much. I stuck a note on your door about poker night tonight," Bryan said as he followed me up the stairs to our floor.

"Sorry. Been busy." *Yeah, busy wallowing.*

"That's cool. How's Cade?"

"He's fine, thanks." We reached the top of the stairs, and Bryan stood behind me as I fumbled to get my door unlocked with my two fists full of mail. "See ya around." I entered my condo and thought better. "Actually, probably not."

I shut the door behind me, leaving Bryan in the hall gulping like a fish out of water. That kind of antisocial, rude behavior would horrify my mother, but I'd already pissed off my father by not returning his numerous calls, my coworkers by blowing off Happy Hour, and Josh for canceling our plans to watch the final round of the NBA Playoffs, so he could get in line.

Yawning, I pulled my phone out of my pocket and tossed it next to the stack of mail and keys on my kitchen table, grabbed a beer, and sat my unhappy ass on the couch. Switching the television on for background noise, I closed my eyes, lay back, and tried to figure out what to do about Cade.

I missed him. Fuck, did I miss him. But, damn, every time I thought about how long he'd kept his secret, my chest burned. My heart battled itself constantly. It shouldn't be possible to feel so much want and so much anger toward the same person at the same time, but I'd been here before—four years ago . . . in a dive bar in Mexico.

All those emotions kept flooding back. The loneliness. The distance. Leading up to that trip, I was convinced if we could get away together, things would be better. Now that I knew what he'd been going through at the time, it all seemed so selfish. But, God, every time I thought about the sheer volume of gaslighting he'd put me through. Every time he'd dismissed my concerns and made me feel it was all in my head. Told me I was overreacting. Anger boiled up in me, and I wasn't sure I should ignore it.

That whole time he was . . . Well, I still wasn't clear on what he'd been doing. I'd read up on eating disorders, but there were different diagnoses, and when I searched for information about anorexia, I couldn't see beyond the pictures. Cade never looked like that. Not once. He was thin. Very thin at times, but never seemed sick.

I couldn't decide how much his being sick excused what he'd done. Guilt kept me up at night. Some nights because I hadn't noticed what he was going through and others because I had noticed and ignored it. And in my darkest moments, the realization that there'd been times I'd encouraged it.

I'd never thought of my attraction to extremely petite men as a problem, but from the porn I'd watched to the guys I'd dated, they'd all been uber-twinks. If Cade believed he had to compete with that . . . I swallowed with the thought, shame burning through me.

While I'd never told anyone they should lose weight, I'd certainly never encouraged any of them to gain weight either. What did it say about me that I liked sex with small men because they'd made me feel more masculine? When I closed my eyes, I saw the outline of Cade's spine through his skin. Had I pushed my concern aside because I was too afraid of upsetting him or because I'd been too turned on by him to stop and ask if he was okay?

Either way. That wasn't healthy. For either of us.

It was like Rachel's whole triaging analogy, only in reverse. It was bad enough when I thought I was the screaming in pain guy, but to think I'd basically been the doctor who let the appendix rupture too. Even if I could forgive Cade, it felt like a pretty clear sign that I wasn't the right guy for him.

I stayed like that for hours, dissecting every sign I'd missed. Reliving things I'd said or done. Things I hadn't said and hadn't done. How many comments had I made about liking his size? How many times did I ignore his weird comments about Brady's weight loss or his strange eating habits? How many guys had I shown off, trying to make him jealous? I didn't know how long I lay there, but when I glanced around, the moonless night had plunged my family room into darkness, and I still didn't know what I wanted to do.

My phone dinged. As I rose to retrieve it, I already knew it was my good night text from Cade. I still hadn't answered him, but receiving them had become essential in my ability to function. Without those updates, I'd be too worried about him to deal with the complexity of the emotions swarming around inside me. Before I could check it, I poured two-fingers of whiskey, imbibing the amber liquid in one long swallow.

I went to group today. We had to talk about what is taking our focus and what we want to feed in our lives. I can't stop thinking about it. I wanted to say I'm sorry, baby. I'm sorry for all the times I didn't value you. I know there have been a lot.

I pressed the reply box, thumb hovered over the keyboard and mouth twisted in indecision. Of all the messages he'd sent, that one was the clearest sign I needed to make a decision. I'd sworn to myself in Hawaii this was our last chance. If we didn't get it right this time, I had to get off the ride. But the thought of actually doing it, especially when Cade was going through so much, made it hard to breathe.

A quick swipe of the screen and I closed the reply box with a sigh. I wasn't sure I was ready yet. I heated a slice of pizza and poured another whiskey. One glass later, my phone was again in my hand, scrolling through the other text messages he'd sent over the past week. The ones I'd been using to gauge my spot on Cade's triage list.

You don't have to answer me, but I wanted to let you know I've told Sid. I'm sorry, baby. I love you.

I wanted to let you know I found a therapist. I love you. Hope you're okay.

Saw my doctor today. She's pleased with my progress and my labs looked good. Good night, love. Sleep well.

Hayley's home! Maura is over the moon. I left them snuggling on the couch. Good night. I love you.

First therapist visit went well. I like her.

Hayley and I read for hours and finally finished Little Women. She loved it. I miss you. Good night.

I started a new book that made me think of you. Definitely going to keep me up late tonight reflecting on it. Can't wait to talk to you about it. Good night. I love you.

Tossing my phone down next to me, I pushed out a long breath. I needed a distraction.

I started with the family room, picking up dishes that had accumulated over the week and placing them in the sink. Since I rarely used it, it'd been a while since I'd checked the hall bath. I popped in and wiped the counters down, then brushed the cobwebs out of the corner behind the door. When I exited, I found myself face-to-face with the door leading to Hayley's room.

Wait. Not Hayley's room. Cade and I hadn't lived together, and I'd made a space for his niece, who didn't even live with him. I thought my parents knew how to run a pressure campaign, but I could give them a run for their money.

I walked inside, tossing on the light switch by the door, and took a seat on the still unused daybed.

When I'd bought the condo, I had an office for Cade in mind. He was always talking about writing, and I thought he'd like to have his own space. Now, I wasn't sure what I'd use it for. I didn't need an office. All my programs were on my laptop, and I hated sitting in a sterile room to work, preferring the couch or recliner. My complex had a gym, not that I used it. I'd been a member of Canal Street Gym since college.

I sat there, racking my brain for how I should use the space, but all I could come up with was a guest room. My parents and siblings didn't visit, and if they did, they were way more likely to stay in a hotel. I hadn't kept in touch with many friends from Atlanta, so all my friends lived in town. But guest room it was. The little girl motif needed to go because I couldn't stand it anymore. I found a box and tossed toys and books into it but stopped midway through the first shelf. Not quite ready to admit that Cade might never live there, that Hayley would never need a place to stay when she slept over.

Tomorrow.

Tomorrow, I would pack up all the things I'd bought and donate them. Or take them to Hayley. She should at least get to use them. Tomorrow, I would decide. I sighed, my head swimming a bit.

Switching off the light and closing the door behind me, I wandered my small condo, picking up and discarding clutter along the way. On top of the stack of mail was a pet store ad. I picked up the flyer, smiling at the Goldendoodle puppy with the red bandana. Perhaps I should get a dog? I'd never had a pet before. Company would be good for me. Cade and I . . . I sighed. *Cade would love this dog.* I closed my eyes, picturing his face if I surprised him with Milo, the name we'd picked years ago after discovering we'd both loved *The Phantom Tollbooth* as kids.

Cursing myself, I tossed Milo in the garbage and continued sorting through the large stack. A pale pink envelope slipped out from inside the folds of a grocery store advertisement onto the table. My pulse jumped. There was no return address, but I'd recognize Cade's handwriting anywhere.

I walked with it to the couch and sat down, tapping it on my leg before deciding that opening it required another drink. But I could only stare at it. It sat on the coffee table, next to the tumbler directly in front of me. Cade had never sent me a letter. Not one. I glared at it as if some magical force could reveal it to be a good letter or a bad letter.

Pink was not the color of a Dear John letter, right?

I rechecked my texts.

I went to group today. We had to talk about what is taking our focus and what we want to feed in our lives. I can't stop thinking about it. I wanted to say I'm sorry, baby. I'm sorry for all the times I didn't value you. I know there have been a lot.

That was not the text of a man who wanted to end things. Biting my lip, I slid a finger under the fold and swallowed.

My hands trembled as I took a swig of my watered-down whiskey and clutched the stationary, filled from top to bottom in loopy cursive swirls.

Dear Adam,

I've been sitting here in my room staring at this blank page for the better part of three hours, trying to figure out how to put what I'm feeling onto this page. Despite my writing aspirations, I'm afraid when it comes to you, my love, words too often fail me.

I understand that I've hurt you, but I'll save that conversation for when we can talk in person. However much you need to talk about it, I'm prepared to do it. To answer whatever questions you may have without running away or getting angry. You deserve those answers from me and I'm so sorry I've kept them from you. But this letter isn't meant to deliver the apology you deserve. It's making sure you fully grasp what you mean to me. It's all the other things I didn't say. Or couldn't. I'm not sure anymore. I know I go to bed every night thinking of you and wishing I'd told you how much I need you.

That's it, I think. The thing that made me panicky inside whenever I got too close to you again. Or when you asked me to move in. Whenever you do something—these big, amazing gestures—to show me how much you love me. It brings my absolute need for you front and center in my brain. I've been so scared to need you. Because if I admit I need you, then what would happen to me if you didn't want me anymore?

You've changed my life, Adam. In so many ways.

From the first time we spoke. I was sitting on the stage in the common room still in my ridiculous can-can dress, covered in sequins and loose feathers falling off me. I'll never forget the way my heart pounded when the tall guy with the dreamy blues eyes tapped me on the shoulder. No one had ever looked at me like you did that night. No one had ever treated me like I was special. Not special enough to invent entire classes to have a reason to speak with me. Special was an entirely unknown emotion for me, but more than that, you gave me a sense of belonging. Confidence. As much as my heart or my lungs, I needed that more than you'll ever know. It changed me. No one thought I would make it in college—not my counselor, or my social worker, not even Aislinn or Maura. Not really. But here was this guy, who had money and a family and every advantage I thought made someone "college material," and he was asking me about Louise Weber and Moulin Rouge and I had the answers.

I love how you build me up. How you let me shine. You introduced me to the people you'd met like you were the lucky one. Everyone at Loman Hall, man, how they looked at you. I noticed minor things after we started hanging out. At first, it was how people would approach me differently. They'd ask me, "You're Adam's boyfriend, right? What's your name again?" Usually they'd tell me I was so lucky. But somewhere along the way it became "They're so lucky." I realized people weren't envious of me because I'd captured the attention of the hottest guy in the building—they were jealous of us, because of how we loved each other.

I could go on. Tell you the million ways your love, your support, your pride in me gave me what I needed and helped pushed me to be better, to follow my dreams. Yours is always the voice I hear when I need to make an important decision. The one that gives me not only the confidence, but the freedom to take risks, because if I jump, you're right there to catch me. No matter how many times I pushed you away, when I needed you, you ran to me.

It's why I'm putting this in a letter. Because this time, I don't want you to come running because I need you. I want to be someone you run to because you need me just as much.

You should have felt my love for you every day. You should have heard it. I'm committing myself to making sure you never wonder how much I love you.

In therapy they tell me to counter negative thoughts with positive ones when I'm eating. To remind myself that I need food to survive. I'm trying to do that with us. To take all those thoughts about how you deserve someone better and channel them into being someone better. I strive to be that man for you. Because you deserve to get from me what you give to me.

And because of you, I'm sure I can be that man. For the first time in my life, I'm ready to be that man. It's why I will get healthy again.

Why I know I can trust you and be someone worthy of your trust. How I know this time is different. I'm here, baby. Whenever you're ready. I'll be waiting with arms open. Ready to love you.

All my love,

Cade

When I finished, I folded the letter carefully, tucked it back into its envelope, and set it next to the empty tumbler on the coffee table.

Whatever anesthetic property the whiskey had given me suddenly wore off.

All the indecision and angst. All the guilt and regret I'd been trying to push down to drink away the past week. All the feelings I'd been painstakingly sorting through. None of it mattered anymore. The people we were. The mistakes we made. Irrelevant. I knew in my heart that what mattered was the Cade who wrote that letter and the Adam who responded to it. That's what would determine our future.

Chapter Twenty

Cade

"**Y**ou're doing wonderful, Cade." Dr. McNamara finished my exam and helped me sit up. "Your usual labs, plus the STD panel you requested, all came back normal and your weight is progressing. I'm incredibly pleased."

I swung my legs over the table, letting them dangle. "Thanks. Eating is getting much easier. The anxiety meds are working. I'm hitting my targets every day. Some meals take less effort than others."

She nodded, wheeling over to make a note in my medical record. "And your support network? Last time we spoke you indicated you planned to tell your partner. How did that go?"

"Adam knows, so that's been a tremendous relief for me. Group is helpful, and my best friend, Siddharth, has been supportive. Plus, my sisters are checking in. I'm keeping an eye on my niece three days a week since my sister returned to work part-time. Hayley is a nice distraction."

"That's wonderful. How's the new therapist working out?"

"Well. Thank you for the recommendation. Also thank you for working with me on the payment arrangements. It's been a godsend. I should be able to get caught up soon." As soon as Adam was done processing, I planned to talk to him about my financial situation, but in the meantime, Maura going back to work had helped.

Dr. McNamara smiled. "I'm sorry we're no longer in network for you. Fighting insurance companies is my least favorite thing about this place. Keep up the excellent work. I'd like to see you again in a month, or sooner if you start to have a resurgence of symptoms."

"I was wondering if you thought it was too soon to exercise?"

She frowned. "Walks are okay. No more than twenty minutes. We can talk about resuming a more regular program next month."

I nodded, accepting the paperwork with a half smile. I was hoping she'd clear me for some gym time, if nothing else to keep myself busy while I waited for Adam. I walked out of the exam room and down the hall to check out with Jill. When I pushed open the door to the waiting room, there she was. The same girl who'd been in the waiting room when I'd first returned. She wasn't in my group, so I hadn't learned her name, but I met her eyes and, after it was clear she recognized me too, I winked.

"Here you go, dear." Jill handed me my appointment card. I debated if I should say anything to the girl, but as I passed her, she peered up and smiled.

"Hey," I said.

"Hey," she responded meekly.

"I'm glad you came back."

She nodded. "You too."

It was a passing comment, nothing more personal than a *How are you?* to a stranger in an elevator, but I smiled a little brighter as I exited the building. I'd been wrong about her. My disorder had colored so many of my thoughts a month ago. In a small way, it let me trust the incessant optimism now going on in my brain. A truly foreign concept for me.

It'd stuck with me since my last therapy appointment. I realized the first time I got healthy was for Maura. No question. The second time was because I was afraid to lose Adam. This time, though. This time, I was getting healthy for me. Because I wanted to be someone Maura, Hayley, and Adam could depend on. My therapist likened it to the oxygen mask on a plane. They tell you to put yours on first before attempting to help others. So that was what I was doing. I was putting my oxygen mask on.

When I slid inside my car, I checked my phone. I was surprised to see my principal had called and left a message for me to return his call. But that would have to wait because there was a text message.

From Adam.

My first one all week, and he'd sent it about ten minutes before. No two words had felt more consequential.

Call me.

My heart collided with the front of my chest as I scrambled to pull up my favorites and tapped his name. The phone rang three times, each a million times longer than usual.

"Hello." His voice sounded okay. Not exactly strong, but not angry either.

I cleared the emotion from my throat. "Hi. It's me."

"How are you?"

My eyes cast toward the building, desperate to find something to focus on other than how fast my heart was racing. "I'm good. Leaving the doctor's office. You?"

"Good." A long beat of silence begged to be filled.

"Did you—"

"I got your texts and your—" We both laughed. "Sorry. You go first."

"No. it's okay. What were you going to say?"

"Just that your letter meant a lot to me."

I held my breath, waiting for the *but* and when it didn't come, my heart soared. "Adam, I meant it. Every word. I'll wait, no matter how long. Take as much time as you need, but I'm in such a different place now. I feel so much more ready for us."

"Brady and Josh want us to come over to dinner next weekend. Sid and Matt are coming too. I didn't know what to tell them."

"If you're not ready, I can make an excuse. Or we can tell them what's going on together. It's up to you. Whatever you're comfortable with."

"No . . . I don't know why I said that, actually. I want to see you, but not . . . Can I see you? I think I need to see you."

"Of course. When?"

"Are you on your way home now?"

"Yeah."

"Good. I'm in front of your apartment. I'll wait."

"You're . . . there? Like now?"

"Yeah."

"Okay. I'll be home in like fifteen minutes."

"Okay. Drive carefully."

"I will."

"Um . . . I love you."

My chin quivered. "I love you too. I'll be there as soon as I can."

Land speed records were broken, but I pulled into the parking lot of my building and saw him sitting in his car. My hands tried to put the car in Park, pull the keys out, take off my seat belt, and open my door all at the same time. It took a minute to remember the proper order of the steps.

Calm down, I willed myself, but fuck the exercise restriction—as soon as I made it out of my vehicle and he noticed me, I couldn't get to him fast enough.

"Hey," I said breathlessly as he stood from his car. I was on my toes, rocking toward him before I realized he didn't plan to kiss me. Skin crawling with electricity that only he could ground, I actively worked to keep my hands from him.

"Hi," he said. "You okay?" The first touch of his hand landed on my forearm. A little jolt of awareness sped up my skin.

"Yeah. I'm good. I'm, um, God, it's . . . I'm happy to see you." I pulled back as much as I could to avoid jumping on him like an excited puppy.

"I'm happy to see you too. Can we . . ." He gestured toward my building. I realized I had trapped him between me and his car door.

"Oh, yeah." I stepped back so he could close his door. "Sorry."

I followed him to my apartment, unable to stop staring at him. Handsome as ever, he still had on work clothes, and the notes of his cologne—vanilla and mint—made my mouth water.

My hands trembled as I worked to free my key from my pocket and inserted it into the lock. I pushed the door open and gestured for Adam to enter. "Come on in."

"Thanks." He stepped inside, and something about having him in my space again filled me with relief. I believed him that a time-out meant a time-out and not a breakup, but if he *were* going to end it, he could have kept us in the parking lot. Lord knew we'd called it quits on multiple blacktops over the years. Still, I didn't care for the way his eyes darted around nervously, like a guest waiting for an invitation to sit. He was nervous, so I did the only thing I could think of to set him at ease.

A brush of my hand on his cheek was all it took. The straight line of his brow broke, and the light came back to his eyes. His hand covered mine, holding it there for a moment.

"I missed you," I whispered.

If my hand hadn't been on his face, I would have missed the almost imperceptible nod of his head that followed. "Me too, Gou." He lowered our hands and kept mine clutched in his as he led me to my couch and pulled me down next to him.

A little smile flashed before me. That smile—it was like a life preserver tossed to a drowning man.

"Do you want to talk?"

Adam breathed in and out, his palm perspiring in mine. "I did. I came over here to. Now I can't remember what I needed to say. I want to look at you."

I gasped, fighting back my hopeful smile. "I am completely on board with that plan."

Adam stiffened, his eyes drifting over to the book on my end table. "Is that the book you started reading? The one you texted me about?"

I followed his gaze. "Yes."

"Did you finish it yet?"

"Yes. It was sort of life-changing. I think you'd like it."

Adam gave a tentative nod, like he wasn't sure if he wanted to ask about the book or talk about what he was feeling. Fear that he'd say he'd come over too soon and needed more time kept me from asking. I would give it to him, but having him with me—even if things were uncomfortable, even if I had to answer for what I'd done—was all I'd wanted.

"Are you hungry? I was planning to make some dinner for myself, but there is plenty for both of us." He didn't answer, just continued to stare at my book. "Adam?" I prompted, gently touching his arm.

He shook his head slightly as if to clear his thoughts. "Oh, sorry. Yes. I'm hungry. Thanks."

"Okay. Why don't you relax? Find something on the television. It's one of those meal kits, so it shouldn't take long. Do you want some wine, or I think I still have some of your whiskey?"

"Ugh. No alcohol," he said, his mouth puckered like he'd eaten something sour. "Water is good."

"Okay. I'll get it." I handed him the remote and nudged the coffee table closer to him so he could put his feet up. When I returned to bring him his water, he had his shoes off and feet up. He took a careful sip, still acting too much like a visitor for my heart to accept this was going to be the end of our time-out.

I worked quickly, consulting my meal plan notes from the fridge before chopping the vegetables. I added some pats of butter to boost the fat count when I sautéed them. Now, the meat. I disliked handling raw meat, but there was no way to get the calories in without it. I cringed as I pulled the breast from the plastic bag and patted them dry. "Babe, I'm adding this sriracha and sour cream sauce to the chicken. Is that okay with you?"

When he didn't answer, I finished seasoning the chicken and turned around to find him watching me. "Hi," I said, a bit surprised. "You want yours with sriracha sauce or plain?"

"Why did you think I'd like this book?" He held up the copy of Desmond Tutu's *The Book of Forgiving*.

I smiled gently. I wiped my hand on the kitchen towel and motioned for him to hand it to me. Flipping the pages, I turned to the passage I'd read so many times I'd practically memorized it and handed it back to him. "Because of this."

He read quietly while I finished prepping dinner. The highlighted passage about the revenge cycle that perfectly described our roller coaster of a relationship wasn't that long, so I figured he'd kept reading. I wondered if he'd reached the part about forgiving yourself.

"Do you believe in all this? This fourfold path?"

I placed the chicken in the oven and straightened. Feeling the fear and doing it anyway, I looked him in the eyes. "Absolutely. I think now that everything is in the open, we can actually talk about it and forgive each other."

"We've tried so many times."

"*You've* tried so many times. You couldn't do it alone, Adam. I had to do my part. By keeping my anorexia secret, I didn't fully tell my story, so I was never able to explain how your cheating hurt me and, like that passage says, a harm felt but denied will always find a way to express itself."

Adam bit his lip, considering my words briefly before nodding in agreement. "I've been educating myself on anorexia. I understand now why you didn't tell me. How hard recovery is. I said things . . ." Adam choked up.

"You're not responsible for things you didn't know about. I have to tell you if you say or do something that is triggering for me, and that's on me, okay? It's not your fault, no more than I'm at fault for my mother being an addict or my sister being bipolar. The book talks about how once you've forgiven, the fourth step is to renew or release the relationship. I want you to be able to talk about how my keeping my anorexia from you hurt you, because I know it did. Once we've done that, then hopefully we can renew our relationship and get out of this revenge cycle."

Adam nodded. "I may need you to keep reminding me of that."

I smiled. I'd been hoping that the passage would resonate with Adam as much as it had for me. When I'd read the book, every page was like peeling back one more layer of what Adam and I had put each other through. Then once I understood how my secret had held me back from truly forgiving him, it had all clicked. "Which part?"

"That it's not my fault. I can't believe I didn't see it."

"As much as you need. Do you want to borrow it? I really think you'd like it or, if you want to, we can read it together. Like we used to."

Adam smiled, and the deep breath he took seemed to take him by surprise. "Thank you for giving me time to get my head wrapped around all this and for the letter. It was . . . It made a huge difference to me."

"I have a book of them."

"A book of letters?"

I smiled and nodded enthusiastically. Every time I wanted to say something to him, I wrote it down instead. "Letters to you. I didn't want to overwhelm you, but I kept writing them because they were therapeutic. You can read them, but I'll warn you they're pretty sappy."

Adam smiled, tenderness morphing his face into something I recognized. "I kind of like you sappy."

I set the timer and walked to the bedroom to grab the journal I'd started, then returned to him. "The letters are intermixed with some of my journaling. Some of this is my internal dialog, so they may not make much sense to you, but here."

"Really?"

I nodded. "I actually prefer it to talking. I'm way better at expressing my feelings this way. Far less bitchy."

Adam laughed and took the book. "I'm intrigued."

"I'm going to fix my supplement drink. Have at it. Ask me any questions you want."

As I turned to leave him, he reached out and grabbed my arm. "Cade."

"Yeah?"

"I can ask you whatever I want?"

I nodded, letting his fingers slide down my forearm and interlace with mine. "Anything."

"Can I kiss you?"

I smiled. "Anytime you want."

The corner of his lips curved up as he drew me into him. His head dipped, and he took one ragged breath against my ear and whispered, "I won't ever leave you."

Overwhelmed by how much I needed to hear the words, I retreated, enough to see his determined jaw and steadfast eyes. My throat wouldn't work, so I nodded until I managed to say, "I may need you to keep reminding me of that."

This time, a slight nod and a burgeoning smile. Confidence surged between us. I pulled my mind away from what work we still had left to do. We had plenty of time to figure it all out, to carve out a better, more productive path forward. What mattered was him. What he needed in this moment. What reassurance I could give to him I was okay and that we could do this. All I could do was lean into that moment.

His breath against my lips was restorative. The faintest brush of his lips—soft and pliable—against mine. I put my hands on his waist and slid them, firm but gentle, around his body and caressed up his back, massaging the hard muscles under my palms.

He moaned, and suddenly, we were *really* kissing. It went on for a long time, neither of us willing to be the first to stop. His arms closed around me, his tongue dancing with mine, and his body pressed hard against me. It was familiar and new. Arousing and comforting. Fierce and forgiving.

Fire *and* earth.

"Oh God," he groaned when the timer beeped. His breath was shaky as he stroked his palms over my cheeks, I pushed against his hand, like a cat, searching for deeper contact. He drew away and stared into my eyes as he tucked a lock of my hair behind my ear. "Fuck. I missed you."

He kissed me again, this one brief but meaningful. The punctuation mark at the end of a chapter's last sentence.

"I missed you too." I placed a hand on his chest, holding him in my gaze for a long stretch, only the beeping kitchen timer and the thought of burning chicken enough to take me out of the moment. "I need to rescue dinner." I slipped on a potholder and removed the pan, setting both on the stovetop before turning back to Adam.

Adam picked up my journal from the table and held it out to me. "Did you actually want me to read this or is it some sacrifice you're making because you think I need it to forgive you? If it's part of therapy—"

I closed my hand over his and pushed it back to him. "It's up to you. If you decide not to, I keep it by my bed, and you're welcome to read it whenever you want and ask me questions. It's private, yes, and a lot of it's embarrassing, particularly the stuff about my body issues, but I want you to understand."

"I'm worried about doing something wrong. I don't want to make things worse. Like make comments about your size or that stupid nickname. I don't want to say the wrong thing."

"Oh, baby. You will. We both will. We're going to hurt each other's feelings and say things we don't mean, and argue. I guarantee we will have conflict because at some point Maura will drive you up the wall."

"I meant what I said. I won't leave you."

"I know. I trust you, Adam. I meant what I wrote in my letter, I want to be the kind of man you deserve. You deserved my forgiveness when you asked for it. I'm sorry I couldn't give it to you. I want you to be able to talk to me too. When I was reading the book, I kept thinking about what happened with Bryan—you told me what was up, and at the first opportunity, I used it against you. I know it makes it hard for you to trust my reactions, but I promise I'm really working on it. If I've hurt you or dismissed your feelings, I want to hear about it."

Adam nodded. "Rachel recently opened my eyes to the fact that I haven't been particularly good at asserting my needs. At least not in a way that seems to be working for us. We both need to do better, but that's the thing about us, Cade. That's why that letter meant so much to me. If we both want to be better for each other, I think that's why we can do this." He took a deep breath, letting it out in one lingering exhalation. "So there is something I do need to get off my chest."

"I want to hear it."

"I need you to stop telling me how I should feel or what I should want. *You* are the only person in my life I've ever put this much effort into building a relationship with. I do it because you're messy and complicated, not despite it. It pushes me to be better, less selfish, and more empathetic. I don't enjoy being the guy who got a Mustang for a C average or who throws a tantrum because my parents hired a new chef. That doesn't make me proud. But fuck, Cade . . . when you tell me I've made an excellent point about a book or when I make you laugh or make you come undone . . . God, it just lights me up inside. I feel like I can do anything. So, I need you to stop thinking that, okay? Don't take that away from me. Don't tell me the things that make me feel good about myself are crap. Can you do that for me?"

I smiled because Adam's request caused me no feelings of bitterness or anger. One of the ways the book said you know you've truly forgiven someone. "A big part of my recovery is not striving for perfection, but I can honestly say I can do that one."

"Thanks, Gou . . . I mean, Cade." Adam cringed, but I quickly kissed the concern from his face.

"I love my nickname. I am a glutton for you. I need you. So much it scares the hell out of me sometimes. But I'm done keeping that a secret from you."

Epilogue

Adam

I'd definitely been wrong about the floral arrangements. They absolutely did transform the space. I stood in front of a dramatic stone fireplace, the dark oak hearth covered in tapered candles and draped in cascading greenery and pale pink roses. The small ceremony, simple and intimate, was the culmination of months of planning. I couldn't help imagining if Cade would want something similar.

"Adam." Cade cleared his throat. The audience laughed as I stared at Brady's open hand for a second too long. *Oh, sorry*, I mouthed, retrieved the ring from my pocket, and handed it to Brady.

Cade threw me a quick wink before prompting Brady to take Josh's hand to say his vows.

"Josh, I love you. I promise to be your faithful husband, to love you through the best and the worst, through the difficult and the easy. I promise you my unconditional love and I give you my unwavering trust. When you look at this ring, remember that I love you always." Brady slid the ring onto Josh's finger, and a murmur spread over the small audience as the ceremony came to its crescendo.

Cade beamed at both of our friends. There was a lot of hand wringing and second-guessing, but he'd been determined to honor his commitment to them. Multiple scripts and so many rehearsals I'd memorized all the readings months ago, but he'd blended all the traditional elements Brady and Josh requested into a genuinely personal testament to their enviable and inspiring love story. I knew he was pleased with the way the ceremony had gone.

"Josh and Brady, it is my honor and delight to declare you married. This poem expresses our parting hope: 'Now you will feel no rain, for each of you will be shelter for the other. Now you will feel no cold, for each of you will be warmth to the other. Now there is no loneliness for you. Now you are two bodies, but there is only one life before you. Go now to your dwelling place, to enter into the days of your life together, and may your days be good and long upon the earth.' You may now kiss your husband."

I choked up as Josh launched himself at Brady and the crowd of about fifty clapped and cheered. The reception was in the same room and we'd already taken pictures, so the party started nearly immediately. Brady and Josh disappeared into a room set aside for a few private moments together.

Brady's mother, Joy, and her husband, Tom, approached Cade before I could pull him away. "That was beautiful, Cade," she gushed.

"Thank you." Cade took my hand as we mingled for a few minutes.

We made the rounds, greeting old friends from college, most of whom were surprised we were not only still together, but had at last moved in together. Food was served, but Cade was in full social butterfly mode: laughing and carrying on. It made my chest clench to see him so happy, so full of pride and receiving well-deserved accolades.

The release of adrenaline had erased the earlier tension from his face, and while I didn't monitor his food intake, on a busy day, he still needed an occasional reminder to eat. I made my way to the buffet and fixed us each a plate.

"So, Cade told me you might want to sell your condo soon." I turned to find Maura, untethered from her recent boyfriend, David, for the first time in months.

I laughed nervously. I knew a Cade and Maura conspiracy plot when I heard one. "Maybe, when the market gets better."

"You think maybe next summer? I'm interested, but Hayley needs to finish elementary school first. The summer would be a good time to make a change."

"Uh. Yeah. It's a ways off."

"Then you and Cade can buy a house, and you can get that poor boy the dog he is dying for."

"We haven't really discussed that yet."

Maura laughed, and I followed her gaze to where Cade was very obviously watching our conversation with interest. "This is all his idea, but you didn't hear it from me."

With my lip tucked between my teeth, I balanced both of our plates and rolls of silverware and carried them to the table Cade had secured.

"God, I'm starving." He took one of the plates. "Damn, this smells good." We sat down and settled in. I watched him take a few eager mouthfuls. I'd learned in his journal that the first couple bites were the biggest challenge for him when he heard that voice in his head. After we talked about it, we agreed that when concerned about his symptoms or the level of stress in his life, I should watch for initial hesitation to reassure myself he wasn't struggling.

"So," I said. "Your sister had some interesting questions about my condo."

"Oh?" Cade responded with a barely contained grin and a highly suspicious level of surprise.

"Yeah." I fought to keep a straight face. Once we'd merged households, our joint income had gone much farther on paying down all our bills. We were making progress toward our financial goals, and I had some recent news about that I hadn't shared yet, but I played along to see where his head was at. "I thought we agreed we would wait on the house until after we paid off my credit cards and your student loan and medical debt." We'd finally paid off Dr. McNamara last week. It meant a lot to me when Cade had asked for help with his medical bills.

"Well, so the thing is Maura wanted to find a place where Hayley would be zoned for my school and I could make sure she gets the best teachers."

"Naturally," I said. It still drove Cade crazy that they'd placed her in the regular reading class, rather than the advanced reading class where she so clearly belonged. I could only imagine how he'd feel if she was assigned a sub-par teacher when Hayley attended his school.

"And it's a buyers' market right now."

"I get that, which is why I rented my place instead of selling it, but Maura would really have to stretch her budget to afford it."

"David is going to give her the money for the down payment."

"Are you sure that's a good idea?"

"No, but I like David. He's good to her and to Hayley, and he has it to give. I told Maura I thought they were moving fast, but you know her. She was quick to point out that not everyone takes eight years to figure out how to communicate. I want my sister to have this, and I want us to have our own place where we can have a dog. The mortgage would be about the same as her rent if she can clear the down payment issue, and Aislinn agreed to cosign for her, so it's all doable. Plus, I'm not having to pay any of Maura's bills now, which means I'm putting all that extra toward my loans."

"Okay. Okay. Yeah. We can run the numbers when we get home. Maybe ask for some advice from Sid or Matt, since they understand way more about the real estate market than we do."

"Ask me what?" Sid took a seat at the table. "Josh and Brady still haven't emerged from the groom's suite. You don't think they're—"

Cade laughed. "Oh, for sure. We'll give them ten more minutes and then knock on the door. And Adam and I are talking about buying a house. Maura might buy Adam's condo this summer. Between what he'd make on the sale and the rate we're saving, we should have enough for a small down payment by then. I wonder if there's anything in our price range for sale in your neighborhood? We couldn't afford anything turnkey, but maybe there's a fixer-upper?"

Sid grinned at me and shook his head. "I told you not to keep it a secret from him."

"Wait. What?" Cade gasped. "What are you not telling me?"

I'd been keeping the news to myself, but it wasn't a secret. Cade and I were doing great, and I didn't want to put pressure on him by making a grand gesture. This was a decision I wanted to make together when the time was right.

"My dad wants to give me a boatload of money," I blurted out, unable to wait to see his reaction, which turned out to be utter confusion, so I explained. "Apparently, my parents decided that since they paid for Rachel's medical school and R.J.'s law school, plus helped them buy their first places, they should give me money to even it out. My dad planned to buy my first place and they tried to invest in a business for me, but I bought the condo without telling them and I like my job, so . . . yeah, they told me they'll write me a check or I'll get more when they die. Either way, it's going to be mine. Rachel told me I'd be insane to turn down a hundred grand and that money is how they show they love us, so I should do something—"

"A hundred grand!" Cade screeched. "Oh my God."

"You think I should take it?"

Cade sat back in his seat, clearly as overwhelmed by the offer as I was. "Do you think you should take it?"

"I think it would make me feel amazing to buy you a house like Sid's."

Cade tsked. "Adam, I've never lived in a house before, let alone own one like Siddharth's. If you aren't comfortable taking the money from your parents, we can wait. You don't need to do something like that for me."

"You were willing to let David do it for Maura."

He shook his head and I stopped pushing.

The truth was I'd accepted that this was the only way my parents knew to show me they cared. When you had means, grand gestures were easier than doing the hard work in a relationship. I didn't want to take the easy route with Cade. "We don't need to decide tonight. Come here. I want to dance with you."

I led Cade onto to the dance floor and, surrounded by our friends, held him close while we swayed to the music. Our height difference made things a little challenging, but like everything else, we did the best we could to overcome.

By the end of the night, my back was sore from dancing, but it was the most fun I'd had in a long time.

"You ready?"

Cade looked up from where he sat laughing with Sid and Matt, his shoes kicked off and feet up on the chair. He'd gone hard all evening, but Brady and Josh had taken off nearly twenty minutes ago, and almost everyone else had departed right after. "I settled the bill. My last best man duty is complete."

"And we loaded all their gifts in my car, so I think I'm done too," Sid said. We followed them out and said our farewells.

I wrote off Cade's introspection on the way home as exhaustion. When we were inside our apartment, Cade fixed his supplement shake and downed it in three gulps.

"You okay, Gou?"

"Yeah," he said, sleepily.

I bent down to kiss him good night, pausing an inch from his face when he yawned and covered his mouth. "Sorry," he mumbled, mouth stretching the boundaries of his palm.

I pulled back, chuckling at his drowsy grin. "I warned you not to stay up grading those literature papers last night." One of Cade's colleagues had retired suddenly and, due to budget cuts, wasn't going to be replaced. Cade had been asked to take one of the new electives his school had offered; unfortunately it was an additional assignment instead of a replacement for the two he already taught.

"I promise next year I will figure out how to stagger their research papers. I will totally rally if you want it."

"Come on." I laughed, taking his hand. I led him toward our bedroom.

He collapsed on the queen-sized bed and kicked off his shoes. With some coaxing, he stood long enough to finish removing his clothes. I took off my suit and held out my hand for his jacket, so I could hang it up. Cade was down to his underwear in no time, and I paused to admire his healthier physique. I helped him remove the extra pillows and pulled the comforter back.

We settled into bed and Cade turned to me, as he did every night since we ended our time-out, to make good on his commitment. Sometimes he'd remind me he loved me and why, but other times, he'd tell me something he was worried about so I could reassure him. On the rare times we fought, we used it to talk though our feelings. Tonight I expected a comment on the money from my parents, but instead he sighed happily and said, "Thank you for dancing with me today even when your back started hurting and for teaching Hayley how to do the Electric Slide—she got a huge kick out of that. I love that you're such a good uncle to her. It means so much to me that she has stable adults in her life she can count on."

"You're welcome, Gou. I love you too."

We kissed lightly before switching off the bedside table lights and turning in.

In the dark, I sighed a little louder than I'd meant to, still a bit restless from the unanswered question of the money and the house. I sighed again, trying to wrap my brain around all that had changed in the last six months and how much I wanted to do this for him. I knew what my childhood home had felt like compared to the place my parents now lived. There was a difference between having a roof over your head and having a home. I wanted Cade to know it. Know what it was like to put down roots and build something with someone who he could count on.

When I stirred a third time, Cade's bedside table light came on.

"Come here," Cade beckoned, grabbing our book from the nightstand. He opened his arms to me. I snuggled into him, curled up around him with my head on his chest. With one arm around my shoulders, he placed the book on his lap and then used the same hand to put on his reading glasses. I lifted my chin, glancing up at him with a knowing smile, and opened to the page we were on.

"I've only got one chapter in me," Cade warned.

"That's enough." I smiled.

"Chapter twelve . . ." He started reading. His deep voice lulled me into a state of relaxation. His fingertips played in my hair, lighting up my skin with goosebumps. Just as I was drifting off, he placed the book on the nightstand and switched off the light before attempting to slink down.

"Baby." He rubbed my shoulder, but I was too comfortable to move, so he gave up and shifted so he was spooning me. His hand came to rest on my chest, and I clutched it, holding it tight to my heart. "If you wake up covered in my drool, I don't want to hear any complaints," he whispered into my ear.

I chuckled, but his warning worked. I rolled over and waited for him to settle into our more natural sleeping position: both on our right sides, with me holding him and his drool on his pillow.

"Good night," I whispered into his ear and pressed my lips to the warm flesh of his neck.

"You know," Cade said in the darkness, sounding far less sleepy than he had been moments before. "If we bought a house, we could have a king bed."

"We could probably fit a king bed in here now," I countered. "But I enjoy sleeping close to you."

"Yeah, but if we had a king-sized bed and a yard, we could sleep close *and* still have room for two Goldendoodles."

I laughed and kissed his temple. I loved when Cade shared his dreams for our future, even when he elaborated upon them. "Oh, it's two Goldendoodles, now? Let me guess. Josh and Brady told you they were getting a dog when they get back from their honeymoon?"

"We can't let Brady and Josh take back 'most domesticated,'" Cade teased. We'd long ago stopped comparing our love to theirs except to make an occasional joke about reclaiming our status as the happiest couple of the group. The faux competition—mostly kept alive because of Josh, Cade, and Bloody Marys—turned out to have some highly entertaining, borderline obscene categories.

"Well, in that case wouldn't we need a king-sized bed and a yard, two Goldendoodles, and a wedding?"

"Yes," Cade said, so softly I wasn't sure I'd heard him.

"What did you say?" I asked, and he rolled in my arms to face me, his expression shifting from teasing to serious.

"Yes," Cade said more firmly. "We should do it. We should get married."

I tsked. "We're not getting married just because Josh and Brady did."

Cade's brow furrowed. "No, not because of that. Because I love you and you make me want it all—the house, the dogs, and the husband. I want everything with you. Marry me, Adam? I'm completely serious. I'm asking."

My heart swelled, and I broke into a smile no earthly force could contain. I pushed a blond strand of hair behind his ear and left my palm resting over his cheek. "You really want to marry me, Goulue?"

"Yeah. I might even want to have your babies someday, Mr. Creedon." Cade's grin matched my own.

"Kids?" I swallowed, practically giddy as I rolled over to reach in my bedside table and retrieved the box I'd bought not long after we'd moved in together. I'd been waiting for a sign that Cade was ready, but having him actually propose was far more definitive than I'd dreamed of. "Well, *that* would be hard to beat, but let's not get carried away.

For now, you'll have to settle for whatever house you want that's in our budget, one fur-baby, and a lifetime of my unconditional love and support, because I will absolutely marry the fuck out of you, Mr. Doyle. I'll even throw in a ring, so don't get greedy." I opened the black velvet box, and Cade gasped.

In a flash, he pushed me onto my back, straddled my hips, and kissed me hard. When he sat up, his joyous laughter swelled my heart until it threatened to burst with pride. He beamed down at me as he slipped the platinum band on his finger and admired it. "No promises. After all, I do have a nickname to live up to."

Explore more of the *Love We Find* series at:
riptidepublishing.com/products/the-weight-we-carry

the weight we carry

LOGAN MEREDITH

Dear Reader,

Thank you for reading Logan Meredith's *The Secrets We Keep*!

We know your time is precious and you have many, many entertainment options, so it means a lot that you've chosen to spend your time reading. We really hope you enjoyed it.

We'd be honored if you'd consider posting a review—good or bad—on sites like **Amazon, Barnes & Noble, Kobo, Goodreads, Twitter, Facebook, Tumblr,** and your blog or website. We'd also be honored if you told your friends and family about this book. Word of mouth is a book's lifeblood!

For more information on upcoming releases, author interviews, blog tours, contests, giveaways, and more, please sign up for our weekly, spam-free newsletter and visit us around the web:

Newsletter: riptidepublishing.com/newsletter
Twitter: twitter.com/RiptideBooks
Facebook: facebook.com/RiptidePublishing
Goodreads: tinyurl.com/RiptideOnGoodreads
Tumblr: riptidepublishing.tumblr.com

Thank you so much for Reading the Rainbow!

RiptidePublishing.com

Also by Logan Meredith

About the Author

Logan Meredith began writing as a teenager when beautiful boys started keeping her company at night. Unfortunately, the voices she heard were imaginary, and their conversations resulted in horrible insomnia. They only let her sleep when she started typing their words down. Thankfully, being awkward as hell and a head taller than anyone else in school afforded plenty of spare time for writing.

At first, she tried to make them play with characters from her favorite television series or books. She found her lost tribe with a ravenous, crazy group of fan fiction lovers online and started sharing her stories. Then something amazing happened: new characters arrived and demanded their own stories. Only they wanted their own world to play in, and they wanted to find their true loves. So between her day job and making time for her family, she tries to keep up with the requirements of her beautiful men for their happily-ever-afters.

A native of San Antonio, Texas, and a graduate of the University of Texas at San Antonio, Logan is an accomplished cross-country mover having honed her skills bouncing between five states. She currently resides in Houston, Texas. In addition to writing, she spends her time reading and rereading her favorite books, cheering for the San Antonio Spurs, playing Words with Friends, and procrastinating pretty much everything else.

She is a proud member of the LGBTQA community and vocal advocate for mental health awareness, suicide prevention, and equality campaigns.

Logan welcomes the chance to interact with readers.
Twitter: @ll_meredith

Enjoy more stories like
The Secrets We Keep
at RiptidePublishing.com!